JENNIFER JOYCE is a writer of romantic comedies. She's been scribbling down bits of stories for as long as she can remember, graduating from a pen to a typewriter and then an electronic typewriter. And she felt like the bee's knees typing on *that*. She now writes her books on a laptop (which has a proper delete button and everything). Jennifer lives in Oldham, Greater Manchester, with her husband Chris and their two daughters, Rianne and Isobel, plus their Jack Russell, Luna. When she isn't writing, Jennifer likes to make things – she'll use any excuse to get her craft box out! She spends far too much time on Twitter, Pinterest and Instagram.

You can find out more about Jennifer on her blog at jenniferjoycewrites.co.uk, on Twitter at @writer_jenn and on Facebook at facebook.com/jenniferjoycewrites

M000158687

Also by Jennifer Joyce

The Single Mums' Picnic Club
The Wedding that Changed Everything
The Little Bed & Breakfast by the Sea
The Little Teashop of Broken Hearts
The Wedding Date
The Mince Pie Mix-Up

The Accidental Life Swap

JENNIFER JOYCE

ONE PLACE. MANY STORIES

HQ
An imprint of HarperCollins*Publishers* Ltd
1 London Bridge Street
London SE1 9GF

This edition 2019

First published in Great Britain by
HQ, an imprint of HarperCollins*Publishers* Ltd 2019

ISBN: PB: 978-0-00-834868-7
EB: 978-0-00-834865-6

For more information visit: www.harpercollins.co.uk/green

Typeset by Palimpsest Book Production Ltd, Falkirk, Stirlingshire

To the Joyces –
Chris, Rianne and Isobel.

Chapter 1

He's used my toothpaste again. The tube is flat in the middle and twisted. *Twisted?* What has he been *doing* with my Colgate? Other than using my stuff without permission – *again*. I'm not having it. I'm not. As soon as I've brushed my teeth, I'm going to march into his bedroom, *without knocking*, and I'm going to tell my flatmate exactly what I think of him.

Lee Williams, I'll bark in the way my boss has perfected, the way that makes me have to cross my legs so I don't do a little wee of fear at my desk. *You are an inconsiderate, lazy, selfish pig. I regret the day I ever moved into this disgusting little flat with you. If I could afford to live anywhere else, I would. In a heartbeat. Half a heartbeat. You make me want to vomit with your rarely washed body, your farting in the kitchen and your bogey-flicking. I especially dislike the way you walk around the flat wearing nothing but a pair of crusty underpants and a look of indifference, not even registering my discomfort, never mind giving a damn about it.*

Perhaps I will knock on the door before I venture into his bedroom, after all. I fear what I may encounter if I catch him unawares.

I can't stand you, Lee. Sometimes I even despise you. And I'm a nice person. I don't usually despise anyone, not even Sonia at work, who has lodged herself so far up Vanessa's bum, only the tips of her knockoff Manolo Blahnik mules are visible. But I dislike you. Very much so. You are ignorant and sexist and like the sound of your own voice far too much. I am not your wife or your mother or your maid. It is not my 'duty' to fill the fridge with nutritious food for you to pilfer so you don't have to go to the shops yourself. It is not my responsibility to clean the entire flat myself (and it is a pointless task anyway because no matter how much I scrub and vacuum and dust, the place is permanently grimy due to the years of neglect before I foolishly came along, and your continuous slovenliness). It is not my obligation to provide you with bloody toothpaste.

I'm working up quite a lather as I release all the pent-up frustration of living with an untrained animal for the past three years on my teeth. I'm going to tell him about his reprehensive behaviour and make it clear that it has to stop. I tried once before, about three months into our flat-share, in the form of a polite note pushed under his bedroom door. I later found the note stuck to the fridge door, with a giant penis and hairy balls scrawled across it in black marker. I don't think my charming flatmate had taken much notice of my requests for him to buy milk every once in a while or to turn his pounding music down after 11 p.m. on worknights before he defaced the note.

Still, I'm going to put things straight now. Better three years late than never.

Popping my toothbrush into my washbag (I never leave my toothbrush unattended in communal areas, having learned the hard way when I discovered Lee's even grubbier friend working on his molars with a toothbrush of mine back in the early days), I throw my shoulders back and lift my chin high before marching into the dimly-lit hallway and heading towards Lee's bedroom. The door is flung open before I have the chance to reach it, revealing an almost naked Lee and a cloud of musty fug.

Right, this is it. I'm going to let rip and unleash the tirade I've been rehearsing in my head. He won't know what's hit him!

2

'Morning.' Flashing the briefest of minty-fresh smiles, I scuttle off to my own bedroom with a sense of shame so severe it makes my stomach ache.

I'm a wimp. A great big wuss. A sissy pants without a backbone.

Why am I so pathetic? Why can't I stand up to him and demand a tiny shred of respect? I've put up with his disregard and insolence for three years and I don't think I can take much more of it. Either Lee has to change or I have to move on, and the only way to do that is to finally bag the promotion I deserve at work. I've already started to squirrel tiny amounts of money away into my savings each month for a deposit on a new flat, but if I could earn a bit more cash, I could move out of this hovel and away from my revolting flatmate much sooner. Plus, it would mean I'd finally earned the respect of my boss.

I've been working as the personal assistant to Vanessa Whitely at her events management company since I graduated from university three years ago, but I'm keen to take on a more creative role within the company. I have so many ideas, but I've yet to voice them in a way that will grab Vanessa's attention. I need to make her listen to me. Be firm, more assertive and all the other strong, positive terms I've been reading about in the pile of self-help books crammed onto my bookshelf. There's a big event coming up, an autumn festival taking place on farmland in the Yorkshire Dales, and I've been working on ideas for weeks, perfecting and polishing them until they're shiny enough to present to Vanessa. This is my chance to show my boss what I'm capable of. That I have skills beyond answering the phone, making coffee and juggling her diary.

I'm going to do it. Today. Before it's too late. I'm going to take a huge, positive leap forward in my career. I'm going to march into Vanessa's office with the file I've compiled, set it on her desk and exhibit my ideas with passion and expertise. She'll be so bowled over, she'll add me to the team with immediate effect and I can start looking into new accommodation as soon as possible.

And who knows – maybe I'll be moving out of this dingy flat within the next month!

*

There are a couple of things I need to do before I march into Vanessa's office. My first task is to sort out my appearance as I'm currently sporting a pair of lemon check pyjamas and the worst case of bedhead I've ever witnessed. I need to present myself as immaculately as my festival ideas, so that Vanessa can take one look at me and instantly see me in the role I covet. Vanessa always appears chic and professional, so I need to emulate her look as best as I can with my limited resources. While Vanessa dresses as though she's about to step on the catwalk at London Fashion Week, I don't have *quite* the same budget for clothes and accessories, but I'll do what I can. Reaching into my wardrobe, I pull out a sleeveless black dress, cut to just below the knee, that is classic and sophisticated and definitely the sort of look Vanessa would go for. I team the dress with a gold belt and pair of lace-up peep-toe ankle boots that are similar to a pair I've seen Vanessa wearing (but while hers undoubtedly cost at least a month's worth of my salary, I bought mine from the supermarket, marked down to less than twenty quid because of a scuff on the heel, which I've coloured in with a Sharpie pen).

My hair takes a bit more effort. It really is an unruly mop and refuses to stay in any of the styles I twist and grip it into. Vanessa favours sleek up-dos, but my hair is not playing along. In the end, because I'm running out of time, I'm forced to gather it into a messy bun and hope with every fibre of my being that it works with the overall look. I have just enough time leftover to swipe on a layer of mascara and smear on my favourite nude lip gloss before I leg it for the bus. I may be attempting to copy Vanessa's style, but there's no way I could get away with her bold red lipstick.

We're advancing into late September, still technically summer, but it's already turning chilly and I zip up my coat as I hurry along the street – not quite jogging but as close as I'm going to get in these heels. The boots may be pretty but they're not very comfortable and my exposed toes are in danger of becoming frostbitten. Little white clouds puff into the air on each ragged exhale as I urge my body to move faster towards the main road. If I miss my bus, there'll be a twenty-minute wait for the next and bursting into the office late is not the sort of impression I want to make on this of all days. I have my autumn festival file tucked under my arm, but it'll be of little use if I don't catch the 8.22 bus.

I'm almost at the main road when I hear the distant rumble of a double decker bus. Gah! Pushing myself and praying I don't break an ankle in the stupid boots, I make a dash for it, gasping and rasping for breath as I sprint towards the bus stop. Yes! There's a sizeable queue waiting to board, giving me a few more valuable seconds to reach the stop. This must be a good sign of things to come, surely, even if it means I'll probably have to stand for the entire fifteen-minute journey.

I make it onto the bus, sweating despite the chill, and collapse onto the one remaining seat at the back. I take the available seat as another good sign of things to come, even if it is the seat in the middle, which means I spend the next fifteen minutes in fear of flying down the aisle of the bus every time we turn a corner or brake. I'm not catapulted from my seat (a third Good Sign) and the traffic is pretty smooth going (Good Sign #4), meaning I have plenty of time to get from the Piccadilly Gardens bus stop to the office without breaking another sweat. This is definitely a Good Day. I'm feeling so positive, I practically skip along Lever Street and offer my cheeriest of hellos to the barista as I step into my favourite independent coffee shop. I order three coffees – a gingerbread soya cappuccino, a cinnamon latte with whipped cream and brown sugar, and a salted caramel mocha. Spending my hard-earned cash on fancy coffees is a big indulgence for me, but I feel a Good Day like today deserves it, and so I barely whimper as I slot my debit card into the card reader and jab my pin into the number pad.

Carrying three hot coffees – even if they are helpfully slotted into a cardboard tray – means I can no longer skip, but my mood is still lifted as I make my way to the office. Vanessa Whitely Events is located on the third floor of a converted red-bricked Victorian terrace and while the outside has kept its historical charm, the inside is airy and modern, with exposed brickwork, shiny white desks and chrome lighting fixtures in every conceivable place. The reception area has huge tub chairs in a rainbow of colours, and I can still taste the fear of waiting to be called for my interview three years ago every time I step inside.

'Morning.' Emma smiles brightly from behind the reception desk, raising a hand in greeting as I elbow my way through the glass doors. 'Need a hand?'

Emma is one of the loveliest people I know. Permanently chirpy and always willing to listen to me moan about Vanessa's lack of faith in me, or Sonia's latest catty remarks, or life in general, Emma is often the only thing that keeps me going at work. She isn't just a work colleague; she's my best friend and I'd be lost without her. I felt a bit out of place when I stepped into the big, wide world of events management alone, but Emma was like a life jacket from the moment she arrived behind the reception desk two years ago, propping me up with friendship and gin.

'I'm okay.' I dodge out of the way of the door, allowing it to close behind me as I right the tray of coffees that is slipping from my grasp. 'Just about.' I scamper towards the reception desk to relieve myself of the tray and the file that I've somehow managed to keep tucked under my arm. 'Cinnamon latte?' I de-wedge one of the coffees and hold it out to Emma, whose eyes widen as she grasps the cardboard cup.

'You're the best! I am so in the mood for a decent coffee.'

I give a one-shouldered shrug, as though the cost of the coffees hasn't taken a scary chunk out of my weep-inducingly low bank balance. I *really* need this promotion. 'I thought we could do with a treat.'

'Amen to that.' Emma raises her cup before she takes a sip, closing her eyes to savour the taste. 'God, yes. I need this today. Vanessa's already on the warpath and it isn't even nine o' clock.'

'She is?' My stomach churns. This information doesn't bode well for me. I need Vanessa to be in good spirits – or at least neutral spirits – when I present my ideas to her. If she's in a bad mood, she's more likely to toss my file aside to 'take a look at later' – which never happens – or dismiss them outright.

Bugger.

'Any idea what's set her off?' If I can smooth things over, I could nudge my chances of promotion back on track. Emma is the font of all knowledge when it comes to Vanessa Whitely Events; she usually knows what's happening and when and to whom, so if you want up-to-date gossip, she's your woman. But Emma shakes her head.

'No idea, sorry. She stormed in here earlier, yelling into her mobile, but I couldn't get the gist of it.'

'Maybe this will help calm her down.' I pick up the tray of coffees. 'Wish me luck.' Slipping my file of ideas under my arm, I head towards Vanessa's office, chin held high in determination as I rap on the door.

Chapter 2

Vanessa is sitting behind her desk, her face pinched as she rests her chin on a clenched fist. Her mobile has been tossed aside, landing on the edge of a stack of paper so that it's being propped up, face-down, on the desk. Her hair – unusually for Vanessa – is looking a bit bedraggled, as though she's been clutching at her head in despair, disrupting her sleek up-do. Do I mention it? Earn myself a few extra brownie points for my honesty and for saving Vanessa from looking anything but flawless? Or will that put me in the firing line? Perhaps it's best to keep quiet, just until I've established why Vanessa is so clearly distressed, if there is a way I can help, and if my mentioning the state of her hair will be a help or hindrance to my cause.

'Well? What do you want?'

I'm still dithering by the door, but Vanessa's bark spurs me into action. Stepping fully into the room, I march purposefully across the large office, noticing with alarm that a pot of pens has been swiped from the desk and is currently strewn across the polished floor. This is not good.

'Coffee.' My voice comes out all squeaky, so I clear my throat and try again. 'I brought you a coffee. Soya cappuccino. Gingerbread.' I clear my throat once more and step over the scattered pens. 'A gingerbread soya cappuccino.'

Vanessa's shoulders rise as she heaves in a breath through flared nostrils. I suspect she's either going to burst into tears with gratitude or roar that a gingerbread soya cappuccino is no longer her coffee of choice. I'm not sure which option I'd prefer, but it's a third option that Vanessa plumps for, releasing her breath with a heavy, disdainful sigh. She snatches a cardboard cup from her desk and wafts it at me.

'I already have a coffee, thank you very much.' Although Vanessa is using pleasantries, the words are fired at me with a sneer.

'I could tell Vanessa needed a pick-me-up this morning.' Sonia's voice makes me jump, and the file slips from under my arm, joining the mess of pens on the floor. I didn't realise my colleague was in the office, skulking in the corner. She smiles sweetly – almost patronisingly – at our boss. 'She's having a tough time.'

'Oh?' Dumping the coffee tray on Vanessa's desk, I crouch down to pick up the file. Luckily, none of the pages have come loose. 'Anything I can help with?'

Sonia snorts, and when I steal a look behind me, she's shaking her head at Vanessa while rolling her eyes. She emerges from her corner by the window and perches on the edge of Vanessa's desk, as though they're the best of buddies. Equals. Sitting in such close proximity, I realise how similar the pair look. Both have bleached white-blonde hair, stark against their defined brows and tanned skin (Vanessa's due to three weeks in Barbados, Sonia's courtesy of Sunny Dayz, the tanning shop she rushes to every lunchtime to keep her tan topped up). They're even dressed alike this morning in silk shirts with pussy-bow collars, Vanessa's a navy, long-sleeved shirt while Sonia has opted for an indigo-and-white striped sleeveless version. I attempted to emulate Vanessa's style this morning, but Sonia has gone one better. She's beaten me, again.

'This problem is going to take more than a coffee run, sweetie.' Sonia crosses her arms and her eyes flick upwards again. Snotty cow. I wish I was the kind of person who could call others out on their rudeness, but I'm not. I'm a pushover. Always have been, always will be, no matter how much it frustrates me.

Sonia and I started working at Vanessa Whitely Events on the same day. While I'd been offered the role as Vanessa's PA, Sonia had joined the company as one of the receptionists. We'd both recently graduated, and this was our first proper job. We should have bonded, but instead battle lines were drawn as Sonia made it her mission to rise to the top as quickly as possible, trampling on anyone she had to on the way up. While she was quickly replaced by Emma on the reception desk after being promoted to event planner, I'm still Vanessa's assistant, with no say in the events the company managed, no matter how many ideas I have whirling around my head.

'I don't know about that, actually.' Vanessa sits upright, her movement so sudden and unexpected that I almost topple backwards in my crouched position. 'Maybe you *can* help.'

'She can?' Sonia's brow furrows as she looks from Vanessa, to me, and back again.

'I can?' I leap up from my squatted position and beam at my boss. Vanessa is tapping her chin with a manicured finger, her eyes narrowed to thoughtful slits.

'Yes.' Her lips spread out into a wide smile until her veneered teeth are displayed, hungry shark-like. 'Yes, I think you may be the perfect solution, Becky.'

'It's, um, Rebecca.' My response is mumbled – what the hell does it matter if she calls me Becky? She can call me Bogey-Face if she wants to (my flatmate certainly does, and finds it hilarious). Vanessa has just declared – with a witness – that I, Rebecca Riley, am the *perfect solution* to her problem. Not Sonia. Not any of the others on the team. *Me*.

'Can you give us a minute to discuss the matter?'

I assume Vanessa is dismissing me, and start to back away from her desk, careful not to step on any of the pens still littering

10

the floor, but it's actually Sonia she's addressing. Sonia seems as shocked as I feel, her mouth slowly forming a large 'O' as she blinks at Vanessa.

'Go on.' Vanessa wafts her hand, almost shooing Sonia away from her perched position on the desk. 'You need to prepare for the team meeting anyway.' Vanessa flicks her wrist to check the time on her chunky watch. 'Shoot. We're already running late. Give me five minutes?'

Sonia closes her gaping mouth and manages a grimace-like smile. It switches off immediately as she meets my eye. 'Fine. I'll make sure we're ready to get started as soon as you've finished here.'

'Thank you, Sonia.' This time, Vanessa's pleasantries are met with a corresponding smile. 'What would I do without my right-hand woman?'

Usually, I'd be silently seething at those vomit-inducing words, but right now I'm floating on a cloud of pure happiness. Because while Sonia is Vanessa's right-hand woman, *I* am the perfect solution to her problem. I will solve whatever hiccup has sent Vanessa into a rage. I will be the hero that saves the day, and Vanessa will finally value my contribution to the company.

Promotion, here we come.

Chapter 3

Vanessa pulls her shoulders back so she's sitting straighter, the frown lines that were moments ago intersecting her forehead all but gone as she turns a mega-watt smile in my direction. She indicates the chair on the opposite side of her desk with an upturned hand as she reaches to align her mobile with the other.

'Please sit, Becky. We have lots to discuss.'

I do as I'm told, but only after I've scooped the scattered collection of pens from the floor and arranged them in their pot, setting it in its rightful place on the desk. I really can't help myself, but I think Vanessa appreciates the act, even if she doesn't voice it and merely watches me with an eyebrow cocked in bemusement.

'So, how can I help?' I've finally plonked myself in the seat and Vanessa is grinning at me again from across the desk. I'm not sure I like it. I've worked for Vanessa Whitely for three years and I've never seen her beam like this. So toothily. Like a crocodile about to snap up its dinner whole. I'm unnerved, but I'm trying not to show it. I want Vanessa to see me as an equal, or as close to an equal as possible while still being the boss. I want her to see me as she sees Sonia and the others, not as the trembling imbecile I feel inside right now.

'Is it about the Heron Farm Festival? Because I've been working on some ideas …' I'm sliding my file across the desk towards Vanessa but pause as she starts to shake her head. Her hair is still askew, but we've gone way beyond the point where I can point it out by now.

'This isn't strictly work-related.' Vanessa thrusts her chin in the air and narrows her eyes ever so slightly. 'But it is extremely important to me.'

'What is it?' I lean forward, my forearms resting on the desk in front of me. I can't say I'm not disappointed that I haven't been catapulted straight into the autumn festival's plans, but I am intrigued.

'I bought a little place last year, practically in the middle of nowhere. There isn't a Waitrose for miles, which sounds hideous, I know, but also a bit romantic, don't you think?' Vanessa poses the question, but she doesn't give me the chance to respond as she ploughs straight on. 'I couldn't live there full-time, obviously – can you imagine the commute?' Her eyes widen momentarily, and she gives a little shake of her head. My eyes linger on her abused hairdo as a stray wisp wobbles on top of her head, and I have to drag my gaze away before I draw attention to it. 'It's more of a weekend getaway, a place I can escape to when I need to unwind. You know how it is.'

Vanessa and I clearly live in different worlds, but I bob my head up and down in understanding, as though I, too, am in a position where I can waltz off to a second home to chill out for the weekend.

'The house is a bit like my sister-in-law; absolutely stunning on the outside but a big ugly mess on the inside.' Vanessa presses her lips together and her shoulders shake with a suppressed giggle. She clears her throat and she's back to being professional Vanessa, the bitchiness locked back inside. 'Anyway, like I was saying, the house is in need of some major TLC. I've been working on it for *months*. My project manager has been *brilliant* though.' She heaves a massive sigh and leans on the desk, jelly-like. 'Unfortunately, she was involved in that pile up on the M60 last night?' Vanessa's voice goes up at the end, turning her statement into a question. Her eyebrows rise too as she awaits a response.

'Oh my God, is she okay?' Of course I'd heard about the accident – it was all over *Granada Reports* last night and splashed across the front of *The Metro* this morning. A haulage truck had ploughed into a car at rush hour, killing the driver and seriously injuring her two young children, and causing a major pile-up on the motorway. Three people had been airlifted to hospital, while several more had been transferred by ambulance.

'She's fine.' Vanessa gives a wave of her hand and the knot that's been tightening in my stomach starts to unwind. 'Cuts and bruises, mostly, and a broken femur.'

Vanessa says the last bit so matter-of-factly that I almost miss it. 'A broken femur?' My eyes are wide, my mouth wider. I'm shocked and horrified in equal measure. But it's a sigh of irritation that hisses from Vanessa.

'Yes, which means hospital and surgery and casts and all that.' Vanessa sighs again and folds her arms across her chest. 'Which is incredibly frustrating when we're so close to finishing the house renovations.'

The chasm that is now my mouth widens even further. *Frustrating*? What about the traumatic ordeal? The pain she must be in? None of that seems to be registering at all with my boss and I feel my blood start to boil as she witters on about schedules and timescales and catastrophic delays.

'I'm throwing a housewarming party, you see, to showcase my beautiful new home.' Vanessa reaches for her handbag, rifling inside before pulling out a cream card embossed with sparkling bronze writing. She slides it towards me, jabbing a finger on the date printed on the front. 'That's in one month's time, when Nicole *promised* me the house would be ready.'

How inconvenient. I'm sure Nicole is as furious with her broken promise as Vanessa is.

I want to say this out loud, my tone so thick with sarcasm the words would almost get wedged in my mouth. But I don't. I silently seethe while Vanessa spits venom about her ruined party plans.

'And the invitations have already gone out to everybody I know!' Vanessa snatches the invite back and shoves it into her handbag. My invitation must have been lost in the post, I suppose.

'The thing is, I don't have time to find another project manager to get the job finished by my tight deadline.' Vanessa pushes herself out of her seat and strides towards the window. 'Especially if I have to go on a waiting list.' Vanessa shakes her head and the wayward strand of hair has a wobble. I fear she's going to catch its reflection in the windowpane and demand to know why I haven't warned her that she looks like she's been on the receiving end of an electric shock.

'You said I could help?' I only give her the reminder so she'll turn away from the window, but I soon wish I'd kept quiet when the crocodile smile makes a return.

'Yes, I did, didn't I?' Vanessa strides away from the window and perches on the edge of her desk, looking down at me.

'Do you want me to get in touch with everyone from your guest list and rearrange the party for a later date?'

The answer to the question is clearly a big fat no as Vanessa's mouth gapes open in outrage. She places a hand on her chest as she gives a humourless laugh. 'I am an *events manager*, Becky. I can't *postpone* my party – what kind of message is that sending out? If I can't organise my own party, what hope is there for paying clients?'

'These are extenuating circumstances. I'm sure if you explain the situation with the accident and …' My words tail off as Vanessa leaps from the desk and marches back towards the window. She isn't listening to me anyway.

'Postponing isn't an option. The party must go ahead, and it must be *spectacular.*'

'You want me to plan your party?' I'm almost breathless. *Vanessa wants me to plan her party*! This is the most exciting thing that has ever happened to me! Of all the event planners in this building, Vanessa has picked *me* to organise her house-warming celebration. This is it. My big chance to prove to Vanessa that I can be a creative asset to this company. No wonder Sonia was looking ticked off as she left the office. She must want to puke with envy.

'No, sweetheart.' Vanessa is giving me an odd look, as though I've just sprouted an extra head before her eyes, and she's speaking to me rather slowly. 'I want you to project manage the final stages of the house renovation.'

Chapter 4

I watch Vanessa carefully, the corners of my mouth twitching, eager to rise into a smile as soon as Vanessa bursts into the laughter I know she's holding deep inside. Because I know she's kidding. I'm a PA. I have a degree in events management. And I know *squat* about restoring houses, other than the occasional viewing of *Homes Under The Hammer* when I'm too hungover to reach for the remote. Let me tell you, I am no Lucy Alexander. I cannot see potential in knackered old buildings. I don't care about original period pieces and I'm as likely to gush over Lee's sweat-dampened socks left strewn across the bathroom floor as I am a ceiling rose.

Vanessa's good, I'll give her that. Her poker face is amazing as she faces me with an unwavering facade, her features as still as a mask cast in plaster.

'You'll need to get in touch with the head builder – Victor, I think his name is. Or maybe Vance?' Vanessa bites her lip, and I suspect this is the moment she is going to roar with laughter. She's trying so hard to keep the amusement in, but it has to burst out at some point. Right? 'I haven't got round to filling him in about Nicole, so you'll need to update him on the situation.' She twists her wrist to glance at her watch. 'I really must dash off,

I'm afraid. I'm *so late* for this meeting. Victor's details are in my contacts and I'll arrange to have Nicole's paperwork couriered over to you ASAP. You'll just have to wing it until it arrives, I'm afraid, but at least the builders won't slack off if you're around to keep them in check.'

She's striding towards the door without a hint of delight at her little joke. I watch her reach for the handle, fully prepared for her to spin around and laugh at me.

Except she doesn't. She strides straight through the door without a backwards glance. When she fails to poke her head back round the door to perform her *gotcha!* moment, panic starts to bubble inside. She isn't *serious* about me taking over the role of project manager, is she?

I laugh to myself, but I don't sound particularly joyful. I sound afraid and slightly manic.

'Vanessa! Wait!' Leaping from my seat, I tear off across the office, almost slipping on the polished floor in my stupid peep-toe boots. Yanking at the door handle, I'm relieved to see the back of Vanessa's head, the strands of hair still sticking up, as she marches towards the meeting room. 'Vanessa!' I yelp as my foot slips again, but I keep going, grasping hold of a startled-looking Vanessa as I reach her. 'I can't do this. I'm not a project manager. I have *no clue* what to do.' I spread my arms out wide. 'No clue at all.'

Vanessa's foot starts to tap as she observes me, one eyebrow quirked unnaturally high on her forehead. I lower my arms slowly as she continues to scrutinise me, resting them by my side as Vanessa's other eyebrow rises to join the first in its piqued position.

'I beg your pardon?' Vanessa's voice is a low growl and I suddenly realise I'm desperate for a wee.

'I, um … the thing is, Vanessa …' I cross my legs as a sharp pain crosses my belly. 'While I'm absolutely flattered that you think I'm capable of overseeing the refurbishment of your new house, I don't think I'm up to the job.'

Vanessa's head tilts to one side and she rests a hand on her hip. 'You don't think you're up to the job?'

I give a rapid shake of my head as I concentrate really hard on not wetting myself outside the meeting room.

'You're not up to the job an untrained monkey with a clipboard could do?'

I'm not sure what to say to that. If I answer no, I'm admitting that I'm less capable than an untrained monkey. But if I answer yes, that I am up to the job after all, then I'm landing myself with a new, albeit temporary, job description for the next few weeks.

'Well?' Vanessa's foot is tapping again. I need to answer quickly, before she loses her temper for the second time this morning.

'I guess I'm a fast learner?' I wish my voice hadn't come out sounding quite so weak, that it had been a strong statement of my abilities rather than a meek question.

'Good.' Vanessa gives a curt nod and I train my eyes on her mouth so I neither have to look into her searing eyes or watch the stray hairs wobble. 'Because I wouldn't want to have to find both a new project manager *and* a PA at such short notice.' If I could bear to meet her gaze, I'm sure Vanessa would be piercing me with a warning look: refuse to take on this role at your peril.

'So, we're perfectly clear?' The eyebrows are reaching for Vanessa's hairline again. I feel I have no choice but to nod. 'Fabulous. I'll reimburse you for your petrol and other expenditures, obviously, but we'll have to sort that out later as I'm *extremely* late for my meeting now.' She gives a pointed look at the meeting room door, but I can't let her go just yet.

'I don't drive, and I have no idea where this house is.'

Vanessa heaves an enormous sigh at the inconvenience of these minor details. 'Then you'll have to catch the train or something. You're more than welcome to stay at the house for the duration, if it's easier than travelling back and forth. It's completely weatherproof, though unfurnished, I'm afraid. There's always the guesthouse, I suppose.' She shrugs and takes a step closer to the meeting room. 'My set of keys are in my handbag, and you'll find the address of the house in my diary from when I went for a viewing, around the middle of January. It's in Little Heaton.' She reaches for the meeting room door, but I haven't *quite* managed to iron out all the details.

'What about my job here?' I point towards my desk, which is portioned off outside Vanessa's office. 'How will you manage without me?'

Vanessa gives me an indulgent smile. 'I'm sure we'll cope, sweetheart. And Emma can step in and help out if needed.'

Emma's head pops up from the reception desk as she hears her name and Vanessa briefly fills her in.

'Of course I'll help out.' Emma smiles at Vanessa, but the corners of her mouth droop as a frown takes over. 'Um, what's going on with your hair, Vanessa? It's a bit …' She wafts a hand above her head while Vanessa's eyes widen. My stomach lurches as Vanessa reaches up and discovers the unruly strands. I should have told her earlier, as soon as I stepped into her office. Why couldn't I be more like Emma? There's no way she would have allowed Vanessa to attend a meeting looking a hot mess.

There's a strangled cry as Vanessa scurries away from the meeting room, only pausing to glare at me before she pushes her way into the ladies'. She's going to be super late for that meeting now.

'Um, Rebecca?' Emma peels a pink post-it note from the pad in front of her and waggles it in my direction. 'Your sister called. Again.' She flashes me an apologetic smile, knowing I've been avoiding Kate for the past few weeks. When I'd ignored her calls enough times, she'd changed tactic and started to badger me at work.

'I haven't got time for that.' I wave away the slip of pink paper and start to back away towards Vanessa's office. 'I've got a train to catch.'

*

The sun is out now, shining bright in the almost cloudless sky, but it is *freezing* as I stand on the platform at Piccadilly train station, my hands shoved deep into the pockets of my coat. I'm still wearing the ridiculous peep-toe boots and I can feel every breath of the wind that is whistling along the platform, my toes turning blue with the chill. I should have changed into more suitable footwear whilst I was at the flat, but I barely had time to shove a few essentials into the holdall before I had to jump into the taxi beeping with irritation outside. I've packed enough to last me until the weekend, when I'll make the journey back home, because Vanessa can't seriously expect me to uproot my life for a whole month – however tempting the thought had been when I'd stepped into the flat and caught the lingering whiff of my flatmate. Having a little break from Lee is the only silver lining of this whole debacle. I toyed with the idea of leaving my absence to his imagination – had I been kidnapped? Run over and left for dead on the side of the road? – but I was afraid he'd have rented out my room by the time I returned if I didn't let him know I'd be back soon, so I've left him a note on the fridge.

Tugging my hands from my pockets, I rub them together to try to create a bit of warmth as I peer down the tracks, hoping to glimpse the train that was due eight minutes ago. I'd rushed to make it to the station but I needn't have been so speedy as there's no sign of the train. I'm half-tempted to nip to the kiosk at the top of the steps to grab a cup of coffee to warm me up but I know without a doubt that the train will have pulled up and left again by the time I've clattered back down the steps, probably spilling hot liquid down myself in my haste. So I'm forced to stand, teeth chattering, while I wait for a train I don't even *want* to catch.

This is absurd. Why am I putting up with this change in job role? I should have been firm. Said no, I will absolutely *not* take on the task of project managing a house renovation in the middle of nowhere, and if you even *think* of firing me over the matter, I will drag you to court for unfair dismissal. But I didn't, because I'm as firm as unset jelly, and now I'm about to board the train that is rumbling down the tracks towards me at last.

I feel a bit sick as I bend down to grab the holdall at my feet. This is it. I'm really doing this. I'm actually taking a break from my role as Vanessa's PA, moving away from the office and my dream profession, to oversee the transformation of a house I have zero interest in. How am I supposed to earn a promotion now I've been shoved out of the way? I can't impress Vanessa with my ideas from Little Heaton. This is career suicide!

Unless … Hooking the holdall onto my arm, I join the melee of people waiting to board, scanning the crowd for the end of a queue to join. Or any hint of a queue in the chaos, at least. There isn't one and I find myself jostled out of the way as a D-bag with a briefcase barges past with his elbows out. I apologise (what the hell?) before edging my way back into the pack, earning myself a glare from a woman with a pushchair, who runs over my exposed toes before I can leap out of the way. I'm silently seething by the time I limp onto the train, shuffling along the carriage in search of an empty seat with my holdall clutched to my chest. This day *sucks*. I thought Lee using my toothpaste without permission had been bad enough, but the morning has been on a steady decline since I stepped into Vanessa's office and spotted her dishevelled hairdo. So much for those good vibes I'd fooled myself into feeling on the way to work.

I make my way into the next carriage and the feeling of dread lifts ever so slightly when I spot a free seat at the end. Not only is the seat free of either body or bag, it is a *window seat* and it is *facing forward*. The positive me from this morning would have taken this as a Very Good Sign, but all the buoyancy has been sucked out of me by now so I simply slot my holdall into the luggage rack above my head and sink gratefully into the seat. The voice over the tannoy system announces the opening of the onboard kiosk, but although I'm in desperate need of a coffee for both the caffeine injection and the warmth, I'm fearful that my seat will have been appropriated by the time I get back. No, it's safer to remain where I am, as settled as I can be whizzing past fields of sheep at a hundred miles an hour. Besides, there's something more urgent than my need for coffee prodding at me. I can't put my finger on it, but it's bugging me, a thought that I can't quite grasp hold of.

My phone beeps in my pocket and I see a message from Emma when I pull it out.

Good luck with your 'new job' – show Vanessa what you're made of! xxx

And that's when it hits me. The thought that's been niggling at me since I picked up my holdall on the platform. I need to use this as an opportunity to really impress Vanessa, to show her that I have all the skills required of a good events planner: exceptional organisation, the ability to multitask and problem-solve while working under pressure, and meeting tight deadlines while retaining a high level of attention to detail. I'm going to be the best, most efficient project manager and keep the refurbishment on track. I'm going to prove to Vanessa that I have what it takes, that I would be an asset to her team if she would only give me the opportunity to shine. I'm going to earn myself that promotion, get a foot back on the career ladder and find myself a decent flat-share so I can finally live the life I dreamed I would when I left home and moved to Manchester. This is the start of a brand new life and a brand new me.

Chapter 5

Vanessa hadn't been exaggerating when she'd said Little Heaton was in the middle of nowhere; I haven't seen any sign of civilisation for at least fifteen minutes as we delve further into the Cheshire countryside. Even the sheep-filled fields have given way to wild moorland and I'm starting to panic that instead of taking me to the address I'd hastily jotted down earlier and am now clutching in my hand, the taxi driver is finding the perfect spot to bury a body. My body.

I know I'm being paranoid – or at least that's what I'm telling myself as I take deep, even breaths while watching the meter clocking up pound after pound – but I'm not the most adventurous of people. I'd felt super-sophisticated when I moved to Manchester from the tiny town I'd grown up in, though any sense of refinement diminished rapidly when I moved into the flat with Lee, obviously – but I was still proud of the leap I'd made. Now, though, I want to take a giant step backwards. I want to return to a place of safety. A place I know, even if I don't particularly love it. My grubby little flat doesn't seem so bad when faced with the prospect of being transported into the wilderness with a maniac.

The taxi driver hasn't given me any hint that he's a maniac.

In fact, he'd seemed quite pleasant as he'd hefted my holdall into the boot of his car, and he'd attempted to make small talk as we'd left the town somewhere on the outskirts of Warrington behind, only giving up when it transpired it would be easier getting blood from a stone than having a two-way conversation with me. It wasn't that I didn't *want* to talk to him about the weather or how many weeks there are until Christmas, but I found all my attention was focused on not having an anxiety-fuelled vomit over the backseat of his car. I'd bought a bottle of water once I'd disembarked the train at Warrington and have been taking tiny sips of it ever since, but it's doing little to ease the nausea I've been feeling since I stepped onto the hot, stuffy bus that eventually led me to a town I'd never even heard of until I'd Googled how to get to Little Heaton. From there, I'd managed to locate a taxi rank to take me the rest of the way. Or at least that's what I hope is happening right now. The taxi driver is pleasant and I didn't spot a shovel in the boot of his car earlier, but you just never know. I should ask if it's much further, to try to gauge the driver's intentions, but I find myself mute and clammy-handed as I sit ramrod straight in my seat, wincing as the meter continues to tick over.

'I don't come this far out very often.'

I jump a mile as the driver's voice suddenly speaks over the radio, interrupting Mike and the Mechanics urging the listeners to appreciate their loved ones while they're still with us. Seriously though, why am I worrying so much? A taxi driver who listens to Mellow Magic is hardly a threat, right?

'Breathtaking, isn't it?' The driver nods his head, indicating the scenery surrounding us. To the left of us, the greenery curves up high, the hilltop reaching for the blue, clear sky, while to the right there is a sharp drop where we can see down into the valley, as one field merges into the next, with only the odd ramshackle outbuilding breaking up the greenery. There are no other cars on the road, no people or animals that I can see from my vantage point. Nobody to hear me scream. It is beautiful and eerie all at once.

'So peaceful, innit?' The taxi driver shakes his head in wonder without waiting for an answer to his original question, as though he knows I couldn't speak even if I wanted to. 'I used to come up here a lot with the missus, back in the day. Walked for miles, we did.' He laughs and pats his rounded stomach, accentuated by the belt tethering him to his seat. 'Long time ago now, though. Don't think I'd have it in me anymore.'

I nod and twitch a smile at him, though I say nothing. My mouth is dry, my tongue fat and sluggish, my mind a garbled mess unable to put together a sentence. I take a sip of my water. It's almost gone.

'Not much further now, love.'

'Really?' My voice is a rasp, despite the water. I haven't uttered a word for miles, not since the meter was displaying below a fiver.

The driver is watching me through the rear-view mirror, his bushy eyebrows raised. 'Five minutes, I'd say. Ten, tops.'

My shoulders relax, even as the fleeting thought that he's toying with me – all part of his sick game – flashes across my mind. I screw the lid back onto my water and slip it into my handbag before taking out my phone to text Emma. I haven't dared to communicate with the outside world since we entered the deep depths of nowhere, in case the driver knew I was on to him and was raising the alarm.

I am an idiot, but in my defence, this has been a really weird and extremely stressful day so far.

'You on holiday then?' Having coaxed one little word from me, the driver is having another stab at small talk and I feel I owe him after thinking the worst of him.

'I wish.' A holiday would be nice. I haven't been away since I was little, back when my parents were still together and we spent a couple of weeks in Italy. I remember the heat and the gelato and the feeling that life couldn't get any better than this. It didn't.

26

My parents split up shortly afterwards and we never returned to the glory days of that summer holiday.

'Oh?' The driver is raising his eyebrows at me in the rear-view mirror, and I assume he isn't enquiring about my desire to jet away to sunnier climes.

'I'm going to Little Heaton for work.'

'I see.' The driver nods, his eyes back on the road. 'What kind of work?'

I'm about to explain that I'm in events management, but that isn't strictly true anymore. But I can't tell him I'm in property development either, as I'd feel like a fraud.

'I'm helping out with a house refurbishment.' This is much closer to the truth of the situation, and luckily the driver doesn't probe any further. Instead, he regales me with tales of his own home improvements, from DIY disasters to DIY triumphs. He's in the middle of a story about the dodgy plumbing he discovered beneath his kitchen sink when I spot the first sign that we are indeed on the right track. We've wound our way down the hillside and though I have yet to see another human being, there are at least fields of sheep and cows again. And then, nestled in an overgrown bush and only just visible through the foliage, is a hand-painted sign:

Buy fresh eggs @ Little Heaton Animal Sanctuary

There's an arrow pointing ahead and everything. We're almost there!

A couple of minutes later, we've turned off the tarmacked road and onto a little lane that is barely more than a dirt track. We jiggle and bump over the loose rocks and potholes until we reach a bridge stretching over a canal. I strain to look out over the side as we drive over, the knot in my stomach loosening for the first time since Vanessa landed this gig on me. Little Heaton is beautiful. The water of the canal is sparkling in the sunshine, throwing out shades of green from the trees and hedges lining the towpath. All is still apart from the ripples following a pair of swans as they glide alongside a moored barge.

We cross the bridge, emerging fully into the village. There is so much green, from the lush, leafy trees, the beautifully presented gardens sitting proudly in front of quaint cottages, and the hills in the distance. We are a world away from the bustling city centre I'm accustomed to.

I finally spot my first human for many miles; a dog-walker in hunter green wellington boots pulled over worn jeans. He raises his hand in greeting as we pass, pulling tight on the lead to keep his dog away from the tiny lane we're passing along.

'Now then.' The driver slows as he peers at the sat nav. 'Can't be far from here.'

We pass an assortment of houses, from squat, crumbly-looking cottages to three-storey newbuilds, until we reach the high street. There's a small community garden in the centre, facing a terrace of shops. There's a tanning shop, which jars against its picturesque surroundings, but it makes me think of Sonia, who is probably laughing her socks off at me back at the office. There are more houses, lots of greenery and even a castle in the distance, which makes me do a proper double-take as I catch sight of it. We pass a couple of pubs – which I fully intend to make use of during my stay – then end up back alongside the canal. The car stops and I peer out of the window, my brow creasing with confusion. There are no houses here, just the water and trees.

'Just give me a minute, love.' The driver is tapping at the screen of his sat nav, tutting and sighing as he jabs harder and harder.

'Are we lost?' Just when I thought things were looking up. Maybe this isn't the right place after all.

'Ah, no, nothing like that.' The driver is still stabbing the screen with his finger. 'It's just this stupid thing …' He shakes his head. 'It's sending us that way.' He points across the canal. I look both ways, looking for another bridge, but there is nothing but the narrow wooden footbridge we've parked alongside. 'We must have taken a wrong turning somewhere.' He jabs at the screen one last time before he spots another dog-walker heading our way. Winding down the window, he leans right out and waves a hand to catch her attention. It's as she approaches the car that I realise she isn't a dog-walker at all. The animal plodding behind her isn't of the canine variety but of the woolly kind. She's taking a *sheep* out for a stroll. What the …?

'We're looking for Arthur's Pass, love, but the sat nav's playing up.' The driver thrusts a thumb at the malfunctioning equipment. 'What's the best way to go?'

The woman stoops to pet the sheep. She's only young, early twenties at the most, with long blonde hair plaited to the side. She's wearing bright red wellies over skinny jeans and a matching parka with a furry hood.

'You'd need to go all the way back to the iron bridge.' She pulls an apologetic face, as though she's responsible for the balls up. 'Arthur's Pass is on the other side of the canal and we only have the one access across the bridge for vehicles. It's a bit of a nightmare, actually, but you sort of get used to it.' She shrugs and pets the sheep again. 'Are you just dropping off?' She's looking at the side of the car, at the taxi's markings. 'Because you'd be better off jumping out here and walking the rest of the way.' She's peering past the driver now to address me. 'It's just over this footbridge and down the lane.' She points across the canal, towards a cluster of trees. 'I'm heading that way myself so I can show you.'

'That would be so kind, thank you.' As much as I appreciate the driver getting me here safely, without turning out to be a bloodthirsty maniac, I don't fancy driving all the way back through the village. I'm still feeling a bit queasy and desperate for a bit of fresh air.

I pay the driver, fighting hard not to wince at the number of notes I'm forced to hand over, and grab my holdall from the boot. With a cheery wave goodbye with one hand and the receipt for the journey clutched in the other, I set off across the footbridge with my volunteer tour guide and her woolly friend.

Arthur's Pass is a tiny, tree-lined lane that leads to a clearing in which stands what can only be described as a manor house. The house is made of pale stone, with wide stone steps leading up to the heavy wooden door, which is set under its own pitched roof. The house is magnificent, but it isn't the only building on the land. Set back from the main house is a long, one-storey building, with three large windows and a smaller version of the wooden front door. Both buildings are angled so they're facing the gorgeous, unobstructed view of the canal, and there are a couple of smaller buildings to the side. Clusters of trees surround the land, creating a barrier to the outside world.

'Here you are.' I'm so in awe of the building before me that I'd forgotten about my companion. She's led me the short distance from the taxi to Vanessa's place, chatting about the village and its amenities once she learned I was new to the area. 'It's such a gorgeous house, isn't it? It's been empty for years, though. I'm glad someone's finally giving it the TLC it needs to bring it back to life.' She starts to back away, whistling at the sheep so it follows. 'I'm sure I'll see you around, but if you need anything, I'm just along the lane.' She lifts a hand in farewell and I copy the gesture briefly before I'm drawn back to the house.

Wow. I can't believe I'm going to be staying here for the next month. I'd already decided that I wouldn't be making the arduous journey back and forth over the next few weeks as I allowed the paranoid thoughts to attack me during the taxi ride over, but this just seals the deal.

Welcome to your new home, Rebecca, I think – rather smugly – as I make my way towards the front door.

Chapter 6

Although the front door looks as though it's an original feature, the lock is more modern, meaning there isn't a rustic, easily identifiable key on the bunch I grabbed from Vanessa's office earlier. The only way to gain entry is to try each key in turn until the lock gives and I'm able to push the heavy oak door open.

The door opens into a vast hallway, with a wide staircase opposite and light flooding in from the huge windows either side of the door. The space is bare, with exposed brick walls and stripped woodwork, but I can tell this is going to be an amazing welcoming area when it's completed. I can picture smooth, plastered walls painted in a warm, creamy shade, a coat stand in the corner, perhaps a bench under the window with storage for shoes underneath, and there is more than enough space for a massive tree at Christmas beside the staircase, all lit up and festive. I get a warm, fuzzy feeling despite the freezing temperature inside the empty, unheated house.

My footsteps echo on the bare floorboards as I move across the room, slowly and carefully, as though I'm an intruder, which I very much feel like right now. I expect to hear noises within the house; hammering, drilling, a too-loud radio, voices at the very least. It's already past lunchtime and there are a couple of vans outside, so I'd assumed the builders were here, but the house is eerily lifeless as I move from room to room. What was once a kitchen has been updated with bi-fold doors that look out onto the land at the back of the property, where there's a humongous, overgrown garden lined with trees to give a feeling of seclusion, and another outbuilding that has definitely seen better days.

I back away from the sheet of glass, jumping at the sound my foot makes as it meets the concrete flooring. I tiptoe my way through the rest of the house, marvelling at the amount of space available. The ceilings are high and most of the rooms are larger than my entire flat. I make my way up to the top floor and open the door that leads to a small balcony. It's cold outside but the view overlooking the canal is stunning, the air fresh and earthy and instantly relaxing. I can feel the stress of the surreal morning being plucked away as I close my eyes, taking deep, greedy breaths as I listen to the soundtrack of the countryside. Gone are the roars of traffic, the dozens of conversations mingling into one incessant hum, the busy lives and dramas of people packed in tight. Here, there is nothing but the mesmerising rustle of the wind tickling the leaves and the sing-song chirrups of unseen birds. A smile flashes onto my face as I take another lungful of the untainted air. Imagine living here, with all this space and beauty, instead of being stuck in a hovel with a semi-feral flatmate. I need this, or something reasonably close but still attainable. And to do that, I have to succeed with my new role as project manager.

*

'Have you tried the pub?'

'The pub?' I sit down on the bottom step of the grand staircase and try to stop my teeth from chattering. It really is bloody freezing in this house.

'Maybe they've gone for a skive since they're unsupervised?'

Emma gives a throaty laugh down the phoneline. 'I know I'd slope off for a gin if I could get away with it. Instead, I'm stuck at this reception desk as usual. I almost wish I could swap places with you.'

I've been in Little Heaton for over an hour and apart from the vans still parked in the driveway and a small digital radio perched on the cistern in the main bathroom on the first floor, there hasn't been the tiniest hint of the builders.

'Believe me, you don't want to trade places with me.' I rub at my nose. It's so cold, it's hurting. 'It took *forever* to get here. I'm definitely staying here for the duration.' If I can stand the cold, that is. Vanessa mentioned a guesthouse; I hope it has some sort of heating system installed. 'Anyway, I'd better go and find the pub and see if they're in there. We passed a couple on the way, so hopefully your hunch is right.' And if not, I can at least warm up for a bit.

Pushing the phone into my pocket, I make my way out of the house, locking up even though there's only a paint-splattered radio to nick. It actually feels a little bit warmer outside with the sunshine and the brisk walk to the nearest pub. I manage to find the Farmer's Arms quite easily by retracing my steps over the footbridge. Being the middle of the afternoon, I expect the pub to be quiet, empty even, but I'm blasted by noise as soon as I push the door open. The jukebox is playing a George Ezra track, interrupted by the clunk of pool balls colliding, and there's the general murmur of conversation. Emma was right. The builders are here, enjoying a day off by the looks of it as they sip pints around the pool table. There are three of them; one older, maybe mid-forties, one who must be early thirties, and a baby-faced kid who has to be late teens at the most. I obviously don't know for sure that these are Vanessa's builders – or builders at all – but with their heavy-duty boots and plaster-ingrained jeans, I highly suspect they are. Emma is a genius who is wasted behind that reception desk. She definitely deserves that gin.

'Everything okay over there, duck?'

I'm still hovering by the door, but I make my way over to the barmaid, whose face breaks out into a friendly smile as I clamber onto one of the high stools at the bar.

'What can I get you?' The barmaid places her hands on the bar, displaying a rainbow of fingernails as each one is painted a different colour. I'm tempted to order something large and lethal, but I still have a job to do.

'Just a diet coke please.' I sneak a look at the builders as I reach into my bag for my purse. They're still playing pool, ribbing each other as tricky shots are missed, completely unaware that I'm here. I should probably march up to them and demand they get back to work (after ascertaining that they are, in fact, Vanessa's builders) but I find myself furtively observing them as I sip at my drink. The older one claps the youngest on the back before he ambles towards the bar, his hand fumbling in his pocket for change. He orders a round of pints before counting out the pound coins in his fist.

'Won the jackpot earlier.' He nods towards the fruit machine and my cheeks burst into flames. I hadn't realised I'd been staring.

'Well done.' I offer a tiny congratulatory smile before I turn away completely, concentrating on my drink and willing my face to cool down. Just minutes ago I'd been about to succumb to frostbite and now I may as well be sunning myself on a Mexican beach in the midst of a heatwave. I should introduce myself, let him know the impromptu day off has come to an abrupt end. But I don't. I sit and stare at my diet coke.

'You're new around here.' The barmaid gives a statement rather than poses a question as she sets the first pint down. 'Sorry.' She gives a one-shouldered shrug and grabs another glass. 'It's a small place.'

'It's okay. I've only just got here.' I sneak a look at the builder as I continue. 'I'm here to take over as project manager for the refurbishment on Arthur's Pass.'

If I had any doubts that these guys were my team of builders, they disappear as the eyes before me widen to unnatural proportions.

'You're taking over? What happened to Nic?' He shoots a look over his shoulder, where the others are still playing pool. The younger one is swaggering towards the table, slowly chalking the end of his cue, while the other is shaking his head and telling him he doesn't stand a chance, but in much more colourful language.

'There was an accident.' I hold up a hand as his eyes widen again. 'Nicole's okay. Hurt, but she'll recover.' I slide off the stool and hold out a hand. 'I'm Vanessa Whitely's PA.' There's a roar from the pool table as the never-gonna-happen shot does indeed happen. The young lad is jumping around giving a victorious cry, while the older one, still shaking his head, flails his arms around as he tries to convince his pal that it was a complete fluke (again, with more colourful language).

'You're Vanessa?' The builder's eyes are like saucers as he turns back to me after the interruption. 'It's so good to finally meet you after all those emails early on.' He takes my hand and pumps it up and down, his eyes still very much rabbits-in-headlights wide. 'You're probably wondering what we're doing here, right?' He gives a chuckle while I simply frown back at him. He thinks I'm Vanessa? The bellowing from his team obviously cut off the end of my introduction, so I've been inadvertently upgraded from PA to the boss herself. I'm jolted by the realisation that I was supposed to get in touch with this guy to explain about the Nicole situation and how I – *Rebecca* – would be replacing her for the last few weeks of the project. Bugger. I never forget to carry out tasks set by Vanessa – I'd be a pretty poor PA if I did – but I did forget to do this during the panic and disorder of the morning. I need to rectify this, and fast.

The laughter dies as the builder lets go of my hand. 'We're not slacking off or anything. We went to the house. Waited ages. Even

35

phoned Nic, but there was no answer. So we came here to wait for her. No key, you see. There isn't much we can do without access.' He chuckles again, but it's much weaker this time and he turns towards the pool table. 'Hey, guys. Get over here.'

'Run out of cash already?' The older of the two stops his tirade so he can turn to his boss with a smirk. 'I'm skint, pal. You don't pay me enough.'

'Did you see that shot?' The other builder grins, his whole face lighting up and somehow making him look even younger.

'That was nothing.' The smirk falls from the older builder's face as he leans over the table with his cue. 'Check this out.'

I reach out to touch the head builder's arm lightly, the frown still furrowing my brow. 'Excuse me, but there's been some sort of misunderstanding. I'm not …' My words are swallowed as another roar goes up from the pool table, but instead of victorious, this roar is of the mocking variety. The older builder is elbowed playfully in the ribs as his mate falls about laughing at his terrible shot.

'Guys! Seriously, get over here.' The head builder flashes me an apologetic smile. I open my mouth to try to explain who I am – or rather who I'm *not* – but he's already turned back to the lads. 'Come and meet Vanessa Whitely.' I see his eyes bulge as he attempts to convey the importance of his words. It works like magic. The lads stop mucking about, their faces turning to stone as they stand upright and rush towards the bar, each thrusting their hand at me to shake in turn.

'Hi Vanessa. It's a pleasure to finally meet you. I'm Harvey.' The older of the two pool-playing builders is acting as spokesman as he points out his workmate. 'And this is Todd.'

'And I'm Vincent Mancini, obviously.' The boss shakes my hand again and I see his forehead is starting to shine with sweat. 'I should have said that earlier. Sorry. You can call me Vince. If you want to, that is.' He chuckles, though the sound is strained rather than joyful. 'I'll answer to anything, really.'

I'm astonished by the reaction my mere presence has caused. Or rather, the reaction *Vanessa's* presence has caused. I should clarify who I am, but I'm rather enjoying the power Vanessa clearly holds, so I keep it zipped. I'll tell them later, obviously, but not until I've chivvied them along and got them back to work.

'Shall we get going then?' I tap my watch in a way I've witnessed Vanessa do many times. 'We've lost half the day already.'

'But my pint …' Todd, the youngest builder, looks longingly at the bar. I could relent, let them finish their drinks, but I feel a surge of authority shoot through me, straightening my spine and raising my chin.

'You can have a pint on your own time, not mine.'

I have no idea where those words came from, but I quite like the firm, assertive tone they're accompanied by, and I get a real kick when the builders march out of the pub instead of snubbing my request. Being Vanessa is strangely satisfying.

Chapter 7

'I'm afraid I don't have any of Nicole's paperwork yet and she's too poorly for a catch up, so if you could give me a brief rundown of where we're up to with the project?'

We're trooping through the village, Vincent and I walking side-by-side while Harvey and Todd are just ahead, having some sort of friendly disagreement that involves a lot of nudging and an attempted wedgie. I've explained about Nicole's condition as best as I can, but now we must get down to business. My career depends on keeping this project on track.

'Once the plastering's finished, we're going to crack on with the fixed flooring. There's only the hallway, kitchen and the family bathroom on the first floor to do, and we would have made a start already, but like I said, with no access …' Vincent scratches the back of his neck as we reach the footbridge across the canal.

'Don't worry about it.' Having worked with Vanessa for three years, I know she wouldn't have appreciated the lack of work, no matter the circumstances, but I really don't see what he could have done, other than break into the property. 'We've still got a few hours left of the day, so I'm sure you and the lads will do your best to catch up.'

'Oh, yes. Absolutely.' Vincent bobs his head up and down

rigorously and I realise my words came out with a vaguely threatening tone rather than the placatory one I'd been aiming for. Perhaps being Vanessa has gone to my head a bit. 'And we'll put in a few more hours to make up for it.'

'There's really no need for that,' I say, but my words are swallowed by the griping up ahead as both Todd and Harvey put their cases across as to why that won't be possible. Harvey, it seems, has football training (he plays five-a-side at the park at weekends if I fancy being his cheerleader – short skirt and pompoms most definitely required) while Todd needs to take his gran to bingo.

Harvey snorts. 'It's the other way around, more like.' He hooks an arm around Todd's neck and pulls him close before running his knuckles over his scalp. 'Didn't your mum get you a personalised bingo dabber for your birthday?'

'Gerroff.' Todd wrestles himself free and tries to smooth down his ruffed-up hair. 'And no, she didn't. It was from my gran. She's got one herself.'

Shaking his head, Harvey gives Todd a gentle shove. 'You're such a loser.'

I think it's quite sweet, but I don't voice my opinion as matching bingo dabbers definitely isn't something Vanessa would appreciate.

'You can both stay behind.' With his shoulders thrown back, Vincent starts to stride ahead across the bridge. 'Oliver too.'

'Who's Oliver?' I quicken my step, scuttling after Vincent over the wooden boards as he overtakes Harvey and Todd. Vanessa would never scuttle after anybody but I don't want to lag behind.

'He's the other builder.' Todd waves a hand in the general direction of the house. 'But he's fixing his sister's fence. Ow!' He rubs his arm, where Harvey has just thumped him.

Vincent holds up a hand, silencing his teammates as they start to squabble. 'He hasn't got time to be messing around with Stacey's fence. We need to get on with the plastering.' He sneaks a glance at me and lifts his chin. 'Get on the phone to him and tell him to get his butt back to the house, pronto.'

Todd is still rubbing his arm as Harvey makes the phone call, singing the nursey rhyme about a man with a dog named Bingo as he waits for the other builder to answer. They're acting as I assume brothers would growing up. Not that I'd know. I only have one sibling, an older sister, and we were never close growing up. Kate and I barely speak even now we're adults, and we meet up even less. Being a doctor, she has a busy life that I just can't seem to fit into. Besides, we have nothing in common other than shared parentage.

'Did you have a look at the house earlier?' Vincent asks as we make our way along Arthur's Pass. 'I know it probably doesn't look like much has happened since you were last here, but we've had to gut the place and start again.' He's scratching his neck again and I want to pull at his arm to stop him.

'It looks great, honestly, and I'm sure it'll start to look more homely soon.'

'Absolutely.' Vincent bobs his head up and down. 'Once the flooring's laid, we can start to put the house back together again. Make it look like a home rather than a shell.'

We reach the clearing and I find myself sucking in my breath at the sight of the house again. It really is magnificent.

'I'm going to be staying on-site for the duration of the project, rather than commuting to and from Manchester every day. Less hassle.' I study the outbuildings, trying to work out which one is the guesthouse. Hopefully it isn't the ramshackle shed at the back. I peeped in earlier and it was less than ideal for human habitation.

'So no more late starts and early lunches then.' He winks at me to show he's kidding, but he's scratching at the back of his neck again. 'I take it you'll be staying in the guesthouse and not the main one. Bit bare and chilly in there at the moment. I'll get Todd to take your luggage through, if you haven't done so already?'

He glances across the drive and turns to me with a puzzled look. 'Where's your car? You haven't parked it out on the lane, have you? Because that thing's so narrow, you won't have wing mirrors left by the end of the day.'

'I didn't drive over.' Which sounds most unlike Vanessa, who'd drive to the corner shop. 'I'm trying to be a bit more green, you know?' I'm about to add that I don't need Todd to help with my luggage as I've only brought a holdall before I realise Todd's help could guide me to my accommodation. I can't *ask* where the guesthouse is as Vanessa would already know and I'm enjoying being her far too much to admit who I really am at the moment. I'll tell them later, once I'm settled in the guesthouse and they've made a start on the flooring.

*

The guesthouse, like most places, is bigger than my flat. It turns out I'll be staying in the long, one-storey building and not the dilapidated shed. This outbuilding has been fully restored and furnished and I gape at the spacious dwelling as I follow Todd inside. Before us is a modern open-plan living and dining area with two huge windows overlooking the canal. There's an L-shaped kitchen in the corner, with a breakfast bar separating the cosy seating area, complete with a massive, wall-mounted TV and a cabinet stuffed with DVDs.

'Where shall I …?' Todd lifts the holdall and glances around the room. I've been too busy gawping to take it from him.

'Thank you for your help.' I relieve Todd of the holdall and lead him back towards the door. 'I'll pop over to the house in a little while to see how you're getting on.' Again, my tone comes out rather menacing and Todd bolts from the guesthouse, stumbling over a large loose rock on the drive in his haste. I've never had this effect on anybody before and I only wish I could bottle it up to dispense on Lee when I get back to the flat.

Closing the door, I take in the room again, noticing all the little touches, from the exposed polished beams, plush carpet and log burner that give the place a snug, homely feel. I feel like weeping when I picture my flat waiting back in Manchester, with its drab, peeling wallpaper and flaky paintwork, the plumbing that likes to announce its presence by squealing every time the hot tap is turned on, and the flatmate whose idea of good hygiene practice is brushing his teeth sporadically with *my* toothpaste and washing his clothes when the smell starts to bother him (which is long after it's started to bother everybody else). But no, I will not cry, because I have a whole month to enjoy the luxury of living without Lee in a beautiful home. Why did I ever think being Vanessa's project manager was a bad idea?

Flopping onto the sofa with a contented sigh, I prop my feet up on the coffee table in front of me and spread my arms out wide. This whole sofa is mine. This whole *room* is mine. I can watch what I want on the TV without having to turn the volume up to its maximum to drown out Lee's racket. I can cook without having to hunt for crockery beforehand. I can cook without replacing the ingredients that have been stolen from the fridge. What extravagance!

My feet are aching from the silly boots, so I ease them off before padding towards the door leading off the living area, the thick pile of the carpet caressing my sore, battered feet. As suspected, the door opens to reveal the bedroom. And what a bedroom it is. I actually gasp out loud when I clock the huge four-poster bed that reaches up to ceiling height. There are more beams in here, and another huge window overlooking the canal. A red and blue barge is passing slowly, decorated with painted flowers and swirls, and a little dog sits on its roof, watching the world pass by.

At the opposite end of the room is a pair of French doors that lead to what was once a small garden but is now a series of pots full of weeds and the last wilting flowers from the summer. There's another log burner in here, and an oversized mahogany wardrobe that looks like it could lead to Narnia. Another door leads to a small but opulent bathroom, with a claw-footed bath taking centre-stage. I can have a bath without having to pluck pubes from the plughole beforehand. I can leave my washbag unattended. I can use a towel before having to give it a tentative sniff first. The indulgence!

I'm overwhelmed with the urge to fill the bath with hot, bubbly water and sink into it, but I have work to do. I need to unpack. I need to find a shop for supplies. And I need to reintroduce myself to the builders before I find myself in a super-awkward situation. But first, I need to take a few photos and send them to Emma. Hopefully she'll show them to Sonia, who will be *green* with envy.

I'm in the middle of sending a bunch of smugtastic photos to Emma when I hear a knock at the front door. Todd is standing on the doorstep with a small box of PG Tips in one hand and a bottle of milk in the other. A jar of coffee and a bag of sugar is tucked under each arm.

'I don't suppose I could use your kettle?' He flashes me a sheepish look as he waggles the box of teabags in my direction. 'Nic used to let us make brews in here.'

I reach out and take the teabags from him. 'Let me do that. I'll bring them over to you.' It's the least I can do after I dragged them away from their untouched pints earlier. 'What am I making?'

'Three coffees – one black, no sugar, the others with milk and two sugars.' Todd follows me into the kitchen, dumping the coffee, milk and sugar on the counter. 'And one tea. Milk, no sugar.'

I repeat the order back to Todd, to make sure I've got it right in my head, before sending him back to the main house. I slip my boots back on while I'm waiting for the kettle to boil, pretending I don't feel the now familiar pinch as I hobble back to the kitchen. There's a small collection of matching mugs in the cupboard and I find a tray tucked beside a set of saucepans. Loading it up with the drinks, I carry the tray carefully across the uneven drive to the main house, setting it down on the steps so I can open the door. The sound of upbeat music hits me as soon as I step into the hallway, and I follow the sound into what will one day be the kitchen again.

'Tea break!' I raise my voice to be heard over the radio and the drill with attached paddle that Vincent is using to mix up a large batch of plaster. He switches off the drill and swipes at his forehead with the back of his arm.

'You're a pet. You should have made this one do it.' Vincent thrusts a thumb towards Todd before he drags himself to his feet. He grabs the black coffee and takes a tentative sip before turning to Todd again. 'Take Oliver his tea up before it gets cold.'

Todd scrambles to his feet and reaches for the tea, but I move the tray out of the way. 'I'll do that. You have a break and enjoy your coffee.' Todd shrugs and takes the remaining coffees, handing one to Harvey, who is still on the floor but now lounging, his legs spread out before him. 'Where is Oliver?'

Vince takes another slurp of his coffee. 'He's making a start on the first-floor bathroom. Up the stairs, second door on your left.'

My footsteps echo loudly on the uncarpeted stairs, even as I take careful steps to avoid spilling the tea. I'd forgotten how cold it is in here and I shiver as I reach the top. I'm not surprised when I see the thick jumper the builder in the bathroom is wearing, the collar of a T-shirt visible at the neckline. I'd need a few more layers to stand working in the cold, and it's clear why Vincent risked a scalded tongue by drinking his coffee so quickly, eager for some source of warmth.

The builder has his own radio up here – the small digital one I'd spotted earlier – and it's currently blaring out The Bangles' 'Walk Like an Egyptian'. It's so loud, he hasn't heard my ascent up the stairs and has no idea I'm observing him from the doorway, watching as his bottom jiggles to the music. And it's a lovely bottom; round but firm and full of rhythm, it seems. Setting the tea down carefully on the floor, I grab my phone and open the camera. Emma will never believe just how perfect a bottom this builder has, so I need photographic proof.

'What are you doing?'

Stepping back with a yelp, I only just manage to avoid kicking the cup of tea over. 'I, er, I was just …' I look down at my phone and discreetly close the camera app. 'I was just making a phone call.' My thumb taps on the contacts app a split second before I turn the phone to show him the screen.

'No.' Oliver shakes his head as he folds his arms across his chest. 'You weren't. You were trying to take a photo of me.'

I don't like his accusatory tone, even if the thing he's accusing me of is absolutely spot on.

'I beg your pardon?' I too can adopt a shirty tone. Even if I'm in the wrong, and even if said shirty tone has been pilfered from Vanessa's repertoire of snotty attitudes. 'I can assure you I wasn't taking a photo of anything, and especially not of *you*.' I'm quite proud of my sneering use of the word 'you', and the way my lip curls in distaste.

'Whatever.' Oliver twists and reaches for the radio, shutting off the music. 'Who are you, anyway? And does Vince know you're up here snooping?'

Snooping, indeed! My mouth starts to gape before I snap it shut. Vanessa doesn't gape. Ever.

'Yes, Vincent does know I'm up here.' Tilting my head to one side, I arch an eyebrow as high as I can manage. Admittedly, it isn't very high as I haven't had much practice in the art of snootiness. 'And I wasn't aware you could snoop in your own home.'

I expect Oliver to falter, to start falling over himself in his eagerness to please, like the others had in the pub earlier. Maybe he could wipe the palms of his hands down the thighs of his jeans while I stand by and enjoy his slack-jawed reaction to my statement. I'm usually the flustered one, so it would make a welcome change to be the cool, calm, collected one for once.

Except this dude doesn't give me the satisfaction of wavering. There are no sweaty palms, no slow realisation that I am The Boss. He is the cool, calm collected one as he narrows his eyes ever so slightly and looks me up and down.

'So you're the infamous Vanessa Whitely then.' He gives me another full-length once-over before giving a lazy shrug. 'You're not what I was expecting at all.'

'And what were you expecting?' Cruella De Vil, I should imagine, and I smile sweetly at him, watching him through lowered lashes, to show that I'm far from the hard-nosed picture he's built up in his head.

'I'd thought you'd be more rottweiler than chihuahua.'

I'm not sure whether this is a compliment or not, but by the sly smile creeping onto Oliver's face, I assume it wasn't intended to be flattering. Instead of the fierce, don't-mess-with-me guard dog, he sees me as a tiny, quivering pooch who's more likely to make a puddle on the carpet than defend its property. I should unleash the Vanessa Whitely effect and put him in his place, but I've never been very good at confrontation. I'm definitely more chihuahua, not that I'll tell him that.

'I take it you're Oliver?' I attempt an air of indifference, to try to claw back a bit of poise.

'Oliver Rowe.' He holds out a hand, and I'm worried mine will be trembling as I reach out to take it. I make the handshake as swift as possible to mask any of the anxiety I'm feeling over the exchange.

'It's lovely to meet you.' I smile sweetly again, even though Oliver's glowering at me. 'And about earlier ... shall we just forget that and start again?'

'Forget that you were perving on me, you mean?' Oliver folds his arms across his chest. 'Because I'm pretty sure that's sexual harassment in the workplace.'

'I wasn't perving on you. I was making a phone call.' I waggle the phone at him, even though the screen is locked by now. 'I wasn't trying to take a photo of your bottom as you so arrogantly assumed.'

'I never said anything about my bottom.' A smug smile creeps onto Oliver's face while I will the ground to open up beneath me. This is not going well at all. I need to get the upper hand back and quickly.

'I actually meant we should forget about the fact that you accused me of snooping around my own home.' There, take that, you smug git! 'Now just get back to work.' Giving him my best withering look, I march from the room, only to sneak back to pick up the cup of tea. If he wants a tea break, he can make his own bloody refreshments.

Chapter 8

I should probably head back to the guesthouse to unpack but I find myself wandering from room to room, sipping Oliver's tea as I take my time to have a good nosy at the first floor of this magnificent house. It felt a bit creepy earlier when I was alone in the bare bones of a giant, cold house, but knowing Oliver is just along the hall and with the sound of the radio drifting from the bathroom again, I feel more at ease. I've counted six bedrooms so far, three with en-suite bathrooms, and I know there are more on the second floor. I'm about to head up there for another mosey around when something catches my eye out of the huge arched window at the end of the hallway. The window looks out over the land at the back of the property and there is something moving out there. I'm not sure what it is, other than non-human and far too large to be a dog. I scurry closer to the window and gasp when I realise what I'm seeing.

'Oh my God.' My eyebrows have all but lifted off my face as I cover my gaping mouth with my hand. I can't believe it. Surely it isn't …

'What's the matter?'

I turn at the sound of Oliver's voice. He's standing in the bathroom doorway with a plaster-covered trowel and board in hand.

'Is it just me, or is there a *donkey* in the garden?' I point out of the window, where the beast is ambling across the long grass, tail swishing.

Oliver joins me at the window and I'm relieved when he nods. I'm not hallucinating then.

'That's just Franny. She must have found the gap in the fence I was fixing earlier. Don't worry, I'll sort it later.' He's striding back towards the bathroom while I remain at the window, staring at the donkey as she bends her head to nibble at the overgrown grass. 'I'll take her home now and then I'll patch up the fence as soon as I've finished here this evening.' Having deposited his equipment back in the bathroom, Oliver is striding along the hallway towards the stairs. Tearing my eyes away from the donkey, I scurry after him.

'Where does she live?' I'm not sure why I'm so interested in this donkey – probably because it's such an unusual sight. It isn't as though you see donkeys wandering around in Manchester. An unleashed dog, perhaps, and plenty of pigeons, but no donkeys or other farmyard friends.

'Just along the lane.' Oliver has already reached the bottom of the stairs while I'm still carefully treading down each step so I don't slip in my silly boots and break my neck.

'Can I come and meet her? Before you take her back?' Forgetting to channel Vanessa for a moment, a huge grin spreads across my face and I risk a tumble down the stairs as I pick up speed to join Oliver in the hallway.

'Do what you want.' Oliver shrugs. 'It's your house.'

Oliver's words are hardly warm and welcoming, but I almost whoop out loud as a rush of pure joy erupts inside me and I'm transported back to the days of being a carefree child, of plodding along the sand on the back of a gentle donkey, of feeling content and unburdened. Of feeling so happy I could burst. I can't recall the last time I felt so jubilant; perhaps it was when I was offered the job at Vanessa Whitely Events, back when I assumed I'd managed to get my foot through the door to my dream career. When I assumed I'd soon have a more inspired input in the business.

'Give me a minute.' Holding up a hand, Oliver strides into the kitchen but I tiptoe after him, catching the end of a conversation he's having with Todd.

'Why didn't you tell me *she* was here?'

The way Oliver spits out the word 'she' is as though he's just scraped it off the bottom of his shoe and caught a rank smell. Oliver Rowe, it seems, is not Vanessa's biggest fan and I've done nothing to persuade him to change his perception.

Todd shrugs as he piles plaster onto his board under Vincent's supervision. 'You didn't ask.'

Oliver throws his hands up in the air as Vincent shrugs. 'I assumed he'd told you.' He tuts at Todd. 'You're really as thick as mince sometimes, boy.'

I feel a bit sorry for Todd, especially as neither Harvey or Oliver jump to his defence and he simply gets on with the job of plastering the wall.

'I could have got myself sacked up there just now.' Oliver's words are hissed and poor Todd flinches.

'Why?' Harvey sniggers. 'What did you do? You didn't hit on her, did you?'

'Of course I didn't hit on her. Why would I?'

I feel a bit stung by Oliver's instant dismissal at the very *notion* of hitting on me. The cheek!

'You know what she's like though. You've seen the emails she sent to Vince back in the beginning, and the way she treated Nic. The woman's a Grade-A bitch.'

I don't want to hear any more, whether it's about me or Vanessa; I don't think my ego could take another bruising. Creeping backwards, I make sure my heels clip-clop to their maximum as I march back towards the kitchen to announce my presence.

'That donkey's still out there, you know.' With my hands on

my hips, I'm projecting pure rottweiler. Oliver responds by saluting me, which isn't quite the reaction I was hoping for, but at least he starts to move across the kitchen. Flashing poor Todd one last reproachful look, Oliver leads the way through the hallway, swinging the heavy oak door open and holding it for me to go through. It's a gentlemanly act, but I don't thank him for it. His words to the others are ringing in my ears on a loop.

Oliver leads me around to the back of the house without a word. Franny is still munching on the grass and seems in no hurry to leave.

'The grass must taste better on this side of the fence.' I'm trying to make light of the situation because the silence stretching between us is so awkward it's making me itch.

'Probably because she doesn't have to share with the others over here.' Oliver forges ahead while I tread over the damp grass as carefully as I can. My toes are already soaked and no doubt filthy. Open-toe boots are even less practical in the countryside than they are in the city.

'The others?' I wobble a bit, but luckily Oliver is too far ahead to notice.

'At the sanctuary.' Oliver slows down and for a moment I fear he's going to try to take my arm to steady me, but luckily he moves ahead again. I don't need his help. And I don't need him to hit on me either, the arrogant sod.

'There's a donkey sanctuary here?' I try to quash it, but there's that joyful feeling again, bursting from the pit of my stomach and spreading into my chest. Who knew, as I stepped on the platform at Piccadilly train station this morning, that I would find such happiness with this project?

'Not just donkeys. There's all sorts, really. In fact, there are only two donkeys – Franny and Daisy.' Oliver stops and turns to give me a strange look. 'You did know you were moving in practically next door to a bunch of animals, right?'

Too late, I realise I'm supposed to be Vanessa, who more than likely would know this fact, and that actually I *did* know there was an animal sanctuary nearby. There was a sign on the roadside. Something about eggs?

'I did know, *obviously*.' I roll my eyes and plant the heel of my hand against my forehead. 'But I can be such a scatterbrain sometimes.' I roll my eyes again for good measure before moving on towards the donkey.

'Have you been over to the sanctuary?'

I don't know. Has Vanessa been to the sanctuary? I can't imagine her being overly excited at the prospect of being in close proximity to any animal other than her prized pug, Angel, who has to be the most pampered pooch in the Greater Manchester area. Angel, whose miniature paws I swear have never touched the ground, is a world away from the robust-looking donkey before us. Franny is tall with spindly but sturdy-looking legs and long, twitching ears. Most of her fur is brown, but she has a creamy underside and face, which creates a stark contrast with her big brown eyes. She is beautiful.

'No. Not yet.' I take a punt and hope it was the right choice.

'You haven't met my sister, Stacey then?' He doesn't wait for an answer before striding ahead, which I'm grateful for as I have absolutely no idea whether Vanessa has been introduced to this woman. 'Hello, Franny. You know you're not supposed to wander off. Stace will be worried sick when she notices you've gone.' Oliver has adopted a mock-stern tone, but he's stroking the donkey with a gentle touch. This Oliver is a world away from the man who has just fumed at his workmate and called Vanessa a Grade-A bitch. 'Come and meet Vanessa and then we'll get you back before Stace has kittens.' He pats the donkey a couple of times on the side before beckoning me to come closer. I edge my way over, suddenly wary now we're up close. 'It's okay. She won't hurt you. She's a big softie, aren't you, girl?' He scratches the donkey in the space between her ears before holding a hand out to me. I take it, surprised it's so warm after being in the chilly house, and step closer to the donkey. She barely moves, too interested in the juicy grass in front of her.

'Hello, Franny.' I feel a bit foolish talking to a donkey, but Oliver smiles in encouragement and I reach out to stroke her fur. It's silky soft and warm and I find myself taking another step closer.

'See? There's nothing to be afraid of. Franny wouldn't hurt a fly.' Oliver stoops to plant a kiss on the top of her head. 'Shall we get you home, girl?'

Franny is wearing a bright red harness, which Oliver takes hold of and starts to gently guide the donkey towards the house. She cooperates fully, willingly giving up her grassy snack to plod alongside us.

'You're really good with her.' I can't help but feel impressed with the confident way Oliver is handling the donkey. As docile as she seems to be, there's no way I'd dare to even *try* to coax her to move, but Oliver is definitely in charge here.

'It comes from years of experience. Plus, we're best buddies, aren't we, girl?' He scratches at the space between Franny's ears as he guides her around the side of the house. I much prefer this Oliver to the smug one in the bathroom. 'Franny was the first animal taken into the sanctuary. In fact, she started it all off. It wasn't even a sanctuary at all back then, just a house with an old, disused barn and a big back garden. Franny was found wandering along the track near the iron bridge. Nearly got herself run over by a tractor. The poor girl was so thin, we didn't know if she'd survive.'

'But she did survive.' I cringe inwardly at my observation. Of *course* she survived – she's walking beside us right now. Oliver must think I'm completely dense. Or as thick as mince, as Vincent would say.

'That's all down to Stace.' We've reached the drive now, and Oliver pauses, his brows lowering as he nods towards the house. 'I won't be long and don't worry – I'll make the time up later.'

He seems to have reverted to the old Oliver, the Oliver who despises me. Or Vanessa. Or both of us.

'Can I come with you?' I'm intrigued by the animal sanctuary, and I also want to experience a bit more of the nice Oliver. If I can keep chatting to him while he's under the influence of Franny, while he's being cute and charming, maybe we can make up for the bad start we've had.

'Whatever.' Oliver shrugs, his tone sullen, but at least he hasn't said no. We carry on along the drive, taking it slowly over the uneven rubble covering on the ground.

'So what happened to Franny after she was found?' The donkey seems to be a safe topic, so I decide to keep our focus on her as we head towards the lane.

'Stace took Franny in, kept her warm and fed, and she got stronger and stronger. We tried to find the owner, but nobody ever came forward to claim her, so she became a permanent fixture in the barn. From there, word spread and any waif and stray was brought to Stace to look after. She loves it though and I'm so proud of the work she does for the animals. I help out when I can, but it's Stace who does most of the hard graft.'

I quite like the way he speaks about his sister, the pride not only in his words but in the tone of his voice and the way his face has lit up. I can't imagine Kate would ever speak about me in that way. I'm more of a disappointment than someone to aspire to.

I reach out to stroke Franny's soft fur, trying not to picture the state she was in when she was found out on the track. It's heartbreaking to imagine the suffering. Oliver and Stacey are good people for taking her – and many others – in and taking care of them. Oliver may not be my cup of tea in the way he speaks to his workmates, or the way he assumes people are drawn to his bottom (even if they are) and certainly not the way he dismissed me so rapidly, but that doesn't mean he's a bad person. And yes, I have to admit he's a good-looking bloke. He's tall and broad-shouldered with a confident manner (even if it sometimes nudges into arrogance) and there's definitely a cheeky twinkle in his eye. And I do like the way his dark blond hair is just a little bit too long and is starting to wave. And have I mentioned his bottom?

We reach the lane and although it's narrow, we're at least on firmer ground, which is good news for both Franny and my boots. Oliver tells me more about the sanctuary as we make our way towards the next property, and how they mainly rely on fund-raising and donations to keep the sanctuary running.

'And here we are.' Oliver stops in front of a gate between two sets of tall hedgerows and swings it open. 'Welcome to Little Heaton's Animal Sanctuary.'

Chapter 9

The animal sanctuary isn't at all what I was expecting. It looks like a regular house. A very pretty house, with a cherry-red door between two large, sashed windows, but a regular house all the same. There's a small garden to the front, with two oblong patches of manicured lawn sandwiching a cobbled path that leads from the wide iron gate to the front door. On closer inspection, I notice that the door knocker is a brass, floppy-eared rabbit, but the only other indication that this is an animal sanctuary is the small plaque proclaiming so above the letterbox.

'Wow. This looks lovely.'

And it really does. If you told me to close my eyes and picture a countryside dwelling, this is the image I would conjure. Chuck on a bit of snow and a wreath on the door, and you've got yourself a classy Christmas card right here.

'It isn't as grand as your house, but we like it.' Oliver closes the gate behind the three of us and leads Franny along the path. 'It was my grandparents' house. My gran left it to us six years ago, shortly before this little lady came to stay.'

Bypassing the front door, Oliver leads the way to a tall wooden gate to the side of the property before he hands the harness to me. My eyes widen in fear but I automatically grab hold of the strap.

'I won't be a minute. Just need to go and unlock the gate from the other side.' Oliver is already backing away from me, even as I open my mouth to protest. Nothing comes out and so I stand there with a gaping mouth until he disappears around the corner. I stand stock-still, willing Franny to do the same until Oliver returns. What would I do if the donkey decided to take another stroll? Other than scuttle after her? I'm a pushover when it comes to humans and although it's never been tested, I'm pretty sure I'll roll over and take whatever decision this donkey makes too.

Thankfully, Franny remains calm during the short time it takes Oliver to move through the house and into the back garden, but I still heave a massive sigh of relief when I hear the sound of a lock being released on the other side of the gate. It swings open, but instead of Oliver standing on the other side, it's the blonde woman who helped me find the house earlier. She doesn't have the sheep with her this time but she's still wearing the bobble hat and wellies.

'I'm so sorry about this.' She reaches for the harness and gives a gentle tug, and Franny responds by plodding through the gate. 'I didn't even realise she'd gone walkabout – I thought she was in the barn, the little tinker.' She indicates that I should follow and locks the gate behind me. 'We met earlier. Arthur's Pass, right?'

Oliver is suddenly beside Stacey, his arm slung around her shoulders. 'This is my sister, Stacey, the mastermind behind Little Heaton's Animal Sanctuary.' Stacey rolls her eyes, but she's smiling at the compliment. 'And this is your new neighbour.' Oliver removes his arm from Stacey's shoulder so he can hold it out towards me. 'Vanessa Whitely.'

The smile vanishes from Stacey's face and I cross my fingers behind my back, hoping with all my might that Stacey and the real Vanessa haven't met previously.

'Oh.' There's a flicker of a smile on Stacey's lips as she holds a hand towards me, but it doesn't last. 'We finally meet.' Her eyes are as cold as Vanessa's barren house as we shake hands. 'I hope Franny hasn't caused too much trouble?' She looks from me to Oliver, her tone rising to form a question.

'No trouble at all.' I stroke Franny's head, feeling braver now I'm not in control of the harness. 'In fact, it was lovely to meet her.'

Now we're on the other side of the gate, the animal sanctuary is clear to see. The garden at the property is quite large, but most of it is taken up by the barn at the bottom of the plot, with two wooden sheds and a series of hutches and coops to the side. A couple of chickens are wandering around, pecking at the ground, while the sheep I met earlier is munching on a patch of grass. There are hand-painted signs indicating where each set of animals is kept, plus another to the side of the back door to the house, directing the way to the café and gift shop.

'Well, feel free to pop over any time you like. We're always happy for volunteers to lend a hand.' Stacey starts to walk towards the barn at the bottom of the garden and Franny plods along beside her with little encouragement needed. 'And don't worry – we've always got plenty of spare pairs of wellies on hand.'

My gaze drops down to my feet, where I see my toes have taken on a blotchy, bluish hue, visible in patches beneath the mud I've accumulated along the way. These boots really aren't suited to countryside living. Vanessa's designer footwear won't stand a chance.

'I'm not sure mucking out donkeys is Vanessa's thing.'

I'm about to agree with Oliver's assessment of my boss until I realise with a start that he's talking about me. *Judging* me. And I don't like it. I don't like it one bit.

'I don't know about that. It might be fun?' I don't want Oliver to be under the impression I'm some sort of dirt-averse princess. I live with an untamed flatmate who leaves his toenail clippings on the arm of the sofa; if I can cope with discovering that grue-some collection as I sit down to watch the telly, I can certainly cope with cleaning out a barn.

'Okay then. Why don't you come round tomorrow morning?' Stacey twists so she's walking backwards, the harness still loose in her hands. 'I'll start you off gently with the chickens and I'll even throw in a free breakfast. How does seven o'clock sound?'

'You don't have to.' Oliver aims a dark look at his sister. 'I'm sure you're very busy.'

'No, it's fine.' I fold my arms across my chest and meet Stacey's eye with a steely determination I didn't even know I possessed. The real Vanessa wouldn't back away from a challenge and this fake one isn't going to either. Perhaps pretending to be Vanessa is rubbing off on me.

*

I finally sink into the claw-footed bath later that evening, once the builders have packed up their van and trundled away and I've had the chance to wander into the village in search of a shop. I eventually discovered a mini market on the high street, sand-wiched between a tanning shop and a charity shop, and I was able to pick up a few essentials and a ready meal – I couldn't face cooking after the day I've had. The warm, bubble-filled water is glorious and I allow myself to sink down until I'm almost fully submerged. I wriggle my toes to get the circulation going again as a combination of the boots and the cold have numbed them during the course of the day. My shoulders rise before I release a long, audible sigh into the steamy bathroom. I can't tell you how comforting it is to know that Lee won't try to shoulder his way through the door as he describes the state of his bowels two minutes into my soak.

I remain submerged until I start to shiver from the cool water and I resemble an old, wrinkly prune. I found a huge towel on the shelving unit inside the wardrobe while I was unpacking earlier, and I've left it warming on the radiator. Another huge sigh escapes as I wrap it around my body. I'm not sure how to light the fire, but I'm toasty warm anyway when I emerge from the bedroom encased in my fleecy onesie and fluffy dressing gown. The guesthouse is completely silent, but I break the stillness by jabbing at my ready meal with a fork and the hum from the microwave is familiar and soothing. While I wait for the microwave to zap my lasagne, I switch on the massive telly and flick through the channels until I find a repeat of *Would I Lie To You*. Lee Mack is tossing a teabag across the studio, aiming for a mug on the opposite desk, when the microwave pings. I turn the volume up to drown out the silence – there isn't a sound from outside, not even the distant murmur of traffic which is pretty eerie after living in a busy town – before I grab my lasagne and settle down for an evening of watching whatever the hell I want without complaint from Lee, or competition from his too-loud music.

I wish I'd thought to buy a bottle of wine from the mini market, but I make do with a cup of coffee and the slab of Dairy Milk I *did* have the forethought to purchase from its prime position at the till. The novelty of being alone is already starting to wane, so I send a quick text to Emma and selfishly hope she hasn't got such a fulfilled social life that it'll prevent her from replying. Thankfully, Emma responds within seconds and we end up chatting until the strangest day of my life takes its toll and I can no longer keep my eyes open. I remember to set my alarm so I'll be up and out of the guesthouse for my date with the chickens at seven the next morning, and it's just as my brain switches from conscious to snoresville that I realise I should have come clean about my true identity, that I shouldn't have spent the day tricking everyone into believing I'm someone I'm not. I'll tell them tomorrow. First thing. Everyone has been so nice and welcoming to me – apart from Oliver and his *'Of course I didn't hit on her. Why would I?'* comment, and Stacey *was* a bit frosty – but it feels wrong to deceive them. Not that I've been lying *per se* – it's simply a mistake I've been slow to rectify. That's all.

Chapter 10

When Vanessa tasked me with the role of project manager, I assumed I'd spend a few days at a time in Little Heaton before returning home for the weekend, so I haven't packed a great deal, and my footwear is limited. As well as the peep-toe boots, I've brought a pair of ballet flats with me, but neither are suitable for cleaning out chicken coops, so I hope Stacey wasn't kidding when she said they had spare pairs of wellies at the animal sanctuary.

It's a chilly morning again, so I zip my coat right up to my chin and shove my hands deep into my pockets as I make my way across the drive. It's still eerily quiet and I find myself longing to hear the rumble of an approaching bus as I make my way along the lane, but there isn't any hint of traffic at all, not even a bicycle. I find myself matching my serene surroundings, taking small, gentle steps along the narrow lane, avoiding the leaves that have already started to litter the ground in case they crunch underfoot. My ballet flats, it seems, are much more suited to creeping around the countryside than my boots.

I stand at the gate for a moment when I reach Stacey and Oliver's house, admiring the property. It isn't nearly as big as Vanessa's house, but it's charming with its yellow stone façade and red tiled roof, a small patch of ivy stretching up between the front door and the sashed window to the side. This house is a world away from the grotty flat above the takeaway I share with Lee and despite my determination to earn a promotion at work, this sort of home feels so far out of reach it makes my chest ache with longing.

The curtains have already been thrown open and I can see somebody pottering around in one of the downstairs rooms. I haven't got a clear view from here, but I can tell it is neither Oliver nor Stacey from the short, curvy build. Deciding it's time I stopped hovering, I push my way through the gate, jumping at the sudden sound as it clangs shut behind me. Turning to shush the inanimate object, I don't see the front door open.

'You came then.'

I jump again, my hand thumping against my chest as I turn around. Stacey is standing on the doorstep, eyebrow quirked as she watches me scuttle along the path towards her.

'Of course.' My voice is a squeak, so I clear my throat and throw my chin into the air, channelling Vanessa. 'Why wouldn't I?'

Stacey gives a lazy shrug before she opens the door wider and steps aside so I can follow her into the house. 'Cleaning out chickens isn't for everyone, and from what I know about you, I'd say it's as far away from your comfort zone as you can get.'

My brow furrows as I close the front door behind me. 'We only met briefly yesterday. What could you possibly know about me to make that judgement?'

Okay, fair enough, I'd been wandering around the countryside in a pair of unsuitable boots the previous day, but that doesn't mean anything. I came to the village in a professional capacity. I wasn't expecting to be volunteering at the local animal sanctuary. I'd have rocked up in my old, saggy jogging bottoms and greying trainers if I'd had an inkling.

'This is a pretty small village.' Stacey leads the way along the hallway, turning to make sure I'm still following. 'There's no such thing as a private life around here. Gossip is rife. It's a local pastime.'

'But there's nothing for people to gossip about when it comes to me.' We've reached the end of the passageway, which has broadened to form a small entryway. There's a shoe rack full of wellies below a row of waterproof jackets. 'I'm really not that interesting.'

The corner of Stacey's mouth flickers up before she presses her lips together to stop the smirk from fully forming on her face. 'If you say so.' She gives another shrug before she eyes my footwear. 'What size are you?'

'Five.'

Stacey is wearing the cherry-red wellies again. She selects a pink pair with white hearts from the rack and hands them to me before turning towards a set of drawers and opening the top one. 'Thick socks. Don't worry – they're clean. We always have plenty of spares.' She opens the next drawer and pulls out a yellow bobble hat. 'You might need this. It's pretty nippy out.' She reaches into the drawer again and hands me a pair of chunky gloves. 'I'll meet you outside when you're ready.' She points at the back door before she slips out of it. There's a chair against the wall opposite the shoe rack, so I sit down while I pull on the socks and wellies. I'm not sure about the bright yellow bobble hat, so I wedge it into my coat pocket and make my way out into the back garden, yanking on the gloves as I go. The chickens are already out of the coop, stalking around the small lawn and scratching at the ground.

'How many chickens have you got?' I only saw a couple yesterday, but there are at least half a dozen out here now.

'Eight.' Stacey rolls her eyes. 'We only started off with two. Ex-battery, in pretty poor condition. Bianca and Patty.' She points out a couple of the chickens. 'Poor girls. I didn't have a clue how to care for them, but you learn quickly, and Oliver put together the coop for me. It helps having someone handy with wood and nails on hand, believe me. Saves a fortune.' Stacey hands me a wicker basket and leads me towards the open coop. 'We'll collect any eggs first. Mrs McColl will be starting her cake baking soon, so we'd better be quick. You don't want to get on her bad side.' Stacey grins at me and I'm not sure whether to be reassured or not. I have no idea who Mrs McColl is but I'm keen to get the eggs in the basket ASAP.

The coop is wide, with a closed house-like structure at one end and a long, meshed run at the other. There's a box attached to the side of the wooden house, which Stacey lifts open. Nestled in the straw are five eggs, which we gently place in the basket. I've never handled an egg so fresh and as long as I don't think about where it has just come from, I'm fascinated.

'I'll get these inside to Mrs McColl so she can get started on her baking.' Stacey takes the basket from me and starts to head back towards the house. 'Can you gather the water containers and give them a quick scrub at the tap?' Stacey has reached the back door and she points out the tap further along the building. I give a thumbs up, my smile bright and confident, but it slips as soon as Stacey disappears inside. What if one of the chickens sees me messing around their coop and comes to investigate? What if all of them suddenly become interested in the stranger on their property? I've never been up close and personal with a chicken (unless I've been sticking one in the oven) but they seem very beaky and scratchy and I don't fancy my chances going up against one of them, let alone eight of the feathered beasts. I think about channelling Vanessa again to bolster my confidence, but there is no way Vanessa would be in this yard cleaning out chickens. For now, I will have to make do with being Rebecca Riley. She is capable. She is reliable. She is also actually quite terrified of chickens, it seems.

With a yelp, I'm across the yard, stumbling in my unfamiliar wellies. One of the chickens, a scrawny-looking, rusty-coloured one, is stalking towards me, its evil intentions clear in its small, beady eyes.

'That's just Chow Mein.' Stacey steps through the door again as I reach it, a bemused look on her face. 'She's curious, that's all. She won't hurt you, will you, sweetie?' Bending, Stacey scoops up the chicken and brandishes it towards me. I fight the urge to leap away and instead hold out a slightly trembling finger, touching it briefly to the chicken's soft feathers. I clocked the look of bemusement on Stacey's face as she caught me cowering by the door and I won't give her the satisfaction of seeing me spooked again. For some reason, Stacey seems to be trying to push my buttons, testing me to find my limits.

'Chow Mein?' I take the opportunity to look away from the feathery beast and focus on Stacey instead. '*Chicken* Chow Mein?'

Stacey rolls her eyes. 'Oliver named her. Thought it was amusing.' She shrugs, the corners of her lips flicking briefly into a small smile. 'Which it is. A little bit.'

'She's lovely, really, isn't she?' I don't dare stroke Chow Mein again, but I do stoop to look her in the face. Her eyes don't look quite so beady now she isn't chasing me across the yard. 'Quite cute for a chicken.'

'She's gorgeous. I've had her since she was a chick, so she's extra special to me.' Stacey releases the chicken and leads me back to the coop, where we gather the plastic water containers. Once they're clean and full again, we sweep out the old bedding, replacing it with fresh handfuls. I'm warm from the exertions of cleaning out the coop but my ears feel as though they're about to pop off through the cold. I'm itching to snatch the bobble hat from my pocket, but I'm sure Stacey would chalk that down as another victory.

Giving a satisfied nod at the clean coop, Stacey starts to wander back towards the house. 'Let's wash up and then Mrs McColl will make you a breakfast to die for.'

She leads me back into the house, indicating a small downstairs loo near the shoe rack. I give my hands a thorough scrub with the coconut-scented handwash before joining Stacey again, changing back into my own footwear while Stacey washes. I'm quite glad to be out of the wellies, but my feet are already mourning the thick socks as I slip on the ballet flats.

'We run a small café for our visitors.' Stacey emerges back into the hall and leads the way along the passage. 'Mainly tea and cake and the odd bit of veggie soup or stew. Mrs McColl is one of our volunteers who mans the kitchen. I don't know what I'd do without her.'

'You'd get along perfectly fine and you know it.' The booming voice comes from within one of the rooms leading off the passageway and Stacey turns to roll her eyes at me.

'I can barely boil an egg. Wait until you try Mrs McColl's freshly baked bread. You'll be in heaven.'

'Hardly. I just throw a bit of flour and water in the oven.' We've reached the café now, which I guess was once a regular dining room but is now filled with four round tables. Mrs McColl is standing by the doorway, her arms folded across her ample chest. 'Anyway, what can I get you? I could probably stretch to a poached egg today, but only one each, mind.'

Stacey reaches for a chair at the nearest table and pulls it out. 'We try to use our own produce as much as possible, but Mrs McColl has first dibs at the eggs for her cakes. Not that anyone complains about that. Mrs McColl puts Mary Berry to shame.'

Mrs McColl snorts and shakes her head. 'Excuse me a moment while I climb down from that pedestal you've put me on. I need to go and get that *to-die-for* loaf out of the oven.' She tuts as she passes by, heading across the room to another doorway and disappearing from view.

'She isn't a fan of compliments, no matter how deserved they are.' Stacey sits down and grabs a menu from the middle of the table, handing it to me once I'm seated opposite. 'I'm going to go for the toast with jam. The jam's homemade too, using the fruit from our allotment.'

'That sounds great.' I pop the menu back into its little wooden holder in the middle of the table. 'I'll have that too.'

It turns out that Mrs McColl really does deserve all the compliments. The thickly-cut bread is divine, while the blackberry jam is the perfect balance between sweet and tart. I wolf down both wedges at lightning speed, washing them down with strong, sweet tea. I'm usually content with a small bowl of cornflakes in the morning, so it must be the fresh, country air making me so ravenous.

'I'd better be getting back over to the house.' I have no idea what time the builders usually start, but I'm hoping to be there before them. I reach for my purse but Stacey holds up a hand.

'Breakfast is on me. As a thank you for helping out with the chickens.' She takes a sip of her tea before setting it down gently on her saucer. 'Same time tomorrow then?' She raises an eyebrow in challenge, and although I have no idea why Stacey has decided to test my willingness to muck out chickens, I find my chin jutting out in defiance.

'Why don't we make it a bit earlier? That way I can help out with Franny too.'

Stacey's mouth stretches into a wide grin while I mentally kick myself. 'Great idea! Shall we say six-thirty?'

I must be a fan of self-flagellation because I find myself giving a curt nod. 'I'll see you tomorrow, bright and early.'

Chapter 11

The silence of the lane is broken by the rumbling of an engine as I make my way back to the house, and I'm both glad of the familiar sound and afraid of the narrow track at the same time. I press myself as far into the bush running alongside the lane as I can as the van nears, somehow entangling my hair in the prickly branches. I'm trying to extricate myself when Oliver toots his horn and waves cheerily from the van's driver's seat. I wave back, yelping as the bush attempts to scalp me as soon as I release my grip. I resume my battle with the bush as the van turns onto Arthur's Pass and disappears from view, but my phone ringing in my pocket pauses my endeavours again. I manage to reach into my pocket without tearing out my hair and leaving a brunette mop on the branches like a badly-crafted bird's nest, and jab at the answer button while trying to untangle myself with my free hand.

'Vanessa! Hi!' I'm aiming for a bright and breezy tone, but the task of freeing myself from the badly-behaved bush is taking its toll and it comes out strained and raspy. 'How are you?'

'Better than you by the sounds of it. Is everything okay?'

I'm shocked by my boss's concern; she's never once asked

after my well-being, not even the time I dragged my aching carcass to the office while in the full throes of a bout of the flu. 'Everything is ...' I tug at a twig and hear it snap, leaving a small spike behind like a cave woman's hair grip. 'Fine. Great, in fact.'

'Then why do you sound like you're battling the crowds at a Primark Boxing Day Sale?' Vanessa sniggers at her own little joke. The woman has never ventured a designer-clad toe inside a Primark store, so how would she know what it's like?

I try to change position but wince in pain as my hair is pulled tighter. 'I'm, erm ...' I move slowly back to my original position. 'Jogging! I'm jogging. The countryside is so beautiful, I thought I'd make the most of it.'

'Right.' Vanessa doesn't seem convinced but I'm too busy trying to dislodge a twig that's doing its best to penetrate my scalp. 'Whatever. The reason I called is to apologise for my behaviour yesterday.'

The sharp twig scrapes the palm of my hand as I finally disentangle it from my hair, but I barely feel it as I'm so shocked by Vanessa's words. 'You want to apologise? To me?'

Vanessa never apologises to her staff, and even when she brings herself to apologise to clients, she's never sincere, despite the sugary tones she adopts for the purpose.

'Yes, which I know is totally out of character.' Vanessa gives a self-deprecating laugh while I'm thinking what an understatement that is. 'But Ty pointed out last night that I may have been a bit ... bulldozer-like in my approach.'

Wow. Tyler Johansson is one brave young man. And he *is* young compared to his girlfriend. While Vanessa is in her 'early thirties' (I'm her PA and privy to her private info. She is *only just* clinging onto her thirties and it'll be a downright lie when she reaches her next birthday), Tyler is a twenty-two-year-old part-time model she met at a charity event three months ago. I've only met him a couple of times, when he's dropped by the office to see Vanessa, but he seems decent enough and he's obviously got balls of steel to go up against Vanessa Whitely.

'I admit I may have been a bit forceful and that threatening to sack you if you didn't take on the project manager role was wrong of me. It's just that this project is very dear to me. You've seen the house – isn't it magnificent? So just imagine how glorious it will be once the work is finished. I can't wait to show it off!'

'It is a beautiful house.'

'Isn't it?' Vanessa breathes a contented sigh down the line. 'So you see why I'm so determined to stick to my original plans? I need that house finished in time for the party. There is *no way* I can postpone. You see that, don't you?' I open my mouth to respond, but Vanessa ploughs on before I have the chance to utter a word. 'But I shouldn't have dropped you in the deep end like I did. That was unfair.' There's a pause for me to react to Vanessa's statement, so I make a slight murmuring sound, neither agreeing nor disagreeing in case I back the wrong horse. You never quite know where you stand with Vanessa and I don't want to rile her, even when we're miles apart. 'I'm going to come over, to do all I can to smooth the transition. Now, I can't make it today – you of all people should know how incredibly busy I am. But I'll get Emma to go through my diary and find a slot when I can give you my undivided attention. Is that okay with you, Becky?'

I ignore the unwanted shortening of my name – I've allowed everyone in Little Heaton to think I'm Vanessa since I arrived, so what does it matter? 'That would be great. Thank you.'

'It's the least I can do for behaving so terribly.' She gives that self-deprecating laugh again. 'Speak soon!' And then she's gone. I slip my phone back into my pocket and resume my bid for freedom. Vanessa, I think as I de-tangle a particularly barbed twig from my ponytail, would never find herself being assaulted by a bush. Finally free, I treat the bush to a death glare before I stomp my way to the house, humiliated, irritated and throbbing from numerous scratches and gouges.

*

'What happened to you?'

I find the builders gathered on the steps in front of the house, Todd trapped under Harvey's armpit in a headlock while Vincent is chatting animatedly on his phone. Oliver has jumped up from the steps and is heading towards me. He grins as he looks me up and down.

'You look like you've been dragged through a hedge backwards.'

Funny that. I feel like it too and have the injuries to prove it.

'*You* happened to me.' I jab an accusatory finger at Oliver. 'Do you make a habit of running people into bushes?'

Oliver huffs out a humourless laugh. 'What the hell are you talking about?'

'Out there.' My finger is now jabbing towards the lane. 'You ran me into the bush and *this happened*.' I hold out my arms, which look as though I've picked a fight with a tiger and lost.

'Are you blaming me for the lane being so narrow?' Oliver laughs again and shakes his head. 'You really are unbelievable.'

'And you're …' I want to tell him that he's a great big knob-head, but that would be unprofessional. '… late for work.' I jab at my watch, wincing as I spot a long, scarlet scratch across my knuckles that suddenly starts to sting like hell. 'Can you just get to work, please?' I don't mean to snap, but I'm really not feeling myself right now. I've just gone through what feels like ten rounds with a bush, my hair must be an absolute state, and I'm on the verge of bursting into self-pitying tears.

Oliver holds his hand up in surrender as he starts to back away. 'There's a first aid box in the guesthouse, in the cupboard under the sink. If I'm allowed to tell you that before I clock on?'

'Yes. Thank you.' I reach into my pocket with my non-injured hand and toss the keys to him. I should apologise for being snippy but I really, *really* want to get inside so I can patch myself up and maybe have a cry.

Chapter 12

The scratches turn out to be pretty superficial, and I'm feeling much better once I've had a cup of tea and disposed of the leftover chocolate from last night. So much so, I'm full of shame for the way I spoke to Oliver and pluck up the courage to head over to the house to offer a full, heartfelt apology. The builders have moved from the courtyard, but they haven't made it very far. I find them in the hallway, Vincent still chatting on his phone, his free arm flailing as he makes a point about some 'braindead ref', while Oliver is having what appears to be a nap in the corner and Harvey and Todd are entwined like a human pretzel as they tussle near the staircase. There isn't a tool in sight and even the paint-splattered radio is silent and abandoned on the windowsill. I stand in the doorway for a moment, my mouth slowly gaping as I take in the scene. Vincent swears loudly, his arm flinging in the air as the expletive echoes in the barren space, and the sudden sound captures Todd's attention. Looking up, he's caught off guard so that when Harvey twists his foot around Todd's ankle and gives him a gentle push, he falls to the concrete floor. Seizing his chance, Harvey elbow drops onto his colleague, winding Todd and causing him to wheeze and splutter while he clutches at his middle.

'That's enough!' I can't stand by and watch this anymore. Not only are these buffoons neglecting their duties, they're taking roughhousing too far and somebody could get seriously hurt. 'What do you think you're doing? You're grown men behaving like silly little boys!' Marching towards the staircase, I reach out a hand to help Todd to his feet as Harvey certainly isn't going to be of any assistance. He was almost crying with laughter at his antics until my booming voice startled the mirth right out of him. I'm not sure where that voice came from; it doesn't belong to me, though I suppose the echo of the empty hallway helped a bit.

'Sorry, Vanessa.' Harvey can't meet my eye as he springs to his feet and brushes down his dusty jeans. 'We were just messing about.'

I'm about to correct Harvey – it's about time everyone knew I wasn't actually Vanessa – but I stop myself before the words come out. Vanessa wouldn't let these guys get away with this. She'd be wearing their danglies for earrings if she caught her staff behaving like schoolboys on her time, but I don't have a tiny portion of Vanessa's boldness and not one shred of her authority. Rebecca Riley is spineless. She's afraid of her own shadow and never, ever sticks up for herself.

So I simply won't be Rebecca Riley at this moment in time. If they think I'm Vanessa Whitely, with all her pluck and clout, then let them. Then maybe, just maybe, they'll do some actual work.

'I'm not paying you to "mess about".' I do the air quotes and everything, just as I know Vanessa would, even adopting her sneer. 'I'm paying you to refurbish my house, on time and on budget. And you.' I turn on my heel and march towards Vincent, who's had the decency to end his call at last. 'You're supposed to be in charge of these chumps. You're supposed to set an example. *What on earth do you think you're playing at?*'

I'm shocked at the anger that spills out of me, but it does the job as Vincent digs his hands into his pockets and looks down at his boots.

'Sorry. It won't happen again.' Vincent sneaks a look up at me and I fix him with my best Vanessa glower until he looks back down again.

'I hope not. Now, get to work. The lot of you.' I turn to the Chuckle Brothers – Todd has stopped wheezing, though he's still looking rather pained – and pierce them with The Glower. 'I'm going to go and chase up Nicole's paperwork, so I can see *exactly* where we're supposed to be. I'm trusting you.' I turn to Vincent again, The Glower firmly in place. 'Don't let me down.'

I'm not really chasing the paperwork. It's just an excuse to get out of the house and shut myself away in the guesthouse for a few minutes because I'm a little bit shaken up right now. That was way more confrontation than I'm comfortable with. My hands are trembling and I feel like I could throw up at any second, but my rant seems to have paid off. When I eventually calm down enough to head back over to the main house, the radio is on full blast while the builders are busy working on the plastering in various rooms. They don't even stop for a tea break until I insist they take one late in the morning, and they're back from their lunch break promptly, getting straight back to work without any prodding from me at all. Perhaps I should play the role of Vanessa Whitely for a *tiny* bit longer. After all, my career is depending on this refurbishment …

It turns out there isn't a great deal for me to do as project manager at this moment in time. Without the paperwork, I'm clueless as to what is supposed to be happening and when, so I spend the majority of my time watching daytime TV in the guesthouse, which isn't a bad way to spend the working day, if I'm honest. I do dash across to the main house during the ad breaks, to make sure the builders are actually working and not practising their WWE moves on each other, or to ferry over cups of tea and coffee. By mid-afternoon, however, I'm totally bored of antique dealing and people airing their filthy laundry for the nation to see, so I grab my phone from the coffee table and check for any message that may have slipped by unnoticed. Nothing, and Emma hasn't even seen the message I sent over WhatsApp almost an hour ago, though I know how busy she is now she's essentially doing both our jobs while I lounge about all day. Guilt prods at my gut but I try to push it away. I didn't *choose* to be here, so if anybody should be feeling guilty about Emma's work-load, it should be Vanessa. The real one.

Opening my phone's browser, I tap out a search for Little Heaton's Animal Sanctuary and find the website. I'm not being nosy or stalkerish – I'm simply curious, especially since I've signed up to help out again tomorrow. There are photos of all the animals, some of which I've already met, plus a rather nice snap of Oliver looking pretty damn handsome in a red checked shirt.

The website looks modern and professional, with tabs for sponsorship and rehoming as well as fundraising events and educational visits. There's an event coming up at the weekend, right here in Little Heaton. A sponsored fun run in the park, with the proceeds going towards the development fund, whatever that is. I find myself bypassing the link for that to tap on the 'About Us' section instead, hoping to find out a bit more about Oliver, but it's mainly about the sanctuary's charity status, which is disappointing. Closing the browser, I toss the phone onto the sofa and slump in my seat. I'm not sure what I was hoping to find. His hobbies? Relationship status? Not that it would matter if he was in a relationship – he's already made it perfectly clear he doesn't find me attractive ('Of course I didn't hit on her. Why would I?') and even though I fancy him the *teeniest, tiniest bit* (it can't be helped. It seems I have a bit of a thing for pale stubble, full lips and booty-shaking to Eighties pop), I would never, ever act on it in a million years. That's not my style at all, which explains why I haven't had a boyfriend since uni. Perhaps this is why Stacey has taken a dislike to me. Could she have picked up on some subtle hint that I fancy her brother a little bit? Oh, God, I hope not. How embarrassing. I will have to make it perfectly clear that I have no interest in Oliver – other than his building skills – when I help out at the sanctuary tomorrow.

A message pings onto my phone. It's finally a reply from Emma:

Sorry! Rushed off my feet today. V has asked me to help out with some stuff. She's asked me to schedule a time for her to visit you. Is Mon morning okay with you? Around ten? Also, Kate phoned again! E xx

Completely side-stepping the Kate issue, I reply that Monday morning is fine. It's a few days away, which isn't ideal, but at least I get to pretend to be the Big Boss for a little while longer. Trembling-through-confrontation aside, it's quite fun having such influence.

Chapter 13

Why is my alarm attempting to pierce my eardrums in the middle of the night? I'm sure I only closed my eyes a few minutes ago and yet I'm being rudely awakened by the stupidly chirpy tone I always set on my phone in the hope that it's perkiness will transfer itself into me first thing in the morning, making early get-ups much more pleasant. Needless to say, it never, ever works.

Reaching out, I grab the phone and bring it mere centimetres from my face, squinting at the time as the alarm continues to chirrup away. It isn't *quite* the middle of the night – but not far off. Why on earth is my alarm going off at *5.30 a.m.*? I don't even get up at this time back in Manchester, where my commute is much longer than a quick dash across the drive.

Oh no. I groan as realisation dawns. Stacey. The animal sanctuary. I agreed to help out again, but at an even more ridiculous time of day. What an idiot I am! But I don't have to get up right this second. A few more minutes won't hurt, will it? I can snooze the alarm and still have plenty of time to get ready for the arranged time. My eyes are already clamped shut as I slide the phone back onto the bedside table, my body already slipping back into slumber.

I'm rudely woken eight minutes later, but it's the snooze button

I jab at, taking several attempts until I hit the right spot and my phone is gloriously silent again. A few more minutes, that's all I need …

I groan as my alarm springs into life again, muttering incoherent words of malice as I roll over to snatch the phone from the table. I squint at the display, fighting bleary eyes that want nothing more than to pull down the shutters and return to dreamland. I think I make out the numbers, but they can't possibly be right. Pulling the phone a fraction closer, I widen my eyes in an attempt to get a clearer view.

6.02 a.m.

What? How? It isn't possible! I snoozed the alarm at 5.38 a.m., so how has so much time passed? I couldn't have snoozed it a couple more times without realising. Could I? Unfortunately, I don't have time for an internal debate between unconscious snooze-button-pressing and some weird time-zapping phenomenon so I simply have to get on with things, which means rushing to the bathroom to have the swiftest shower known to man. I don't have time to wash and dry my hair, so I give my body a quick scrub before hastily drying and dressing in a pencil skirt and silk blouse, which isn't ideal for cleaning out the chicken coop but I don't have many options left. I really must put a wash on later.

I wish I'd had the foresight to bring a can of dry shampoo with me as I gather my hair into a high ponytail and twist it into a messy bun. There is no way Vanessa would be seen out in public with anything but salon-perfect hair. Still, there's nothing I can do about that now and at least I have a ruby lipstick in my make-up bag that should divert attention away from my not-so-freshly-washed locks. The lipstick was a freebie from a cosmetics company's event we planned earlier in the year but I haven't been brave enough to actually try it out until now. I apply the glossy lipstick, blotting most of it away with a tissue before I look in the mirror.

Wow. That's making a statement, though of what, I'm not entirely sure. It's certainly eye-catching and a shade Vanessa would rock, so I fight the urge to scrub it away and replace it with my clear lip balm and scuttle out of the guesthouse before I can change my mind.

I avoid the bushes as I head to the sanctuary, more or less walking in the middle of the lane, but there isn't any hint of traffic. Or people. It's still dim, though the darkness is starting to lift, and there's a slight chill in the air. Summer has undeniably drifted away and I tuck my hands into my pockets as my fingers start to feel the bite.

'Hello again.' Mrs McColl is ahead of me on the lane, about to reach for the sanctuary's gate. She nods in greeting but doesn't crack a smile. 'You're here early this morning. Most volunteers don't make it in until at least nine.'

'I need to start work before then.' I quicken my pace as Mrs McColl opens the gate, so I can grab it before it swings shut again. 'Especially as I found the builders mucking about yesterday. I won't be making that mistake again.'

'You need to watch that lot.' Mrs McColl rummages in the handbag looped over her forearm. 'Oliver's a decent sort, obviously, but the rest of them?' She shakes her head, sending her doughy jowls into a wobble. 'Vincent sent that young apprentice of his to my house over the summer. Needed a bit of brickwork mending on my front wall. Quick job, it should have been. Took the great lump three days.' She tuts loudly before producing a set of keys from the handbag. 'Make sure you crack the whip. It's the only way you'll get the job done.' She selects a key and inserts it into the front door's lock. 'I take it Stacey's expecting you?' Her eyes are narrowed with suspicion as she turns to me, key still in the lock, door still shut.

'She is. It was her suggestion that I help out again.' Although I was the nitwit who'd bartered for such an unreasonable time.

Mrs McColl pushes open the door and steps into the hallway,

pausing on the doormat and blocking my path. 'Stacey? You have a visitor.' She turns to me again, eyes still narrowed. 'What was your name again?'

I open my mouth, ready to introduce myself. My mouth is forming the letter R before I realise what I'm about to do. Do I tell her my name, or do I allow the misunderstanding over my identity to continue? I don't want to lie, but I also want to keep the builders in check and I know that without the Vanessa pretence acting as a shield, I'll shrink back to my normal pushover state of mind.

'Well? Do you have a name or don't you?' Mrs McColl's eyebrows jump towards her greying hairline as she observes me. My mouth opens again, but I still don't know what to say. 'For goodness' sake!' She bends down towards me and speaks *very slowly*. 'What. Is. Your. Name?'

'This is Vanessa Whitely.' Stacey appears behind Mrs McColl and ushers the older woman out of the way. 'I introduced you yesterday, remember? Vanessa's doing up the house at Arthur's Pass.'

'I knew she was working on the house but I didn't know she was the owner herself.' Mrs McColl sniffs as she unwinds the scarf around her neck and hooks it onto the coat stand behind the door. 'She could at least identify herself instead of standing there flapping her lips like a goldfish. I thought you said she was assertive. Bossy, I think those were your words. And you certainly made her sound like a she-devil.'

'I did not.' Stacey laughs, convincing nobody, before she pulls me into the house, bright smile plastered on her face. 'Shall we get started? I thought you could help with Franny and Daisy today.'

My eyes flit from Stacey to Mrs McColl – who is still observing me with deep suspicion as she unbuttons her coat – and back again. 'Sounds good to me. And I brought my own socks this time!' I delve into my pocket and pull out the balled pair. They're not as thick as the ones I borrowed yesterday, but at least I know whose feet (only my own) have been in them previously.

'Let's get you kitted out in wellies and leave Mrs McColl to her breadmaking.' Stacey winks at Mrs McColl, who sniffs loudly before turning her back on us to hang up her coat.

'I'm starting to get the impression Mrs McColl doesn't like me very much.' We've moved along the passage to the little area by the back door while Mrs McColl has disappeared into the café, but still I lower my voice to barely audible levels.

'Oh, don't worry about that.' Stacey selects the same pair of wellies as yesterday and hands them to me. 'It's just her way. She was my gran's best friend, so I've known her all my life and I've got used to her manner, but she really doesn't mean anything by it.' She pulls open one of the drawers and grabs a hat – a neon pink monstrosity with a white bobble on top – and tosses it my way. I reluctantly catch it but shove it straight into my pocket. I would rather suffer frostbitten ears than entertain even the idea of wearing it.

'I still think I'll try to keep out of her way.'

Stacey snorts as she tosses me a pair of gloves. 'Most people do. I love the woman to death, but she wasn't at the front of the queue when they were giving out likeability.'

I sit down on the wooden chair and unlace my boots. 'It sounds like she was standing behind my boss then. She's definitely lacking in that department.'

'Your boss?' I look up to see Stacey frowning down at me. 'I thought you ran your own company. Nic said something about party planning or something? She actually gave me your card, in case I wanted to hire someone to plan our party when we finally expand. I think I still have it here somewhere …' She reaches for the back pocket of her jeans and pulls out a wallet, rummaging inside until she finds a slightly dog-eared business card. 'See?' She holds it up to me. It's the familiar ivory-coloured card with gold embossed lettering that I've seen a million times, with *Vanessa Whitely Events* taking centre stage. There is no doubt at all that Vanessa is at the very top of the food chain, meaning I've put my foot right in it.

Chapter 14

This could be the perfect opportunity to come clean, to tell Stacey about my mistaken identity, which we would laugh about because it's so silly to think that I could be mistaken for the hard-nosed Vanessa Whitely. But Stacey would obviously pass on the information to her brother, who in turn would reveal all to his workmates and I really, *really* need to keep those guys on track. Vanessa's visiting in a few days and I can't let the schedule slip even a tiny bit. I need her to see that I am capable and reliable, that I deserve the promotion I've coveted for the past three years. I can't let the mask slip just yet.

'I meant my old boss, before I set up my own company.' I roll my eyes. 'She was a real bitch to work for.' I slip my boots off and un-ball the socks. 'And I'm in events management, not party planning.' I sound snooty, but there's no way Vanessa would have let that one slide.

'Sor-ree.' Stacey shoves the business card back into her wallet, causing it to crease diagonally, cutting right through Vanessa's shiny, gold name. 'I'll meet you outside, down at the barn. Don't take too long – there's a lot to do this morning.' Stalking from the entryway, Stacey shuts the back door roughly behind her. I shove my socks and the wellies on, which don't feel half as comfortable as they did yesterday while I was wearing the cosier socks, and it's only when I stand up that I realise how ridiculous I must look in the get up of a pencil skirt and heart-printed wellington boots. If I'm going to be staying in Little Heaton until the house is completed, I'll need to go home and pick up some more clothes over the weekend. The thought of the lengthy and tiresome journey to Manchester and back again fills me with dread, but not nearly as much as the thought of returning to the dingy flat – and the dingier flatmate – does. I'm pondering the state the flat will be in during my absence when the back door flings open. Stacey is standing on the threshold, one hand on her hip and lips pursed.

'Are you coming to help or not?'

'Yes. Sorry.' Grabbing my boots, I place them neatly next to the wellies on the rack and scuttle after Stacey. A couple of the chickens are already out on the lawn, along with the two donkeys and the sheep.

'Is that Oliver down there?' Although the body on the perimeter of the garden is hunched over the fence, it does look familiar. Especially the bottom.

'Yep. Patching up the fence. *Again.*' Stacey stops to watch him work for a moment. 'We could do with replacing the whole lot with something a bit sturdier but all our money's going into the new development at the moment.'

'You're developing the sanctuary?' I can understand why; the lawn is already pretty crowded and there are only five of the animals out of their shelters.

'As great as Gran and Grandad's house is, we've outgrown it. I have to take Claude over to a nearby field to graze every day as there just isn't enough on offer for him here, and we always get an influx of hedgehogs over the autumn months, so they're going to take up most of the education room.'

'You have an education room?'

Stacey points back at the house. 'It used to be the living room.'

86

She laughs and shakes her head. 'But the sanctuary has taken over the entire downstairs. If we don't get the land up for auction …' She points back towards Oliver, at the land sitting between her property and Vanessa's. 'Then we'll have to start taking rooms from the upstairs too. Who needs a bedroom, right?' She gives a wry smile before she starts to move down towards the barn again. As both of the donkeys are already outside, we get to work straight away, clearing out the old hay and … other stuff I try not to think about or smell. Stacey tells me more about the vacant land sandwiched between the sanctuary and Vanessa's property as we work. It's a relatively narrow plot but it contains two sizeable outbuildings, which Oliver would convert into a new education suite for visiting schoolchildren and community groups and host a new site for the café and gift shop, both of which bring in valuable revenue.

'Any extra land could be used for grazing and housing some of the smaller animals, and we could maybe grow some of our own crops here instead of at the allotment. Don't get me wrong, we appreciate having that space so much.' Stacey stops scooping up the hay to swipe at her brow with the back of a gloved hand. 'But it's only a small plot and it would be much easier to have the crops on site, especially when it comes to the visiting kids. At the moment, we have to trek across the village, which isn't ideal with thirty plus children, believe me.' Leaning on the shovel, she sighs as she looks out of the barn's door. 'I just hope we get the winning bid.'

'Is there much competition?' The plot was ideal for expanding the animal sanctuary, but would anybody else want a sliver of land with no current access to the lane?

Stacey shrugs before resuming her shovelling. 'Who knows? But I hope not as our funds are pretty tight. We've been fund-raising for this ever since the land first went up for sale three years ago. It was way beyond our budget back then, but we're hoping to get a bargain at the auction. Even still, we're fundraising now. We're having a fun run in the park tomorrow for a last-minute push. You should come along. It's probably too late for you to get sponsorship organised, but we could use all the volunteers we can get our hands on to help out.'

'I'd love to, but I have to head back home tomorrow to sort some stuff out.' I heft a shovelful of hay into the wheelbarrow. 'But let me know if there's anything else I can do to help. Other than mucking out first thing in the morning, obviously.'

Stacey almost smiles at me but catches herself just in time, giving a curt nod of her head instead. 'I'll let you know if I think of anything.'

*

Lesson learned; if you're going to muck out animals, having a shower *beforehand* is a complete waste of time and clean clothes. I'm sweaty and stink of donkey so I'm in desperate need of another shower before I start work. I have one clean outfit left, so I bung a load into the washing machine while I jump in the shower. Although Vanessa wears a lot of dry-clean only clothes, most of mine can be tumble dried, but I'll still need more than a handful of outfits to rotate while I'm in Little Heaton for the next few weeks – so though an expedition to Manchester and back doesn't appeal in the slightest, it is inevitable. I'll set off first thing in the morning and hopefully arrive at the flat sometime before sunset.

The washing machine has completed its cycle by the time I've showered, dried my hair and changed into my shirtdress (which is a little on the casual side for work but I don't think the builders will either mind nor notice) so I throw most of it into the dryer and drape the rest on a maiden that was folded up and tucked beside the fridge freezer. I'd be able to dry these items a bit quicker if I was brave enough to set the fire going, but I'm more used to the plumbed-in gas variety and this is a proper log burner that

I'm sure I could quite easily burn the guesthouse down with. The only other heat source is the radiator in the bathroom, which is currently drying my towel.

The vans are already parked in the drive as I make my way over to the main house, and I'm pleasantly surprised to find the builders hard at work. Being Vanessa is definitely paying off, so it'll be a shame to burst the bubble on Monday morning, but reverting back to Rebecca Riley is unavoidable and maybe I can keep the spirit of Vanessa with me afterwards, if not the name and prestige.

Oh, who am I kidding? I'll wilt as soon as Vanessa rocks up in her red Mini Cooper and takes charge, letting everyone know what a fraud I've been over the past couple of days. I'll be lucky to get the builders to show up at all, never mind on time and ready to work.

'Morning, Vanessa.'

It takes me a moment to realise Vincent is calling out to me over the sound of Meat Loaf on the radio, but I'm hoping he puts my delay in responding down to aloofness rather than gormlessness. Or even the truth that I'm not who I claim to be.

'Good morning, Vincent. It's nice to see you raring to go.'

'He didn't want another bollocking.' Todd grins at me, but it dies a quick death as he clocks the glare from his boss. 'And he's dedicated to the job and stuff.'

'Glad to hear it.' I wink at Todd, even though it isn't something Vanessa would ever do in a million years. 'Shall I go and put the kettle on?'

Vincent rubs his hands together. 'I wouldn't say no. I'm parched.'

'I'm starving.' Todd aims his grumble towards Vincent. 'It's Friday. We *always* have a bacon butty before we start work on a Friday.'

'Not today, mate.' Vincent shrugs an apology at his apprentice. 'Not when we've got a big job on.'

'When has that ever stopped us?' Todd clamps his mouth shut as he receives another glare from Vincent. With a huff, he returns to his task. The rustic flagstones they've been busy laying are already looking fantastic in the kitchen, but I'm not sure how much progress would have been made if the fake Vanessa hadn't been in charge and the builders were more interested in their bacon butties. It's going to be a shame when I have to give her up.

Chapter 15

I have to admit that I'm feeling a bit sorry for Todd and his lack of a Friday breakfast, so when I realise there's only a drop of milk left in the fridge at the guesthouse, I decide to treat him – and the other builders – to a bacon sandwich. Rather than forking out on several pre-made sandwiches, I go down the more budget-friendly route and pick up a pack of bacon and a loaf of bread along with my milk and a ready-meal-for-one at the mini market. I'm making my way back to the guesthouse when the mannequin in the charity shop window catches my eye. It's looking very stylish in a burgundy leather pencil skirt and a simple but elegant black polo neck sweater. There's even a pair of matching knee-length boots standing alongside the mannequin, completing the look. I'd always assumed charity shops were stuffed to the gills with musty granny clothes, but this outfit is modern and stylish and definitely something I could add to my meagre workwear collection. And if they have more outfits like this, it would mean I could postpone my trip back to Manchester!

I'm pleasantly surprised by the lack of the stale air I was expecting as I step inside, but my optimism drops when I clock the rails of old-fashioned garments. I can't see anything resembling the outfit in the window.

'Can I help you, my dear?' The elderly woman behind the counter smiles encouragingly at me. 'Looking for anything in particular?'

'I saw the outfit in the window.' I point towards the display behind me. 'The leather skirt and polo neck?'

'Ah, yes.' The woman eases herself off the stool she's sitting on behind the counter and shuffles towards me. She's wearing a tweed skirt, a scratchy-looking jumper and a pair of pink slippers. 'Came in this morning. I thought it might draw you young ones in.' She chuckles as she passes me by and heads for the window. 'Haven't had time to put the rest out. All needs steaming, you see, and we're short-staffed. Betty's back has seized up again, poor love.'

'There's more like this?'

Hope starts to bubble up again. If the clothes fit – and they're reasonably priced – we could be onto a winner here.

'Oh, yes.' The elderly woman reaches for the mannequin with a slightly trembly, liver-spotted hand. 'Bin liner full of them out the back. Someone's had a clear-out, I should imagine. Either that or … Well, never mind. Here we are, love.' She wriggles the polo neck off the mannequin and hands it to me before wrestling the skirt off. 'Changing room's just back there. Do you want the boots as well?'

With the outfit and boots, I make my way into the changing room, which is a miniscule space behind a flimsy-looking curtain. The skirt and top fit perfectly but the boots are a size too big, unfortunately. I slip my peep-toe boots back on and appraise the look in the mirror. Perfect!

I quickly change back into my shirtdress and head back out into the shop. I really want to have a look through that bin liner for more treasures, but my conscience won't allow me to hang around the charity shop any longer when poor Todd's tummy is rumbling and I have a pack of bacon waiting in my carrier bag.

'Any good, my dear?' The elderly lady is back behind the counter, perched on her stool.

'Perfect, thank you, apart from the boots. They're a bit too big.' I place the skirt and top on the counter but hand the boots over to the woman, who places them behind the counter.

'That's a shame, but we do have more footwear.' She points out a display of shoes against the back wall. 'Maybe you'll find some in your size there?'

'I'll just take these for now, but I'll try and pop back.' Would it be cheeky to ask for the bin liner of clothes to be held back? Possibly, and I don't have the nerve to ask. I can't even channel Vanessa as she wouldn't be seen dead in second-hand clothes.

'That's just twelve pounds ninety-eight then, my dear.' The elderly woman doesn't see my jaw drop as she's busy folding the clothes and neatly placing them into a bag for me. I can't quite believe it. Thirteen quid for an entire outfit, including a real leather skirt that is not only in good condition, it looks as though it hasn't been worn at all? I will definitely be back to have a rummage through that bin liner!

*

Todd falls on his bacon sandwich as though he hasn't eaten for a week when I head over to the main house with a tray of refreshments, but Oliver's appreciation is much more muted. He barely looks up from his crouched position on the bathroom floor, where he's fitting the tiles as promised as he instructs me to shove it on the side of the bath.

'Okay.' I do as I'm told, placing the foil-wrapped sandwich and cup of tea on the corner of the bath, where it's wide enough to hold them. I back into the doorway, watching as Oliver slots the next tile into place. I am absolutely appreciating his workmanship and not his peachy bum.

'Was there anything else? Because I'm kind of busy here.' Oliver doesn't look up as he fires his frosty words at me, and I'm taken aback by his tone. What *is* his problem? So Vanessa fired off some snotty emails months ago – so what? I deal with the woman on a daily basis and I manage to retain my professionalism and manners.

'No, not really.' My tone has its own cold edge as I straighten my spine and fling my chin into the air. 'I am *ever so sorry* for disturbing you.' My voice is thick with sarcasm, and I'm quite proud that I haven't scuttled away with my tail between my legs. Channelling Vanessa has finally given me a spine that isn't made of jelly.

'You can pretend to be nice all you want, Vanessa, but I see through you.' Oliver finally turns to look at me, and I see that his eyes are as cold as his words. 'It'll take more than a bacon butty and cleaning out the chicken coop to fool me. I know what you're really like, and you sacking Nic has proved it.' He shakes his head and grabs another tile from the stack beside him. 'She didn't deserve that. She was hardworking, dedicated, and she took everything you threw at her, however unreasonable.'

'What are you talking about?' My tone isn't quite so cold, not so imposing. I try to swallow but find my throat is too dry. 'I didn't fire Nicole. She was in an accident. The pile-up on the M60 …' I trail off as I mull over Vanessa's words, trying to recall the exact details.

'What a convenient excuse.' Oliver dumps the tile back on the pile and turns to me with a shake of his head. 'I can't believe you would use that as a cover story. Somebody *died*. How sick are you?'

'Are you saying Nicole wasn't involved?' Because I can't believe Vanessa would stoop so low. Yes, she's domineering and she has a manipulative streak, but she wouldn't lie about something so tragic, surely.

'That's exactly what I'm saying.' Oliver lifts himself up onto his feet and snatches up the bacon sandwich and cup of tea. 'You sacked her because she fell behind schedule. She worked so hard to get this house to the condition it's in now, but your deadlines are ridiculous. The poor girl never stood a chance.' Squeezing past me, Oliver stomps out of the bathroom. 'I'm going on my break.'

There's a lump of dread in my stomach as I watch Oliver slope off along the hallway. If true, that explains the attitude towards me, but I'm hoping with every fibre of my being that he's mistaken.

*

'A parcel came while you were up there.' Todd pokes his head out of the kitchen when I eventually creep down the stairs. I've been skulking up on the top floor, mostly hiding out on the balcony and watching a group of ducks glide past as I waited for Oliver to shut himself back in the bathroom. 'We left it on the bottom step for you.'

It's hardly good sense to leave a box on the staircase where it's a trip hazard, but I let it go and retrieve the parcel instead. It's pretty hefty but as I don't have a clue what's actually inside, I decide to heave it over to the guesthouse to open it in private.

'Who's Rebecca Riley?' Todd saunters over and jabs a finger at the label. Panic causes me to stagger backwards with the parcel, and I almost drop it as I attempt to twist it away from Todd's sight.

'She's nobody.' I stagger backwards a bit more, heading for the door. 'Just somebody who works for me.'

'That's a nice way to speak about your employee.' I twist again, pushing my hands tight against the cardboard box to keep it from slipping from my grasp, and see Oliver sloping down the stairs. 'A nobody? Was Nic was a nobody too?'

I squeeze my eyes shut, hoping that when I open them again, he'll have disappeared in a puff of smoke. No such luck. He's still there, approaching the bottom step. Why did Vanessa have to lie about Nicole? Why did she have to make *me* lie about Nicole?

'The Nicole thing was an unfortunate misunderstanding.' I glance behind me and am relieved to see the door is just a couple of steps away.

'Do you need a hand with that parcel?' Todd is already striding towards me, but I shake my head, the movement and the heavy box causing me to list to one side.

'I'm fine, honestly.' I lurch towards the front door. 'But if you could just open … Thanks so much, Todd.' He's a good kid. I'm going to make it my mission to stop Harvey tormenting him while I'm here.

I regret declining Todd's offer of help as soon as I step onto the uneven drive. The loose stones, coupled with my heeled boots, make staggering across to the guesthouse with the heavy box extremely difficult. But I do make it across, albeit with jellied arms and a stone lodged between my toes, and dump the box on the coffee table with a groan of relief. I use my keys to cut along the thick tape and open the box to find three box files absolutely stuffed to the gills with loose papers, along with an equally stuffed lever arch file and five plastic wallets that will no longer close due to the sheer amount of paperwork jammed inside. There's a quick note scrawled onto a scrap of paper on the top:

Nicole's paperwork. Good luck with the project! E xx

I don't know where to start. I realise none of the files or wallets are marked as I pull them out of the box and lay them on the table. In the office, I'm a big fan of sticky labels and Post-it notes, but Nicole clearly isn't and if she had a system going, it isn't plain to see. I'm just going to have to dive in and work it out myself.

I decide to work from one end of the coffee table to the other, picking up the box file furthest left and settling down on the sofa with it. The box is only just keeping hold of its latch as the contents fight for freedom, and it pings open almost before I even touch the button. There's an invoice on the top, dated two weeks ago. I need to mark the box accordingly and I'm wondering if the mini market on the high street sells sticky labels or even Sharpie pens as I idly flick through the papers, but all thoughts of stationery fall from my mind as I take in the absolute horror show before me.

What the hell?

This isn't a box file of invoices. Yes, there are invoices in here, but there are also scribbled-on to-do lists, rough costings, quotes and contracts. It's a jumble of paperwork and not one piece of it seems to be in any sort of order, not even date-wise. Grabbing the next box, I'm equally as horrified to find another administration mishmash. The third box is the same and I want to weep after a quick peep into the wallets. It's a random, unorganised mess and I have to somehow make sense of it all. I'm going to need more than sticky labels and Sharpie pens to get this job done.

Panic is building up inside me, threatening to burst forth like the paperwork spilling from the box files. I'd thought I was in trouble when I'd been thrown into the deep end of this project without any kind of floating device, but it turns out it's the paperwork that's going to drown me.

I've read so many self-help books over the past couple of years and I'm trying to conjure their advice as my body threatens to give in to the distress of the situation. I can't let this beat me. I have to focus on the big picture. My career. The promotion I will have more than earned if I pull this off. The new, Lee-free home I won't have to dread going back to. I *have* to do this, somehow. There is no other option.

Gritting my teeth with determination, I grab the nearest box file and march over to the breakfast bar. I will sort this mess out, one sheet of paper at a time. Invoices will go in one clearly marked box, organised by date and then I'll categorise every other bit of paperwork there is, no matter how long it takes me.

The panic subsides as I get to work. I have a clear plan and

I'm focused on the task at hand, even if I'm not entirely sure what I'll do with all this paperwork once it's organised to within an inch of its life. I get through the first box relatively quickly, so I'm feeling pretty gratified with my efforts as I grab the first handful of papers from the next one. *I can do this.* I've spent the past three years organising Vanessa's work life, so I can certainly bring a bit of order to this mess. I'm actually feeling on the verge of smug as I swiftly send each piece of paperwork to its corresponding pile on the breakfast bar like a Vegas poker dealer – whoosh, whoosh, whoosh, next set of papers, please! But one set of papers drains every bit of complacency away and I feel the panic start to simmer again. This is a to-do list, which isn't unusual as Nicole has made lots of them, bullet-pointing every minute detail of the project, which will come in handy once I decipher her scribbled notes and diagrams. But this to-do list is different to the rest. It's legible, for a start, and printed from a spreadsheet. And it's also dated, each job broken down and allocated a time and date. This must be a culmination of all the scrappy to-do lists currently piled up on the breakfast bar, neatly presented and up to date. Which is terrifying because, according to the timeline, the project is currently three weeks behind schedule and there's no way it'll be ready in time for Vanessa's all-important housewarming party. And if Vanessa did indeed fire Nicole for falling behind schedule, there's no reason at all she won't fire me when I fail to live up to her expectations too.

Chapter 16

This is not good. Not good at all. The only reason I'm here at all is because Vanessa is desperate for the party to go ahead as arranged, and although being behind schedule isn't my fault as the delays didn't take place on my watch, I know this won't matter to Vanessa. She wants that party, no matter what, and if I can't deliver a completed house, I will have failed in my mission and can kiss goodbye to that promotion and, like my predecessor, my job.

Still clutching the printed-out schedule, I walk zombie-like to the sofa and flop down, my whole body crumpling with defeat. *Three weeks.* I can't make up that time. It would mean non-stop graft from the builders and no-nonsense management to keep them on an even tighter leash, and I don't have it in me. Right now, those guys are scoffing bacon sandwiches and, more than likely, using the hallway as a makeshift wrestling ring because although I'm waltzing around the place pretending to be Vanessa, I'm not her and I don't really have the prestige she has or the ability to terrify people into carrying out her bidding. Because if Vanessa were here, she'd have those guys working their little socks off until the job was done, with time to spare. She wouldn't be sitting on the sofa about to sob because all her hopes and dreams had just flown right out of the window.

My fingers release their grip on the papers and they drop onto my lap, slowly sliding until they flutter to the ground. My promotion. Moving out of the flat. It's all been snatched away and it isn't even my fault. I shouldn't have come here. I should have stood my ground, because at least then I wouldn't have failed before I'd even really begun.

I need to speak to Vanessa and admit the original timescale isn't going to happen. She won't be happy – far from it – but I can't bury my head in the sand, especially as she's coming to visit on Monday and she'll see for herself that the development isn't as far along as it should be. Honesty has to count for something, right?

I know I'm kidding myself, as evidenced by my trembling hand when I reach for my phone. Vanessa won't care about honesty. She'll care that someone – anyone, it doesn't matter who – has stuffed up her plans and she'll have to push back the party. My thumb hovers over the call button. She'll be *livid* at having to reschedule the party and I'll be on the receiving end of her fury, however unjust. She'll pour every last bit of venom down this phone line, and she won't hesitate over getting rid of another project manager. But if I don't let her know now, if I put it off until she sees for herself on Monday, I will still have to face her wrath eventually. I may as well get it over and done with, no matter how much I'm shaking at the prospect.

Taking a deep breath, I jab my thumb at the button, squeezing my eyes tight as I press the phone to my ear.

'Good morning. Vanessa Whitely Events!'

My breath rushes out of my body so fast it makes me feel a little bit woozy, and I collapse against the sofa cushions. Although I'd dialled Vanessa's direct number, it's Emma's upbeat voice that has answered, giving me a few more precious seconds before the onslaught begins.

'Hi, Emma. It's Rebecca.' I try to sound brave but my voice starts to crack and I know I'm going to fall to pieces as soon as Vanessa is on the other end of the line. I haven't felt this scared since my dad found out I'd only got a D in my mock GCSE for maths. Still, that had worked out in the end. Sort of. I'd worked really hard and managed to scrape a B in the final exams, even if Dad saw that as a failure just because my super-brainy sister absolutely smashed her way through her exams.

'Is everything okay, chick?' Emma's voice is soft and soothing, which only makes me crumble even more. I know that if she were here in Little Heaton, she'd have her arms around me and a tissue at the ready while the kettle boiled for a comforting cup of tea in the background.

'Not really.' I draw my knees up to my chin and wrap my free arm around my shins, pulling them in tight. 'I need to speak to Vanessa.'

'She isn't in the office at the moment. Tyler came to take her for an early lunch.' Emma giggles and I find my lips twitching at the sound, even if I don't manage an actual smile. 'Although I don't think they actually had food in mind. I don't expect her back for a while, if at all today.' There's the sound of clicking in the background. 'In fact, it looks like she's cleared her diary for the afternoon. Wow, I didn't think she even knew how to work her diary. She's had me doing everything for her this week. Honestly, I don't know how you cope with her. I'm exhausted! When are you coming back again?' Emma giggles again, clearly kidding about that last part, but it only reminds me of the mess I'm in.

'I'm not sure I will be, actually.' I take a deep, shaky breath and will the tears to hold off for now.

'What do you mean?'

Squeezing my eyes shut again, I take another deep breath before I tell Emma about the files, including the plan that is way behind schedule, and the real reason Nicole needed replacing at such short notice. Of course, I don't let slip that I'm pretending to be Vanessa.

'Oh, chick.' Emma tuts. 'Don't you feel bad about any of this. It isn't your fault at all. You know that, don't you?'

'It doesn't matter what *I* think. Vanessa is going to be so mad, and we all know how unreasonable she can be. I'm going to get it full-force, whether it's my fault or not.'

'Hmm, you're probably right.' Emma's words are like a punch to the stomach, even though she's only echoing my own thoughts. 'But maybe she doesn't have to know.'

I snort. 'I think she'll be a tad suspicious when she and her guests arrive for a housewarming party and they find the house is only half-finished.'

'Not if you get the project back on track.'

I laugh, but the sound is void of any hint of humour. 'Didn't you hear what I said? We're *three weeks* behind.' Springing forward, I grab the schedule from the floor. 'Next week, we're supposed to be installing the white goods, except *there isn't a kitchen to install them in*. The floor isn't even finished yet!' I frisbee the schedule towards the coffee table but it sails past and smacks into the log burner. If only I'd figured out how to light it, because burning the damn thing would at least be cathartic.

'Come on, Rebecca.' Emma's soothing tone has disappeared and has been replaced with something more robust and rousing. 'You've got this. You're the most organised person I know – I'm sitting in Vanessa's office right now, so I can see what a tight ship you run. Vanessa would be lost without you on a permanent basis, even if she doesn't realise it.'

'But being a PA and a project manager are two completely different things.'

'Are they that different, though? Okay, so you have to manage a slightly bigger team, but you're organised and hardworking and far more capable than you think you are. You're so talented, which is why you can't give up now.'

'You really think I can do this?' It would be nice not to unleash the dragon in Vanessa, and it'd mean I could show her that she can trust me with more than filing, but there's so much to do and not enough time to do it in. I'd have to redo Nicole's schedule, set new goals and ask an awful lot of Vincent and the team. I'd have to go into full-on Vanessa mode to get the job done, especially with Oliver, who clearly despises me already. I'd have to be bold and demanding and everything I'm programmed not to be.

'I really think you can do this.' Emma's tone is firm and I find myself nodding along.

'I can do this.' I stand up, my free hand planted on my hip. 'I'm going to do this.'

Emma whoops. 'Good girl!'

'There's just one problem.' I slump onto the sofa again. 'Vanessa's visiting on Monday. She's bound to want to look at the plans and see where we're up to.'

'Leave that with me, chick.' I can hear the tapping of a keyboard in the background. 'I'll create a diversion or an emergency or something to keep her away.'

'You think you can pull it off?'

'Absolutely. You concentrate on getting that house party-ready and leave Vanessa to me.'

A minute or two ago, I was in desperate need of a comforting hug, but now I'm all fired up. I'm going to do this. I'm going to channel every bit of Vanessa Whitely that I can and whip those boys into an efficient, diligent dream team. The party is firmly back on track – and hopefully it'll bring that promotion with it.

Chapter 17

I spend the rest of the morning organising the files, and I pore over every to-do list, deciphering Nicole's own brand of shorthand code, until I have a better grasp of where we're up to in the development. The white goods are being delivered on Thursday, to be installed in a kitchen that was supposed to be fitted and plumbed in three weeks ago. According to Nicole's paperwork, the plumber and electrician are due to start work on the kitchen, bathrooms and heating system on Monday, after already being rescheduled due to the backlog of work still to be done. The fixed flooring needs to be completed before they arrive, otherwise it'll mean more delays.

'Nope.' Vincent shakes his head when I ask if the flooring will be finished for Monday morning. 'No way. We're looking at Tuesday at the earliest.'

Tuesday is no good, and there's no way Vanessa would accept the answer being given if it didn't suit her agenda. Lifting my chin, I adopt Vanessa's no-nonsense tone. 'The thing is, Vincent, we can't go ahead with the kitchen and bathrooms until the floors are laid.' Why Vanessa couldn't stick down lino like the rest of us instead of having ceramic tiles and flagstones laid, I'll never know. 'So we're going to have to work something out.' I narrow my eyes ever so slightly as I observe the builder, the silence growing uncomfortable around us. It's a trick Vanessa uses, and it always works back in the office. Her silent rages are far scarier than her most boisterous rantings.

'I suppose we could put some overtime in.' He scratches at his armpit. 'Stay behind a bit later in the evenings.'

'That's a start.'

'A start?' Vincent frowns. 'What else do you want us to do?'

I smile at Vincent, but there is no warmth there. 'I'm so glad you asked, Vincent. And here come your workforce, just in time.' Todd, Harvey and Oliver have wandered into the hallway to go on their lunchbreak, but I'm not ready to let them go just yet. 'Gather round, guys. It's about time you learned what Vanessa Whitely is all about.'

*

My legs are still a little wobbly as I make my way across the canal's footbridge, as though my kneecaps have been replaced with soggy sponges, but I allow myself a small whoop of victory after making sure there's nobody in sight, my bunched fists thrown up towards the cloudy sky. I did it! I went into full-on Vanessa mode, telling those builders what was to happen next, leaving no doubt that my wishes were their command. Every last flagstone and ceramic tile will be laid by Monday morning, *no matter what*. If it means working well into the night, so be it. If it means starting at the crack of dawn, they will do it. And if they have to work every single hour during the weekend, that is what they will do. The builders did their best to wriggle out of the last one, but I was firm. Unmoving. *I was bloody amazing.* I may as well have been possessed by the actual spirit of Vanessa the way I stood my ground and I couldn't be prouder of myself, even if the confrontation has shaken me to the core. I hid my uneasiness at the conflict well, keeping my trembling hands tucked under my

105

armpits as I crossed my arms in a steady stance until I was out of sight. Only then did my body crumple, with only the wall to the side of the house keeping me upright. A few deep breaths and a wipe of my brow later and I was ready for the next stage of my plan. Just about.

My knees have stopped knocking by the time I make it to the high street, where I rush straight to the charity shop. If I'm going to do this, if I'm going to drag this project back on track, I need to be in Little Heaton for the duration. I can't waste time trekking back to Manchester, which means I'm going to need a few more outfits to tide me over. My fingers are mentally crossed as I push the door to the charity shop open, hoping that the bag of clothes out the back is still here and hasn't been snapped up, because I'm going to struggle otherwise. I'm all for staying in the village but if it means sporting calf-length pleated skirts in a palette of beiges and browns and scratchy jumpers, I'll have to re-evaluate my plan.

'Won't be a minute.' The voice that calls through from the back room is familiar, but it doesn't belong to the little old lady who served me earlier. 'We have CCTV here, you know, so no funny business.'

I head for the window display, hoping to see another modern outfit on the mannequin but she's dressed in an embroidered blouse and a voluminous skirt that I can't imagine was ever in fashion. I can't see anything contemporary on the rails, so either the bag of clothes hasn't been sorted out yet, it's all been sold, or the leather skirt was an anomaly.

'Looking for anything in particular?'

I turn away from the rail of woollen cardigans to see Mrs McColl striding towards me. There's a moment of recognition, where she blinks rapidly at me before she twitches the briefest smile at me like she's got a tic.

'I didn't expect to see you in here.' She changes course, circum-navigating a rail of bedding and curtains and stopping in front of a bookcase. 'Thought you'd be into all that designer gear. Not that you'll find any of that in Little Heaton.' She tuts loudly as she picks up a haphazard pile of novels and slots them back into place on the shelf.

I shrug. 'I like to support local businesses, especially charities. That's why I've been helping out at the animal sanctuary.'

Mrs McColl dusts off her hands as she walks towards me again. 'I suppose you have shown your charitable side, though from what I've heard, it isn't in abundance very often.' There's that tic of a smile again, as though she hasn't just insulted me. I guess she's heard about the Nicole thing too. 'Now, what can I help you with today?'

'I bought a leather skirt and a top this morning.' I point towards the window, even though the mannequin now looks like her earlier guise's great-aunt.

'And you wish to return them?' Mrs McColl heaves a sigh as she heads towards the counter. 'I take it you have the receipt? Because I can't give you a refund without one, I'm afraid.'

'No, I don't want to return them.' I scurry after Mrs McColl, who is quite speedy despite her advanced years. 'I'd like to buy more, if you still have them. There was a whole bag of clothes donated, apparently, which the skirt and top came from. The lady who served me this morning said they hadn't been sorted yet. They were still out the back.' I glance towards the closed door to the back room, hoping with all my might that it's still tucked away there.

Mrs McColl throws back her shoulders and observes me through narrowed eyes. 'We have been awfully short-staffed today. I don't usually work on Friday afternoons but I was asked to cover. So there may be a backlog. Which is highly unusual, I should add. We're a very efficient team.'

'I don't doubt it.' I give a quick scan of the shop and nod my head. 'It all looks extremely ordered.'

'It is. I pride myself on my organisational skills.' Mrs McColl's shoulders relax as she moves from behind the counter. 'Now, you wait here and I'll go and have a look in the back. We don't usually leave the shop floor unsupervised but Elsie's on her lunchbreak and needs must.' She jabs a finger towards the ceiling. 'CCTV, remember?'

I wander over to peruse the books while I wait, but Mrs McColl has returned before I've even read the blurb of the first novel I pick up, hefting a bulging bin liner with her.

'None of this has been steamed yet, so you'll have to take it as it is.' She heaves the bag up onto the counter. 'And it hasn't been priced, so you'll have to bear with me if you see anything you like. I'll leave you to have a good look through while I get on with my dusting.' She shakes her head. 'You can't trust the morning volunteers to do a decent job of it.'

The bag is stuffed with garments and footwear, which look largely unworn and all contain a high-end label. Like the skirt and top I bagged earlier, the clothes are all in my size. I've hit the jackpot! I pull each item out of the bag, scrutinising it before placing it on the yes or no pile I've set up on the counter. Once the bag is empty, I take the yes pile into the changing room before returning triumphantly to the counter with six for-keeps outfits that I can mix and match with the garments I have back at the guesthouse. There's even a pair of jeans and a grey striped T-shirt, which will be perfect for when I volunteer at the animal sanctuary, and I can't resist the nude leather bomber jacket. I also pick up a pair of brown ankle boots from the footwear section and a couple of pretty scarves. And I get the lot for under a hundred quid. Bargain! I'll have to borrow the money from the savings I've been accumulating to use as a deposit when I can finally move out of my current flat-share, but I have to look at it as an investment. If these outfits make me feel and look the part of Vanessa, that can only be a positive step to achieving my plan.

Chapter 18

I'm bunging a load of my new clothes in the washing machine when there's a tentative knock on the guesthouse door. I'm expecting it to be Todd, sent over on a tea break mission, but it's Oliver standing awkwardly on the drive. His hands are tucked deep into his jeans pockets and he's looking everywhere but directly at me.

'Can I have a quick word?' Oliver scuffs the toes of his boot along the gravel, his gaze somewhere to my left. 'It's about tomorrow.'

'Okay.' Intrigued by Oliver's change in stance, I move aside so he can step into the guesthouse, watching as he wipes his boots once, twice, three times on the mat before shuffling towards the sofa. 'Let me just make you some room.' Paperwork is littering the length of the sofa, so I gather the sheets up and shove them on the coffee table. There's an uncomfortable silence as we settle ourselves on opposite ends of the sofa, and I'm about to prompt Oliver when he finally clears his throat and speaks.

'I know you want us to work this Saturday.' Oliver still can't look at me and is currently eying the DVD collection on the shelf across the room. 'But we've been planning a fun run to raise money for the animal sanctuary's development *for months*. It's all organised; permission to use the park, sign ups and sponsorship, the lot. And now, the *day before*, you decide to stamp your authority and pull four of the runners out so we can lay your flooring.' While Oliver started off his little speech trite, somewhere along the way his voice has risen and has become more powerful. 'Do you know how much money we're going to lose in sponsorship? I mean, it's probably nothing to you. You probably spend as much on a pair of shoes.' His eyes flicker to the bags in the kitchen, and there's a flicker of a frown as he spots the charity shop branding before he recomposes himself and jabs a finger at his chest. 'But it's important to us. *So important*. We need to raise every penny we can tomorrow to go towards the auction in a couple of weeks.'

I could kick myself. I knew about the fun run. Stacey told me all about it this morning, but it slipped my mind in all the drama of getting the project back on track. Obviously Oliver will be taking part, but I had no idea the other builders were too.

'I'm sorry.' Vanessa would never apologise in this situation and nor would she do what I'm about to, but I can't lose every scrap of my humanity to this project. 'And you're right. You should take part in the fun run.' I purse my lips as I do some calculations in my head. 'What time is the fun run?'

'It's in the afternoon. From two o' clock.'

'How about a compromise?' A dirty word in Vanessa's book, but needs must. 'You guys still work in the morning, get as much of the flooring down as you can, and then finish up in time for the fun run. Would that work?'

Oliver blinks at me, momentarily mute, but then he nods. 'Yes, I suppose that would work, but I was going to help set up.'

'I could do that, if that's okay with you and Stacey? I'm not going back to Manchester this weekend after all, so I could lend a hand. I can help clear up afterwards, and not just so that you can get back to the flooring.' I try out a smile in Oliver's direction and I'm relieved to see his features have softened, even if he doesn't return the gesture. 'Just tell me what you need me to do and I'll do it.'

'Okay.'

I only get one simple word in response, but I'll take it. We both get up and head for the door.

'Is Vincent really taking part in the fun run?'

A bubble of laughter spills out before Oliver can block it with his hand, but he cuts it off by clearing his throat and giving a solemn nod.

'Really?' I can't imagine Vincent running for pleasure, or even charity. I've heard his rasping puffs of breath from climbing the steps up to the house.

'Yep.' Oliver is still battling the mirth as a rare smile plays on his lips. 'He's asked us to have a medic on standby.'

I was hoping the builders wouldn't see my backing down as a sign of weakness and slow down, but it has the opposite effect. Grateful that I'm giving them the afternoon off, they work even harder and later than I expected and arrive early on Saturday morning, ready to work without needing a revitalising cup of tea. I'm so impressed, I don't feel any reservations in leaving them to it while I head over to the park to help Stacey set up.

'You came.' There's a hint of a frown as Stacey sees me walking towards her, but it smooths away quickly and she attempts a smile. She still doesn't trust me, but then why should she? She's heard nothing but horror stories about Vanessa and then I rock up and confirm the rumours.

'Have you met Julia?' Stacey leads the way to the tent set up in the middle of the park, where there's a bar set up inside.

'From the Farmer's Arms?' I recognise the barmaid from my first day in the village. Her arms are full of wooden bangles, which clink together each time she reaches for the crate beside her to stock the fridge.

'That's right.' Julia stands up with a wince and brushes at the knees of her skinny jeans. 'We're sponsoring today's fun run, plus supplying drinks for the thirsty masses afterwards.' She winks at me. 'I'm sorry, I don't think I caught your name?'

Naturally, my actual name forms on my lips, but I stop myself in the nick of time. 'Vanessa Whitely.' I thrust my hand out towards her. 'I'm doing up the house at Arthur's Pass.'

'About time someone did something with that place.' The bangles clink as Julia pumps my hand up and down. 'Ellie and Tom gave it a go, bless 'em, but it's a big job. The plan was for them to live in the guesthouse while they did the main house up, but they never made it out of there and in the end they had to sell up, and pretty quickly it seems. They were here one minute, gone the next.' Julia frowns. 'They still owed me a couple of quid for the footie card.'

Their swift exit explains why the guesthouse is fully furnished, I guess.

'Shall we get on with setting up?' Stacey starts to guide me away from the bar before she lowers her voice. 'She'll gossip all day if you let her.' She rubs her hands together. 'And we've got lots to do. Can you help me with these tables?'

There's a pile of half a dozen folding tables stacked up just outside the tent, and we grab an end each of the first table, with Stacey leading the way.

'The route is pretty easy to follow – it's just once or twice around the perimeter of the park, depending on age, ability or optimism.' Stacey comes to a stop and we lay the table on its side so we can pull the legs out into place. 'But we'll put some cones out, so there's no confusion. These tables are going to be set out at intervals with bottles of water, just in case people forget to bring their own, and there'll be one at the start and finish, for registration and the medals.'

We set out the tables and cones with the help of a few more volunteers and then I'm tasked with helping out with the registrations and handing out the numbered stickers for the participants to attach to their tops.

'There's quite a turnout,' I say when Oliver arrives at the table. The race doesn't start for another half an hour, yet there are over a hundred people either warming up at the starting line or downing some ill-advised Dutch courage in the tent.

'We've been lucky.' Oliver peels the backing off his sticker and presses it to his T-shirt. It's quite a tight T-shirt but I try not to notice the way it clings to the contours of his body. The rather nicely sculpted contours that his physical job – and perhaps the gym – has earned him. 'The whole community has come together to support us. They've been amazing.'

'How's everything been at the house?' I probably shouldn't bring it up right now, but although I'm confident about the effort the builders were putting in earlier, I can't ignore the flutter of butterflies in my stomach. My career is depending on this, after all.

'Great.' Oliver gives an enthusiastic nod of his head. 'I think we'll be done with a final push tomorrow.'

'Really?' I press my hands together as though in prayer. 'That would be incredible. Thank you so much.'

Oliver gives a one-shouldered shrug before he moves on, calling over his shoulder as he goes. 'It's what I'm paid to do.'

Once the registrations are complete and the fun run is about to start, Stacey sends me to the first water station. The race starts and I see a few familiar faces jog by; Stacey and Oliver are running side-by-side, closely followed by an enthusiastic-looking Todd, who is wearing a one-piece lycra bodysuit that is so tight, I can practically see every bone of his skeleton. Harvey is jogging alongside a group of women, doing his best to be charming while keeping his breathing steady, and Vincent, bless him, is almost the last of the pack, with only a crew of elderly ladies bringing up the rear as they stroll along the route. Mrs McColl is leading the silver-haired strollers, powering slightly ahead of the woman who sold me the leather skirt in the charity shop this morning.

Stacey and Oliver pass me a second time, still side-by-side, and Harvey and Todd have opted for two laps of the park too, though Todd is less enthusiastic now as he half-staggers, half-jogs his way past, clutching his side and looking as though he'd quite welcome death to put him out of his misery.

Stacey makes a short speech once the race has finished, and the crowds pile into the beer tent for some well-earned refreshments afterwards. The clean-up starts straight away, and I help to fold and load the tables into the van waiting at the entrance of the park before setting off with a bin liner and a litter picker. My back is aching by the time I've patrolled the perimeter of the park, and I'm starting to feel guilty that I sent Oliver and the others back to the house to carry on working after their run, even though I know Vanessa would have no qualms about it. By the time Stacey has thanked me for my help and dismissed me, I've made up my mind. Returning to the house, I gather the builders in the hallway.

'Are you sure the flooring will be completed tomorrow?' I ask Vincent, glad I have someone else to focus on other than Todd, who is still wearing the lycra bodysuit along with his work boots. He looks absolutely ridiculous and I have to avert my gaze every time he bends over.

Vincent nods. 'Absolutely.'

'Great.' I clap my hands together. 'Then I think we should head back to the park for a celebratory drink. And the first round is on me.'

Chapter 19

The beer tent is still pretty full when we arrive back at the park, minus Todd who has sloped off home to change. I tried to be diplomatic as I suggested that he might want to change out of the lycra bodysuit, but it took Harvey's less tactful observation that Todd 'looks like a knob' for him to take the hint. As promised, I buy the first round, as a thank you for the builders' hard work over the past couple of days.

'You know what?' Harvey leans against the bar as he takes a sip of his pint. 'You're not so bad once you take that stick out of your arse.' He winks at me, a slow smile playing at his lips. 'And you're pretty fit.'

I'm not sure how to react. I'm sure it was meant as a compliment, even if it was delivered in a sleazy manner and Harvey's gaze has dropped to my chest, but it definitely leaves me feeling uncomfortable and a bit icky. What would Vanessa do in this situation?

'My eyes are up here, pal.' Reaching out, I take Harvey's chin between my thumb and index finger, squeezing them together with slightly more force than is strictly necessary, and tilt it until our eyes lock. 'And I'm paying your wages. Don't think you can cross any lines.'

Harvey sighs as I release my grip on his chin. He shakes his head as he lifts his pint, pausing before taking another sip. 'And the stick is firmly back in place.'

'We will get this job finished on time, you know.' Vincent hands me a glass of wine shortly afterwards. I didn't know he was buying another round, but I'm grateful. The first glass went down very nicely and I can feel the tension slipping away from my bunched-up shoulders.

'I hope so.'

Vincent holds his pint aloft. 'I give you my word.' And then he downs his drink in one, which doesn't bode well for our early start tomorrow. I keep quiet, not wanting to be a party pooper and prove Harvey's analysis of the stick and its location right.

Todd turns up in a pair of jeans and a checked shirt, which is a much better look than the bodysuit, and the group decide to move onto the pub as it starts to grow dark. I watch them amble away, teasing and ribbing each other, and weigh up whether it would be wise to order one more drink before I go home. I'm not a big drinker but I am enjoying the effects of the wine and, if I'm honest, I'm not relishing the thought of a Saturday evening on my own in the guesthouse.

'Vanessa?' Todd has somehow un-wedged himself from Harvey's signature headlock and is looking back at me. 'Aren't you coming?'

I wasn't aware that I'd been part of the plans to move onto the pub, and I'm still not sure I'd be a welcome addition as I gauge the reaction from the others. Oliver is looking down at the ground while Harvey is shooting daggers at his wrestling buddy.

'Why not?' Not only will I show Harvey that I do not have a stick lodged anywhere about my person, I'll also avoid the long, lonely stretch of evening ahead.

*

The evening turns out to be surprisingly fun as we feed money into the jukebox at the Farmer's Arms and try to outdo each other with the cheesiest song choices. The more wine I drink, the more relaxed I feel, and I even succumb to Harvey's gentle goading and knock back a couple of shots of tequila, which I haven't done since my student union days. The battle lines Oliver and I have marked out over the past few days start to blur as the evening draws on, and when he chooses Tight Fit's 'The Lion Sleeps Tonight' on the jukebox, I join in with the merriment as we stagger around the pool table in a sort of conga line with added animal moves.

Gosh, I must have drunk more than I thought as I'd usually be too self-conscious to throw myself around with such abandonment in public, but it's actually quite freeing. My arm is held up in front of me, swinging like an elephant's trunk when I stumble into the corner of the pool table and end up on my bottom, laughing at the hilarity and trying not to pee myself.

'I think it's time we got you home.' Oliver holds out a hand and heaves me to my feet. I stumble again but manage to stay upright. 'Where did everybody go?'

I glance around the pub for a familiar face, but apart from Oliver, who is holding me steady, and Julia behind the bar, I don't recognise anybody. I know Vincent left earlier after several phone calls from his other half, but I'm sure Harvey and Todd were here a moment ago, prancing around like a gorilla and a gazelle respectively.

'Maybe they're in the bogs?' I shrug and grab my handbag, which I'd dumped on a table earlier, almost taking out a couple of empty glasses like a wrecking ball. 'Can we get a kebab on the way home? I really, *really* fancy a kebab.'

'You're in Little Heaton, remember?' Oliver guides me away from the pool table, making sure I don't propel myself into a table full of drinks or trip over my own feet. 'There aren't any takeaways around. There's a fish and chip shop, but it's over by the cricket grounds and there's no way I'm propping you up that far.'

'Hey.' Placing my hand on Oliver's chest, which feels firm and *delicious* even in my drunken state, I push myself away from him. 'I don't need propping up, mister.' Which is when I walk straight into a low stool and almost catapult over it.

'Really?' Oliver's smirking as he grabs me around the waist and guides me towards the door.

I scrunch up my nose. 'I think I've had too much to drink.'

A laugh splutters from Oliver as he opens the door, but it isn't the derisive sound I'm used to hearing from him. 'I think that's an understatement. I never thought I'd see Vanessa Whitely dancing to The Cheeky Girls. By the way, don't tell Stacey you asked Dominic Blackwood to touch your bum. She'll scratch your eyes right out.'

The door swings shut behind us and Oliver places his arm around me so he can take some of my weight. It's quite nice to lean on somebody, and not just because I'm hammered. It takes an age for us to totter towards the footbridge, and when we do get there I insist that I'm perfectly able to walk unaided. I proceed to ricochet from the rail on one side of the bridge to the other like a pinball machine, which is *hilarious* for me, but not so much for Oliver, who has tasked himself with keeping me from hitting the deck.

'I've seen a different side to you tonight.' Oliver takes hold of me again and guides me towards Arthur's Pass. 'I thought you were super stuck-up. Conceited. And definitely a ball breaker. But tonight you seem different.'

'You thought I was a Grade-A bitch.' I tap Oliver's chest with my index finger, punctuating each word.

He groans and screws up his face. 'You heard that?'

'Yup.' I give my head a good old bob up and down, which makes me feel a bit queasy so I'm forced to stop. 'I heard it. But that isn't me, you know. I'm not the bitchy, manipulative woman

118

you think I am. I'm not this either.' I hold my arms out wide and stumble as we reach the loose gravel of the drive. 'I'm actually timid and … *boring*.'

Oliver snorts. 'You really are drunk.'

I shake my head. Too much. There's that queasiness again. 'It's true. I don't get drunk. I don't sing and dance in the pub. That was fun, wasn't it?' Wriggling free from Oliver's grasp, I launch into another verse, warbling about the lion sleeping at the top of my voice as I throw my body around in a one-person conga as Oliver tries to shush me. Dodging his arm as he tries to hook me around the waist, I stumble, this time falling down onto the ground. It hurts. A lot. And when I look down at my knee, it's oozing blood and I'm in real danger of throwing up.

*

'Brace yourself. This might sting a bit.' We're sitting at the break-fast bar in the guesthouse, a well-stocked first aid kit open in front of us. After my fall, Oliver scooped me up off the gravel and is now tending to the gash on my knee.

'S'okay.' I shrug as Oliver tears open an antiseptic wipe. 'It already hurts like – aaarrgghh. Jeez, that stings like a mother—'

'Told you.' I hiss as Oliver presses the wipe to my knee again. 'Sorry, but it has to be done. You don't want that gravel getting in and infecting your knee.'

I bite my lip in preparation for the sting, but it isn't nearly as bad the third time. 'There we are. All done and it doesn't look so bad now. No stitches required anyway.' Oliver releases my leg so he can rifle through the first aid kit. 'You definitely need a Mickey Mouse plaster though.' He holds the strip up before tearing one off and placing it ever so gently on the wound. Still, I wince as it makes contact.

'How did you know about the first aid kit?'

Oliver holds out his left hand. There's a pale pink line above the knuckle on his index finger. 'I had a fight with a Stanley knife. Nic patched me up. Luckily it didn't go too deep.'

'Did Nic stay here then? In the guesthouse?'

'No, but we all used the kitchen and the, er … facilities over here.'

I flinch as Oliver applies another plaster as the cut is quite long. 'What have you been doing for the past few days?'

'Sneaking over to the Farmer's. Julia doesn't mind and we didn't want to bother you.' Oliver grimaces. 'I'm pretty sure Harvey has been making use of the big bushes at the back.'

'Lovely.' I pull a face. 'You should just use the loo here from now on.' I'll just have to be extra careful not to leave my bras lying around the bedroom as the builders will have to pass through to the en suite bathroom.

'Thanks.' Oliver balls up the antiseptic wipe and gathers up the packaging. 'There. Your knee's all done. How are your hands?' He takes my hands in his and turns them over to inspect the palms but although I broke my fall with my hands, they seem to have survived unscathed.

'You should be a nurse, not a builder.'

Oliver laughs, his whole face lighting up, and my tummy goes all topsy-turvy. My hands are still in his as neither of us have moved away, and I can't stop looking at those lips, wondering what it would be like to kiss him. It's madness. Utter madness. Oliver hates me – or the person he thinks I am – and his words from a couple of days are still reverberating around my brain. *'Of course I didn't hit on her. Why would I?'* So why then am I leaning in towards him, my eyes closing as I bring my lips closer to his?

'Vanessa.' Oliver's tone is firm without being harsh as he finally extricates his hands and places them on my shoulders, gently pushing me away so I'm left pouting into the air. 'You're drunk.'

I am, very much so, but all the alcohol in the world couldn't numb the abject humiliation as Oliver jumps away from me, already backing away towards the door before I've had the chance to un-pout. He can't get away from me fast enough and I stare in horror as he sprints across the room. I think he says something – goodnight, perhaps? – before the door swings shut behind him but I can't be sure as the realisation of what has just happened rains down on me.

I tried to kiss Oliver. And he rejected me. How can I ever face him again?

Chapter 20

The radio, as ever, is blaring in the main house, which my pounding head doesn't appreciate one bit, but my hangover – and it's a biggie – pales into insignificance when Vincent delivers some very good news. I've been walking around like a zombie ever since Kate woke me up by calling just before nine this morning (which was a blessing as the builders were due to start work in a few minutes), feeling as though I could throw up or die every time I moved.

'Isn't it amazing what you can do when you put your mind to it?' I pad carefully around the kitchen, mindful of the brand new tiles, my churning stomach and my sore knee. By some miracle, the flooring is complete and it's only mid-afternoon.

'And isn't it amazing how patronising such a tiny woman can be?' Vincent quirks an eyebrow at me, but there's a hint of a smile on his face.

'Sorry. I didn't mean to be patronising.' I turn slowly to take it all in. My knee is throbbing beneath the Mickey Mouse plasters, but I've sort of got used to it throughout the day and it's now a background niggle. 'It looks great, though. It all looks amazing.' While most people would be happy with carpet, laminate flooring and lino, the majority of the rooms in Vanessa's giant house are now laid with either flagstones, ceramic tiles or solid wood flooring. 'And now we're ready for the plumber tomorrow!' I clap my hands together. I can't quite believe we've managed to pull it off. 'And we can really crack on with the rest of the refurb. I've got a new schedule I want us to go through first thing tomorrow.'

'I'm looking forward to it already.' Vincent bends to pick up his toolbox before he lifts a hand in farewell. 'I'll see you tomorrow then.' He yells for Harvey and Todd to 'get their arses in gear' if they want dropping off at home as he trudges towards the front door, grabbing the now blissfully silent radio on the way. There's a flurry of movement in the hallway as the builders race to catch their lift, leaving just Oliver and I in the house. I can hear him on the stairs and I wonder if I can hobble out of the front door and across the drive before he makes it down to the hallway. I've managed to avoid him all day, sending Todd up with his cups of tea and generally moving about the house like a hungover ninja. If I can just evade him one more time …

No such luck. He's on the bottom step before I even make it halfway across the hallway.

'How's your knee?'

I look down at my knee, as though it will whisper the words I need while I'm so flustered by Oliver's presence. I can still feel the light pressure of his hands on my shoulders as he pushed me away and my face is burning with the humiliation of being rejected. I wish I could wave a magic wand and wipe the memory clear.

That's it! I am a genius!

'You know about my busted knee?' Tilting my head to one side, I frown at Oliver. Memory loss will save my pride, even if I have to fake it.

'I was there when you fell over. I cleaned it up and patched you up.'

'Oh, that was *you*.' I laugh in wonder, which is maybe laying it on a bit thick. 'I can't remember a thing after that second shot of tequila.' I give a 'what are you gonna do' shrug and make a rather slow beeline for the door. 'Anyway, I thought I'd head over to the sanctuary since I was too hungover to help out this morning, so I guess I'll see you tomorrow.'

'I'm heading that way myself so I'll walk with you.'

Of course he's heading that way too, because *he lives there*, you numpty.

Oliver strides ahead, opening the door for me. I smile in thanks while inside I'm shrivelling in shame. I may be refusing to acknowledge the attempted kiss but that doesn't mean it didn't happen.

'We got some new guests in last night.' Oliver waits at the bottom of the steps while I hobble down them as best as I can with a knee covered in plasters. 'Three kittens. They're adorable.'

'Aww, how cute. I love kittens. They're so tiny and fluffy, aren't they? I'd love a cat but my flat is so small and I wouldn't trust my flatmate not to torture the poor thing while I was out.' I'm babbling to mask my discomfort as we head across the drive, not realising I'm putting my foot in it until Oliver manages to get a word in.

'You don't strike me as the kind of person that would have a flatmate. Successful businesswoman and all that. Fiercely independent. I thought you'd want your own space.'

I do, desperately, but only because I share a flat with a buffoon.

'She's not a flatmate as such. More a temporary houseguest. She's my best friend and she needed a place to stay for a few weeks, until she gets herself sorted.'

Oliver frowns. 'You suspect your best friend would torture your pet if you had one?'

Damn it! Why do my lies keep coming back to bite me on the arse?

'She's, um, going through a tough time. A bad break up. It's made her a bit …'

'Unhinged?'

'Prone to acting irrationally. Out of character.' This imaginary best friend is starting to sound familiar. Almost as though I'm describing myself since I arrived in Little Heaton (cat torture and bad break up aside). 'She's muddling through as best as she can though, and if she does act a little … oddly … it isn't done with malicious intent. She's just doing what she can to get through this difficult time.'

'Fair enough.' Oliver gives me a sideways look, a smile playing on his lips. 'Still wouldn't trust her with a cat though.'

I nudge him with my elbow and for the briefest of moments, as we both try and fail to contain a giggle, I forget all about last night.

*

The kittens are, as I suspected they would be, utterly delightful. There are three of them, each small enough to fit in the palm of your hand, and my heart melts at the mere sight of them as they snuggle together on a fleecy blanket. It's the first time I've been upstairs at Stacey's house, which has been transformed into a flat as the animal sanctuary has taken over the ground floor.

'You're just in time to help me feed them.' My hangover has abated to the extent that I at least feel vaguely human again, but Stacey looks exhausted. 'I've made up the formula and it should be cool enough by now.'

'They have to have formula?' And I get to help feed them. My heart is a puddle in my chest.

'Yep. They're only a few days old and should be with Mum.' Stacey kneels down at the coffee table and starts to fill a small syringe with formula. 'Unfortunately, we don't know where she is. These poor little mites were left outside a vet's in Altrincham so we're looking after them until they can be rehomed.'

'Who would abandon them like that?'

Stacey shrugs as she pushes a tiny drop of the formula onto her wrist. 'Desperate people, I guess. And at least they left them in a relatively safe place instead of ...' She shakes her head and beckons for me to join her at the table before handing me the syringe. 'This is perfect. Let me just grab Tommy and I'll show you what to do.'

Tommy is a tiny bundle of marmalade fur with fine white stripes along his paws and tail. He's so small, with his eyes still closed, and I fall instantly In Love. Stacey places him on his belly on a fluffy towel in front of me, carefully lifting the kitten's head and instructing me to place the teat at the end of the syringe into his mouth.

'You want to apply a little bit of pressure on the plunger. We don't want to fill him up too quickly.' Stacey nods as I press down gently. 'Try to match his rhythm. That's it. You're doing brilliantly.' Tommy has started to suckle and I feel such an overwhelming surge of pride as he takes in his feed. No wonder Stacey loves taking care of all these animals if this is the sense of satisfaction you get.

'I think he's had enough now.' Tommy has started to turn his face away from the syringe, so Stacey takes it away, making a note of how much formula he's taken on a chart. 'Look at your messy chops, mister.'

I didn't think Tommy could look any more adorable, but I was wrong. The fur around his mouth is matted with milk and I could burst with the cuteness of it right now.

'There we go.' Having cleaned Tommy with a baby wipe, Stacey returns him to the fleecy blanket and picks up the next kitten. 'This is Timmy. He's a little wriggler, so I'm going to wrap him up like a burrito, otherwise we'll never get any food into him.'

Timmy is indeed a wriggler, but together we manage to feed

him a full syringe of food, even if it takes a little longer than his brother. When we get to the third kitten, however, I discover that Timmy's feeding was speedy in comparison. Stacey takes over, expertly holding the kitten's tiny head while feeding her one drop at a time as she refuses to latch onto the teat.

'I have to do this every two hours,' Stacey says once all three kittens have full tummies. 'Which is why I'm walking around like a zombie.'

'I can help out more.' Oliver peers at the little bundle of fur, reaching out to gently stroke Timmy. 'I'll take care of the night feeds.'

Stacey shakes her head, even as she's yawning. 'Thanks, but you've got a full-time job to be getting on with for this tyrant.' Stacey grins at me, to show she's joking. At least I hope she is. 'Anyway, I'm starving, so let's eat before I have to start this all over again.' She turns to the kittens, but she's smiling and clearly adores them, and rightly so. 'You'll stay and eat with us, won't you, Vanessa? Mrs McColl has left a vegetable hotpot warming in the oven and it smells divine.'

I'm about to decline Stacey's kind offer. It doesn't feel right accepting such hospitality from these people when I've been lying to them since my arrival, plus there's the added bonus of Oliver's rejection of my drunken pass last night to contend with. But then I recall the aroma as I stepped into the house earlier, the smell of the dish in the oven creating an irresistible sense of nostalgia, taking me back to childhood dinners, of sitting around the kitchen table, warm and cosy and happy, before Mum left and Kate went off to uni and it was just Dad and I and the coldness remaining. I should say no, but I'm desperate to cling onto those memories, for just a little while.

'I'd love to. Thank you.'

We eat downstairs in the sanctuary's café, which has closed for the day. Mrs McColl's hotpot is as delicious as the memories it invokes, especially when dunked with chunks of leftover homemade bread. I thought things between Oliver and I might be awkward, but it seems he's as willing to forget the whole thing ever happened as I am, so I start to relax, enjoying my new friends' company. We chat and laugh over the meal before Oliver suggests a game of Monopoly. I think it's a splendid idea, though it's met with a groan from Stacey.

'Oh, come on. We never get to play it anymore.' Oliver starts to gather up the dishes, making room for the board game.

'That's because you're terribly competitive to the point I would happily strangle you.' Stacey grabs a stack of dishes and carries them into the kitchen, with Oliver and I following with the plates and glasses. She's started to stack the dishwasher, but she turns to me with a wry look on her face. 'Do you know, he once had a major tantrum over a lost game of Kerplunk?'

Oliver rolls his eyes at me. 'I was a kid.'

Stacey gives a hoot. 'You were seventeen and you didn't speak to me for a week afterwards.'

'It was a few days at most.' Oliver nudges his sister playfully. 'And I'm way more mature now. Go on, you know you want to. And Vanessa wants to play too, don't you?' Oliver shoots me a pleading look, but it isn't needed.

'I'm up for a game of Monopoly.' I give a nonchalant shrug, but inside I'm rubbing my hands with glee. Oliver may think he's competitive but he's met his match. I'm not over-competitive in everyday life, but I'm pretty cut-throat when it comes to board games. One of the things Dad taught me was to play to win, and I fully intend to.

*

We start off playing as a trio, but Stacey has to pop back upstairs to feed the kittens and tells us to carry on without her, which I'm more than happy to do as we return her money and property cards to the bank, meaning Mayfair is up for grabs again. I have

Park Lane in my portfolio, but it's pretty useless without its purple partner. I have a full set of green properties, each with a hotel, so if I can get my mitts on the Holy Grail of Monopoly properties, Oliver will be toast when he passes along the last quarter of the board.

'Oh my God, are you still playing?'

I'm about to roll the dice, but I look towards the doorway, where Stacey is standing with her arms folded across her chest. She's shaking her head at us, a look of pure bewilderment on her face.

'Of course we are.' Oliver indicates that I should go ahead and roll. 'There's still plenty of life in the game yet. Look, Vanessa still has money. Not much, admittedly ...' He flashes me a smug grin and gives a one-shouldered shrug. 'But the game doesn't end until I've taken the shirt off her back.' His eyes widen and he holds up his hands. 'Not literally, obviously.'

'I may not have much money *right now*, but that's because I've been heavily investing in my properties. Plus, I have enough to buy Mayfair and I'm only ...' I count the spaces on the board. 'Seven spaces away and it's my turn to roll.' I give the dice a vigorous shake before spilling them onto the board. A four and a ... six. Damn it! Oliver whoops as I snatch the battleship piece and move it to the Super Tax space, rubbing his hands together as I slide a hundred-pound note from my meagre stack and throw it into the bank.

'Better luck next time.' Oliver scoops up the dice, still tittering to himself as he rolls.

'Guys, it's almost ten o' clock. You've been playing for *hours*.' Stacey steps into the room, and I put a protective arm around the board, in case she's planning to tidy the game away before we're ready. 'I've fed the kittens twice, for goodness' sake. You need to stop.'

'Not just yet.' Oliver moves his counter, safely landing on his own property and purchasing another house.

'I've got a busy day tomorrow.' Stacey pulls a chair out and flops down onto it. 'I've got Dianne Baxter coming over to discuss the Brownies' role in the open day and Mrs McColl wants to plan the cake stall. I need to sleep.'

'Then sleep.' Oliver waves her away but Stacey doesn't move.

'I can't leave you down here. I know how obsessed you get, and who do you think will have to deal with Mrs McColl when she finds you cluttering her café in the morning?'

I'm about to snatch up the dice but pause and look at Stacey. The poor woman does look exhausted and I'm overstaying my welcome.

'Stacey's right. It's getting late and I should get going.'

Oliver's grin is wide, his eyes shining and his hands clenched into tight fists. 'Are you forfeiting?'

'Absolutely not.' I wouldn't dream of it. Dad didn't raise a board game quitter. 'Count your money.'

Oliver snorts. 'Is that really necessary? I've clearly got more than you.'

'Yes, it is necessary.' Hooking my handbag with my foot, I scrape it towards me and rummage inside for my phone. 'Because we're not done yet, pal. We're only just getting started.' Opening the camera app on my phone, I take a snapshot of the board. 'Let's get this over to my place so I can continue to whoop your butt.'

'*Continue* to whoop my butt?' Oliver snorts again. 'When did you start to?'

Oh, I'm going to wipe the floor with this smug git and I won't even have to unleash Vanessa Whitely to do so.

'You're not seriously going to take that over to your place and set it up again, are you?' The bewildered look is back on Stacey's face.

'We seriously are.' I waggle my phone at her. 'And we're going to carry on where we left off.'

'You're both insane.' Stacey stands up and tucks her chair back under the table. 'But at least I won't have to witness it.'

130

Chapter 21

It physically hurts to open my eyes when my alarm goes off the following morning. I've only managed a few hours of sleep after the Monopoly game, but I'm determined to drag myself out of bed without hitting the snooze button. After a rocky start with Stacey and Oliver, it feels as though there was an unspoken truce between us yesterday and I'm hoping it continues. Spending time with them yesterday was fun and if I'm going to be here for a few more weeks, it would be nice not to be so isolated and make some friends.

Stacey's in the middle of feeding the kittens, so it's Mrs McColl who lets me into the animal sanctuary. Wanting to make myself useful – and possibly prove myself – I decide to head straight out into the yard to get started on the daily routines. Changing into a pair of wellies and pulling on a pair of gloves and a hat (it's far too cold for vanity this morning), I head outside, ignoring the swirl of apprehension I feel as I ease the chicken coop open. Chow Mein, the chicken who herded me across the yard a few days ago, is out first but this time I stand my ground and she plods past me without so much as a sideways glance. Patty is next, startling me and making me take a step backwards as she ruffles her feathers, but she's simply having a morning stretch and continues on her way to the patch of grass. I take a deep breath. I can do this. If I can persuade Vincent and the guys to finish the flooring over the weekend, I can deal with a few chickens.

'Come on, girls.' The remaining chickens have yet to emerge from the coop but, as brave as I'm telling myself to be, I don't want to be sticking my hands in there with all those beaks. I clap my hands as best as I can inside the thick gloves in a bid to encourage the emptying of the coop. Would whistling work, or is that only a dog thing?

'Please?' I crouch down, wincing as my knee is still sore. 'Come out and play with your sisters so I can clean out your house.' Stacey will be down soon and I don't want her to catch me pleading with her chickens. I'm supposed to be in control. Strong. Gutsy. I'm not supposed to be a wuss. 'Fine. We'll do this the hard way.' I can't quite believe what I'm doing, but I appear to be reaching into the coop. I try to muffle a squeal as I give one of the chickens a gentle nudge. Amazingly, the chicken toddles out into the yard leaving me with all five fingers intact. I did it! I'm more capable than I think I am, which is a valuable lesson I'm going to need over the coming weeks if I'm going to get this house party-ready in time.

I'm on a bit of a high after managing to clean out the coop without being pecked to death, and I have a definite swagger of confidence as I make my way across the drive later that morning with one of the lever arch files tucked under my arm. Vincent has just pulled up in his van, and he jumps out, laughing at something one of the others has said, but the amusement fades away, his features taking on a more serious look when he spots me. He nods in greeting and waits for me to catch up while Todd and Harvey shuffle towards the steps.

'Good morning, Vincent.' I give a curt nod of my own. 'Ready for our little chat?'

'I've been on tenterhooks all night, ma'am.'

'Ma'am?' I purse my lips before beaming at Vincent. 'I know you were being sarcastic, but I like it. Why don't we give it a trial?'

Vincent's mouth gapes. I walk past him, trying not to giggle as I make my way up the steps. I unlock the door and make my way through to what will one day soon become the living room. It's a bright, airy room, with super-high ceilings and bi-fold doors leading out onto the garden overlooking the canal, and my heels clip-clop on the newly laid solid wood flooring.

'The decorators are due in two weeks.' I decide to get straight to business. It's what Vanessa would do. 'And we've got a lot to get done before then. The plumber will be arriving at any moment to make a start on installing the boiler and fit the radiators, and the electrician will be joining us on Wednesday. I've revised the list of jobs your team needs to be getting on with and the time-scale I expect them to be completed by.' I give Vincent my sternest look, to show him that I won't be making any allowances or accepting any excuses as I open the file and take out a copy of the new to-do list and hand it over. 'I know it's a tight schedule, but this job will be finished on time because I have a very important event planned here and you wouldn't want to let me down, would you, Vincent?'

Vincent shakes his head, his eyes still working its way down the list. 'No. Of course not.'

I lean in close to Vincent, trying my hardest to keep a straight face. 'What happened to *ma'am*?'

Vincent tears his eyes away from the list, his eyebrows pulled down low. 'You weren't actually serious about that, were you?'

I close the file and tuck it back under my arm, already walking away without answering the question. 'Sounds like the plumber's here. You should be making a start on that list.' I only make it as far as the doorway before something occurs to me and I turn back around. 'Where's Oliver, by the way?'

Vincent shrugs. He's looking down at the list again, but I can see the corners of his lips lifting. 'Maybe he had a late night? Or maybe he's worn out.' Vincent looks up now, locking eyes with me. 'You know, from the fun run?'

'That was two days ago, and he seemed okay yesterday.'

Vincent nods, and his lips are twitching again. 'He did, didn't he? Maybe something else happened to, er, wear him out?' He starts to whistle as he makes his way into the hallway, only pausing to yell for Todd and Harvey to join him.

With the builders and the plumber busy working on their respective jobs, I head over to the guesthouse, waving as Oliver's van swings onto the drive, so I can get on with some paperwork. Although I've made good progress with the mess Nicole left behind, there's still a lot to get my head around. I'm staring at the array of invoices and receipts in bafflement when my phone starts to ring. I'm hoping it's Emma as I haven't had the chance to chat to her since Friday, before I made a complete fool of myself with Oliver. He thinks I've forgotten all about it, but my insides still burn with shame whenever the image pops into my head, which it does far too often. Emma will make me feel better. She'll do her best to convince me that I'm not an ogre, that the reason Oliver rejected me is because I'm simply not his type. I won't believe her, but it'll be nice to hear it.

But it isn't Emma and I feel a knot of dread when I see my boss's name on the display.

'Hi, Vanessa!' My bright tone belies the tightening knot in my stomach. 'How are you?'

There's a slight pause before she speaks, and I can imagine she's frowning, wondering why I'm asking a question I never have before. Vanessa and I don't do pleasantries. She doesn't have the time or inclination for it. 'I'm absolutely fine.' There's another pause, where I imagine she's asking herself *why wouldn't I be?* 'Anyway, I'm just calling to reschedule my visit. I take it Emma told you I couldn't make it today? There was an appointment I didn't see on the calendar. Stupid thing.' She mutters the last bit before continuing in her usual brisk manner without waiting for confirmation that I did indeed know about the change of plan. 'I thought we could do Wednesday instead.' It isn't a question. Vanessa is coming on Wednesday, which isn't ideal. The electrician is due to start that day and although this means we're making progress, we're still far behind where we should be at this point. I need a bit more time to catch up, to at least appear like I have a handle on the project.

'Aren't you terribly busy with the Heron Farm Festival?' I'm clutching at straws, but this is quite a substantial one. The Heron Farm Festival is a big event, one Vanessa and the team have been working on for weeks and which I'd hoped to be a part of. The knot in my stomach constricts again when I think about how much effort I put into the ideas that will never see the light of day.

'Sonia's really put herself forward on the project over the past few days and brought some wonderful ideas to the table, and Emma's on board to take care of the admin side, so I can spare an afternoon.'

Emma's working on the Heron Farm Festival? She never said anything to me about it, just that Vanessa had asked her to help with some 'stuff', which I took to mean *my* 'stuff'. Emma's my closest friend, but I can't help feeling a bit sick that she's getting to work on the project I coveted. I know I shouldn't be jealous of her success, that I should be happy for my friend, but I can't help feeling the bite of disappointment that Emma's been given this opportunity in my absence, even if it is only an administrative role.

'So I'll see you on Wednesday afternoon then.'

'I'm looking forward to it.' I'm lying, but Vanessa has already hung up anyway.

Vanessa is visiting in two days' time. We're nowhere near ready for her to clap eyes on the property. And the team think I'm her. I'm in a *major* pickle here.

Chapter 22

Work is coming along nicely over at the main house when I pop over with a tray of refreshments, and I'm bowled over when I return later in the day and see how quickly the kitchen is progressing. The units and the large island are starting to take shape, and although the walls are still bare plaster with wires sticking out ready for the light fittings and sockets to be fitted, you can really see how the finished space will function. The whole house is going to be stunning when it's finished and it'll pain me to return to my grotty flat-share.

'I hope you haven't forgotten about our rematch this evening?' The plumber has left for the day and Vincent is packing up the van while Harvey and Todd thumb wrestle on the drive so I've managed to catch Oliver on his own.

Oliver makes a 'pfft' sound and gives me an odd look. 'Of course not. Just let me nip home for a wash and a change and grab something quick to eat and I'll be ready to kick your butt. *Again.*'

Oliver won the game of Monopoly last night, but only because he managed to buy Mayfair and block my plan for world domi-nation. I suggested a rematch and Oliver was happy to oblige.

I raise my eyebrows, but I don't rise to the bait. 'Why don't I cook for us?' Too late, I realise it sounds like I'm proposing a date. And a cosy one at that. 'I mean, I say "cook"…' I use air quotes and everything and immediately feel like a prat. 'But I'm really only offering a ready meal that we can eat off our laps. That way, we can play and eat at the same time. Kill two birds and all that. Give you more time to "kick my butt".' There are the air quotes again, followed by a look of disdain that suggests it wouldn't happen in a million years.

I couldn't resist that bait after all.

'Okay.' Oliver gives a lazy shrug. 'Fine by me. But don't think I'll go easy on you just because you've fed me.'

My jaw drops. 'I wasn't expecting anything of the kind. When I thrash you – which I absolutely will – it'll be because I'm a far superior player than you.'

Oliver makes that 'pfft' sound again as he starts to walk away. 'Keep dreaming, mate.' I stick my tongue out at his back but quickly retract it as he turns to face me. 'Don't think I can't see your reflection in the window.' I remain silent, my face the picture of innocence. 'I'll see you in about half an hour then?'

I wait until Oliver has disappeared from view before I lock up and tear across the drive as quickly as I can with my still-busted knee and the loose stones. Half an hour isn't much time when the living room of the guesthouse looks like a tornado has passed through a filing cabinet and tossed every scrap of paper in the air, leaving them to flutter and land wherever the wind has taken them. Plus, I should probably change out of the restrictive pencil skirt I chose from my new collection of clothes this morning, which was fine for appearing professional but not very comfortable for an evening of Monopoly. My jeans haven't been in the wash yet and they still smell like donkey, so I grab a pair of leather-look leggings and a burnt orange asymmetrical top.

I've just set up the Monopoly board and plumped the cushions on the sofa for the third time when there's a knock at the door.

Smoothing down my top and throwing my shoulders back, I stride towards the door with a confidence that is full-on fake. Even though I know this isn't a date – and Oliver *definitely* doesn't consider it a date – I'm nervous. But at least I won't be drunk this time and therefore less likely to make a fool of myself.

'Change of plan.' I step aside as Stacey waltzes into the guesthouse, leaving Oliver to mouth his apologies in her wake. 'We're all going to the pub instead of playing that.' She wafts a hand in the direction of the Monopoly board. 'And I don't want to hear any arguing or excuses. Oliver's already tried and it won't wash.' I look at Oliver, who gives a shrug of defeat. 'One of my regular volunteers has offered to watch the kittens for a couple of hours, so come on, chop chop. I'm on the clock here, people.'

'My sister can be a bossy cow at times,' Oliver mumbles as Stacey powers ahead towards the lane.

I zip up my jacket, having not been permitted the two seconds to do so back at the guesthouse. 'Maybe we can play later?'

Oliver grins at me. 'There's no need, unless you don't like Scrabble?'

I give him a sideways 'puh-lease' look. 'I am the *queen* of Scrabble.'

'Good.' Oliver rubs his hands together, and not because it's chilly. 'Because there's a set behind the bar of the Farmers.'

*

Stacey isn't happy that we've hijacked her evening in the pub with our game of Scrabble (even though *she* hijacked our plans first) and she lets us know every thirty seconds or so, either by sighing loudly or telling us outright. She's refused to take part and is currently grumbling into her gin and tonic about what a pair of losers we are as I place the word 'wheezily' onto the board while trying not to look too smug that my Z is on a double letter square.

'You didn't get out much as a kid, did you?' Stacey's voice is dripping with disdain and although I know she's playing the part of the disgruntled spectator and probably doesn't really mean it, it hits a nerve. Dad's strictness meant my social life was seriously lacking until I left for uni.

'Like we did, you mean?' Oliver has noted down my score on the pad and is studying his own tiles. 'How old were you before you left the village on your own? Nineteen?' Oliver smirks at his sister. 'And you only made it as far as Cheshire.'

Stacey gives him a hard shove. 'I went to college way before then, and it isn't my fault we were brought up in the middle of nowhere.'

Oliver snorts as he picks up one of his tiles and places it on the board. 'The middle of nowhere? There's a town a couple of miles away.'

I sit up straighter. 'There is?' There'll be shops. A Rymans or WHSmiths. Maybe even – dare I hope – an Asda. I could stock up on all the stationery I need. And buy tights to stop my legs turning blue in the cold. And underwear, so I don't have to wash, dry and wear the same handful of knickers I packed for 'a few days away'. 'Is there a bus that'll take me there?'

Stacey wrinkles her nose. 'There is, but it only runs every couple of hours. If you're lucky. I used to end up walking home from college most days, until I learned to drive.'

Oliver snorts as he places three more tiles down on the board. 'Gran used to pick you up, you mean.'

Stacey shoves him again, but Oliver is too pleased with himself to pay her any attention as he tots up his score. FAQIR, on a double word square. Damn it.

'I could give you a lift.' He gives the tile bag a shake before delving inside. 'At the weekend?'

'Really?' I've clearly been isolated in Little Heaton for too long because although it's been less than a week, the prospect of pushing a trolley around a supermarket is making me giddy. 'That would be great, if it isn't too much trouble?' I cross my fingers under the table.

Oliver places his new tiles on his rack. 'No trouble at all. Like I said, it's only a couple of miles away.'

'You can't go on Sunday, remember?' Stacey's attention is caught by the pub door opening, and it's held by the bloke who's now walking towards the bar. He looks vaguely familiar but I can't place him. Stacey clearly can as she's basically salivating.

'Is Saturday afternoon okay with you?'

I pull my gaze away from the bar to find Oliver giving me a quizzical look. 'Saturday afternoon would be perfect.' Unlike the selection of Scrabble tiles I have in front of me, which are far from ideal and I'm twenty-six points behind. AERIE is the best I can manage and although it only earns me five points, it's better than forfeiting my turn to swap my tiles. Oliver, however, can hardly contain his glee, performing a joyful little wiggle as he adds my meagre points to my tally. I dig my hand into the bag and pull out four new tiles, squeezing my eyes shut until the very last second as I hope for better letters this time.

No such luck.

Two more vowels, plus a Z and an X.

Why am I even bothering?

Because you never, ever give up, I hear my dad's voice boom inside my head. *You keep fighting until the bitter end, unlike that so-called mother of yours who ran off at the first hiccup in our marriage. Bloody quitter. Don't ever be like her, Rebecca, do you hear me?*

'The game isn't over yet.' I rearrange the tiles in my rack, as though it will actually make a difference. 'Far from it.'

'And on that note …' Stacey drains her gin and tonic and stands up. 'I'm going to the bar.'

Oliver doesn't take his eyes off his tiles, but I see him smirking. 'Say hi to Dreamy Dominic for me.'

Stacey fake laughs, but then she gives a genuine smile as she

140

crouches next to her brother. 'I wasn't going to say anything, but you do know there's a rumour going around about the two of you, don't you?' She waves a hand between Oliver and I, her smile turning sly when it transpires neither of us has the foggiest what she's talking about. 'Apparently, you were seen sloping away from Arthur's Pass *very* early this morning.' She places a finger to her chin. 'Where could you possibly have been sneaking away from? And what had you been up to, hmm?'

'We were playing Monopoly.' Oliver rolls his eyes. 'Take your mind out of the gutter.'

Oh, God. I recall Vincent's strange behaviour this morning when I asked about Oliver's whereabouts. He must have heard the rumour too.

'Try convincing the village gossips that's all you were doing.' Patting her brother on the back, Stacey sashays away towards the bar, leaving an awkward atmosphere in her wake.

The only way to get through this, I decide, is to pretend it isn't happening and concentrate on the game of Scrabble. I manage to claw my way back and swoop the win when I place the word 'ZAX' on a triple word square. Stacey is chuffed for me, but mainly because it means we can put the game away and enjoy one more drink before she has to get back to the kittens. She offers to get another round in, but I suspect it's just so she can make cow eyes at the bloke propping up the bar.

'That's Dominic Blackwood,' Oliver tells me when my nosiness gets the better of me. 'Runs one of the farms down the road.'

'What's their deal?' I open the little cloth bag while Oliver lifts the board and tips the tiles into it. 'Stacey clearly likes him, but does he like her?'

Oliver shrugs as he folds the board in half. 'No idea. I try not to examine my sister's love life too closely. But I do know Dominic's wife left him for their much younger farmhand about a year ago.' Oliver shakes his head and takes the bag from me, setting it down in the box. 'Poor guy was pretty messed up. I think that's why Stacey holds back, but like I said, I try not to think about that kind of stuff.'

I watch as Stacey throws her head back to laugh at something Dominic has said, grabbing hold of the end of her ponytail so she can twist it around her finger. If Dominic can't take the hint that Stacey has a massive crush on him, the dude must be blind. I'm about to remark as such to Oliver when my phone starts to ring. It's my sister, again, who is another one who can't take a hint.

'Are you going to get that?' Oliver nods down at my phone, which is still ringing in my hand.

I shake my head and send the call to voicemail, knowing Kate won't bother to leave a message.

Chapter 23

I'm a bag of nerves as I pace the living room, the clip-clopping of my heels echoing in the vast, empty room. The builders, plumber and electrician are all up on the first and second floors and I'm surprised I can still hear the radio blaring from up there over the thumping of my heart. My chest hurts, my skin is prickling with sweat and I'm struggling to control my breathing. If there wasn't a very good reason for the severe apprehension I'm feeling right now, I'd swear I was having a heart attack.

What am I going to do? I move to the bi-fold doors, my heels clip-clopping at a pace, before turning sharply and marching back to the window at the front of the property, peering out onto the drive. Vanessa will be here any minute and whatever game I've been playing over the past few days will be up. The builders will discover I'm not Vanessa, that I'm simply her pushover PA, and it will be clear for Vanessa to see that I know nothing about property development, despite watching *Homes Under The Hammer* very, very carefully every morning since I got here.

I'm going to get fired, just like poor Nicole. I'll be jobless, penniless, and I'll be forced to slope back home to Dad and admit that he was right all along. I'm a failure. I shouldn't have ignored Dad's advice and followed my own path. Just look at Kate – she'd never find herself in a situation like this. My sister's life is sorted while mine is falling apart.

I'm about to turn and stalk back across the room when a familiar cherry-red Mini swoops onto the drive, loose pebbles scattering as it swings in front of the house. Oh, God. She's here. She's actually here, right now. My hand flies up to cover my mouth as I watch my boss's legs swing elegantly from the open door. Flicking the car door shut, she starts to tread carefully over the uneven drive in a pair of needle-thin heels that would make my eyes water even if I wasn't already on the verge of tears.

Springing into action, I throw myself out of the house and barrel my way down the steps before she can reach the door. 'Vanessa, hi!' I clamp a hand over my mouth again. I can't go around shouting that name. 'Why don't you come this way?' Hurtling towards her over the gravel, I wave a hand in the general direction of the guesthouse. 'We'll have a cup of tea and then I'll give you the grand tour.'

Vanessa looks from me to the house and back again before giving a shrug. 'I don't drink tea.'

I nod effusively, the rhythm matching the ferocious beat of my heart. 'Of course. I know that.' I give a strangled laugh, cutting it off when I see the startled look on Vanessa's face. 'Sorry. I'm just so excited that you're here. How about a coffee?' I usher Vanessa into the guesthouse, checking we haven't been clocked before closing the door behind us. I know I'm only delaying the inevitable, but self-preservation has kicked in. 'Take a seat and I'll put the kettle on. I'm afraid we only have instant.'

Vanessa smiles tightly. 'That's fine.'

I know that it isn't, but cheap coffee from the mini market is the least of my worries. 'I bet you'll have a state-of-the-art coffee machine in the house when it's finished.'

Vanessa smooths down the seat of her trousers before she lowers herself carefully onto the edge of the sofa. 'Speaking of the house, how is it all coming along? I spoke to Nicole at the weekend – she's still in the hospital but recovering well, apparently – and she said everything was all going to plan before the accident.'

What a liar. I should pull my boss up on her porkies, but of course I don't.

'It's going great!' If my tone is too enthusiastic – which I suspect it is – Vanessa doesn't pick up on it.

'So we'll be ready for the party?'

'Absolutely!' I shove my head into the cupboard to pick out a couple of mugs and also to hide the shame that is surely written all over my face. Vanessa isn't the only fibber.

'Good, because I'm going to start planning the party in earnest next week.'

The mugs clatter onto the worktop. 'You are?'

'Well, obviously.' Vanessa scrunches up her face as she looks at me as though I'm a spanner short of a toolbox. 'The party is in a couple of weeks so I'm already cutting it fine. It's just that the Heron Farm Festival has been taking up so much of my time. Thank goodness for Sonia! And Emma too. She's been a godsend.' She sucks in a deep breath before letting it out slowly while shaking her head. 'I don't know what we would have done without my right-hand girls, to be honest.'

I know that I should be happy for my friend for getting some recognition, but I can't help feeling a pang of jealousy. Here I am, stepping completely out of my comfort zone and it's Emma and Sonia getting all the praise. I can feel that promotion slipping away from me even if I do somehow manage to cling onto my job after the disastrous refurb.

'I could take care of the party planning!' It comes to me in a flash of inspiration, my hands flying outwards like I'm inviting a hug, such is my enthusiasm. It's the first time I've been so forthright, the first time I have put myself out there so explicitly, and I don't know whether to be so proud of myself that I can't help but dance around the kitchen or whether I should pick up one of the mugs and clunk myself over the head with it. Repeatedly.

'You?' Vanessa's eyebrows inch ever so slightly up her forehead. 'But you're a PA.'

Yes, I want to scream at her. *I am a PA, but I also have a degree in events management. And also, my job as a PA didn't stop you bunging me into an alternative role to suit your needs.* But I keep silent, obviously, and concentrate on spooning economy coffee granules into the mugs.

'This place is quite nice, isn't it?' Vanessa is up and inspecting the living room when I place the coffees on the table. 'I didn't really pay any attention to it when I was viewing the house, but it's a nice little bonus.'

'Would you like a tour?' I've been quite good at making sure there are no bras or knickers loitering around the bedroom since the builders started using the facilities, but I'm suddenly gripped by fear that I've left the contents of my washing basket strewn about the place.

'No thanks.' Vanessa gives a quick shake of her head. 'I really don't have time for that. Ty's taking me to the opening of a new club tonight and I need to get my roots done.' She runs her fingers through her hair as she gazes around the room. 'It's a decent size though, and it'd make a lovely holiday let, don't you think?' Vanessa reaches into her tiny handbag and pulls out her phone, tapping at the screen as she wanders towards the kitchen area. 'I'm just going to have a quick look on Airbnb. See what the deal is.' She leans against the breakfast bar as she swipes her finger on the screen. 'It doesn't need much work, and if we replace that manky old sofa with a sofa bed, we could charge more.' Stepping away from the breakfast bar, she yanks open the oven door. 'This could do with a clean.' Her eyebrow quirks as she looks at me with mild disgust, and I want to tell her that I haven't even touched the oven since I've been here, never mind cooked with it, so any griminess is down to the previous occupants. But I don't. I simply stand back while she opens the cupboards, examining the contents briefly before flicking the doors shut again.

'It's all self-contained. I've had no problems with living here, apart from not being able to light the fire.'

Vanessa glances at the blazing fire. The eyebrow is quirked again.

'Oliver showed me how to do it.' I don't mention the fact I was afraid to attempt it by myself in case I burned the place down, in case she chalks it up as incompetence.

'Oliver?' Vanessa quirks the eyebrow again, but she has a bemused look on her face to accompany it this time. 'Been getting friendly with the locals, have you?'

'No, not like that anyway.' I hop up onto a stool at the breakfast bar, which is a big mistake as the image of me leaning in to kiss Oliver in this very spot imprints itself into my brain. My face is aflame, which is damning evidence as far as Vanessa is concerned if her dirty cackle is anything to go by.

'Of course you haven't.' She pats my shoulder while performing an elaborate wink before moving on to inspect the washing machine.

'I really haven't. Oliver is one of the builders.' I should have kept my big gob shut and let Vanessa assume I've been working my way through the male population of the village because mentioning the builders only reminds Vanessa why she's here.

'Ah, yes, the builders.' Vanessa slips her phone into her miniscule handbag as she strides towards the door. 'Shall we go over and take a look at the house? I'm dying to see how it's all coming together.'

So this is it, I think as I shuffle after her. Time's up. It's time to come clean and face the music.

Chapter 24

I creep into the house as though I'm the next victim in a horror movie, with the killer lurking behind any one of the doors. The radio is still blaring from upstairs, which is good as the builders may not hear us skulking about down here. If I can keep Vanessa downstairs and the others upstairs, I may just get away with this.

'I don't understand.' Vanessa is turning in a slow circle as she takes in the hallway, and I have to lean in close to hear her over the music. 'It looks so … bland. It's still a worksite. There are wires hanging from the ceiling!' She jabs a hand at the offending wires before marching towards the living room, squeaking with alarm when she spots the bleakness that greets her. The bare plaster. More hanging wires. A vast, echoey space.

'I was expecting …' She shakes her head as she turns in another slow circle. 'I was expecting … *Something*. This looks exactly the same as when I viewed the place six months ago!' Her hands are covering her cheeks as she performs a second turn.

'That isn't true. The place was gutted, pulled back to its bare bones before being built back up again.' I know this because I've picked my way through every single bit of paperwork contained in the numerous files. 'So although it may not look like much work has taken place, it absolutely has. This room in particular was riddled with damp, which needed to be sorted before any restoration work could take place. And the joists needed replacing because of the damage the damp caused to the floor.' I point down at the newly fitted flooring. 'And look at the bi-fold doors. They're going to give you a stunning view once the garden has been landscaped.' I shouldn't have mentioned the bi-fold doors, because while I'm heading for the door to move the tour onto the more aesthetically pleasing kitchen, Vanessa is wandering towards the huge panes of glass.

'Oh, my God.' She turns to me with wide eyes, and I'm about to explain that the jungle of a garden will be tamed *very soon* when she points into the distance. 'There's a *donkey* in my garden. Becky, why is there a donkey in my garden?'

I check over my shoulder, making sure the others haven't sneaked down the stairs and overheard Vanessa's use of the name Becky, least of all because *it isn't my name*, before I hurry over to the doors. 'It's okay. That's just Franny.'

'Franny?' Vanessa is still peering out into the garden, a hand at her throat, looking as though she'll soon be in need of some smelling salts.

'She lives at the animal sanctuary along the lane.' I try to guide Vanessa away, but she's dug her needle-thin heels in.

'But what is it doing in my garden? Why isn't there a fence to keep it away?'

I try once more to guide her away, and this time she's more yielding. 'There is a fence on the sanctuary's side but Daisy, the other donkey, is a bit mischievous. She manages to sniff out any weak spots and break through, leaving Franny to wander out and take the blame.' I titter but Vanessa doesn't join in the mirth. We're back in the hallway, so I give her a gentle nudge towards the kitchen, where there at least units and worktops and a giant island to admire. 'There'll be a new fence put up soon, once the vacant land is bought, so it won't be a problem for you.'

'Vacant land?' Vanessa runs a hand along the smooth, cool

149

marble of the island, but her eyes are on the kitchen's matching bi-fold doors. Or rather on Franny, who is nibbling at the over-grown grass.

'The land between your property and the sanctuary is empty, so Stacey and Oliver are going to buy it and expand. There'll be a new fence – a better, stronger one that Daisy won't be able to exploit. There didn't seem to be much point in putting up a new one before your garden was landscaped anyway. Oliver and Vincent agreed it would be best left until then.'

'But it will be sorted before the party?' Vanessa absently opens and closes a cupboard door.

'The auction is next weekend.' I hold up my entwined fingers. 'So, if all goes well, the fence will be in place well before your guests arrive.'

Vanessa nods, eyes still on the donkey. 'Right. Well, I think I've seen enough for now.' She glances around the kitchen. 'Are you *sure* the house will be ready in time? It seems like there's an awful lot to do …'

'Absolutely.' I steer Vanessa back into the hallway at a gallop, heading straight for the front door before she changes her mind and asks to see upstairs. 'This is just how refurbishments go. Slowly, slowly and then boom!' I clap my hands together, but not too loudly in case it arouses intrigue from upstairs. 'It comes together all at once.'

'Hmm.' Vanessa bites her lip. 'I'll pop over again next week, just to keep tabs on the progress. I need to get a feel for the place anyway so I can plan the party. Get Emma to book a time in the diary, okay?'

I nod, practically pushing Vanessa out of the door. If I can get her into her car without encountering the others, I'll have survived to fight another day. I'll worry about her next visit later.

'You would tell me, if there was a problem, wouldn't you?' Vanessa is at the bottom of the steps. So close to her car, fob in hand.

'Of course I would.' The smile plastered to my face is making my cheeks ache. 'But there's absolutely nothing to worry about. Everything is on track.'

Vanessa nods once before she pushes down on the fob. I hold my breath until she's climbed into the mini, checked her make-up in the rear-view mirror and set off along the drive. I'm almost blue in the face by the time the breath gusts from me and I suck in a lungful of fresh air, but at least she's gone and I haven't been rumbled.

*

I survived Vanessa's visit, but I can't completely relax just yet, even as I slide into a hot bubble bath later that evening. My body unwinds, my muscles unclenching as the water soothes them, but my mind is still a hive of activity as I try to figure out a way to explain to everyone who I really am. Because although I got away with it today, I doubt I'll be so lucky next time. I have to come clean about my true identity, sooner rather than later, and definitely before my subterfuge is exposed. I'm hoping the builders will see the funny side, and that they'll continue to give me the respect they show 'Vanessa'.

Oh, who am I kidding? There's still so much to do before the party deadline, and there's no way I can keep them under control as my true self. Rebecca Riley has the authority of a wet blanket and Harvey will have Todd in a half nelson on the hallway floor before you can say 'false identity'.

It's all too tempting to let myself slip under the bubbly water, but fortunately there's a knock at the front door that has me hauling my body from the tub. Wrapping myself in the nicely warmed towel from the rail, I head for the door, glad of the fire I lit earlier as I step into the toasty living room. Thanks to Oliver's guidance, I haven't set fire to the guesthouse in my bid to keep warm.

Checking the towel is secure, I open the door to find Oliver on the doorstep, brandishing a Battleships box.

'We need a decider.' He pushes the box towards me at the same time he registers the fact I'm wearing nothing but a towel. His face blanches as he takes a step back, his jaw almost dropping to the gravelled driveway, and I'm not sure whether he's embarrassed or appalled by the sight of my near-nakedness. Either way, I jump behind the door so only my head is peeking out, which is probably what I should have done in the first place.

'Sorry. I didn't know that you, um …' Oliver is scratching at the back of his neck but he stops to waft a hand in my direction. 'I shouldn't have just come here unannounced like a complete turnip. I'll, er …' He backs away further and is about to turn around when I open the door the tiniest fraction more.

'Wait. You're right, we do need a decider.' Our board game scoresheet is currently one all after my victory at Scrabble in the pub last night. 'And Battleships is an … interesting tiebreaker. Come in.' Clamping a hand over my chest to ensure the towel remains in place, I swing the door open fully and step aside. 'Give me five minutes? You can even put the kettle on while you wait.' I grin at Oliver to mask how awkward I feel in my undressed state. It's been a long time since anyone has seen me wearing so little, other than Lee who doesn't respect boundaries.

Scuttling into the bedroom, I cringe when I spot my reflection in the full-length mirror attached to the wardrobe's door. My skin is blotchy from the heat of the bath (plus the embarrassment reddening my cheeks further) and my hair is piled on top of my head like a particularly haphazard pineapple. No wonder Oliver had wanted to run a mile!

Pulling the bobble from my hair, I run my fingers through it as I head to the wardrobe and fling the door open. I'm all set with professional pieces but I really could do with something more casual to wear on occasions such as these. I'd had no idea I'd have anything resembling a social life when I'd shoved a few items in my holdall so a couple of pairs of leggings and a T-shirt or two will be on the top of my list when we go into town at the weekend.

I make do with a shirtdress and give my hair another ruffle before joining Oliver in the living room. He's set up the game on the coffee table, placing two of the plumpest cushions on the floor at opposite sides, and there's a steaming cup of tea waiting for me.

'Have you eaten?' I haven't yet and my stomach is quietly grumbling. If I leave it much longer, it'll be a full-on roar. 'I can't offer Michelin-style cooking, but I do have a selection of ready meals.' I open the fridge with a flourish. Oliver joins me in the kitchen, his eyebrows rising when he clocks the rows of plastic trays.

'You really don't like cooking, do you?'

I shrug. 'I don't mind cooking. I'm no Nigella, but I usually do better than this.' I point at the trays I stocked up on earlier. 'But I'm not sure I trust the so-called fresh food from the mini-market. Furry tangerines may be a delicacy in Little Heaton, but I'll pass, thanks.'

Oliver pulls a face. 'I see your point. But we do get online deliveries, you know.'

'You do?' Why did nobody tell me this before I'd consumed more mediocre shepherd's pies than you could shake a stick at? 'Can you get Waitrose to deliver here?'

Oliver shrugs as he reaches for a lasagne. 'I'm more of a Tesco man myself, but probably.'

'Vanessa will be ecstatic if they do.' I close my eyes as I realise what I've done. Bugger. 'Because Vanessa can't live without her Waitrose groceries.' I place a hand on my chest and giggle, as though I'm some kooky idiot who talks about herself in the third person. Luckily, my phone starts to ring from where it's charging on the breakfast bar and I lunge at it, flashing Oliver an apologetic face as I scuttle off to the bedroom, not because I want privacy for the call but because I need a moment to compose myself before I combust through sheer mortification.

What an idiot.

'Emma, hi.' I try to sound upbeat, but it's quite difficult when you're cringing so hard your face is in danger of turning itself inside out. 'Where are you? It's really noisy.' I can hear the cacophony of numerous conversations taking place in a small space, made worse by an echo amplifying the din.

'Sorry, I thought it would be quieter in the loos, but I think the entire female population of the Greater Manchester area has squeezed itself in here. Give me a sec.' I can hear Emma excusing herself and I can imagine her battling through the crowds. The noise is suddenly deafening, and I'm about to tell Emma it's much worse when it dies down again and all I can hear is the occasional car driving past.

'Better?'

'Much.' I flop onto the bed, laying back so I'm looking up at the ceiling. 'Where are you?'

'I'm outside the club. It's way too busy inside. It's like Black Friday in there, but with free drinks instead of discounted TVs.'

'You're at a club on a work night?' That isn't like Emma at all. We sometimes go for an after-work drink, but it's only ever a quick one in a pub close to the office.

'I know, madness, isn't it?' Emma giggles. 'It's this mega exclusive place, where all the celebs are supposed to start hanging out. It's the opening night and Tyler managed to get us all tickets. Sonia's trying to cop off with some bloke from *Emmerdale*.' Emma giggles again and I feel a pang of jealousy that I'm not there with them. I don't particularly want to hang out with celebs, and I definitely don't want to watch Sonia snogging a soap actor (or trying her best to), but I do want to feel like part of the team. I feel out of the loop. Forgotten.

'Anyway, I've only just got your message to ring you back. Sorry. It's so manic at the moment.'

I sit up on the bed, pulling my knees up to my chest. My Mickey Mouse plasters are starting to curl at the edges after my bath. Am I pathetic for mourning the days when I was a top priority for my best friend, before she started to shine in the eyes of our boss while I'm tucked away out of sight and mind? Yes, I probably am pathetic.

'Vanessa's free on Tuesday next week if that's okay with you?'

I start to pick at the Mickey Mouse plaster. 'Sure.'

'Is everything okay?' Emma's voice is so soothing, so like my usual, comforting best friend, it makes me feel pathetic all over again.

'Everything's fine.' I try to pump some cheer into my voice, to be more gracious. I shouldn't begrudge my friend her chance to shine. 'I'm just tired. You go and enjoy your night. Make the most of it.'

'Are you sure?' Emma is hesitant, and I know that if she were here, she'd have her arm around me, doing everything in her power to make me feel better.

'I'm sure. In fact, I've got a date with a ready meal and a game of Battleships.'

Emma puffs out a confused-sounding laugh. 'Okay. That sounds … fun. I'll give you a call tomorrow. Fill you in on how Sonia gets on with her soap star.'

'I can't wait.' Hopping off the bed, I say goodbye to Emma and head back into the living room to kick some Battleships butt, which does sound fun and more up my street than the opening of some swanky club.

Chapter 25

'Why don't we make this more interesting?'

We're sitting on the sofa, facing each other from opposite ends while our feet meet in the middle, because it was too uncomfortable sitting on the floor, even with plump cushions. My feet are bare while Oliver is wearing thick woollen socks, and the urge to dig my toes into the baby-soft wool is strong but I force myself to focus on Oliver's words instead.

'How do you mean?' I reach for my glass of wine, careful not to flash my battleship placements to Oliver.

'Why don't we make a new rule?' Oliver eyes me over the top of his Battleships board and I pull a face. We're a few moves into the game but there hasn't been a hit yet.

'We're not playing strip Battleships.' I shake my head and plonk my wine back down on the coffee table, in case I drink too much and actually agree to go along with it. 'No way.'

Oliver barks out a laugh. 'That isn't what I was going to suggest, but now you mention it …' He grins at me over the board so I toss a scatter cushion at him. It misses by a mile, landing behind the sofa, which makes him laugh even harder.

'What new rule then?'

Oliver shifts into a more comfortable position, his foot

brushing against mine. The wool really is super-soft. 'I was thinking that whenever one of our ships is sunk, we have to tell the other person a secret or confession.'

'What, like truth or dare?'

'I guess.' Oliver shrugs. 'But without the dares.'

'What if I don't have any secrets?' This is obviously a hypothetical question, because I have a massive secret, but I'm not sure a game of Battleships is the best scenario for admitting I'm not really Vanessa.

'Then I'll ask you a question and you have to answer honestly.'

'Why would we do this?'

Oliver shrugs. 'I guess I'm intrigued by you.'

'By me?' I snort. Why would anybody's interest be piqued by me?

'Yes, by you. I want to see what makes you tick, because I can't work you out. I've heard all these things about you …' I raise an eyebrow to perfection. I've been practising in the mirror. 'Not all of it good. In fact, none of it good.' Oliver grins at me, but I doubt he's kidding. 'But then you turn up and you're not as bad as I was expecting.'

I splutter a laugh. 'If that isn't a ringing endorsement, I don't know what is.'

'You know what I mean. You're more fun than I thought you'd be – except when you yell at us for slacking, obviously.'

'Duh.' I nudge Oliver with my foot. 'Then stop slacking.'

'And you do these random acts of kindness. Bacon butties, regular rounds with your tea tray, threatening to nail Harvey's bollocks to the wall if he performs one more atomic leg drop on Todd. That poor boy was tortured before you came along.'

'Okay, but why would *I* agree to play with your new rule?'

Oliver holds his arms out wide. 'Aren't you intrigued about the hidden depths of this handsome chap?'

I groan and cover my eyes with one hand. 'Fine, go on then.' I must be mad agreeing to this, but it does sound kind of fun.

'*Yes!*' Oliver rubs his hands together, the movement almost causing his board to topple off his lap. 'Whose turn was it?'

I stretch my legs out a little more and lean back against the cushions. 'Yours.'

'Okay, here goes.' Oliver taps the top of his board for a moment, figuring out his strategy. 'F5.'

I consult my own board and try to keep a neutral face before I give my verdict. 'Miss.' I waste no time before giving my own coordinates. 'I7.'

'Miss. C5.'

'Miss.' I like how Oliver doesn't mess around, but I don't tell him so. I also don't tell him just how close he was to a hit. 'D3.'

'Miss. I5.'

Damn it! Not only is it a hit, it's a hit on my biggest ship. I'm fuming inside, but I don't allow it to surface.

'Hit.' I say the word with an air of indifference that belies the rage going on inside my head. I don't want Oliver to see how ruffled I am as I pick up a red peg and jab it into my battleship.

'Yes!' Oliver can't contain his glee as he gives a little wiggle of victory as he plucks his own red peg from his tray. I need to locate and sink one of Oliver's ships before he takes mine down – there's no way I want to be the first to reveal a secret. Oliver delivers a second blow to my ship before I manage a hit of my own. He still has three hits until I sink, so if I'm onto a smaller ship, I still stand a chance. I go to take a sip of my wine, but the glass is empty. When did that happen?

'I believe G6 is a hit?' I return the glass to the coffee table without refilling it.

'You sank my battleship.' The smile has completely vanished from Oliver's face as he plucks a red peg from his tray, but his features lift when he consults his board. 'I2, which I believe is not only a hit but a devastating hit.' He grabs another red peg but I hold up a finger to stop him.

'*I* believe, having sunk your ship, you owe me a confession.'

The smile drops from Oliver's face again. 'I do, don't I?' He drops the peg back into the tray. 'Whose stupid idea was this confession thing again?' He gives a wry smile as he reaches for the bottle of wine, refilling his glass. I go to stop him when he stretches towards my glass but change my mind. I'm feeling pretty chilled out right now, despite the upcoming secret I'm going to have to divulge. I'm hoping Oliver's secret will be minor – pocketing a couple of penny sweets from the mini market during his youth – so I can get away with something insignificant too.

'Right then. A confession.' Oliver takes a gulp of wine before settling back down against the sofa cushions. 'Okay, here goes.' Oliver takes a deep breath before looking me in the eye. 'I've been single for four and a half years. I haven't been on a single date since things ended with my ex.'

'Why not?' I can't believe it's due to lack of interest from the opposite sex – the man is hot.

Oliver grins at me. 'Sink another ship and I might tell you.' He picks up a red peg and wiggles it at me. 'I think I'm going to plump for I2.'

I gulp down half of my glass of wine, dragging out this moment, because we both know I'm sunk. Oliver wiggles in his seat, a grin spreading across his face.

'Come on, spill.'

'Fine.' I shrug, taking inspiration from Oliver's own confession. 'I've been single for three years. There are no big secrets though, I'm afraid, and I have been on dates since but they haven't evolved into anything. I was with Daniel for a year and a half through uni, then we went our separate ways. Daniel went back to Newcastle and I stayed in Manchester.'

'Didn't he ask you to go with him? Or what about a long-distance relationship? Newcastle isn't *that* far away in the grand scheme of things.'

I shake my head. 'It was never that serious between us. I think we both just liked having a comfort blanket while we were away from home.'

'God, that sounds grim.'

I shake my head again. 'It wasn't. It was lovely. Daniel was a great guy.'

'But it hardly sounds like a passion-filled relationship.'

I shrug. 'Maybe not, but I don't regret it. The question is, do you regret your last relationship? Because it's obviously had a big impact.'

Oliver taps his board. 'No freebies. You've got to sink another ship first.'

It takes three turns before I manage to hit another ship, and another five before I sink it.

'Right then, mister.' I grab my glass of wine and settle down against the sofa cushions. 'Fess up.'

'Okay.' Oliver shifts in his seat and I'm not sure whether his discomfort is physical or because he's about to reveal something deep and meaningful. 'My last relationship ended four and a half years ago when I asked her to marry me.'

Chapter 26

Deep and meaningful it is then, because proposing to someone is a biggie, especially if they turn you down.

'She said no?' I honestly don't understand why anybody would. Not only is Oliver extremely easy on the eye, he's also fun and caring. Even when he despised me, he still made sure I got home relatively safely from the pub and patched my knee up afterwards. Plus, he hasn't mentioned my clumsy attempt to kiss him, which makes him pretty gentlemanly in my books.

'She said maybe.'

'Maybe?' I frown. 'What kind of wishy-washy answer is that?'

Oliver smiles, but it's forced and there's sorrow behind his eyes. 'It's the kind of answer you give when you're already married.'

My eyes widen and I hear myself sucking in a breath. '*No*. Did you know? About the husband?'

'Of course not.' Lines burrow deep into Oliver's forehead as he reaches for his glass of wine. 'I had no idea, which I feel pretty stupid about, looking back. I should have known.' He takes a sip of wine and although I have a million questions buzzing around my head, I keep quiet. 'Lottie never answered when I called – I always had to wait until she got in touch – and she never introduced me to her friends or family. She said her parents were dead and she didn't see much of her brothers and sister. She never let me visit her because she was embarrassed by the hovel she lived in, so she'd always come and stay with me.'

'No offence, but this is a tiny village. How did she get away with it?'

'She didn't live in Little Heaton.' Oliver returns his glass to the coffee table. It's empty. 'She said she lived in Macclesfield, though how true that is I don't know. I don't know if anything she told me was true. I trusted her completely and she made an absolute mug out of me.'

'How long were you together?'

'Almost two years.'

Ouch. 'And what happened after you proposed?'

Oliver shakes the last drops of wine into his glass. There's another bottle in the fridge but I'm not sure we should open it. Getting drunk is never the answer, even if it helps for a little while.

'She told me about her husband.' Oliver screws ups his face, squeezing his eyes shut. 'And their kids.'

Shifting my Battleships board onto the coffee table, I head into the kitchen and return with the other bottle of wine.

'She said she loved me but she couldn't marry me yet.' Oliver gives a cheerless laugh. 'Like I'd marry her after that little confession.'

'You must have been heartbroken.' I top up both our glasses and settle myself back on the sofa.

'I was devastated. But I also felt like a massive idiot. I mean, you hear about businessmen who lead double lives, setting up homes in different parts of the country, but I never expected to be on the receiving end. I was humiliated. Which is why I've never told anybody the real reason we split up. Not even Stace.'

Wow. That's some major confession, so whatever I come up with next must somehow match its importance. I don't think admitting that I've never watched an episode of *Game of Thrones* will cut it.

'So that's why you've put dating on the backburner.'

Oliver nods. 'It's pretty hard to put your trust in someone after something like that.'

Our feet are meeting in the middle of the sofa, but the contact doesn't seem enough. I want to reach across the short distance and give Oliver's knee a reassuring squeeze, or hold his hand. Anything to take some of the burden. Instead, with the image of Oliver's rejection the other night in my mind, I pick up my glass of wine.

'Why do you think you were able to tell me about Lottie but not your sister? I mean, you don't even like me, so why trust me with your secret?'

'I do like you.'

I quirk an eyebrow as I take a sip of my wine. I'm getting pretty good at this eyebrow stuff.

'Okay, maybe I don't like some of your actions – sacking Nicole for one. And those emails you sent Vince in the beginning were pretty brutal. You really know how to alienate people, I'll give you that.'

'That still doesn't answer my question though.' I need to side-step away from these emails, because I have no idea what they contained and I don't want to trip myself up. 'Why did you tell me about Lottie?'

Oliver lifts up his Battleships board. 'It's in our new rules.'

I shake my head. 'You could have told me anything. Like the time you borrowed your sister's prized mood ring and lost it somewhere between home and school.' I shrug as Oliver tilts his head to one side. 'I was seven and it was way too big. I did look for it, but it'd disappeared. Kate still doesn't know what happened to that mood ring …'

'That doesn't count as one of your confessions, you know.'

My mouth gapes at Oliver, but I have to concede; it hardly

compares to his deep and meaningful revelation. 'Fine. Anyway, stop evading my question. Why me?'

Oliver looks down at his Battleships board. 'I'm not sure. Maybe it's because we barely know each other. I'm not sure I want Stace to know how much of a failure I am.' He gives a one-shouldered shrug, his eyes still fixed on his board. 'Or maybe, despite everything, you seem like a trustworthy person. A good listener. Non-judgemental. I've just told you my deepest, darkest secret but it doesn't seem like you think any less of me.'

'Why would I? What happened was hardly your fault.'

'See.' Oliver looks up from his board to beam at me. 'My instincts were right. Now, come on. Let's get on with the game, otherwise I'll be sneaking down the lane during the early hours and setting off the rumour mill again.'

I've never resigned from a game before – that would have been a cardinal sin according to Dad – but I'm starting to wonder if now would be a good time to forfeit. But no, I can't do it. Oliver has revealed something he's kept hidden from those closest to him, so I have to be as true to my word.

'I haven't spoken to my dad for about six years.'

I feel a huge wave of shame shower down on me as I say the words. My dad is so ashamed of me, he's refused any attempt at contact since I left for university. He won't pick up the phone when he knows it's me, hangs up if I manage to deceive him by using a withheld or unknown number, and has yet to acknowledge any of the emails or letters I've sent over the years. In the end, I gave up trying.

'And the worst bit is, I'm glad. I feel freer without him now.' My gaze drops to my Battleships board, to my duo of sunken ships.

'Why did you stop talking? Did you have a fight?'

I shift position, my eyes still focusing on the ships and pegs on my board so I don't have to meet Oliver's eye. I've never spoken about Dad to anyone. Not even to Emma or my sister. Kate is too similar to Dad and sees me as the failed sister. I'm not as smart as her, not as driven or ambitious and we've never been on the same wavelength.

'Dad and I don't – *didn't* – fight. He laid down the law and I followed it without comment. Except when it came to my choice of degree. Dad's a doctor, you see, and so was his father and his grandfather. My sister's a doctor and studying medicine was expected of me too.' I finish off my glass of wine, and when Oliver goes to refill it, it doesn't even occur to me to stop him. 'But I didn't want to go into medicine. I wanted to do anything *other* than medicine, so when I told him I was doing a degree in events management, he was livid. Proper livid. *Scary* livid.'

Oliver frowns. 'Did he hurt you?'

I shake my head. 'Dad's controlling and a bully, but he never hit me. But I'd never stood up to him, never gone against his wishes – nobody did, except Mum, who eventually had enough and left. But I think he could see there was no way I was going to back down on this one.' He'd threatened me with everything he had at his disposal; he'd disown me, cut me off financially, pack my bags and toss them onto the street himself. But still I refused to bend to his will, so in the end he told me to go, to get the 'silly little degree' and see where it led me. Nowhere, was his prediction.

'He must see how successful you've become though. Doesn't that count for anything?'

I'm confused for a moment. What success? I live in a squalid flat-share and I'm yet to put my degree to good use. But then I realise that's *Rebecca's* life, not Vanessa's. I've accidentally slipped back into reality but it's time to return to the charade I've been playing for the past few days.

'I'm nowhere near a success in Dad's eyes. My sister, now she's a triumph according to Dad. She has it all – the career, the husband, the stature. But this …' I indicate the guesthouse and beyond. 'This means nothing to Dad. The business I've built up means nothing.'

'But you must have built it pretty quickly if you only set it up three years ago? That's got to count for something?'

I almost choke on the sip of wine I've just taken. Why do my lies have to keep sneaking up on me? 'It's medicine or nothing, I'm afraid. I could be a millionaire and it wouldn't make a scrap of difference.'

'It would be quite nice though, eh?' Oliver raises his glass of wine.

'Absolutely.' I clink my glass against his and gulp the rest down.

'Do you miss him?'

I take a moment to consider the question, my fingers fiddling with the white pegs in the little tray on my lap. 'I think I miss the *idea* of him. I don't miss his rules or the yelling or the way he'd belittle us. I don't miss his drinking or the rages, but I miss having a dad, you know?'

'What about your mum?'

I smile sadly. 'We talk, but only occasionally. She left Dad when I was little, which I totally get. He isn't the easiest person to live with. But she met someone else and sort of just got on with her life without me and Kate. We aren't close, unsurprisingly.'

'Are you close with your sister?'

I think of all the missed and cancelled calls from Kate over the past few days and shake my head. 'We're too different. I don't think there's a way to bridge that.'

Luckily, Oliver lightens the mood by confessing next that he once attended a Sugababes concert ('It was a birthday treat for Stace. I was being a good big brother, that's all'), which paves the way for me to admit my teenage crush on George Dawes.

Oliver leans back against the sofa cushions and gives me an odd look. 'Matt Lucas' character from *Shooting Stars*?'

I cover my face with my hands and groan. 'Yes.'

'What the hell?' Oliver is trying – and failing – not to laugh.

'I know.' My hands are still in situ, covering my shame as I let out another groan.

'He was dressed as a *baby*. What is *wrong* with you?'

I catch Oliver's eye and we both crack up – perhaps a bit too much on Oliver's part – before moving on to other embarrassing admissions; Oliver had such a huge crush on his school's textiles teacher, he took a GCSE in the subject, put up with relentless teasing for two years and failed miserably because he can't even thread a needle. I was so nervous before my maths GCSE I chucked up in a bin in front of the whole school year. Oliver once threw up on a girl on an Alton Towers ride.

And so it goes on, even after the ships are obliterated and the wine is all gone. We make each other laugh with our tales of embarrassment and indignity until Oliver reluctantly drags himself off the sofa.

'What happens in Battleships stays in Battleships, right?' It's pitch black outside and a gust of wind whips into the guesthouse as Oliver opens the door.

'Of course.' There's no way I want anybody knowing that I once had a crush on a giant, drum-playing baby. Oliver's secrets are definitely safe with me.

'Tonight's been really fun.' Oliver stoops to kiss me on the cheek. It's an unexpected gesture and I feel heat creep up my neck and start to engulf my entire face. 'I'll see you tomorrow.'

'Bright and early.' I adopt a mock-stern tone to deflect from my reddening cheeks.

With a wave, Oliver heads across the drive, and I think about calling him back for one more confession. What would he say if he knew I remembered my attempted kiss after all? But I do the sensible thing and close the door, keeping that particular can of worms firmly shut.

Chapter 27

It's the weekend but I'm still up ridiculously early, clad in the spotty wellington boots and a dark grey woolly hat with a paler grey oversized bobble that's similar to one I've seen the Duchess of Cambridge wearing. I'm still not entirely comfortable wearing the hat, but it's getting colder, especially so early in the morning, and if it's good enough for royalty …

'You're getting good at this.' Stacey is crouched by the rabbit hutch, wriggling one of the water bottles free, but she pauses to watch me as I make my way to the shed that houses the feed, one of the chickens tucked under one arm. 'Can you imagine you not only voluntarily picking up a chicken but chatting to it just a week ago?'

'I wasn't chatting to her.' I screw my face up as though Stacey is completely cuckoo, even though I *was* just reeling off the to-do list for the house refurb over the next few days to Patty. Patty is surprisingly easy to talk to, and relaying the plans – even to a chicken – is pretty cathartic. I've been stressed since Vanessa's visit a few days ago, but right now I'm feeling as relaxed as I've ever been since I arrived in Little Heaton. It helps that the boiler and heating system is now up and running and the tiling is coming along nicely in the bathrooms and kitchen. It looks like

I wasn't lying when I told Vanessa that the house would all come together suddenly towards the end.

'Seriously, though, you're much more confident with the animals.' Stacey, having freed the water bottle makes her way to the outdoor water tap. 'I think you should be in charge of the chickens tomorrow.'

Stacey's referring to the family open day the sanctuary is hosting tomorrow, and while I've volunteered to help out, I'd assumed I'd be selling Mrs McColl's cakes and biscuits.

'I think we're jumping ahead of ourselves here.' I open the shed and place Patty on the ground while I fill a plastic jug with pellets. She paces around my feet, making it difficult to carry out the job at hand without tripping over her, but I don't begrudge her presence. She's taken a bit of a shine to me over the past few days, which is rather sweet. It's a shame the same can't be said about her feral sister, Bianca, who still views me with deep suspicion whenever I'm in the yard.

'I'd be more comfortable with something a bit less beaky.' With the shed door closed and Patty tucked under my arm again, I make my way back to the chicken coop, doing my best to avoid Bianca as she stalks towards me. 'The hedgehogs, maybe? Or Claude?' The sheep is pretty laid back – I wonder if he talks to the chickens too. 'But definitely not the rabbits.' As gorgeous as Rupert and Honey are, they are also incredibly skittish and I'm sure I'd spend the day darting around the yard after them with the *Benny Hill* tune running through my head. Stacey's hoping to attract a new adoptive family at the open day and my incompetence at handling them won't promote her cause.

'Fair enough.' Stacey shrugs as she turns on the tap and fills the bottle. 'I think I'll put Dianne on chicken duty. She can rotate her Brownie pack to help her out.'

After filling the chickens' feeding trough and water containers, I help Stacey clean out the barn before rushing home to shower and change. The builders are coming over for a few hours and then Oliver and I are going into town to do some shopping this afternoon. As much as I'm growing to love Little Heaton and its quaint ways and stillness, I can't wait to get into town and feel the hustle and bustle of life. Plus, I really do need to buy myself some bits and pieces and payday is just around the corner – with my added expenses – so although I'm not flush, I'm not on the brink of freaking out about money. I've saved a heap over the past couple of weeks anyway since I haven't had to replace all the food that Lee usually helps himself to. I wonder if he's starved in my absence. I wonder if he's even *noticed* my absence, because I haven't been in touch since I left Manchester, or vice versa.

I push Lee from my mind and get on with enjoying my day. The sun is shining and glistening on the canal and from the glorious warmth of the guesthouse, I can pretend we're in the midst of summer. I immerse myself in the fantasy so deeply, the biting whip of the cold breeze is a shock when I head back outside again.

'Winter's on its way.' Oliver rubs his hands together as we crunch our way across the drive towards his car.

'Hush it.' I nudge him gently with my shoulder. 'We're only in October. Autumn hasn't even got started yet.'

'Tell my fingers that.' He blows on them, which I think is being rather dramatic. 'I like winter anyway.'

'You do?' I pull a face. I can't think of anything worse than the seemingly endless months of cold and greyness. Winter means being cooped up inside, counting down the never-ending days until spring, when life seems to reboot itself.

'What's not to love?' Oliver unlocks the car and we climb inside. 'Christmas is in winter, for a start. And then you've got snow …'

'And that's a *good* thing?'

'Er, yeah.' Oliver pulls his seatbelt across his chest and clunks it into place. 'You don't like snow?'

'Why would I?' It's cold and wet and the country seems to come to a standstill at the threat of a single flake.

'Snowmen?' Oliver looks at me as though I've completely lost the plot.

'We weren't a snowman-building type of family.' The idea of Dad bundled up in a bobble hat and thick gloves while he rolls a giant snowball around the garden is ludicrous. He's more of a freshly-pressed-suit-and-tie-at-all-times kind of guy. He reads broadsheet newspapers and heavy novels for pleasure, and mucking about in the garden just wouldn't have occurred to him. The only form of social interaction we had while I was growing up were the grillings over the dinner table, in which I'd usually have to explain a less-than-perfect test score, and the Sunday evening board games that were highly competitive rather than the intended fun, bonding experience they were designed for.

'We can build a snowman together if it snows this winter.' Oliver starts the engine and is concentrating on the road so he doesn't see the weak smile I give in return. It isn't that I don't like the idea of building my first snowman with Oliver. It's that I won't be here during the winter. In a couple of weeks, the work on the house will be finished and I'll be back in Manchester, being Rebecca again instead of the fake Vanessa.

*

I feel like a kid on Christmas morning as we wander along the high street, my eyes wide as I take in familiar shops and brands; is this all mine to play with? There's a Poundland! And a KFC, Boots, and a branch of Santander. I actually squeal and grab hold of Oliver's arm when I spot the huge turquois letters of a Primark, before quickly letting go and pretending it never happened at all. It's like the grandest day out I've ever had, which would feel quite sad if I wasn't overwhelmed with the elation of being out of the village.

I buy three pairs of leggings, a handful of T-shirts, packs of tights and knickers (while Oliver pretends to examine a rack filled with scarves) and push the boat out with a pair of Converse-style trainers before we move onto the supermarket. I fill a basket with fresh meat and vegetables, tins of soup and beans that aren't covered in a fine layer of dust as per the mini market, and a few bits and pieces to pop in the freezer at the guesthouse. I've offered to cook for Oliver tonight, as a thank you for the excursion into town, and then we're going to play Trivial Pursuit, which Oliver has just bought in town. He wasn't impressed when I narrowly won the game of Battleships the other night, meaning I'm in the lead on the game scoreboard, 2-1. I could quit while I'm ahead and claim the victory, wearing my smugness like a gold medal, but I've enjoyed playing the games with Oliver, and it beats sitting in the guesthouse on my own night after night.

'Do you think I should invite Stacey round tonight?' I place my bag of groceries in the boot of Oliver's car, nestling it next to my Primark bag. The idea of cooking for Oliver suddenly feels like a date and I don't want him to think I'm going to lunge at him again over the breakfast bar. Inviting his sister along will kill any romantic connotations.

'It's Saturday.' Oliver places the other bag of groceries in the boot and pulls it closed. 'She'll be down the Farmer's, ogling Dominic Blackwood. He always goes in for a couple of pints on a Saturday, so Stace follows suit.'

*

To change or not to change, that is the question I'm faced with when Oliver drops me off at the guesthouse. As comfortable as my new leggings and a T-shirt combo would be, they don't scream 'Saturday night dinner plans', but I also don't want to come across as though I'm trying too hard in case it gives Oliver the wrong idea about tonight. What would I do if it was Emma I was expecting in twenty minutes?

In the end, I opt for a compromise of a pair of leggings teamed with a loosely draped top, which is comfortable but with a less formal feel, so I won't look as though I'm trying too hard. It feels fantastic to be so unrestricted, to feel like Rebecca again. Never in a million years would I lounge around the flat in a pair of tailored trousers or form-fitting dresses like I have these past couple of weeks and I feel like I can finally breathe again.

'I brought wine.' The game of Trivial Pursuit is tucked under one arm while Oliver brandishes a bottle in the other when I open the door. He's wearing a pair of jeans – but not the tired-looking work jeans I'm used to – and a soft, dove-grey jumper. He's struck the right balance between smart and casual, but I doubt he agonised over his wardrobe choices as much as I did. 'I wasn't sure what you liked so I got Stacey's favourite. I hope it's okay?' He hands me the bottle and I check the label, though I'm no wine connoisseur; I usually just buy whatever's on offer at my local supermarket.

'This looks great. Thank you.' I give a nod of approval, hoping it masks how clueless I am because Vanessa definitely has a wide range of knowledge when it comes to wine. 'Would you like a glass now, or would you rather wait until the food's ready?'

'Let's go nuts and have a glass now.' Oliver grins at me and I have to turn away because his smile is doing funny things to my insides. Which is crazy as I see the guy every day and cope perfectly well, the lunging-in-for-a-kiss incident aside, though I place the blame on that firmly on the amount of alcohol I'd drunk in the pub.

'I think I'll just have a small glass.' Darting into the kitchen, I grab a couple of glasses and pour a regular amount in one and a thimble-sized drop in the other. 'I don't want to be cooking under the influence.'

'What are we having?' Oliver glances past me at the oven devoid of any foodstuff.

'Not ready meals again, don't worry.' I open the fridge and pull out the shrimp and veggies I prepped earlier. 'I hope you like Thai red curry? And shrimp?' I hold up the plates, my lips pressed tightly together as I hope he does. I should have asked him while we were at the supermarket, so I could stock up on alternative ingredients if he doesn't like it.

'Sounds great.' Oliver rubs his hands together. 'Anything I can help with?'

'You could put some music on.' Placing the plates down on the counter, I nod towards the stereo in the living room. 'I'm afraid there's only a couple of CDs to choose from though.' The previous occupants of the guesthouse left behind *Now That's What I Call Music! 35* and Britney Spears' *Femme Fatale* album, both of which I've listened to countless times over the past two weeks. By now, either of those CDs could be my specialist subject on *Mastermind*.

'Oh.' Oliver sounds less than impressed when he picks up the cases from on top of the stereo. 'Any preference? Other than silence?'

I hide my smirk in the cupboard as I reach for the frying pan. 'No, you can choose.' Placing the pan on the hob, I pour in a little of the vegetable oil I bought earlier while Oliver deals with the music. I look over as the opening to The Spice Girls' 'Say You'll Be There' starts up and Oliver gives me an apologetic shrug.

'Well, at least I know what to get you for Christmas.' Oliver slides onto one of the stools at the breakfast bar. 'Some decent music choices.'

I turn back to the frying pan even though I know the oil hasn't had the chance to heat up. I don't want him to see the moment the smile drops from my face, because I won't be here at Christmas and I doubt I'll still be friends with Oliver once the refurbishment is complete. Not after I've lied to him about who I really am.

'How do you know I'm not a massive fan of Britney?' I force myself to turn around again, my eyebrows raised at the query.

'Did I choose the wrong one?' He twists on the stool, looking back towards the stereo, but I reach out to stop him before he gets up.

'I'm kidding.' I reach into the cupboard for the curry paste, squeezing a good dollop into the pan. 'I actually don't mind Britney, but I've worn that CD out while I've been soaking in the bath.'

Mentioning the bath brings up an image of me being naked, and I hope Oliver isn't experiencing the same awkwardness. I send myself on a massive coconut milk hunt as a distraction, even though I know exactly which cupboard it's in.

Fifteen minutes later, we're sitting at the breakfast bar, which Oliver set while singing along to 'If You Ever', taking on both East 17's parts and Gabrielle's when I refused to duet. My glass of wine didn't last long but there wasn't nearly enough alcohol in the tiny measure to allow my inhibitions to lower enough to allow me to sing in front of an audience (even if that audience is just Oliver, who has already seen me at my worst).

'You really know how to cook.' Oliver is tucking into his curry, making all the right noises to show he's enjoying the meal I've prepared. 'How have you coped eating those ready meals for the past couple of weeks?'

I shrug as I top up Oliver's glass. 'They're not so bad, and my cooking isn't exceptional. I've just had a lot of practice, I guess. I learned to cook quite young and you soon get bored of the same meals night after night.'

'Well, I happen to think your cooking *is* exceptional.' Oliver spears a shrimp and pops it into his mouth with an overexaggerated moan of pleasure. I roll my eyes as I add a dash of wine to my glass.

'You've tried one meal, and it's a pretty easy one. You just bung everything into the one pan. Plus, I cheated and used microwavable rice.' I do this often, and it always gives me a little tingle of rebellion whenever I set the timer on the microwave. There's no way Dad would ever have allowed a grain of 'phony' rice on his plate. We didn't even own a microwave while I was growing up, and processed food was never to be seen at our dinner table.

'Do your parents like to cook?' Oliver, thankfully, has stopped his over-the-top moaning and is eating like a normal person. 'Is that where you inherited it from?'

I almost choke on a slice of red pepper. 'My dad can't boil an egg.' At least he couldn't when I still lived at home. Perhaps he's been forced into learning how to feed himself now, meaning my refusal to toe the line was a positive move for the both of us.

'What about your mum?'

I chew slowly as Oliver awaits an answer, drawing out my response for as long as possible. 'I have no idea. I don't have that many memories of when Mum was around, and I probably only see her a couple of times a year, and never at home.' I give a humourless laugh. 'I can't remember the last time I shared a meal with my mum.'

'It must have been tough growing up. I don't mean to sound out of turn, but your dad sounds quite strict.'

I snort. 'That's an understatement. He could be pretty mean at times, and he was of the opinion that the louder you shouted, the more respect you earned.' I'm loading up my fork with curry but pause as I spot Oliver giving me an odd look. 'What?'

'Nothing.' Oliver shakes his head, a smile playing at his lips. 'It's just, that last bit sounds sort of familiar. Not this Vanessa.' He nods at me. 'But the one I thought I knew before you turned up. What's the saying, the one about the apple not falling far from the tree?'

I'm horrified at the thought of ending up like Dad, but Oliver's right; Dad and Vanessa do share some unsavoury qualities. I decide the best course of action is to nudge the conversation on.

'What about you? Do you like to cook?'

'*Like* is pushing it a bit. *Have to* in order to survive is more accurate.' Oliver scrunches up his nose. 'I'm no Jamie Oliver, let's put it that way.'

'I bet Jamie couldn't tile a floor as beautifully as you can though.'

Oliver straightens, his shoulders thrown back and he gives a slow nod. 'I am particularly skilled in that area.' His serious face cracks into a smile. 'Plus, I'm the master at Monopoly.'

'But not Scrabble or Battleships.' I hide a smile as I concentrate on filling my fork with rice. 'Let's hope you have better luck with Trivial Pursuit. I fear for your ego if you lose again.'

'My ego will be just fine, because there's no way you're going to win this one.'

I grin at Oliver. 'Bring it on.'

Chapter 28

There's a good turnout at the sanctuary's family day, with a steady stream of visitors already descending and cooing over the animals. Stacey is leading a small party around the yard while another volunteer is showing a family how to groom the donkeys, and inside is just as busy. The café is full to the brim while the education suite has been transformed into a craft centre as half a dozen kids make peanut butter bird feeders, cereal necklaces for the chickens and DIY rabbit toys out of slotted-together cardboard shapes and hay. The sanctuary is usually so peaceful when I visit first thing in the morning, which is lovely, but it's wonderful to see the place come to life.

I've been placed in the education suite, tucked away in a corner with the hedgehogs. I've been given all the information from Stacey and although I'm not prone to public speaking, I hope I'm living up to her expectations.

'Here at Little Heaton Animal Sanctuary, we work closely with the local veterinary surgery to care for injured or sick hedgehogs, as well as those who have been orphaned. We hope to release them back into the wild once we think they're able to survive.' I've rolled this little speech off numerous times this morning and envisage doing so several more over the course of the day. 'This is Pumpkin, and he was found in the allotment. Can you guess where?'

Half a dozen hands shoot up into the air, wiggling and waving for attention until I choose one of the children at the back to answer.

'Elsie's pumpkin patch?' The answer is faltering, unsure, but totally correct.

'That's right. Pumpkin was found right in the middle of the pumpkin patch. He had a broken leg but he's been nursed back to health by Stacey and the vet and he'll be ready to be released very soon.' I place the hedgehog very carefully into his box. 'And this little cutie is Sophie.' I pick up the next hedgehog, telling the story of how she was rescued after some bad flooding down by the canal. 'One of the first things we do when we take in a hedgehog is to weigh them. Sophie was very small and weak, but she's been well fed and looked after.' I pop the hedgehog on the scales set out on the table in front of me. 'And she'll be released with Pumpkin in the next week or two.'

One of the hands shoots up into the air, the question of the enthusiastic little girl asked before I've had the chance to respond. 'Is it sad to let them go?'

'Maybe a little bit.' I pick Sophie up from the scales, thinking of everything I'll have to let go of when I leave Little Heaton. The animals. The views and peacefulness. Stacey, Vince and Todd – and even Harvey, I guess. And Oliver, of course.

'But it also means the hedgehogs are happy and healthy and ready to go back where they belong.' I give a decisive nod, as though I'm trying to convince myself. 'Which is a good thing. Hedgehogs are wild creatures, not pets.' I place Sophie back into her box. 'We have two baby hedgehogs at the sanctuary at the moment. Rianne and Isobel are very small, so we're going to keep them in their boxes today, but you can have a little look at them if you'd like. They'll be staying at the sanctuary over the next few months and will hopefully be released in the spring.'

Afterwards, once the children have all had a peek at the hedgehogs and are now either colouring in a hedgehog picture at the tables across the room or have moved outside to see more animals, Stacey pulls me aside. At first, I think I've done something wrong but she's full of praise.

'You're a natural. Who would have thought that the Vanessa who turned up here that first morning in those unsuitable boots and ran away from a chicken she was convinced was stalking her would be this Vanessa.' She spreads her arms out and takes a step back. 'You're like a completely different Vanessa now.'

She has no idea.

Stacey leans in close and lowers her voice. 'Shall we sneak upstairs for a brew? I need to feed the kittens, plus you can tell me all about your date with Oliver last night.'

'It wasn't a date.'

Stacey raises her eyebrows at me. 'You cooked for him. That's a date in my book.'

'Just to say thank you for taking me into town. There was nothing romantic about it whatsoever. We played Trivial Pursuit, for goodness sake.'

Stacey stops abruptly to observe me. 'What is the matter with the pair of you? Who plays bloody board games with someone they fancy instead of snogging their face off?'

I open my mouth to deny such an attraction exists, but I find I can't outright lie to her. Again. 'What about you and Dominic? You clearly fancy him but you've never done anything about it.' With the option of denial unavailable to me, I decide to divert attention away from myself and go on the attack.

She stops at the door leading up to her flat, fishing in her pocket for the key. 'It's complicated. He's still getting over the breakup of his marriage and I—'

'Am a big wuss?'

Stacey sticks her tongue out at me as she pushes the key into

180

the lock. We make our way up to the flat, where I put the kettle on while Stacey starts to feed the kittens.

'We're going to the pub later. Once we've finished here.' Stacey places the bottle of kitten formula on the coffee table and gently cleans around Tammy's mouth with a wet wipe. 'You should come with us. I know Oliver would like that.' She kisses the top of the kitten's head before placing her with her brothers and even though I can't see her face right now, I can take a wild guess that there's a mischievous glint in her eye. I decide not to play along.

'Do you think you've raised enough for the auction next week?'

'Who knows?' Stacey shrugs as she sits back down on the sofa. 'That's the downside of auctions, I guess. You never know what the competition is willing to pay, but I've got my fingers crossed.'

'Me too.' I hold them up, to demonstrate.

Stacey makes a note of Tammy's feed before she wanders over to the window. 'It's been a great turnout and we'll be able to do more open days once we've expanded and … whoa.' She moves closer to the window, pressing the palms of her hands against the pane. 'That's insane.'

Placing my cup of coffee on the table, I move towards the window. 'What is it?'

'Nothing major, but the queue for the face-painting is way out of hand. Look at it.' She moves aside and I peer down into the yard. I can't actually see the entire queue of children as it passes beyond our line of sight. There must be at least forty kids waiting not very patiently. 'I should have booked another face-painter, but I didn't expect quite so many people to turn up. I wonder if any of the Brownie leaders know how to do it …' Stacey is already moving away from the window, her bottom lip pinched between her teeth.

'I can do it.' Sort of. I've only ever practised on Emma before, but I managed to perfect the butterfly design and my tiger was rather impressive.

'You can face-paint?' Stacey looks a strange mix of sceptical and hopeful.

'I'm an events manager.' At least, Vanessa is, and I'm being her. 'It's part of the remit. Do you know how many times I've had to step in during an emergency such as this?' I indicate the window, hoping Stacey won't ask for an actual number, because that would be a big fat zero. But I did attend one of Vanessa's events once, about a year into my employment, and the face-painter booked for the occasion called in sick at the last minute. I'd really wished I'd had the skills to step in and save the day so I could impress Vanessa, but I'd never been in close contact with a face-paint palette before. Upon returning home, however, I vowed that I would never be in that situation again and, thanks to several YouTube videos and Emma acting as my guinea pig, I'm confident I can pull it off this time.

'Great!' Stacey marches towards the staircase but pauses to turn and look at me. 'I'm so glad you're here, Vanessa. You're really not the person I thought you were going to be. In a good way, obviously.' She beams at me and I try my hardest to return the gesture but it isn't quite as forthcoming. If only Stacey knew I *really* wasn't the person she thinks I was in the beginning. Would she be beaming so widely if she knew I was lying to her? That I'd been lying to her for the past few weeks? It may just be a name, perhaps a bit of borrowed character every now and then, but I'd be devastated if it turned out the person I'd grown to trust had been deceiving me.

*

'To Vanessa, for saving the day!' Stacey raises her G&T later that evening as we gather in the Farmers for a celebratory drink. It's been a long and rewarding day and we all deserve a pat on the back (and a very big drink).

'I hardly saved the day.' I brush away the compliment, but

182

there's a warm glow inside as Stacey heaps on the praise. 'And it was fun, apart from that kid who kicked off because he said his Hulk looked more like Shrek.' I rub at my shin, where the kid had literally kicked off. Brat.

'Thank you *all* for your help.' Stacey raises her glass again and looks around at the small gathering of volunteers who were able to pop over to the pub after we'd cleared up at the sanctuary. 'We managed to raise a good chunk of money to put towards the expansion fund, and it's all thanks to you.'

'I think you had something to do with it too, my dear.' Mrs McColl raises her glass at Stacey before she downs the large sherry in one. 'Now, I'm going to love you and leave you. *Strictly*'s on and I need to get my Craig Revel Horwood fix.' There's a definite twinkle in Mrs McColl's eye as she hooks her handbag onto her arm. 'I'll see you bright and early tomorrow.' She wriggles her fingers in farewell before marching from the pub.

'Who knew Mrs McColl had a thing for Craig Revel Horwood?' Stacey is still staring at the space the older woman had been occupying a few seconds ago, blinking slowly as her mouth gapes wide open.

'Speaking of having a thing for somebody …' I nudge Stacey out of her stupor and nod towards the bar, where Dominic is waiting for his pint. He looks as though he's come straight from the field, with a pair of green wellies pulled over his (nicely fitting, even I must admit) jeans, waterproof jacket zipped up to his chin and a woollen hat pulled down almost to his eyeballs. With his elbows on the bar and his back to the rest of the pub's customers, his stance isn't exactly warm and welcoming.

'What do you want me to do?' Stacey asks. 'Go over there and drape myself over him?'

'If that's what it takes.'

'Nah.' Stacey shakes her head and takes a sip of her gin. 'He's clearly here to have a quiet pint. I'll just stay here and enjoy the view.' She tilts her head, eyes bulging right out of their sockets as they land on the farmer's bum. Like I said, those jeans are a *nice* fit. I join Stacey for a quick ogle before I start to feel a bit seedy.

'Shall we put some music on?'

'What?' Stacey turns her head towards me, her eyes still fixed on Dominic until the very last second. 'Oh, yeah. Why not?' She rummages in her purse and hands me a pound coin. 'Pick something for me?' Her eyes are already back on the farmer's arse.

'Why don't you just go and talk to him?'

Stacey drags her gaze away from her beau, a smirk forming on her face. 'Why don't you just go and snog the face off my brother? We all know these board games you keep playing are a weird form of foreplay.' My eyes dart towards Oliver, who's thankfully deep in conversation with the leader of the Brownie pack and hasn't overheard. 'You need to stop tiptoeing around now and get on with it.'

'I think that's what they call projection.' I give Dominic a pointed look before heading for the jukebox, selecting some not-so-subtle tracks about having a crush, ending the mini playlist of mad-about-you songs with Elvis' 'Can't Help Falling In Love'.

The Brownies leader has moved onto Stacey by the time I return to our table, dragging her attention away from Little Heaton's most eligible farmer – kicking and screaming, I should imagine – and leaving Oliver thumbing through a beer-stained newspaper.

'I didn't know you were a fan of The Kinks.' He closes the newspaper and dumps it on the neighbouring table. 'You've Really Got Me', the first of my ode-to-Stacey's-crush playlist, is reaching its chorus.

'I'm not really.' I try to catch Stacey's eye but she's resolutely ignoring me, nodding along earnestly to whatever Dianne is saying. 'I just like this song.' I pick up my drink, swirling the dregs at the bottom of the glass. 'It was either this or something by the Sugababes.'

'Hey!' Oliver's eyes widen and he leans in close and lowers his voice. 'What's shared over a game of Battleships stays over a game of Battleships, remember?' He arches an eyebrow at me and I give a nod of agreement. 'That reminds me, actually. I thought that maybe we could have dinner one evening? I owe you after that amazing curry.' Oliver picks up a beermat and picks at the top layer of cardboard. 'I thought we could go to a restaurant this time. I wouldn't subject you to my cooking.' He stops undressing the beermat long enough to grin at me, and my stomach performs a happy little somersault. 'No Monopoly or Scrabble and definitely no Battleships this time. Just the two of us. On a date.' He peels off the beermat's top layer before dumping the whole lot on the table and turning to face me properly. 'What do you think?'

There are several reasons why I should say no – mainly because Oliver doesn't know my true identity and I'll be leaving Little Heaton as soon as the house is finished – but I drop-kick these reasons from my mind for the time being.

'I think I'd like that very much.'

Chapter 29

Oliver and I agree that our first official date will take place on Saturday evening, giving me almost a week to prepare. It's been a while since I've been on a date, and the last one – set up by Emma – was enough to put anyone off dating for an extremely long time (probably forever in my case, had I not met Oliver). It also means I can concentrate on getting the house ready for Vanessa's upcoming visit, which is causing me to hyperventilate whenever it pops into my mind, which is every few minutes. The refurbishment is going well, with the kitchen completely kitted out, including all the tiling work and the installation of white goods, the bathrooms are plumbed in and the electrics are all in order. This week we're focusing on finishing the tiling of the bathrooms and shower enclosures and the snagging (which I had to Google, because I'd had no idea what it was) and I'm finding this stage of the refurb quite satisfying as I move from room to room with my notepad and a real sense of purpose, making a note of any minor faults that need rectifying before the decorators arrive next week. The following week is going to be pretty hectic as the landscaping and the laying of the drive will be taking place too. Ideally, the builders and the gardening team should have finished up by the time the decorating begins, but we're going to have to carry out the three tasks at once, which is doable as long as the builders keep their mucky boots away from the newly spruced up house.

I'm pretty sure I can get away with Vanessa's visit with regards to the house and its progress, but the logistics of keeping my boss away from those who are under the impression that *I'm* Vanessa Whitely (i.e. the entire population of Little Heaton) is keeping me awake at night. Luck was on my side last time, but I don't think I'll get away with it a second time so I need a plan. A solid, can't-possibly-go-wrong plan that will keep Vanessa away from the builders.

'Have you got that list for me?' Vince's words are elongated through a yawn as he scrubs at his eyes with the heels of his hands. The builders have been starting early and staying late in a bid to keep to the schedule, and it's clearly taking its toll. Vince looks knackered, with bags as big as the skips we've hired for next week's jobs under bloodshot eyes.

'Here you go.' I tear off the sheet from my notebook with the list of little jobs that need to be completed before the builders can move onto laying the drive and hand it to Vince, but my mind is on his worn-out state and Vanessa's visit tomorrow. Perhaps there is a way I can keep my identity mishap hidden after all.

*

I usually help out at the animal sanctuary early in the morning, so Stacey is surprised to see me in the yard when she arrives back with Claude mid-afternoon after his daily trip to the Blackwoods' field, though she smooths her features back into a neutral expression as she heads towards me. I've been trying to coax Daisy away from the fence, where I'm sure she's casing out the weak points to work on next, but it's difficult when you're dealing not only with a determined donkey but a menagerie of chickens bobbing

187

around your ankles. It seems I've earned not only Patty's trust but that of most of her feathery sisters, and even Bianca is warming to me. We're not exactly on friendly terms but she no longer pierces me with those beady eyes whenever I rock up at the sanctuary and she hasn't chased me across the yard for over a week now.

'Thank Mother Nature for her fake summer days.' Stacey tips her face up to the sky, shielding her eyes from the unusually bright sun. Just when summer was nothing but a distant memory, out pops a glorious sunny day to lift everybody's spirits. 'I took the long way out of the field and caught a glimpse of a shirtless Dominic working in the next field over.' Stacey fans herself, and it has nothing to do with the heat from the sun. 'I thought I'd died and gone to a Diet Coke break heaven.'

'Are you ever going to ask him out?' Dodging Chow Mein, who's taken a liking to my borrowed polka-dot wellies, I give one last attempt at moving Daisy away from the fence but she's one stubborn donkey.

'Just because you and Oliver have finally admitted that you fancy each other and are going on an actual date, doesn't mean the rest of us can't have our secret crushes, you know.'

I snort. Stacey's crush on Dominic is about as secret as Daisy's appreciation of mischief. I think the only person who hasn't noticed is the farmer himself.

'So, what brings you over here at this time?' Stacey mock gasps. 'Are you *skiving*?'

'Not at all.' I pick my way carefully across the grass, making sure I don't accidentally squish a chicken underfoot. 'I wanted to book a table at the café for tomorrow.'

Stacey frowns as she takes hold of the donkey's reins. 'You want to book a table? At the café that serves half a dozen people at most per day?'

My jaw sets in annoyance as Daisy starts to plod away from the fence with barely any encouragement from Stacey after I've spent a good twenty minutes trying to shift her, but I have more pressing matters than a roguish donkey. 'Yes, I would like to book a table at noon.'

'For you and Oliver?' Stacey winks at me as she reaches into the bum bag attached to her front. 'Shall we make it candlelit?'

'You could, but I don't think Vince and the guys would appreciate the ambience.'

Stacey holds out her hand, a treat sat on her palm for Daisy to take. That's where I went wrong!

'So you're dating the whole gang of builders now?' Stacey looks suitably perturbed at the idea.

'I want to book a table for four. And I won't be there at all.' I sidestep Patty. 'It's a treat for the builders, for all their hard work over the past few weeks.' My plan of action for Vanessa's visit is to keep the builders away from the house by plying them with food under the guise of my eternal gratitude for their labour. It isn't foolproof but it's all I've got.

'Have you spoken to Mrs McColl?'

'Nope.' I swerve around the chickens like a dog swerves around the cones at Crufts, only with less grace. 'And I was hoping I wouldn't have to. The woman terrifies me.'

'Don't worry about Mrs McColl.' Stacey grins at me. 'Her bite's worse than her bark.'

'That's hardly reassuring.'

'She's a pussycat really, once you dig beneath the snarky exterior.' Stacey flings her arm around my shoulders and picks up the pace as we head towards the house. Luckily, we don't maim any chickens in the process.

*

My plan seems to be working; the builders have happily downed tools – they needed very little persuasion – and are on their way to the animal sanctuary for a 'gentleman's' afternoon tea, which

I think is like a regular afternoon tea but with bigger, less pretty portions. Vanessa's arrival is imminent so I'm pacing the hallway, eyes peeled for the cherry red mini. But it isn't Vanessa's car that turns onto the drive. The black Fiesta that pulls up outside the house belongs to Emma.

'What are you doing here?' I tear down the steps as fast as I can in my peep-toe boots and leather pencil skirt, which is making me waddle penguin-like.

'Aren't you pleased to me?' Emma hooks a satchel over her shoulder and aims the fob in her hand at the car.

'Of course I am. Come here!' I pull my friend into a hug, squeezing the life out of her. I hadn't realised quite how much I'd missed her until now, and I'd quite happily burst into tears if I hadn't spent an age perfecting my make-up this morning. 'I was expecting Vanessa, that's all. Is she coming?' I peer over Emma's shoulder but there's no sign of the red mini of doom.

'I'm afraid you're stuck with just me.' Emma peels herself away and holds me at arm's length. 'Wow, look at you! You've gone all corporate-chic.'

'Is that a good thing?' I look down at my outfit, suddenly feeling foolish. I've reverted to my old, comfortable look over the past few days, making use of my new leggings and T-shirts, but I'd been trying to impress Vanessa when I'd selected my outfit this morning, thinking the leather pencil skirt and pussy-bow blouse combo would look professional and sophisticated. And instead of pulling my hair into my usual high ponytail, I've left it loose on my shoulders, loosely pinning it at the sides, and I'm wearing the red lipstick, which now feels too much.

'Are you kidding me? You look amazing.' Emma throws her arms around me again and I feel my shoulders relax. 'Being out here obviously suits you.'

'Do you know what, I think it might.' I give Emma one last squeeze before leading the way up the stone steps to the house. 'I was so mad at Vanessa for sending me here, but it's actually been a lot of fun. I'll be almost sorry to say goodbye to the place.'

'Wow.' Emma stops, her jaw dropping in slow motion, but it has nothing to do with my admission. She's gazing around the hallway in awe, and I can't blame her. Seeing the space every day, I've become immune to its splendour, but it's like I'm seeing it through fresh eyes again. I'd forgotten how vast the space is, how the light floods in through the huge windows, and the wide staircase has been transformed into an artwork with its decorative balustrade and mahogany handrail. The space is luxurious, even with its bare plaster walls, so I can only imagine the grandeur once the decorators have worked their magic and the finishing touches are put into place.

'Vanessa is going to *love* this.' Emma reaches into her satchel and pulls out her phone. 'Do you mind?' She's opened the camera app and is aiming at the staircase. 'Vanessa was afraid the house wouldn't be ready in time for the party, so she asked me to take photos. This will put her mind at rest.'

'Go ahead.' I stand back while Emma takes several shots of the hallway. I'll definitely make sure she takes some photos of the kitchen and bathrooms as they're even more impressive. 'So Vanessa couldn't make it then?'

'Not exactly.' Emma takes a final shot of the front door, taking in the fanlight and the huge sash windows either side. 'She's handed the reins over to me.' Emma lowers her phone and beams at me. 'I'm in charge of organising the housewarming party! How amazing is that?'

My stomach lurches, but I manage to beam back at Emma. Sort of. I only hope it doesn't come across as a churlish grimace. 'That's fantastic. Congratulations! I'm so happy for you.' Which I am, although I'd be happier if Vanessa had trusted me with the role.

'Sonia is *livid*.' Emma slips her phone back inside her satchel and takes out a notebook and pen, jotting down a few notes. 'She thinks she should have been asked to do it since she's been part of the events team longer and I'm "just the receptionist". Emma tucks the notebook under her arm so she can perform the air quotes. 'I haven't dared to accept a cup of coffee from her since, in case she spits in it.'

'Speaking of coffee …' I lead the way into the kitchen, where we now have a kettle and supplies set up so the builders don't have to traipse across to the guesthouse every time they want a brew. 'We even have some biscuits, unless Todd's scoffed them all again.'

'Wow.' Emma's jaw has gone south again, and I can't help but feel a swell of pride. Emma may be planning Vanessa's party, but this kitchen is my legacy. I may not have physically laid the flooring or built the units with my own fair hands, but I was part of the team that created this beautiful room. Plus, I did help to shift the huge American-style fridge freezer into place, and I was first to flick the kettle on once the electrician had assured me it was safe to do so.

'Look at the view!' Emma heads straight for the bi-fold doors, her palms pressing against the glass. She turns to me, a frown creating grooves along her forehead. 'Rebecca, is that a *donkey* in the garden?'

Of course it is. Bloody Daisy! I *knew* she'd been up to no good yesterday.

'That's just Franny.' I give a wave of my hand and head for the kettle, as though having a donkey nibbling at your overgrown lawn is a perfectly normal occurrence. 'She's just wandered over from next door. She's harmless.' It's the other mischief-maker you have to look out for. Well, Daisy's in for a shock next week when the set of iron railings go up. I'd like to see the little madam work her way through those. 'Anyway, come and fill me in on all the goss from the office.'

We have to stand at the breakfast bar with our cups of coffee as installation of the furniture is one of the final jobs of the refurb, and Emma fills me in on the goings on at Vanessa Whitely Events, from the mystery of the phantom non-flusher in the ladies' loos (Emma suspects the new temp on reception) to the cleaner who was caught rifling through Vanessa's drawers (of the desk variety, not her knickers).

'And there's something else.' There's a plate of bourbon creams between us on the breakfast bar and Emma takes one, nibbling at it before changing her mind and placing it down next to her mug. She catches my eye and holds my gaze. 'But she swore me to secrecy so you can't tell anyone else, okay?'

'I won't tell a soul. Cross my heart and pinky promise.' I'm almost giddy with the forbidden knowledge I am about to receive. 'What is it?'

Emma picks up the bourbon cream for another nibble and I have to dig deep to stop myself from slapping it out of her hand and demanding she part with the juicy scandal immediately.

'I really shouldn't say …' She places the biscuit down again with a heavy sigh, and I fear she's going to snatch away the dangled carrot of gossip. 'It's Vanessa.' She sighs again while my giddiness notches up a gear. Gossip about your boss is the *best* kind of gossip as it tips the balance of power slightly in your favour. 'She thinks Ty's cheating on her. With someone from the office.'

'*No.*' My eyes are almost popping out of my head. 'Who does she think it is?'

Emma's nibbling at the biscuit again. I should have left them in the cupboard.

'She thinks …' Emma leans in close and lowers her voice, even though the only other living creature in the vicinity is Franny, out in the garden. 'It's Sonia.'

'Oh my God.' My mouth is gaping with outrage. I *knew* she couldn't be trusted!

'Do you remember that opening we went to? That new club?'

How could I forget? Emma says 'we' but I was excluded from the jaunt.

'Vanessa thinks it started then. Sonia was almost manic in her need to pull a celeb, and Ty's been super attentive towards Vanessa since then, taking her out for romantic dinners almost every evening, whisking her away for weekends away. It's like he's got a guilty conscience or something.'

'But why does she think it's Sonia? Tyler's hardly a household name.' He's a model, but he isn't on anybody's radar outside the world of fashion shoots.

Emma shrugs. 'Vanessa must have her reasons. All I know is that she's keeping a *very* close eye on her. That's why I'm here and not Vanessa. She doesn't want to leave the office unnecessarily. Or rather, she doesn't want to leave *Sonia* unsupervised unnecessarily. I feel a bit sorry for her, actually.'

'For Sonia?' I know Emma likes to see the good in people, but this is stretching her positive nature. 'Even though she may be cheating with Tyler?'

Emma shrugs. 'That's the thing, though. There's no actual proof that it's Sonia. It's just a hunch coupled with office gossip.'

I want to explore this deeper, as it does seem a huge leap to suspect Sonia, but my mobile starts to ring and it's Stacey. Excusing myself, I scuttle out of the room to answer it in case I say anything incriminating in front of Emma and give away my deception.

'Hello?' Slipping into the living room, I gently close the door behind me and scurry to the far end of the room.

'Franny's gone walkabout again.' There's a short sigh on the other end of the line. 'She isn't in your garden, is she?'

She is. I can see her snacking on the grass through the living room's bi-fold doors. But do I tell Stacey this? If I do, she's bound to come over to retrieve the donkey, but if I don't, Stacey's going to be out of her mind with worry as she searches the village for her missing charge.

'Yes, she's here.' I lean against the wall and squeeze my eyes shut. 'But you don't have to pick her up right now. In fact, leave her for a while. She'll be doing the gardeners a favour. There'll be less grass to cut at this rate.' I try to laugh but I can't muster the required enthusiasm.

'I've already sent Oliver round to check, just in case.'

I make a dash for the window, just in time to see Oliver appear at the top of the drive. My stomach lurches, knowing that I'm about to be rumbled.

Chapter 30

I garble something vaguely coherent into the phone before hanging up and taking a few deep breaths to stave off the blind panic that is ready to step in and take over. Watching Oliver's rapid journey across the drive really isn't helping so I move away from the window, barrelling my way into the kitchen, where Emma is working her way through the bourbons.

'Upstairs!' My voice is a rasp, both from the sprint and the fear that is closing up my throat. 'Why don't you have a look upstairs? Photos. Notes. For the party.' I slump against the door-frame. What does a panic attack feel like? And does it count as a panic attack if your lies catching up with you is the cause of the distress?

'Okay.' Emma is giving me a very odd look, which is under-standable under the circumstances but I'm hoping her uncertainty won't hinder her movements. Because I need Emma to be as far away from Oliver as I can get her and time is running out.

'The top floor!' Pushing myself off the doorframe, I scuttle out into the hallway, hoping to encourage Emma to speed up. 'You have to see the top floor. There's a balcony!' Which overlooks both the canal and the part of the garden Franny is currently munching her way through. 'Which is unsafe. So don't go out onto it. Or even near the window. Just in case.' I'm almost running towards the staircase now, though Emma is merely ambling.

'Is everything okay, Rebecca?'

My eyes dart from Emma to the front door. What if Oliver is on the other side, right now? Could he have overheard the use of my real, lie-destroying name? The door is pretty chunky, but still …

'Everything is absolutely fine.' My mouth is smiling reassuringly but the less said about my eyes the better. Needless to say, they aren't exuding calm. 'But you really should take a look upstairs.'

'Right.' Emma is nodding but her face tells me she isn't convinced and she's stopped moving, feet planted in the middle of the hallway. I'm about to usher her forward when the front door swings open. Why didn't I lock it? And bolt it? And build an electric fence around it?

I turn slowly, prolonging the time I have left before the brown stuff hits the fan. Part of me hopes it isn't Oliver standing on the threshold, about to step into the house and kick down the fantasyland I've created for myself. It's a foolish part of me, but I allow it to blossom, to take over and fill my heart with optimism, albeit for a microsecond.

Of course it's Oliver at the door. Except now he's in the hallway, nudging the door closed and shutting us into a situation I can't see a way out of. I have no control over Oliver or Emma, no control over what they say, what they reveal. My fate is in their hands.

'Oliver!' My voice is full of false cheer. Unnatural and jarring. 'You're here for Franny, right?' I'm marching towards the front door, ready to eject him before he can say something I'll regret. 'I'll take you round now.'

'Sorry, I'm disturbing you.' Oliver – praise be – is backing towards the door of his own volition. 'I didn't realise you had company.'

'Not a problem.' As long as he gets out of the house *right now*.

'Hello.' Emma, finally, is moving, but it isn't towards the staircase. She's heading for Oliver, hand outstretched. 'I'm Emma. I'm planning Vanessa's housewarming party.'

Oliver takes her hand and gives it a short but firm shake. 'I'm Oliver, one of Vanessa's builders.' He catches my eye and winks, because he's more than my builder. He's my friend. My ... well, who knows what the future holds, but it probably won't be that date on Saturday night if he finds out the truth. Obviously I'm going to have to come clean about my true identity at some point, but having the truth blurted out here in the hallway isn't how I imagined it would happen.

'It's very nice to meet you.' Emma turns away from Oliver, widening her eyes at me and mouthing '*wow, he's gorgeous*', which I can't disagree with.

'Emma was just going upstairs to have a look around.' With my hand on the small of her back, I give her a little prod towards the staircase. 'Shall we go and sort Franny out?'

Oliver reaches behind him to open the door. 'I can do that. You continue the grand tour.' He smiles charmingly at Emma but I'm too tense to appreciate its beauty. 'Todd practically inhaled the food as soon as it was put down on the table, so the others won't be far behind me and you know how hectic it can get round here. Better get that tour in while you can.'

Damn it! I knew my plan wasn't foolproof but I didn't expect it to crumble so quickly. I'm already coming across as unhinged – if I bundle Emma out of the house now, before the guys descend and without showing off the *utterly amazing top floor*, I'm going to come across as highly suspicious.

'The pub!' There's that overenthusiastic voice again. I need to calm down. 'I forgot to mention it earlier. The afternoon tea was only the beginning of your treat. You should go to the pub.' I left my handbag in the kitchen earlier, dumped on the breakfast bar, so I make the quickest of dashes to retrieve it, mentally crossing my fingers that Oliver and Emma won't strike up a conversation in the few seconds it takes me to return. 'Here. Make sure everybody gets a pint.' I rummage in my purse and hand over a couple of notes. '*Don't* let Harvey have more than one. But don't rush back either.'

'Are you sure?' Oliver looks down at the notes I've thrust into his hand.

'Absolutely.' I sidestep Oliver and widen the door. 'And don't worry about Franny. You can take her back later.'

Oliver tucks the money into his pocket. 'Thanks, Vanessa.' Looking past me, he raises his hand. 'Nice to meet you, Emma.'

If Emma responds, I don't hear it. I can't hear anything other than my fantasy world crashing around me, brick by brick.

The front door closes behind Oliver but I remain fixed to the spot, eyes settled on a knot in the grain of wood. I can't move. I can't turn around and face Emma.

It's over. My lies have been exposed. How did I ever think I would get away with it?

'Rebecca?' I don't have to turn around to see how confused Emma is. I can hear it plainly in her voice. 'Why did he just call you Vanessa?'

Chapter 31

Emma watches me as I explain the whole situation, from Vince's initial mishearing in the pub when I introduced myself, to the downright lies I've told ever since. We're back in the kitchen, fresh cups of coffee in front of us, the plate of bourbons now a plate of crumbs as I've systematically shoved the biscuits in my mouth to try to sooth the apprehension gurgling in my stomach. Emma's eyebrows have been moving up her forehead, a tiny fraction at a time, as my story has unfolded and they're now in danger of disappearing into her hairline. She must think I'm completely bonkers. Or terribly dishonest.

'I know I shouldn't have let it get this far.' I press a finger to the plate, tapping my way across the crumbs before licking them off my fingertip. 'I should have made it clear who I was, right from the very beginning.' Emma hasn't said a word while I've been confessing my faux pas, and there's no indication she's about to break her silence. 'But they seemed to really respect me when they thought I was Vanessa, and I knew I'd never have that sort of influence if they knew I was just mousy Rebecca Riley.'

'You're not mousey.' Emma reaches out, placing her hand gently on my arm and giving it a comforting squeeze. 'You're lovely and kind and all the nice things Vanessa will never be. You should be proud to be Rebecca Riley. I'm proud to be her friend.'

'Really?' There's a giant lump in my throat but I manage to push the word out.

'Really.' Emma gives my arm another squeeze. 'But obviously it's far too late to reintroduce yourself now.'

'Is it?' I swallow against the giant lump. I'd been planning on coming clean to Oliver before our date on Saturday. It's the right thing to do, surely. How can I date a man who doesn't even know who I really am?

'Jeez, can you imagine it?' Emma snorts. 'Hey guys, guess what? I'm not really Vanessa Whitely, I'm her PA, Rebecca. I've been lying to you all this time. Ha ha ha.' She shakes her head, tittering to herself. 'No, you're just going to have to keep up the charade until you leave.'

'But then what?'

Emma gives me an odd look. 'Then you go back to your normal life – your *Rebecca* life – and hope Vanessa never finds out that you pretended to be her.'

'How will she find out?' I reach for the biscuits, realising too late that they're all gone. 'She isn't going to speak to the builders once the house is finished, not when she hasn't bothered to meet them in person during the refurb. She doesn't want to bother herself with the actual mechanics of having a newly refurbished house. She just wants the glory.' I really, *really* wish there were more biscuits. 'And she isn't going to bother making polite conversation with her new neighbours. She won't give them the time of day. She'll rock up here at the weekend, lord it about her manor, and then waltz back to Manchester. If she wants friends here, she'll bring them with her.'

'I hope for your sake that's true.' Emma gathers the mugs and plate and takes them across to the sink.

'She hasn't made any effort to introduce herself so far.' Otherwise I'd never have got away with playing her for this long.

Emma turns on the tap, testing the water until it's hot. 'It sounds like you've got it all under control then.'

I nod, though I'm biting my lip. 'What if I wanted to stay in contact with the friends I've made here though?'

'I don't think you can, under the circumstances.' She gives the mugs a quick scrub under the tap and places them on the draining board. 'If you tell them the truth now, they'll probably think you're pretty weird, to be honest.'

'Even if I explain it like I did to you?'

Emma turns, a wry smile on her face. 'Even then.' She washes the plate before drying her hands on one of the tea towels I brought over from the guesthouse.

'But what if I really liked one of them?'

Emma is folding the tea towel into a neat square but she pauses, looking up to meet my eye. '*Like* like someone, you mean?'

I glance down at the breakfast bar, tracing an invisible pattern with my finger. 'Just hypothetically, but yes.'

'Then you'd be in a hypothetical pickle.' Dumping the tea towel on the side, Emma joins me at the breakfast bar. 'Who is he? Is it that guy who was just here? Because he was pretty cute.'

'Oliver?' I make a strangled spluttery sound that I hope is convincing in its derision. 'No way. And there really isn't anyone. I was just wondering what you would do in that situation.'

'That made up situation?' Emma shrugs and grabs her handbag. 'I guess it would depend how much I liked him and whether I could see a future for us.'

'And if you could?'

'Then I'd have to tell him the truth. Preferably before the wedding ceremony, otherwise that could turn out to be a bit awkward.'

'Wedding ceremony? Steady on there. We've only known each other a few weeks.'

The corner of Emma's mouth lifts into a smirk. 'A few hypothetical weeks?'

'Yes. Obviously.' I clear my throat, tracing that imaginary pattern on the breakfast bar again.

'Okay, *hypothetically* speaking, I'd at least leave it until this job's done.' Emma's eyes flit around the room. 'Because if it doesn't go down all that well, you don't want to jeopardise all your hard work. And then at least Vanessa will only maim you for stealing her identity and not messing up her dream holiday home and messing up her party plans.'

'I've only borrowed her identity.' I desperately need a bourbon cream right now.

'I'm not sure Vanessa will see it like that. Trust me, you're best keeping it zipped for as long as possible.' Emma heads for the hallway. 'Come on, *Vanessa*. Show me the rest of the house before I have to head back to the office.'

*

The lane is littered with leaves as I make my way to the sanctuary in the half-light of early Saturday morning, my hands tucked into the pockets of my leather bomber jacket. Despite wearing the gloves and bobble hat Stacey has insisted I borrow on a semi-permanent basis, I can still feel the bite of the autumn chill in the air and my breath is visible in wispy puffs. The lane is silent, bar the odd rustle of the leaves stubbornly clinging onto branches in the breeze, but it no longer feels peculiar. I don't expect to hear the rumble of a double decker bus or the wail of a police siren as I make my way along the narrow track anymore, but I'll be back in Manchester in just over a week's time and my secondment to the countryside will become nothing more than a distant memory.

It's a sobering thought, which I push away immediately. Today is not a day for sadness. Today is a positive day. A day of new beginnings that should have a skip in its step, because today marks the next stage for Stacey and Oliver and the animal sanctuary. The auction will be taking place this afternoon, and all the hard work Stacey, Oliver and the whole community of Little Heaton will pay off. My stomach dances with anticipation and glee because although I may not be around to witness this exciting new stage, I know for a fact that Stacey will make a success of the development and I'm so proud of my friend.

'She's in a flap.' It's Mrs McColl who answers the door when I reach the sanctuary, a tea towel thrown over her shoulder and a scowl fixed firmly in place. 'Please calm her down before I'm forced to administer a sedative.'

'I'll do my best.' Mrs McColl is already marching back towards the kitchen as I step inside. I make my way to the yard, stopping off to pull on my usual polka-dotted wellies before heading outside. Stacey is sweeping up the old bedding from the rabbits' hutch with gusto, and I know she's throwing herself into her work to take her mind off the upcoming auction. I know this because she's been working away non-stop like the Duracell bunny for the past few days and is in danger of serious burnout. It's exhausting just watching from the sidelines.

'Why don't I take over? You look like you need a break.' I reach for the broom, but Stacey tugs it away.

'I'm fine. Plus, this will be the last time I do this for Honey and Rupert. Their new family are picking them up this afternoon.' She looks fondly at the rabbits before attacking the debris on the ground again. 'I've already mucked out the barn, so could you make a start on the chickens?'

'What time did you start?' It isn't even seven yet and she's carried out the biggest job in the yard?

Stacey straightens and swipes at her forehead with the back of a gloved hand. 'I couldn't sleep.'

'Have you at least had breakfast?'

Stacey shakes her head and resumes her sweeping. 'I'm too nervous to eat, and if I stop working, I'll only think about the auction and want to throw up.'

'It'll be fine. Who else would want a bit of land with no road access?'

Stacey pauses for a moment and nods her head. 'I hope you're right.' And then she's sweeping again, more feverishly than before. I head for the chickens, vowing to make Stacey stop for breakfast once I'm done, even if I have to wrestle the broom from her hands.

But there's no stopping Stacey, and in the end I have to give up trying because as much as I want my friend to take a break before she collapses in an exhausted heap, I have a house refurbishment to manage and a matter of days to complete the project. This is the final push before the decorators work their magic next week and turn the blank canvas into the masterpiece that will hopefully earn me the promotion I surely deserve. The builders have been amazing this past week, and the afternoon tea treat (and, I suspect more so, the pint in the pub afterwards) has really spurred them on to complete the tasks on time. I couldn't be prouder of my team, and it's come as a bit of a revelation that I can get the job done without resorting to Vanessa's unpleasant tactics. It's a bit of a relief, to be honest, as I haven't enjoyed the yelling and the being strict that comes with playing my boss, especially after Oliver pointed out the similarities between Vanessa and my father. People don't respect people like Vanessa and my dad – they fear them, and I don't want to live my life like that. I want to gain respect by being myself.

The thought of being myself has caused a lot of disturbed sleep over the past few days. It's my date with Oliver tonight and I've been unable to decide whether to tell him about my true identity now or later. I need to disentangle myself from the lies without destroying the friendships I've developed in Little Heaton and to do this, I have to own up to the untruths and misunderstandings, but the question is how and when. Tonight? Before the date? Or during? Or do I take Emma's

205

advice and wait until the house is finished, to avoid any repercussions?

My head is hurting just thinking about it, so I push the decision away. I have a job to do. A focus. Surely I'll know when the time is right to fess up so there's no point in stressing over it now.

Chapter 32

My stomach is tingling with anticipation as I send a good luck message to Stacey, but the prickly sensation – which is both unpleasant and agreeable in equal measure – has nothing to do with the auction that Stacey and Oliver are on their way to. Placing the phone down on the coffee table so I won't be tempted to check for messages every thirty seconds, I turn the volume up of the familiar Britney album (which I'm contemplating slipping into my holdall when I leave) and head into the bathroom, where a warm bubble bath is waiting for me. I have several hours until my date with Oliver, but it's been so long since I've been in this situation, I'm going to savour every single moment.

With Britney blasting from the living room, I sink into the water, feeling my body loosen up instantly. The warmth and soothing rose scent is pure bliss and the tension from the refurb, the lies that need clearing up and the thought of returning to a grubby shared bathroom all evaporates in the air as I close my eyes and concentrate purely on the words of Ms Spears. By the time I emerge, skin pink and wrinkled, I feel energised and ready to face the challenges that lay ahead. I'm not going to worry about my confession, not tonight. I'm going to enjoy an evening with a man who makes me laugh and feel good about myself. And the fact Oliver is easy on the eye is inconsequential, obviously …

Selecting the wide-legged jumpsuit from my charity shop haul, I team it with a gold belt and my peep-toe boots. With the help of a YouTube tutorial and several attempts, I manage to braid my hair at the sides, finishing off with a rolled bun at the nape of my neck, which looks stylish but cute. I keep my make-up quite simple, because although I want to make an effort, I still want to look like me, which is ironic given my Vanessa situation, but I elbow the niggling voice in my head away and concentrate on getting my smoky eye just right. A couple of layers of mascara and a nude lip gloss and I'm done. I'm physically ready for my date with Oliver.

I don't know how people do this dating thing on a regular basis. I'm a bag of nerves as I pace the length of the guesthouse. The tension has started to creep back and I have to remind myself – repeatedly – that it's only Oliver I'm waiting for, someone I like, who I feel relaxed with. Someone I've told my secrets to, only omitting the one that could prove problematic if this date goes as well as I hope it will.

I pause my pacing and close my eyes, drawing in a huge, chest-aching breath before allowing it to seep out slowly. My shoulders lower and my stomach unclenches. I am calm. I am relaxed. I am unruffled and ready to enjoy an evening with a man who has so far proved to be good company. Obviously, my new zen-like state crumbles as soon as I hear a car on the drive and, breathing ragged, I leap towards the window. He's here. Oliver is here. Is it too late to change my mind?

I give myself a mental slap on the wrist. I haven't changed my mind, nor do I wish to. I'm just nervous and need to snap out of it. Pulling my shoulders back and lifting my chin, I remind myself who I am. I am Vanessa Whitely, project manager, an all-round kick-ass and capable woman. Vanessa Whitely doesn't tremble behind curtains as she watches her date approach the door. She quickly checks her hair and make-up and plasters on her brightest smile, ready to greet the lucky man in question. She counts to five before she opens the door, so her date doesn't know she's been pacing the floor waiting for him.

'Hi!' My voice is cheery and without a hint of the wobble I feel inside. 'Won't be a sec.' I grab my handbag from the breakfast bar and hook it onto my shoulder before joining Oliver at the door and locking up behind us. He takes my hand as we head for the car and my heart starts to hammer.

Oh my God, we're holding hands.

'You look amazing.'

If I were being Rebecca, I'd have batted the compliment away, probably made a disparaging comment about myself while feeling incredibly awkward. But I'm not being Rebecca. I'm channelling Vanessa, who already knows she looks amazing.

'Thank you. You scrub up well yourself.'

And he does. Oliver looks knee-weakening hot in slim-fitting trousers and a white shirt, open at the collar, sleeves rolled to three-quarter length. I'm used to seeing him in jeans and T-shirts, but I approve of this new look.

'I thought I'd make an effort.' Oliver pulls lightly on his collar. 'I even dusted off the iron.'

'Then I'm honoured.' I'm disappointed when we reach the car as it means Oliver has to let go of my hand.

'Are you cold?' Oliver starts to fiddle with the heating settings once we're in the car and while I'd normally say not to bother, that I was fine (even as the goose bumps grew to epic proportions), this time I'm upfront.

'I'm bloody freezing.' Wrapping my arms around myself, I give my bare arms a vigorous rub. Oliver whacks the heating up and I'm much warmer by the time we leave the village. Maybe I could learn a thing or two while being Vanessa after all. I can leave behind the bad bits – the meanness and manipulation – but being a bit more assertive wouldn't be a bad thing.

I twist in my seat as we head over the iron bridge, watching as the village disappears from view. It's only the second time I've made the outward journey since my arrival, but this time I'm not so desperate to escape. And the next time I make this trip, in a week's time, I may never return again.

*

Oliver has booked a table at a restaurant in town, and it's as the waitress is leading us to our table that I realise I've forgotten to feel any nerves at all since we set off from the guesthouse. Oliver and I have chatted in the car, we've deliberated music preferences and debated the greatest film ever made. We've laughed. We've teased. We've had a brilliant time and we haven't even glimpsed a menu yet. Any wobbles I was feeling earlier have wobbled away.

'Did you manage to sign off all the snagging this afternoon?'

We're seated, drinks in front of us, our food order tapped out on a tablet and on its way to the kitchen when Oliver enquires about the refurbishment. I shake my head and hold up a finger.

'I did, but no more shop talk.' Mainly because I don't want to think about what happens next week when the house is finished and I have to go back home to my regular life.

'You're right, sorry.' Oliver shakes his head, as though he's resetting himself. 'Shall we discuss our next game? Because there isn't a clear winner and look at me.' Oliver scratches the back of his hand. 'It's making me itch.'

He has a point. 'What did you have in mind? A Scrabble rematch?'

Oliver snorts and waggles his finger at me. 'I see what you're doing there, missy.'

I feign innocence, my eyes wide and jaw slack. 'What am I doing?'

Oliver narrows his eyes at me and I try not to giggle. 'You've just picked a game you've already won.'

'Scared of losing again, are we?' I lean back in my chair and fold my arms across my chest, with my eyebrows raised as I await the answer.

'No. Of course not.' Oliver clears his throat and straightens the cutlery that already looks perfectly aligned from where I'm sitting. 'But it should be a new game. A game neither of us has won before. How about Hungry Hungry Hippos?'

I'm taking a sip of my drink when Oliver makes his suggestion, and the ridiculousness of his proposal makes me splutter and choke. Oliver is halfway out of his seat to come to my aid, but I wave his offer of help away.

'I'm fine.' My voice is a bit raspy, but at least I'm breathing. 'But Hungry Hungry Hippos though?'

'What?' Oliver holds his hands out with a laugh. 'It's a fun game. I used to love playing Hungry Hungry Hippos when I was a kid.'

I suppose Hungry Hungry Hippos *would* be a fun way to settle the score. 'Okay then. Hungry Hippos it is then. You don't happen to have the game tucked away, do you?' I'm joking, because what kind of childless, thirty-something owns Hungry Hungry Hippos?

'I do, actually.' Oliver laughs as my jaw drops in horror. He holds his hands up as I struggle to find words. Any words. 'In my defence, it was up in the attic gathering dust until yesterday. I remembered we had a stack of games up there from when we were kids, so had a nose around, found Hungry Hungry Hippos, and thought it would be a laugh. We can also play Guess Who and Ghost Castle if you want? Do you remember Ghost Castle? Oh, and Go For Broke! We should definitely play that. Did you ever play it? Nobody else seems to remember it.'

I hear the question somewhere in the back of my mind, but something else is going on in my brain. A slow acknowledgement of facts as Oliver chats animatedly about his favourite childhood games rediscovered in the attic of his grandparents' attic. The attic in the house that now belongs to Oliver and Stacey. The house that is now half-home, half-animal sanctuary.

I gasp, my hand covering my mouth, and it has nothing to do with Oliver's admission that he never really liked playing Operation because it was too fiddly and tedious.

'The animal sanctuary.' I've uncovered my mouth, my hands now resting on my cheeks in a recreation of The Scream. 'It was the auction today.' I'd forgotten all about it in the panic and excitement of my date. 'How did it go?'

Oliver's shoulders slump and all the joy displayed on his face during his childhood reminiscing only moments earlier fades away. 'Not good, I'm afraid. We were outbid by five grand. There was no way we could match it, let alone beat it.'

'Oh no.' I reach across the table and place my hand on Oliver's. 'I'm so sorry.'

'Thanks.' Oliver smiles at me but there's no pleasure there. I wish we could go back to chatting about Hungry Hungry Hippos, to get that light, carefree feeling back but this is too important to brush away.

'Who was the winning bidder?'

Oliver shrugs and puffs out a sigh. 'We don't know. There were only two of us bidding on the land – Stacey and I and someone bidding online. Stacey's determined to find out, though what she's going to do when she finds out who it was I have no idea.'

'How is she?' It's a stupid question – she's hardly going to be performing cartwheels after losing out. They've been raising the money for this development for years.

'She's devastated, though she's trying her best to hide it with anger and sheer determination in finding out who's bought the land.'

'Poor Stace.' Our starters arrive, the waitress placing our plates of delicious-looking food carefully in front of us, but my appetite has vanished. There's a great big boulder of dismay sitting in my stomach and I'm not sure anything else will fit in there. I should phone Stacey, tell her how disappointed I am for her, offer a shoulder to cry or vent on.

'I'm sorry, I shouldn't have brought it up.' Oliver is prodding at his food, seemingly as disinterested in eating it as I am.

'You didn't. It was me.' I give my own food a prod, accidentally spearing a slice of chorizo. When my attempts to shake it off my fork fail miserably, I give in and shove it into my mouth, trying not to think about how utterly delicious it is. The boulder of dismay shifts over slightly as my stomach rumbles.

'Anyway, what's done is done.' Oliver slices through the scallop on his plate. 'We'll figure something out. Stace won't let this hold her back. It's whoever bought the land I feel sorry for, because when she does find them …' Oliver gives a slow shake of his head. 'They're in trouble. I wouldn't like to get on the wrong side of my sister.'

'She is pretty feisty.'

Oliver snorts. 'You haven't seen anything yet. See this scar.' Oliver leans forward, tilting his head so I can see the faint, tiny mark on his temple. 'That's what I got when I *accidentally* broke the legs off her favourite doll.'

'How do you accidentally break the legs off a doll?' The chorizo really is delicious, I muse as I munch on a second slice.

'The parachute I made out of a Kwik Save carrier bag didn't work when I chucked her out of my bedroom window.'

I almost choke for a second time this evening, this time on a slice of chorizo. 'So it wasn't an accident at all.'

'Of course it was. I released Betsy in good faith, believing the parachute would lower her safely to the ground. How was I supposed to know she'd plummet to the concrete below? Either way, this was uncalled for.' He wiggles a finger at the scar at his temple.

'What did she do?'

Oliver gives a slow shake of his head. 'She went bat-shit crazy and frisbeed my grandad's Simon and Garfunkel record at me. The corner of the sleeve nearly took my eye out. I was lucky, really.'

I shouldn't laugh, but I can't help it, especially when Oliver flashes me a wounded look, his finger gently massaging the barely-there scar. He can't keep it up, however, and we're both giggling when the waitress returns to clear our plates away. I hadn't realised I'd eaten my entire starter, but my plate is empty.

Despite the bad news for the animal sanctuary, we manage to enjoy the rest of our meal before heading back to Little Heaton, where we stop off at the Farmer's. We have to battle our way through to the bar as it seems most of the village's population has squeezed into the pub. I expect to see Stacey lurking somewhere in the crowds when I spot Dominic Blackwood propping up the bar but she's nowhere to be seen, which is proof enough that losing the auction has hit her hard. I'll go and see her first thing in the morning, see if there's any way I can help. I don't imagine there's a whole lot I can do to ease the situation, other than scouring the charity shop for records to use as weapons when she does find the winning bidder, but I can at least offer my support.

'I can't believe we only met a few weeks ago.' Oliver places his pint down on a table near the jukebox, which is only vacant because the table is tiny and squeezed into an awkward corner, and sits down on a wobbly stool, leaving the more comfortable backed chair for me to take. 'Is it just me or does it feel like we've known each other for a lot longer?'

'It isn't just you.' I sit down and take a sip of my wine. 'I feel like I've known you forever.'

'Good.' Oliver smiles shyly. 'I was afraid I was going to make an idiot of myself saying that, but I don't think I've ever met anybody and just known I could trust them instantly. Especially after Lottie.'

Guilt gnaws at my insides, because Oliver's trust is misplaced.

I've been lying to him from the moment we met almost three weeks ago. It started as an accident but I let it continue. I reiterated the lie over and over again. I am not the person Oliver thinks I am. He's put his trust in someone who is the amalgamation of Vanessa and me, someone who doesn't really exist.

'It was hardly instantaneous trust. You thought I was a Grade-A bitch at first, remember?' I go to arch an eyebrow playfully but my heart isn't in it.

'I misjudged you.' Oliver reaches across the table and takes my hands in his. 'Sorry.' His apology only makes me feel worse. 'But I did think you were cute, even when you were yelling at me. Especially when you were yelling at me.' Oliver winks at me, and I can't help the flicker of a smile as he grins at me. 'I was expecting some Miss Trunchbull type to turn up, so I was taken aback when I realised how gorgeous you are. I think that's part of the reason I reacted so badly when you arrived. I was trying to mask how attracted to you I was.'

'Then why did you push me away when I tried to kiss you?' Too late, I realise I'm not supposed to remember that part of the evening. Oliver cottons on quickly, as evidenced by the bark of laughter.

'What happened to your drink-induced amnesia?'

'Shut up.' I nudge him lightly under the table with my foot. 'I was embarrassed that I'd made a pass at you, so I pretended I couldn't remember what had happened. It was less humiliating that way.'

'Vanessa.' I flinch at Oliver's use of my fake name. 'There's nothing to feel embarrassed about. I didn't push you away because I didn't fancy you. Do you know how drunk you were that night?'

I cover my face with my hands. 'Yes. Horribly so.'

Oliver peels my hands away. '*That's* why I didn't kiss you. It would have felt like I was taking advantage, and that isn't me. But it's different now ...' Oliver is moving towards me, and I know that this is where we're supposed to share our first kiss, but this time it's me that can't let it happen.

'It's a bit crowded in here.' I pull away, standing so abruptly my stool almost topples over. 'Why don't we grab a bottle of wine and go back to the guesthouse?' I need to tell him the truth and I don't think I can wait a week until the work on the house is finished. But I can't do it here, packed into the corner of the pub like a sardine, where anyone could overhear my confession.

We thread our way across the pub and it's a relief to make it out into the fresh air. Oliver lends me his jacket to stop me shivering, but it isn't the cold that is making me tremble, and even Oliver's hand in mine as we make our way across the village offers little comfort. I'm about to hit the self-destruct button and even though I'm terrified of the consequences, I know with absolute certainty that it's the right thing to do.

Chapter 33

We reach the footbridge and I instinctively slow down, delaying the inevitable and stretching out this blissful time for as long as I possibly can. I like Oliver, and he likes me, and he was just about to kiss me. I must be mad, I think as we near the middle of the bridge and I look out across the canal. The view before me is so idyllic, with the yellow and magenta-coloured trees reflecting up at us from the water, and it conjures up feelings of romance and cosiness, of an existence far removed from the life I plod through back home. I've hijacked Vanessa's life over the past few weeks and I have no choice but to give it all up. Oliver is going to find out one way or another; either I tell him, in my own words, or he makes the hideous discovery when the real Vanessa turns up.

'We should go on a canal ride.' I hadn't realised I'd come to a complete standstill until Oliver joins me at the rail, his arm slipping around my waist as we look out across the water. 'Maybe next weekend?'

I swallow hard and try to muster a smile. 'That'd be nice, but I'm going home next weekend.' And I doubt Oliver will want to be in such close proximity to me when he finds out that I'm an imposter. How would I feel if the shoe was on the other foot? If

Oliver suddenly dropped into conversation that he isn't in fact Oliver Rowe. That he isn't a builder at all and has a completely different name, a different life to the one he's projected for the past few weeks. Even though he's essentially the same person, with just a few minor tweaks to his personality and backstory, could I brush it under the carpet and carry on regardless? Could I trust him ever again?

'But you'll be back.' Oliver states this as a fact rather than a question. 'For weekends and stuff.'

Vanessa will be, but I'll be back in Manchester, reminiscing about those few weeks when I'd become somebody else and had the time of my life. When I'd found my voice and believed in myself. When I'd formed friendships and found the potential for … what? Romance? Love? Who knows because I'm about to pull the plug on whatever it is.

I don't answer Oliver's question because I don't want to tell another lie. From now on, I'm going to tell the truth, the whole truth and nothing but, as I should have done from the very start.

'Let's get back to the guesthouse.' My hand is in Oliver's again and I move away from the rail. 'I'm freezing.'

We make our way across the footbridge and onto Arthur's Pass, our feet crunching across the gravel as we cross the drive.

'What are you going to do with this place when you move into the main house?'

I step into the guesthouse and switch the lights on. It'd be cosier with the lamps but the stark brightness suits the situation, I think. I want everything to be clear and focused. No shadows. No room for doubt.

'It'll probably go up on Airbnb.' This isn't a fabrication as it was an idea floated by Vanessa herself.

'Good idea.' Oliver closes the door behind him and looks around the room. 'It's a great space.'

'It really is.' I take the bottle of wine we picked up from the mini market from Oliver and head towards the kitchen. I'm going to miss this guesthouse when I'm back home, avoiding dubious stains on the sofa and disposing of the little piles of toenail clippings Lee has left behind.

'Shall I?' Oliver has moved across the room to the stereo and is holding up the Britney album, which I'd been merrily singing along to in the bath only a matter of hours ago. I shake my head. I want to retain the happy memories of that Britney album, not taint it with what I'm about to do.

'I'm not really in the mood for music.' I grab a couple of glasses from the cupboard and open the wine, resisting the urge to glug it straight from the bottle. My heart is hammering so hard as I carry the drinks into the living room area, I'm surprised Oliver hasn't commented on the din, but he's blissfully unaware that anything is afoot as he accepts his glass and settles down on the sofa. Taking a huge gulp of wine, I join Oliver, shrugging off his jacket and draping it along the back of the sofa as he'll need that in a minute or two as he no doubt makes a swift exit from the guesthouse.

'I've had a really nice time tonight.' Placing his glass on the coffee table, Oliver takes my hand in his and gives me a shy smile. I almost wince as the hammering in my chest ups its tempo to dangerous levels. I'm pretty sure he's going to kiss me now, but I can't let that happen, no matter how much I want him to. I want him to kiss Rebecca, not Vanessa, and he deserves to know the truth before anything happens between us.

'Oliver. Wait.' He's leaning in towards me but my hands are on his shoulders, preventing him from moving closer. It's like a reversal of the time I tried to kiss Oliver and he stopped me because I was blind drunk. It would be quite funny if it wasn't so tragic.

'Sorry.' Oliver sits bolt upright and twists away from me, his hand reaching for the glass of wine for a fortifying sip. 'I thought … Never mind. Sorry.'

'Stop saying sorry.' I place my hand on Oliver's arm. '*I'm* the one who should be apologising.'

Oliver shifts in his seat so he's facing me again. 'What for?'

My heart is now hammering so hard, it's surely about to crack through my ribcage. I feel lightheaded, and I'm not sure if it's due to my abnormal pulse or through sheer terror.

'I need to tell you something.' The glass is vibrating in my hand as I place it down on the coffee table.

'What is it?' I think Oliver is frowning at me as he asks the question but my vision has gone a bit hazy. This is it. Confession time. There's no turning back. I open my mouth, though I'm not sure what I'm about to say. There are words buzzing around my head but they aren't in any kind of coherent order.

'I haven't been entirely honest with you.' I'm shocked when the words leaving my mouth are not only logical, they're clear and precise and said without a hint of a wobble.

'What do you mean?'

I don't have the chance to answer as we're interrupted by a hammering at the door that rivals my heartbeat for speed and volume. I'm not sure whether this is a blessing or not, but I jump out of my seat and rush to the door, more than happy to delay my declaration of deceits. Who knows, maybe it's Vanessa herself, here to reveal my pack of lies on my behalf.

It isn't Vanessa at the door. It's Stacey, or someone who looks vaguely like the Stacey I know. This Stacey is wide-eyed with a puce-like hue as she barges past me. Her mouth is screwed up tight, her nostrils flared, and her fingers are curled into fists by her sides.

'Everything okay, Stace?' Oliver edges towards his sister, his hand outstretched. She flinches as he makes contact with her arm but she doesn't pull away.

'I found out who bought the land.' Lifting a hand, one of her fingers unfurls until it is pointing directly at me, just inches from my face. 'It was you.' She turns to Oliver, her finger still aimed at my face, her anger making it quiver. 'Vanessa bought the land, right from under our noses.'

Chapter 34

The room is almost silent, with just the ravaged breath of Stacey audible. She's still pointing that finger at me like a dagger, still looking at Oliver and watching for his reaction to the news that I have betrayed them. But Oliver's face is blank and I can only imagine the thoughts currently buzzing around his head. And none of them are good.

'She. Did. It.' Stacey spits the words, her finger jabbing so close to my face that I'm forced to take a step back to prevent an eye gouging. 'She pretended to be our friend, when all the time she was plotting to snatch the land away from us. And what does she need it for anyway?' Stacey finally removes her finger from the vicinity of my face so she can indicate the space around us. 'She already has the big house and the land, why does she need more?' She turns to me, her eyebrows shooting up her forehead as she directs the question at me.

'I don't know.' It's the honest answer. I have no idea why Vanessa has bought the land. She already has so much and, as far as I'm aware, she doesn't have plans to expand.

'She doesn't know.' Stacey gives a hoot, but she is no way delighted by my response. 'She's bought the land but doesn't know why. Spite, maybe? Do you get your kicks from making people miserable?' She places a hand on her forehead and shakes her head. 'Nic was right about you all along. Why did I ever trust you?'

'You don't understand.' I think about taking a step closer to Stacey but she's absolutely furious and, quite frankly, I'm terrified of her right now. 'I haven't been entirely honest with you since I got here.'

'Is this what you were about to tell me?' Oliver points back towards the sofa, where just moments ago he was about to kiss me. His face is no longer blank. There is confusion there, with an undercurrent of anger.

'No, because I didn't know about the land then.' Stacey gives another hoot, but I carry on. 'But I *was* going to tell you the truth. About who I really am.'

'Oh, we know who you really are.' Stacey snarls the words at me and I find myself shrinking away, both physically and mentally. I shuffle backwards, edging towards the sofa, but the tiny distance I'm putting between us is irrelevant. I'm a little girl again, cornered and powerless and full of fear.

'What is the truth, Vanessa?' Oliver's voice is soft, gentle, but I'm still afraid. I was so sure that telling him the truth was the right thing to do, but I never imagined it would happen like this. It was supposed to be on my terms.

'Well?' Stacey moves towards me, but Oliver holds out a hand, halting her progress.

'Vanessa?'

I can't look at him. I can't look at either of them, so I make my confession to my hands, wringing in front of me in agitation.

'I'm not Vanessa.'

My voice is low and raspy, barely a voice at all, and I'm not sure whether Stacey and Oliver have heard as silence ensues. So I say it again, lifting my chin and making the briefest of eye contact with Oliver before I repeat my confession.

'I'm not Vanessa.' My voice is stronger, even if there is still a slight tremor. 'There was a mix up when I arrived. Vince misheard me and thought I was Vanessa. I should have corrected him, but I didn't. I let him think I was her. I let you all think I was her.' My chin drops again and I'm back to observing my hands, my fingers twisting and flexing wildly.

'Then who are you?' It's Oliver who asks the question. I don't dare look up to see the expression on his face, but if it matches his tone it will be a mixture of shock, disbelief and utter bewilderment.

'I'm Rebecca Riley, Vanessa's PA. She sent me here to take over Nicole's role as project manager. A job I was totally unprepared for.' I give a hollow laugh. 'I have no experience of building or renovation. I've never even wallpapered a room. But none of that matters to Vanessa. If she wants something, she gets it, one way or another.' I sneak a look at Oliver. There are lines furrowed deep into his forehead and his mouth is open as though he was about to say something but has lost the ability to form words.

'So you've been pretending to be somebody else all this time?' Stacey asks, and I sneak a glance at her. Most of the anger has seeped away from her features, but she doesn't look happy.

'Yes. I took Vanessa's name and her influence to get the job done.'

'But why?'

I back away further and sink onto the sofa, relieved that my jellied legs no longer have to hold me upright. 'Because I'm nothing like Vanessa. I have no authority. I don't have the ability to sway people, to get them to do my bidding. I have no leadership skills. If the real me was left in charge, we'd still be laying the flooring three weeks down the line.' I give a slow shrug and manage to hold eye contact with Stacey for more than a few seconds. 'And I needed this job to go well. To prove myself to Vanessa.'

'But to hell with the rest of us, yeah?'

'No, it wasn't like that.' I shake my head, my eyes focused on Stacey and pleading with her to believe me. 'I didn't know I was going to form friendships here. I was supposed to just show up, get the job done and go home again. But by the time we became friends, it was too late. Everyone thought I was Vanessa. I couldn't just reintroduce myself.'

'Tell the truth, you mean?'

I sigh and look down at my hands. They're still fidgety but I'm no longer in danger of dislocating a digit. 'Yes, I guess so. But I was going to tell the truth. Just now.' I look at Oliver for confirmation, but he's still suspended in his baffled state. 'And I swear I had nothing to do with Vanessa buying the land. I had no idea she was planning to bid on it. She never mentioned it when we were talking about the auction a couple of weeks ago. She never even knew about the auction until I brought it up.' My words peter out and my hand claps over my mouth. *I* told Vanessa about the land between the properties. *I* told her about the auction. She didn't have a clue about it until I opened my big gob!

This *is* all my fault.

'Great. Thanks for giving her the head's up.' Stacey gives me one last look of contempt before she turns and walks out of the door. Oliver finally comes back to life, giving his head a little shake before he snatches his jacket from the back of the sofa and strides after his sister. I watch him reach the door, wanting to call out for him to stop, but I'm unable to form any words or movements. He stops before he crosses the threshold, turning slowly towards me.

'I trusted you. Confided in you about things I've never told anybody.' He peers out of the door, in case his sister is still lurking, but Stacey is long gone. 'Has everything you've said been a lie?'

It breaks my heart that he would think that, but I can hardly blame him.

'No, it hasn't all been a lie. I lied about my name, but I've still been me.'

Oliver's chest rises and falls in a huge sigh and then he's gone, the door closing gently behind him.

*

I don't sleep at all. I don't even attempt it. I've betrayed two people I care about and taken a wrecking ball to Stacey's development plans. I've seen first-hand how much that extra land would mean to the animal sanctuary but, because of me, it won't happen at all.

I need to fix this somehow, because I can't stand the thought that Stacey's hard work will suffer because I'm an idiot, and I need to prove to both Stacey and Oliver that I'm a good person, that I *can* be trusted and that our friendship means a lot to me. The hours pass agonisingly slowly, but finally morning arrives, the sun weak and ineffective as it rises above the trees. I know Vanessa won't appreciate a phone call so early on a Sunday morning, but I can't wait any longer and she's brought it on herself.

Surprisingly, Vanessa answers on the first ring, her voice groggy but urgent. 'Ty? Where are you?'

I'd very much like to hang up and abort the plan right now, but I throw back my shoulders and remind myself why I'm doing this. 'It isn't Tyler. It's Rebecca.'

'Who?'

If I had a pillow, I'd be screaming into it right now. 'Rebecca Riley. Your PA?' It seems strange to be using my actual name after weeks of being Vanessa.

'Becky?' Seriously, I need a pillow-scream right now. 'Is everything okay with the house? There isn't going to be a delay, is there? Because most people have RSVPed.' There's a definite warning tone to Vanessa's voice and I wonder why I ever wanted to be more like her.

'This isn't about the house.' I close my eyes and try to summon strength from somewhere deep, deep down. 'It's about yesterday's auction.'

'What auction?' Vanessa attempts to sound perplexed, but she isn't fooling me.

'The auction you bid at and won. For the bit of land between your holiday home and the animal sanctuary.'

'Oh. That auction. What about it?' Vanessa sounds utterly bored, and I can picture her rolling her eyes at being disturbed on a Sunday morning for something she deems trivial. If I wasn't such a wuss and didn't value my job, I'd give her a major ticking off. Instead, I grit my teeth and try to remain as calm as possible.

'I don't understand why you bid. You never mentioned wanting the land, and you certainly don't need any more. What are you going to do with it?'

'First of all, I'm going to erect a bloody big fence. Maybe even a wall. What do you think? Do you think a fence will be sufficient at keeping the animals on their own side?' Vanessa is posing questions, but she doesn't seem to require any answers as she ploughs on ahead without pausing for breath. 'I think the wall, to be on the safe side. Really high and solid.'

'But what about the land? What are you going to do with it?'

There's a pause on the other end of the line. It's unlike Vanessa to keep quiet for any length of time, so I'm about to check we're still connected when she speaks again. 'Nothing, obviously. Like you said, I don't need it. I've got more than enough land for a huge garden at the back of the house.'

My mouth opens and closes several times before I manage to get any words out. 'Then why did you buy the land if you don't plan to do anything with it?'

'It's a buffer, isn't it? A pretty expensive buffer, but worth it to keep those horrible creatures off my property. Can you imagine what they'd do to my new lawn?'

'You bought the land to keep the animals from wandering over into your garden?' My ears can't be working properly. 'Because there's a new fence going up already. The work on the garden starts tomorrow.'

'It isn't just to keep them wandering over. It's the noise and smell as well, isn't it? Who wants a stinky farmyard on their doorstep?'

The neighbouring land is hardly on Vanessa's doorstep, unless it was a bloody big doorstep stretching several hundred feet. And Stacey is robust at keeping the sanctuary – and its occupants – clean and tidy. I don't point this out to Vanessa, obviously, as my wimpish tendencies are in full force.

'You should come and visit the animal sanctuary. See what amazing work they do to look after the sick and abandoned animals. Then you'll see why that extra land is so important to them.'

Vanessa sighs, long and hard. 'Do you think I have time to be traipsing around a filthy yard, looking at filthier animals? I'm a very busy woman, as you know.'

'But you don't understand how vital that land is. It's such a waste to just leave it sitting there when it could be used for something really important.'

Vanessa sighs again. 'Look, I have to go. Ty's just arrived and he has some serious explaining to do.'

'But the land ...' My voice is weak, the fight burning inside nothing but a whimper on the outside. I'm angry at Vanessa, but I'm absolutely livid with myself.

'Fine, I'll think about it.'

I'm jolted by the shock of cooperation from Vanessa but I don't get the chance to press her any further as she's already screeching at her boyfriend, demanding to know where he's been all night, and then the line goes dead. Still, this is a tiny victory, at least. There is hope and I will cling onto it as though my life depends on it.

*

I've cleaned the entire guesthouse, scrubbing every nook and cranny to keep my mind occupied, but I drop the mop and dash across the room when I hear the text tone on my phone, almost slipping on the wet floor. I'm hoping the text will be from Vanessa, or even Oliver, who I haven't heard from since my confession last night. But it's neither. It's Kate, inviting me for Sunday lunch, which is something she has never done before.

Can't. Busy with work.

Tossing my phone on the sofa, I return to the mop, attempting to sing along to the Britney CD even as my mind drifts back to the Vanessa situation. I'm hoping I got through to her earlier, but when has she ever paid attention to me?

My phone beeps once more, but this time I'm in no rush to read the text. As suspected, it's Kate again, offering to pick me up and drop me off home again as soon as lunch is over. I don't bother to reply this time. Kate's never respected my choices in life, so it's pointless trying to persuade her that there are more important things to me than an awkward lunch with people who don't understand me. Ignoring her is the best course of action.

I've run out of surfaces to clean and have moved on to rearranging the kitchen cupboards when Vanessa finally gets back to me with a concession over the land; she's willing to sell the land to Stacey – for a profit.

*

'She wants an extra five grand?'

Stacey, unsurprisingly, doesn't take the news well. I've headed straight over to the animal sanctuary to pass on the sort-of good news and, after being on the receiving end of an icy glare from Mrs McColl that would have frozen Lucifer's spuds, Stacey and Oliver have taken me upstairs for a bit of privacy.

'The auction was twenty-four hours ago, and she wants to

make a five-grand profit?' Stacey leaps off the sofa and marches towards the window, glowering down at the yard below while Oliver sits in the armchair, his arms folded in front of him, face impassive.

'There are fees and stuff …' I sound so feeble, I want to slap myself, so if Stacey makes a move towards me, I'm out of here.

'Are you in this together? Good cop, bad cop?' Stacey turns towards me, but luckily she stays by the window, which keeps me safely out of slapping distance. 'You befriend us and then talk us into accepting her crappy offer?'

'Of course not.' I'm appalled at Stacey's suggestion, but I can hardly blame her for distrusting me. I've brought all of this on myself. 'I wish you'd won the auction, honestly I do. And I'm so sorry I gave her the information about it, but I never in a million years thought she'd buy it herself.'

Stacey shrugs and wanders towards the basket where the kittens are starting to stir after a nap. 'It makes no difference either way. The simple fact is, we haven't got an extra five grand. We haven't got an extra fiver, and there's no way we can get another loan. Vanessa already outbid us – how are we supposed to match that, let alone top it up?' Stacey reaches into the basket, scooping up Tammy. 'You should go now, Rebecca or whatever your name is. And please don't come back. There's nothing more to say.'

'But …' I'm not sure what I'm going to say, but it doesn't matter as Oliver interjects before I've even finished forming that one tiny word.

'We trusted you. Stacey thought you were friends, and I thought …' He shakes his head, as though he can't bear to say the actual words. 'But you've been lying to us all this time. I told you about Lottie …' He sneaks a furtive look at Stacey and lowers his voice. 'About what she did. How she told me nothing but lies, and you're just the same.'

'I'm not. Really.' I move towards Oliver, but he's already out of his seat and marching towards the door. When he yanks it open so forcefully, I'm surprised to see the hinges still attached to the frame.

'I don't know you at all. All I know is, we've lost the land because of you and there's no way we can find the money to buy it now. The expansion can't go ahead.' He indicates the open door and steps aside. 'Now please, I'm begging you, go away and don't come back.'

I do as I'm told, glancing back just as the door closes behind me to see Stacey pressing her face into the kitten's soft fur. The guilt is overwhelming and I clutch the handrail to keep myself steady on the stairs. I've lost my new friends and destroyed the plans they've worked so hard on. There is no way I can ever make it up to Stacey and how can Oliver ever put his faith in me again?

Trudging down the stairs, I'm met by Mrs McColl in the hallway, almost as though she's been waiting for me. She gives a sniff and folds her arms across her chest as she looks me up and down.

'I always knew I couldn't trust you. Right from the very beginning. My instincts are never wrong.' With one last look of distaste, she marches along the corridor and disappears into the café. I want to call after her that her instincts were wrong. That I'm a good person who *can* be trusted. I made a stupid mistake, and if there was anything I could do to put it right, I would. If I had five thousand pounds, I'd give it to Stacey right now. But I don't have the money or the means to raise such a substantial amount.

Or do I? What if I *could* somehow raise the money? I could finally put my skills to good use and organise a fundraising event, which would not only save the animal sanctuary development, it would showcase my skills to Vanessa in a far more practical way than project managing a house refurbishment. I could salvage my friendships, put the development firmly back on track and earn my coveted promotion all in one fell swoop!

Chapter 35

I've already started to formulate a plan as I hurry along the lane, so I'm ready to spring into action by the time I reach the guest-house. I don't have a lot of time to put my plan into action; I'll be leaving Little Heaton in a week, so I have to organise and execute the fundraising event within days. It's crazy. Probably impossible. But I have to give it everything I've got if I want to make up for my mistakes.

I have such a small window of time to carry this out, but I do have one trick up my sleeve, something that will give me a major head start. Before Vanessa sent me to Little Heaton, I'd been working on some ideas for the Heron Farm Festival and while my ideas are obviously surplus to requirements for that project, I could utilise them now by putting on my own autumn festival, here in the village, with all the proceeds going to the animal sanctuary. The ideas are all there, waiting to be put into action. Unfortunately, I left the file behind – I had no idea it would come in useful during a house refurb – so I'm going to have to do the unthinkable and get in touch with Lee back at the flat.

It's a Sunday afternoon, so hopefully he'll still be sprawled on the sofa, recovering from a hangover sufficiently enough for his usual back-to-work-tomorrow drinks in the pub later. The phone rings and rings and I'm about to give up when it's finally answered.

'Yo.' I'd forgotten what a tit Lee is, but I'm reminded by his greeting, followed by a small, gassy burp.

'Hi, Lee. It's Rebecca.' I'm expecting a cry of 'you're alive!' or 'where have you been?' or even a confused 'who?', but I receive no reaction at all. I've been gone for three weeks and nothing. Charming. 'I need a favour.'

'From me?'

I bite back a sarcastic retort, because I really do need his help. 'Yes please.'

'You don't need me to go out and get milk, do you? Because I'm watching *The Simpsons* and it's the Mr Plow episode. I only answered the phone because of the ads.'

'No, I don't need you to go out and get milk.' I'm fighting a sigh so badly right now. 'I need you to go into my room and find a file I left in there.' The thought of Lee in my bedroom makes me shudder, but needs must.

'Oh. Because we do actually need milk. There hasn't been any in the fridge for yonks. I've been having to eat my Sugar Puffs dry.'

As oppose to getting off his arse and buying more milk? Unthinkable!

'Anyway, Lee. The file.'

'What file?'

I really do wish you could strangle people over the phone. 'The file in my room. I need you to get it and courier it to me. I'll set it all up from here, so you don't have to do anything other than hand it over. Okay?'

'It'll have to wait until *The Simpsons* has finished …'

I squeeze my eyes shut and take a deep, calming breath. 'Fine. But let me know as soon as you've found it so I can set up the collection. It should be on top of my chest of drawers. Or maybe on the bed.' I packed in a bit of a rush, so I don't actually remember what I did with it that day. 'But it shouldn't be too hard to find. It's a red presentation file with a clear cover you're looking for. It'll say Heron Farm Festival on the front, plus my name. Got it?'

'Red file. Some festival thingy. Your name. Got it.'

I'm hardly filled with confidence, but I'll have to put my trust in Lee. 'Thank you. I owe you one.'

'S'alright. You couldn't pick up some milk on your way home though, could you'

I close my eyes again. Deep, deep breath. 'I'm in Cheshire. I won't be home for another week. You might want to get some milk yourself in the meantime.'

'What are you doing in Cheshire?'

Deep, *deep* breath. 'Working. I've been here for three weeks.'

'Ah, I see!' Lee sniggers. '*That* explains why there's no food in the fridge. I thought you were on one of your pissy *I'm not here to feed you* campaigns again.' It's so nice to know I've been missed during my absence.

'I left you a note, telling you I'd be away for a few days.'

'Did you?' There's a silence, in which I picture Lee shrugging while he picks at his nose. 'Anyway, *The Simpsons* is coming back on.'

'Please don't forget the file.' My plea comes too late; the line is already dead. Placing the phone down on the coffee table, I drop my face into my hands, allowing myself a moment of despair as I realise my fate and that of the animal sanctuary is now firmly in my flatmate's grubby little hands.

*

I can't sit around twiddling my thumbs while I wait for Lee to finish watching cartoons so I use the time to brainstorm. The festival needs a venue and while the animal sanctuary

234

springs immediately to mind, I soon dismiss it. The family day was a huge success, but this festival has to be on a much bigger scale to raise as much money as possible. There's the park, where the fun run took place, but I'd need to get permission from the council and there's no way I'd be able to get that over the next few days. There's loads of open space around, but I'd need to find out who owned the land before I could even think about requesting permission to use it. There's a lot of space behind Vanessa's property, but I hardly think she'd appreciate me christening her newly landscaped garden with a mini festival.

Chewing on my pen, I'm starting to get the horrible feeling that this is hopeless. I could have a million, fail-proof ideas put together, but every one of them would be useless without a venue. I need land and lots of it to house the entertainment and the food and drink facilities that will draw people in.

Sitting upright and removing the pen from my teeth, I grab my phone and Google Durban Castle, which is just up the road from here. The castle is surrounded by acres of land, which I'm sure was a venue Vanessa has used for one of her events. Isn't that how she discovered her holiday home in the first place?

I find the website and punch the air when I find that the castle's grounds can be hired. This is it! This would be the perfect venue for the autumn festival. I was momentarily derailed but I may just be back on track again.

A quick phone call later and my hopes are not only dashed, they're completely obliterated. Not only is the castle booked for a wedding next weekend, the cost of hiring the grounds is eye-watering. I'm going to have to organise this festival on the tiniest budget from my savings, so the castle is firmly out.

And the bad news keeps on coming when Lee phones to say my file is nowhere to be found (and he looked *everywhere*, he told me with extra emphasis, which leads me to believe he's found a little battery-operated friend of mine in the bedside drawer. I'm now moving out whether I get the promotion or not). I have the file saved on my laptop, so I can print out a new copy, but the original holds so much more, with added snippets from newspapers and magazines, and contact information I'd gathered while researching venues and facilities. I must have left the original file at the office, as I definitely took it with me that morning, so I could ask Emma to look for it tomorrow, but is there any point when I don't have a venue?

*

Sitting in the guesthouse and chewing on my nails as I try to come up with an alternative plan is doing my head in (plus, I've chomped almost down to the knuckles, which isn't a good look) so I decide to go for a walk. Perhaps the fresh air will get the creative cogs turning again. Or maybe I'll just freeze in the biting wind. It's worth the gamble, at least.

Zipping my jacket all the way to my chin, I make my way across the gravel drive that will be excavated tomorrow to make way for the new block paving. The following week is going to be intense, with the drive, garden and decorating all being tackled at once, so I really must be losing it if I think adding another major project on top is in any way sensible, but I can't give up. I owe it to Stacey and the animals to pull this off, whatever it takes.

I pause on the footbridge and look out across the canal, as I did only yesterday, with Oliver. There's a barge moored in the distance, its red and green paint bright against the darkening October evening. I doubt Oliver will be inviting me to join him on a boat trip again any time soon. Whatever potential we had, I've trampled all over it. Sighing, I lean against the wooden rail and squeeze my eyes shut, as though I can block out everything that has happened over the past few weeks. Why did I have to go along with the whole Vanessa thing? I wouldn't be in such a mess if I'd been honest from the start. But would Oliver have liked me? The real me? Timid Rebecca, who can't even stand up to her flatmate or insist her boss listens to her ideas? I'm not so sure about that. Being Vanessa boosted my confidence. She gave me self-worth and made me feel happy in my own skin. She allowed me to believe that someone like Oliver could be interested in me. Without Vanessa, I don't think I would have felt worthy enough to strike up a friendship – let alone anything else – with him because I'm still the girl who doesn't think she's good enough. For her family, for her boss, for anyone.

My eyes open when I hear footsteps on the bridge, and I turn slowly, as though I already know who will be making their way towards me before I see them.

'Hello, Stacey.' My throat is dry and scratchy, but I manage to push out the greeting. It isn't returned. Stacey, stony-faced and seeming to look right through me, marches across the footbridge, her only words those of encouragement to Claude as he ambles after her. They wouldn't have to make this daily trip to and from Dominic Blackwood's field if Stacey owned the neighbouring land, as there would be plenty of grass to sustain the sheep, though I'm sure Stacey would miss the opportunities to glimpse her crush.

I'm jolted by my thoughts, pushing myself upright and away from the rail. The Blackwoods' field! *Of course.* Dominic doesn't use that field, which is why he's happy to let Claude munch his way through it. Would he be willing to let me use the field for the festival? There's only one way to find out.

Lifting my chin and throwing back my shoulders, I set off at a pace. I've been hiding behind the Vanessa persona for long enough. It's time to be Rebecca again. But this time I'm going to be the best version of Rebecca Riley that I can be. It's time to unleash the Rebecca I am inside and see what she can do when she really puts her mind to it.

Chapter 36

I can barely hear myself think with the excavation work going on outside, but I close myself off in the bathroom of the guesthouse, as far away from the noise as I can possibly get before calling the office. The new temp on reception puts me through to Emma, but it's Sonia who answers.

'Hi, it's Rebecca.' It feels odd using my real name. 'Is Emma there? I really need to speak to her.'

'She isn't here. She's gone out for lunch. With Vanessa.' Sonia spits the words 'lunch' and 'Vanessa' as though the very notion disgusts her. 'They're proper pally now, you know. Always together. *Besties*. Nobody else gets a look in. It's like our ideas don't even matter anymore. There's no way Emma's going back on that reception desk. Not now she's Vanessa's right-hand woman.'

'Right.' I stretch the word out as I figure out where to go from here. I don't have time to discuss office politics right now, especially with Sonia. Maybe Vanessa would be friendlier with Sonia if she wasn't sleeping with her boyfriend? 'Can you ask Emma to phone me as soon as she's back?'

With Dominic's help, the autumn mini festival is back on so I need my file as soon as possible, and if it isn't at the flat, it must be at the office. I was ready to literally beg on my knees when I found Dominic in the Farmer's last night, but he didn't need any coaxing at all.

'Sure. Use it.' He'd shrugged and taken a sip of his pint.

'I won't be able to pay you upfront, but once we have all the money from the ticket sales …'

Dominic had held up his hand to stop me. 'Don't worry about it. You don't have to pay me to use the field.'

'Really?' I couldn't believe my luck. Not only had I found a venue, it wouldn't cost me a bean. Being Rebecca Riley was working a treat.

'It's to help Stacey, right?' Dominic had shrugged lazily, but I was sure his cheeks had taken on a rosy glow. 'She's a mate, and we like to help each other out around here.'

Until I have the file, I'll have to work from the bare essentials I have saved on my laptop and use my initiative. I've spent the morning at the house, organising the three teams and their work-load, but now it's time to crack on with the festival. Juggling my responsibilities and this new project is going to be tough, but I'm more determined than I've ever been in my life to pull it off.

After ending the call with Sonia, I make some calls and emails, trying not to feel *too* offended when I'm practically laughed at for wanting to book facilities and acts at such short notice. I do manage to book some portaloos and generators, so at least we'll have power and somewhere to go, but by mid-afternoon I admit to myself that I'm going to need a bit of help. There's way too much to do for one person over a matter of days; at Vanessa Whitely Events, there are whole teams of people working on any given project, with weeks or months to plan. Stacey clearly hates my guts, and she's refused to even speak to me, so there's only one other person I can ask. I've avoided him as much as possible, speaking only to Vince at the house, but I'm going to have to bite the bullet and face Oliver. He probably hates me more than his sister, but I'm hoping he'll take pity on me when he realises what I'm trying to do.

The drive's in a state as I step carefully out of the guesthouse, skirting around the worst of the rubble. I've heard the rumbling outside as I've been hunched over my laptop, but it's been hours since I've actually seen the drive – or what's left of it – and I'm momentarily panicked by the sight. It looks like we're back to square one, but I have to remind myself this is only the outside, that the inside is still intact and the decorators have been beautifying the rooms with colour and print.

'Oliver!' I can see him up ahead, chatting to Vince over by one of the skips. He doesn't acknowledge my call so I wave my hand about and try again. 'Oliver!' This time, he turns towards me, though he doesn't flash the smile I've grown accustomed to over the past few weeks. His face is blank, neither welcoming or hostile. I could be a stranger for all the impact I'm having on his features.

'Can I have a word?' I nod my head back towards the guesthouse. 'It'll only take a minute or two.'

Oliver wipes his hands down his jeans and gives a one-shouldered shrug. 'Sure.' He turns back to Vince and says something I can't hear from the other side of the wreckage between us before making his way towards me. He's looking down at the ground and I'm not sure whether he's avoiding meeting my eye or concentrating on making it across the jagged ground in one piece. Probably a combo of the two.

'Come in.' We've made it to the guesthouse but Oliver is hovering by the door, looking awkward and out of place.

'I'm okay here.' He lifts a foot. 'Dirty boots and cream carpets aren't a good mix.' He's wiped his feet on the mat but they're still caked in mud, though I doubt he's that bothered about the flooring. There's been such a sudden shift in our relationship, that I guess he doesn't want to be anywhere near me, and I can't really blame him. This is the very reason I was so reluctant to tell him the truth.

'Do they know?' I nod towards Vince and the others outside. 'About me?'

Oliver shrugs. 'I haven't told them and they haven't mentioned it to me.'

Blimey, Mrs McColl must be losing her gossipy touch.

'Is that all you wanted to talk about?' Oliver folds his arms across his chest, that blank look still dulling his features.

'No.' I'm hovering by the sofa, hands wringing. Do I sit or remain standing? 'I was hoping you'd help me.'

Oliver barks out a laugh, his features finally forming an expression, though I wish it wasn't such a cruel looking one. 'You want my help? For what? Do you need a cover story? A pretend husband or business partner? Who are you lying to this time?'

I decide to sit, mainly because my legs have turned to jelly. I'm not a fan of confrontation at the best of times, but when it's against someone I was close to just days earlier, it's doubly discomforting.

'I don't need you to lie for me.' I swallow the lump of dread in my throat. This was a bad idea. A very bad idea, but I can't back out now. 'I want to put things right. With the animal sanctuary.' I feel the need to clarify, since it's quite clear I'll never be able to put things right between Oliver and I. 'I want to raise some money, hopefully enough to cover the extra cost of buying the land from Vanessa.' Oliver flinches at hearing the name in reference to its real owner but I move on quickly. 'I want to host a mini festival. This weekend.'

Oliver laughs again, but it's more of a snort than a scornful bark. '*This* weekend?'

'Yes, because then I'll be going home.' Oliver flinches once more – a tiny flicker of regret, perhaps? 'This is my only chance to do it, and I know it sounds insane but I think I could pull it off if I had a bit of help.'

Oliver's silent for a moment, his eyebrows slowly drawing together as he mulls over what I've just told him. 'What can I do? I'm a builder. I don't know anything about organising festivals. You're better off talking to Stace. She's the one who organises all the fundraising events and open days.'

'Stacey can't bear to be in the same room as me.'

'That's true, but I still don't see how I can help. Sorry.' Oliver shrugs before turning and stepping back out onto the drive. There isn't a glance back as he leaves, just the door closing gently. There's no anger or resentment, just a sadness which is worse somehow.

I watch the door for a few minutes, hoping a miracle will occur and Oliver will stride back inside, mouth wide in the smile I know so well. It doesn't happen, of course, so I force myself up off the sofa and put the kettle on. It looks like I'm on my own then, facing an impossible task. But I can't – won't – give up.

*

There are a handful of replies to emails I sent earlier when I'm back at my laptop, all declining the possibility of a booking due to the time constraints. I send off a few more enquiries but my hope plummets further each time I click the send button. I'm drafting an email to a funfair hire company when there's a knock at the guesthouse door.

'Oliver.' My mouth gapes open when I see him standing on the doorstep. Of all the people I was expecting to see on the other side of the door, Oliver is the last.

'Dianne Baxter.' He presses a folded piece of paper into my hand, already backing away before I've even managed to curl my fingers around it. 'She'll be more use than I will.' He turns then and breaks out into a run over the dug-up drive in his eagerness to get away from me. Closing the door, I unfold the piece of paper as I wander back to the sofa and find a phone number scribbled down. Dianne is the leader of the local Brownies, and I know she and her pack are always willing to lend a hand at the animal sanctuary, so perhaps she'll help me with the festival.

I phone the number straight away. Dianne's at work, but she

says she'll come over this evening. In the meantime, I settle down with my laptop and phone, dialling and emailing every contact I can find. My phone starts to ring mid-email and I leap at it when I spot Emma's name, jabbing to answer with more force than is necessary.

'Emma! Hi! It's so good to hear from you!' I need to calm down but I can't help feeling hope start to inflate again. Emma will help me. She'll tell me what to do.

'Sorry it's taken me so long to get back to you. It's been so hectic here, you wouldn't believe it.' There's a whoosh down the line as Emma puffs out a breath.

'It's okay, but I do need your help. Urgently.' I am not calming down any time soon, it seems. 'I'm pretty sure I left a file with ideas for the Heron Farm Festival in Vanessa's office, so can you see if it's in there?'

'I'm sorry, Rebecca, but I haven't seen it, and I've been in and out of Vanessa's office since you left.' Emma's tone is soothing but her words are still a massive kick in the teeth. 'What did you need it for anyway?'

I tell Emma everything, from Oliver and Stacey finding out who I really am, to Vanessa buying the neighbouring land and offering to sell it for a profit.

'I want to organise a mini autumn festival for this weekend, like the Heron Farm Festival but on a smaller scale, so I can raise the money to cover the extra cost. I had some really good contacts in the file that I really need to get my hands on.'

There's a pause before Emma speaks, and when she finally does, her tone is so motherly, I want to curl up on the sofa, snuggling up to the scatter cushions.

'Oh, sweetie. Do you really think you can organise an event like this in … what? Five days?'

'Yes. Maybe. I don't know. But I have to try.'

'But why? These people have turned their backs on you because you told a little white lie. Nobody died. Nobody got hurt.' I think

Oliver was quite badly bruised, but Emma's on a roll so I can't get a word in. 'Why are you putting yourself through all this stress when you're leaving in a few days and returning to your normal, everyday life?'

'Because I feel responsible for the mess they're in. And it isn't just about Stacey and Oliver. I need to prove to Vanessa that I can do this.'

'What, organise an event with little to no money and with just days to do it in?'

'When you put it like that …' It sounds ridiculous. Unattainable. Pointless. 'But I need to show her that I can do it. That I can be creative. That I can put together an event, or at least be part of a team that does. I'm tired of being Vanessa's PA. It isn't the job I want, what I worked so hard for. I need to prove to Vanessa – to myself – that I'm capable.'

It may be an impossible task, but I'm determined to pull it off. To prove I'm worthy of the promotion. To show Oliver and Stacey that they were right to put their trust in me and that I was right to follow my own dreams instead of allowing Dad to dictate the rest of my life.

Chapter 37

There's a minor hiccup over a tin of magnolia paint at the house late afternoon (there is *no way* Vanessa would have chosen magnolia, even if the correct shade – Soft Jasmine Blush – is almost identical in shade), but I'm able to concentrate on the festival for the rest of the day and reinforcements arrive just before seven. I was only expecting Dianne, but she's brought along a small committee who are willing to help out. As well as the Brownies leader, Julia from the Farmer's troops into the guesthouse, followed by Elsie from the charity shop and, most surprisingly, Mrs McColl.

'I'll help out on one condition.' Mrs McColl issues an icy glare as she unwinds the woollen scarf from around her neck. 'You do not tell Stacey about this. *Nobody* tells her, okay? Because I won't let her get her hopes up again if we can't pull this off. Is that clear?'

I bob my head up and down in a terrified acknowledgement as I take the scarf from her. 'That's perfectly clear. And under-standable, under the circumstances.'

I decide now is the best time to explain the 'circumstances', but it seems everybody in the room is well aware of my part in the auction debacle, including my true identity. Mrs McColl refuses to meet my eye, so I assume she's helped in the spreading of the gossip after all. Still, it feels good to have everything out in the open for a change.

'Right.' I clap my hands together once the confession is over and done with. 'Shall we get on with festival planning? We have a very small budget to work with and I'm having trouble sourcing rides and attractions at such short notice, so I'm aiming to provide entertainment for the festival goers as cheaply and innovatively as possible. I have some ideas, but I'd love your input too. Shall I put the kettle on before we get started?'

'I'd love a cup of tea, thanks.' Dianne reaches into her handbag and produces a spiralbound notepad and pen. 'No sugar. Tiny bit of milk, please.' She settles back on the sofa, crossing one leg over the other and opening the notepad. 'I've been thinking about your festival and jotting down ideas.' She smiles at me and shrugs. 'Slow day at the office. Anyway, I can definitely help you out with some bits and pieces we've collected over the years for our Christmas and summer fairs.'

I'm bending down to grab a handful of mugs from the cupboard, but I straighten up, my attention well and truly hooked. 'Like what?'

Dianne consults her notepad and counts off the items on her fingers as she lists them. 'We have a candyfloss machine and a chocolate fountain, which are always popular at this kind of thing, and a popcorn maker. A proper one, not one of the little ones you have for your kitchen. Cost a fortune. We had a Brownie fundraiser for it and everything. Still, it's made its money back over the past couple of years.' Dianne looks back down at her notes. 'And we have a small selection of giant board games – snakes and ladders, drafts, Connect Four, Jenga, that kind of thing. Very family-friendly and won't cost a penny.'

I want to hug her. I seriously want to leap onto the sofa and squeeze the woman until she pops.

But I don't.

Obviously.

That would be weird.

'That's amazing. I don't know how to thank you.'

'I do.' Dianne winks at me. 'I know my pack would absolutely love to help out on the day, and it would really help them work towards their badges. A few of them are working towards their circus performer badge, for example, so if they could showcase their skills at the festival, that would really help them out.'

'Of course. In fact, one of my ideas was a talent contest, so that would fit right in.' The beauty of a talent contest is the festival-goers will provide the entertainment themselves, with only the costs of prizes for me to deal with out of my savings.

Julia raises her hand, as though she's back in the classroom. 'How about a karaoke competition too? You could borrow our equipment.'

'That would be brilliant, thank you.' I shove my head into the cupboard under the pretence of grabbing more mugs, but the truth is I'm getting a bit choked up here. These people are willing to put aside the fact that I've lied to them over the past few weeks and help me out. They're under no illusions of who I am. They know I'm just plain old Rebecca Riley. I have no power or prestige, and I haven't had to scream and shout to get my way.

'Obviously, you can leave the cake stall to me.' Mrs McColl leans in towards Dianne. 'Though if you have any Brownies working towards their baking badge, the help would be appreciated.'

We continue the discussion over cups of tea and coffee, and I'm feeling so positive by the time I'm showing Dianne and the others to the door that I practically float across the living room. Dianne is going to set her pack the task of spreading the word as far and wide as they can, plus Julia and Elsie are going to use their positions within the community to get the word out. Tomorrow, I'll design and print posters and drop stacks off at the church hall, ready for the Brownies to distribute, and the pub and charity shop. I'm also going to set up a Facebook page to publicise the event outside the village and hopefully entice festival goers from further afield.

Maybe, just maybe, I think as I flop down on the sofa, we may just pull this off.

*

I'm impressed by the work that has been carried out in the house, and I feel a sense of pride as I move around the living room. It's my favourite room of the whole house so far. Already a huge space with its double aspect windows and super-high ceilings, the magnolia (sorry, Soft Jasmine Blush) on the walls make the room feel never-ending and full of light. A feature wall is covered in a delicate floral pattern, with the palest pink and mint green shimmering in the light. I can see the progress made on the garden through the bi-fold doors to the back of the room, and already there has been a vast improvement. The grass has been trimmed to create a luscious lawn, the new fence has been put in place, and the trees and bushes have been cut back to reveal an even bigger plot than before. Space has been cleared for the decking and patio areas, and tomorrow we're expecting a huge delivery of flowers and shrubs to fill the garden with colour and life.

Movement out on the drive catches my eye, and I see the builders have arrived back from their lunch break, making their way across the drive where the block paving is starting to take shape. The builders now know about my true identity and have reacted in very different ways; Vince seems let down that I deceived him, though he hasn't said as much and has simply avoided eye contact and conversation as much as possible, while Harvey thinks it's hilarious and has wondered (out loud) whether it would have counted as a threesome if we'd slept together. I'm not sure Todd has fully taken on board the change, bless him.

'Oliver, can I have a quick word?' I'm moving carefully over the newly laid drive, mindful of undoing the guys' hard work.

'I'm a bit busy.' He indicates the stack of paving blocks still to be laid. 'Can it wait?'

'No, it can't.' Taking my key out of my pocket, I unlock the guesthouse door. 'I'm sure Vince can spare you for five minutes. Right, Vince?' I don't wait for an answer and instead step into the guesthouse. Luckily, Oliver dutifully follows, and this time he makes it further than the doormat, throwing himself sulkily into the armchair.

'I need your help.' Grabbing the sketch I've put together for the layout of the festival, I set it out on the coffee table.

'You're really doing this?' Oliver shuffles forward so he can look at the plans in more detail. We have lots going on, from the karaoke and talent contests, to a candlelit pumpkin parade and fireworks display, as well as an array of food and drink options.

'Yep. It's all coming together really well. We have a Facebook page and everything.' I turn the laptop so Oliver can see the screen. The page is already open and I notice we've hit the two hundred likes milestone. There's a real buzz building up in the comments section, with people excited and curious about the festival. We've already had registrations for the talent contest and four bands have signed up to take part in the battle of the bands we're hosting, including Todd's band, which I'd had no idea he was part of until now. We've also had donations for raffle prizes, including a three-treatment voucher from a spa a couple of miles away, admission to a food festival that will be taking place at Durban Castle, and a hamper of fresh fruit and vegetables from the allotment.

The newly formed festival committee have been a godsend, especially with Julia's position behind the bar at the Farmer's. One of her customers has a nephew who runs a burger van, and although he was booked for this weekend, he did provide contact details for acquaintances, and we now have mobile catering booked for jacket potatoes, Mexican food, burgers and hot dogs, veggie fare and donuts. Plus, the bloke who runs the local ice cream van is also a regular at the Farmer's, and he's agreed to pitch up and sell his treats.

Oliver wafts a hand over the plans. 'You've seriously organised all this? For this weekend?'

I nod, my cheeks starting to warm at the awe in Oliver's voice. 'But the thing is, we need a small stage. For the talent contest and stuff.' I place my hands together and adopt my best puppy dog expression. 'Dominic has some pallets and old planks of wood, but he needs help putting it together.' I widen my eyes further, hoping they convey just how much I need Oliver's help and prevent him from telling me to get stuffed.

'Fine.' It's a dull, monosyllabic word, puffed out on a sigh, but I want to perform a happy little jig. 'Tell Dominic I'll be over once we've finished here.' Oliver thrusts his thumb over his shoulder, indicating the drive before he slopes off back to work. With two days to go before Vanessa arrives for the grand reveal and the festival is opened, the builders are almost finished, the gardeners are transforming the outdoor space at a mind-boggling pace, and the decorators have sprinkled a whole vat of fairy dust on the interior. Tomorrow, with the drive complete and clear of debris and equipment, the furniture, household appliances and decorative pieces Vanessa has been holding in storage will arrive, ready to transform the house into a home. I can't quite believe I've managed to pull this project off, though there's no way I could have done it without the builders' hard work. I owe them, big time. But I also need to give myself a pat on the back too.

Grabbing a bin liner from the cupboard under the kitchen sink, I march into the bedroom and open the wardrobe. The space is stuffed with Vanessa-inspired clothes. The burgundy leather skirt that caught my eye from the charity shop's window, the white pussy-bow blouse, the wide leg jumpsuit. I fold them carefully and place them into the bin liner, along with all the other clothes I've accumulated during my stay in Little Heaton that just aren't me. Tailored trousers, leather-look leggings, silk blouses. In the bin liner they go, until all I'm left with are leggings, jeans and T-shirts. I even toss in the peep-toe boots. I never did like them.

It's so satisfying tying the bag, closing off that chapter in my life and shedding the pretence. I will no longer pretend to be someone else and hide behind their personality. I'll drop these items off at the charity shop and then I'll be free to be me. Rebecca Riley. Nothing more, nothing less, because she's good enough. Always has been and always will be.

Chapter 38

It's the morning of the festival, with two hours before the gates will open, and I'm already frazzled. I barely slept last night and when I finally did succumb to slumber, my alarm snapped me awake again almost immediately. There's so much to do, so much to organise, but luckily I've had Dianne and Dominic on hand to help, plus a dozen excited Brownies. Even Oliver's turned up to help with setting up, which I'm both surprised by and eternally grateful for.

The generators are up and running and we have toilet facilities on site, and most of the catering vans are here. Dominic is directing the caterers into the right places according to my plans while I'm busy setting up the Trick or Treat Treasure Trail, hiding the clues the children will soon be following in order to earn their goody bag prizes. We've still got to set up the stalls, place the bales of hay Dominic has provided for seating in strategic places, and put out the oversized board games Dianne has loaned to us for the day. The community has really come together, with villagers taking up stalls to sell their crafty creations, allotment produce, and homemade beauty products.

'Where do you want these, love?' A van driver sticks his head out of the open window as he approaches, and I direct him to the other side of the field, hurrying to catch up so I can held unload the bulk order of pumpkins that will later be carved by festival goers and displayed in a pumpkin parade at nightfall. With battery-operated tealights, it should look magical.

Afterwards, I set up the story time corner for our younger visitors, which was Dianne's idea. A different Halloween-themed children's story will be read by one of the Brownies every hour, which I love because not only does it cater to the family-friendly feel of the festival, it's also cost-free entertainment as we've borrowed the books for the day.

The field starts to fill up as opening time approaches, with the rest of the catering vans finally turning up, along with the balloon modeller and face-painters Mrs McColl organised, having had a sneaky look in Stacey's contacts, and the bands lug their equipment towards the stage. There's already a buzz of activity outside the field as people queue, and I feel a half-happy, half-queasy sensation in my stomach as I realise there are only a matter of minutes to go.

'You've done a great job here, Rebecca.' I press a hand to my chest as Oliver's sudden presence behind me makes me jump. 'I can't believe you pulled it off in such a short space of time.'

'*I* can't believe I managed to pull it off.' And it's true. I never knew I had this in me, not deep down. I never knew I could take an idea and run with it. That I could lead a team, organise an event, be a success. But I did it, and I did it as myself.

'Do you think Stacey will come?' Mrs McColl has popped over to the animal sanctuary to finally break the news about what we've been cooking up over the past few days, now it seems we've pulled it off.

'I hope so.' Oliver looks around, at the stalls and the entertainment we've organised for the day. 'She should see how much effort you've put into all this.'

'Do you think she'll ever forgive me?'

Oliver places a hand on my arm, and I try not to read too

much into the contact but fail miserably and feel a flutter of hope in my chest. 'She knows you didn't do anything maliciously, and we can't really blame you for your boss's actions.'

'Really?' There's that flutter again. Stronger, almost taking my breath away. But Oliver removes his hand and starts to back away.

'Really.' He gives a firm nod, but he's still backing away. 'I'll see you around, yeah?'

I open my mouth, to ask if he can ever forgive me, but I'm pretty sure I'm about to burst into tears. Instead, I close my mouth tight to ward off any sobs, raise my hand in farewell and turn and flee before I make a fool of myself.

*

I don't have time to cry. I don't even have time to think about Oliver and how badly I've messed up as the festival kicks off with an almighty bang, with hordes of people piling into the Blackwoods' field. A couple of the Brownies and their parents are manning the tables acting as a ticket booth, but I step in to help keep the flow of visitors going. It's so busy, I miss the start of the first round of the talent contest, and I have to dash across to the stage in time to catch Harvey's stand-up routine, which definitely isn't family-friendly. Elsie, who has stepped away from her tombola stall to act as one of the judges, is far from impressed and I see her cross out Harvey's name on her notepad with such force, I'm sure the pen cuts through several layers of paper. I hold on long enough to watch the Brownies perform their newly acquired circus skills before I have to slip away from the festival and hurry back to the house as Vanessa is due any minute for the grand tour. I'm nervous and excited to show off the house all at the same time, which leaves me feeling jittery and on the verge of hysterics as I jog across the footbridge.

I have so much to show Vanessa, so much to be proud of, but I know how temperamental my boss can be. Will she still like the wallpaper she picked out for the second floor master bedroom months ago? Will she appreciate the workmanship that went into the coving in the living room? Or the man-hours it took to lay the bespoke flooring? And what will she think about the festival? It seems like a huge success from where I'm standing, but Vanessa may view it differently.

I have to slow down and take deep, even breaths as I reach Arthur's Pass, partly because I'm out of puff due to legging it across the village, and partly because I'm in danger of hyperventilating through fear when I spot Vanessa's red mini pulling up in the drive ahead. She's here. Vanessa is here. It's judgement time.

Picking up speed again, I reach the drive just as Vanessa is emerging from her car, smoothing down the black lace pencil skirt of her dress. With a flick of her wrist, the door closes as she strides towards the stone steps that lead up to the house.

'Vanessa. Hi!' My voice is a wheeze as I canter across the drive, hand waving to catch her attention. She turns to aim her fob at the car and spots me, a look of bemusement on her face as I stagger to a halt in front of her, hands resting on my thighs as I try to catch my breath.

'Are you alright, Becky?' Vanessa peers at me. 'Do you need a glass of water or something?'

I shake my head, still gulping greedily at the air. 'I'm fine. Really. Shall we go inside?' I waft a hand towards the house before it flops back down to my thigh again.

'Ooh, yes.' Vanessa rubs her hands together as she strides towards the steps. 'I'm so looking forward to this! Is it beautiful? Please tell me it's as beautiful as I imagine.'

'It's stunning.' I stagger after Vanessa, handing over the key once we reach the door as I don't have the energy required to gain entry myself. Vanessa slots the key in the door and twists, pausing dramatically before she pushes the door open. She's mid-stride over the threshold when she stops with a gasp, her hand covering her mouth as she gazes around the welcoming space of the hallway. Light is flooding in through the huge windows, making the highly-polished tiles sparkle. With a white, high-gloss finish to the walls, staircase and furniture, the room is gleaming and appears to never end, but there are splashes of colour in the vases of flowers on each windowsill, vibrant hues of pinks and green on the upholstery of the wooden bench and storage unit, and framed prints catching the eye on the walls.

'Well, this is simply divine, isn't it?' Vanessa steps fully into the house, turning three hundred and sixty degrees in slow motion as she takes in every little detail. She moves towards the staircase, her hand resting on the newel post as a tiny sigh escapes. She's beaming when she turns back towards me. I don't think I've ever seen Vanessa genuinely beam before. It's rather unsettling.

'Would you like to see the kitchen?' I'm still feeling a bit jittery but my breathing is more level now. 'There's champagne in the fridge.'

Vanessa looks down at her watch. It isn't yet lunchtime. 'Oh, go on then. But just the tiniest drop for me. I need to be back in Manchester for three – Ty's whisking me off to Vienna for our six-month anniversary. Don't worry, I'll be back for the party next week.' She clip-clops across the gleaming tiles as I do the maths in my head.

'Hasn't it only been, like, four months?'

'Four and a half.' Vanessa gasps again as she reaches the kitchen, this time her delight propelling her forward into the room. 'But Ty's been booked for a shoot, so he's taking me with him for an early romantic getaway.' She runs her hand along the glossy work surface. 'How sweet is that?'

'Very sweet.' I grab the champagne from the fridge and set it down on the island. 'There's something I want to show you, though, before you leave.'

'Hmm?' Vanessa drags her eyes away from the futuristic-looking coffee machine and turns to me, meeting my eye before something catches her attention over my shoulder. She gasps again before scurrying across the room and throwing open the bi-fold doors. 'Oh. My. *Goodness*.' She steps carefully onto the decking, her eyes moving left and right as she tries to take the huge garden in. 'Just look at this. It's … it's …' Vanessa shakes her head, her mouth opening and shutting without producing any more words. I have never known Vanessa to be speechless. This, too, is rather unsettling. 'I just can't believe it.' Vanessa turns to me, beaming again. 'Get that champagne open, Becky. We need to toast this triumph!' She totters back into the kitchen, clapping her hands together. 'The party is going to be *amazing*. I *knew* I could count on you!' She joins me at the island as I place two gold-rimmed flutes on the surface. I offer the bottle of champagne to Vanessa, for her to do the honours, but she shakes her head and waggles her manicured fingers at me. 'I have to say, though, I am looking forward to having you back in the office.'

'You are?' I've never actually popped a cork before, and it isn't as easy as it looks. I'm basically gurning as I twist the bottle, anticipating the sudden pop as the cork is released.

'Gosh, yes.' Vanessa pulls out a stool and hops up onto it. 'Don't get me wrong, I love Emma *to pieces* but she's more of a creative person, you know? She hasn't got a clue when it comes to organising my work life. My filing cabinets are *horrendous*, so good luck with that when you get back.' Vanessa giggles, jumping slightly as the cork pops.

'The thing is, Vanessa …' I pour a drop of champagne into Vanessa's glass and hand it to her. 'I was hoping to move into a more creative role myself when I returned.'

'You were?' Vanessa frowns at me as she raises the glass to her lips, as though baffled by my aspirations.

'I never planned to be a PA forever.' I pour myself a large measure and take a huge gulp while Vanessa sips her thimbleful. 'It was more of a stepping stone. I have a degree in events management.'

'That's right, you do!' Vanessa places her empty glass down.

'And we do need to replace Sonia …' Vanessa taps her chin with a red-tipped finger.

'Sonia's left?' I almost choke on my champagne, the bubbles making my nose sting.

'There was a little … drama back at the office.' She purses her lips, her foot tapping against her stool. 'I may have accused her of sleeping with Tyler behind my back and things got a bit ugly. The next thing I know, she's shouting abuse at me, accusing me of being manipulative and a nightmare boss, and saying she quits.' Vanessa shakes her head, her hand on her chest. 'It was most upsetting.' She sits up straighter and gives my hand a pat. 'Although it means we have a vacancy on the team, I was going to offer the role to Emma. She really has stepped up to the mark these past few weeks, and I'm not sure you're quite ready to move up, but it's certainly something we can look at in the future. Maybe you could sit in on a few meetings?' Hooking her handbag onto her arm, Vanessa starts to move towards the hallway again. 'Come and show me the master suite. I can't wait to see if it matches up to my mood board.'

Pouring a bit more champagne into my glass, I tip it down my throat before dashing after Vanessa, reaching her as she's about to take her first step up the staircase.

'Actually, Vanessa, I do think I'm ready.' My pulse is racing and I feel a bit sick from terror and knocking back the champagne too fast. This isn't me. I don't stand up for myself. I am meek. A pushover. I don't ever go for what I want. But where has that got me in the past?

Squaring my shoulders, I tilt my chin and use my most commanding tone. 'I'm more than ready, and I can prove it.'

Chapter 39

'Why are you showing me this?'

Vanessa and I are standing outside the gates of the Blackwoods' fields, taking in the crowds. And they are vast. There are *so many* people, I can't quite believe my eyes.

'This is Little Heaton's first ever autumn festival.' Vanessa is giving me a blank look, and I hear the slightest puff a sigh. She's a busy woman and I'm keeping her from her exotic, whisking-away-to-foreign-lands plans. I need to get to the point, and fast. 'And I organised it.'

There's a pause as Vanessa looks from me to the festival, her eyebrows inching up her forehead very, very slowly before she turns back to me again. 'You put all this together?' She jabs a finger towards the middle of the field without taking her eyes off mine. 'On your own?'

'Not entirely. I had a bit of help from some of the locals.' I crane my neck, trying to spot Dianne or one of the other committee members, but the field is crammed and I don't stand a chance.

'But you organised it?'

I nod. 'It was my idea.'

'But why?'

I explain about the fundraising motivation as we make our way into the heart of the festival. The first round of the talent show has ended but there's still plenty going on around us. One of Dianne's Brownies is enthralling a bunch of pre-schoolers with a *Winnie the Witch* story in the spooky book corner, and I point her out to Vanessa.

'This is …' Vanessa shakes her head and puffs out a breath. '… incredible. I had no idea you had this in you, Becky.' My smile falters at the shortening of my name, but I manage to push it back into place. 'You've been hiding your talents away all this time, you little minx. We'll definitely be having a chat once I'm back from Vienna.'

I want to jump up and punch the air. I've actually done it! My dream job is practically mine, curled up in the palm of my hand.

'Will you excuse me?' Vanessa places a hand briefly on my arm before she digs into her handbag for her ringing phone. 'It's probably Ty, panicking that I'll be late for the flight.' She rolls her eyes. 'He's such a worrier, bless him.'

I edge away as Vanessa takes the call, keeping her in my eyeline as I check in on Dianne, who's supervising the pumpkin carving.

'The fancy dress parade will be starting in ten minutes.' She wipes her hands on a towel as I glance back at Vanessa. 'Oliver's volunteered to man the ticket booth so Talia can take part.'

'He has?' I'm pleasantly surprised that Oliver has offered his services, but then he is a good bloke and I shouldn't be surprised that he's coming to the aid of the Brownies at all.

'Shall we?' Dianne nods towards the stage, which has been allocated for the meeting point for those wanting to take part in the parade.

I glance back at Vanessa, who's still on the phone. 'Can I catch you up in a few minutes?'

'Of course.' Dianne pats me on the shoulder before she makes her way across the field, gathering zombie princesses, witches and superheroes on the way. Vanessa is still occupied with her call so I take out my own phone and am about to dial Emma's number to share my news when it dawns on me that I may have just usurped my best friend. Vanessa said she was going to offer the role to Emma, but now it looks as though I'm in the running for Sonia's replacement too. Guilt gnaws at my gut as I slip my phone back in my pocket. What am I going to do? I can't steal Emma's promotion from under her nose, but I can't give up on my own dreams either. I deserve this promotion just as much as Emma, so I guess the decision lies with Vanessa. Maybe, if we both prove our worth, there will be a place for both of us on the team.

Ahead, Vanessa has finished her call and is pushing her phone back into her handbag. I hurry to join her.

'The fancy dress parade is about to start if you'd like to watch?'

'There are a couple of things I'd like to clear up first after that very interesting conversation.' Vanessa folds her arms across her chest and quirks an eyebrow. 'I'd *love* to know why you lied to me just now when you told me it was *you* who organised this event. And secondly – and most importantly of all – I'd be *delighted* if you could explain why you've been pretending to be me for the past few weeks.'

I'm so shocked by Vanessa's rapid switch from being enchanted by the festival to being so hopping mad her face is taking on a rather puce hue, her actual words don't click straight away. I simply stand before her, my mouth gaping like a horrified goldfish as she rants at me, her arms flailing and nostrils flaring as she tells me exactly what she thinks of me and the festival that moments ago was 'incredible' but is now a suspicious-looking stain on my career.

'I put my trust in you and you've abused it. You've been sneaky and duplicitous. You've stolen ideas from the company and passed them off as your own. Did you think I wouldn't notice?' Vanessa's arms stops flailing and she opens them wide, her fingers splayed as she awaits my answer. I swallow hard and try not to wet myself under her furious scrutiny.

'I, erm …' I try to swallow again but my mouth has completely dried up. 'I'm sorry, for using your name. That was stupid of me, and I've paid the price, believe me.'

Vanessa snorts. 'Believe *you*? Why on earth would I trust a word that comes out of your mouth now?'

I nod, totally getting her point of view. It's a shared opinion of me in recent days. 'It wasn't a malicious thing. Not at all.' I look around the field, wondering who has ratted me out, because there's no way Tyler knew anything about my identity slip-up. Mrs McColl isn't too far away, but she seems pretty busy on her toffee apple stall, and Vanessa was never out of my sight. 'It was a mistake, to begin with. One of the builders misheard me and thought I was you, and I sort of let him.'

'And stealing Emma's ideas for the Heron Farm Festival?' Vanessa places her arms carefully across her chest. 'Was that a *mistake* too?'

The horrified goldfish is back as I stare at Vanessa. 'I have absolutely no idea what you're talking about. I haven't stolen anybody's ideas. I've only used my own.'

Vanessa unfolds her arms so she can jab a finger at something behind me. 'The Trick or Treat Treasure Trail?'

I turn towards one of the stalls near the entrance to the field, where several children are busily decorating the paper bags that they will collect treats in as they make their way through the festival, collecting a sweet or chocolate whenever they see the treasure trail's pumpkin logo on a stall or attraction.

'That was one of the ideas Emma pitched to us a few weeks ago.' Vanessa reaches into her bag and produces one of the leaflets I handed to her from the ticket booth earlier, which she folded and shoved into her handbag without glancing at. She studios it now before jabbing a finger angrily at the sheet of paper. 'And this! The night-time pumpkin parade. That's come straight from Emma's proposal. And the Monster Hunt. Let me guess – the children have to find the pictures of monsters around the festival, which each have a letter underneath them. Then, once they've found all the letters, they have to rearrange them to make a spooky word and win a prize. Am I right?'

'Yes.' I frown. 'How did you know?'

'*Because you stole the idea from Emma.*' Vanessa leans towards me, speaking slowly and carefully. 'And I bet most of the ideas here have been taken straight from Emma's proposal.'

'What proposal?' Emma never said a word to me about pitching any ideas to Vanessa. She told me she'd sat in on a meeting or two to take notes, that's all.

'Emma came to me a few weeks ago with a proposal for the Heron Farm Festival. It's what earned her a provisional place on the events team.'

Emma has had a creative part on the team? Why didn't she tell me?

'Most of her ideas have been copied here.' Vanessa spreads her arms wide. 'I could fire you for this. I *should* fire you for this.'

A tremor has started, somewhere deep in my belly, and it's spreading out, making my fingers quiver and my knees tremble. The dream of gaining Vanessa's approval and respect, the promotion and finally freeing myself of Lee and the grim flat-share is slipping away from me and I don't think I can clutch it again.

'There's been some mistake.' There's a wobble to my voice as I battle a torrent of tears that are preparing to activate.

'Yes, you've already told me that.' Vanessa shoves the leaflet back into her handbag, not even bothering to fold it this time so it crumples into a corner.

'No, another mistake. One that isn't my fault.' The wobble's still there, but less so. I need Vanessa to hear me and I'm determined to make myself heard this time. 'I didn't steal any ideas. Not from Emma or anybody else. I had a proposal of my own, with all my ideas for the Heron Farm Festival in there. I left it behind at the office before I came here.'

I cover my mouth to stifle a gasp as it all becomes perfectly clear. But no. Emma wouldn't have taken my proposal and passed it off as her own. We're friends, *best friends*, and she isn't that kind of person.

'Was that Emma on the phone just now?' My question is whispered, because I'm not sure I want to know the answer.

'I don't have time for this.' Vanessa snaps her handbag shut and starts to walk away. 'I have a flight to catch. Schedule a meeting for us on Tuesday afternoon and we'll discuss your future at Vanessa Whitely Events – if you even have one, that is.'

The tremor has increased, making my body practically vibrate on the spot. The dream isn't so much slipping away, it's packed its bags and jetted off to start a new life somewhere else, and the worst part is, I'm not to blame this time. I didn't steal Emma's ideas – I had no idea what her input on the Heron Farm Festival entailed until now.

'I can't wait until Friday.' I'm taken aback by the voice that emerges from me, strong and confident and without a hint of the wobble I'm feeling so powerfully inside. 'I need to know what's going to happen to me now.'

Vanessa stops and turns back towards me, but she doesn't move any closer. 'I don't know what's going to happen to you. I need time to mull it over.'

'But this is my life we're talking about.' I squeeze my fingers tight into a fist against the tremble. 'And it isn't fair of you to leave me hanging while you go off on holiday with your boyfriend.' I try not to yelp in fright as Vanessa stalks back towards me, her eyebrows pushing up towards her hairline.

'Maybe I should fire you right now. Save you the injustice of waiting a few days while I decide what's right for my business.'

'Maybe you should fire me.' My knees are like balls of jelly, and should be incapable of keeping my body upright, but somehow I'm still standing. 'Maybe you'd be doing me a massive favour, because my talents are wasted at Vanessa Whitely Events. Just take a look around you.' I throw my arms out wide, ignoring the way they jitter. 'I organised this. Me, not Emma. I didn't steal her ideas. In fact, I suspect she's stolen *my* ideas and passed them onto you as her own.' The thought makes me want to weep and throw up in equal measure, because it can't be true, can it? My friend wouldn't do that to me. 'I'm not a PA, and I'm not a project manager for a property development. I'm an events planner and maybe it's time I moved on to somewhere where I'll be appreciated. Somewhere my boss doesn't lie and manipulate to get what she wants. You push and push, Vanessa, but eventually people will get sick and tired of it and walk away. Like Sonia did.'

Vanessa really is like my father. They're both bullies who don't know when to stop. Just like Vanessa has pushed Sonia too far, Dad pushes away everyone he cares about, starting with Mum all those years ago. With horror, I realise I'm following in his footsteps. I've somehow lost everyone I care about, including the sister who is still reaching out to me. Kate phoned me again this morning and I sent it to voicemail because I was too busy setting up the festival. How long will it be before she gives up and I'll be truly alone? I didn't intend for any of this to happen, but then I don't think Dad pushes people away on purpose either. He has high expectations and dismisses those who fail to live up to them. A bit like Vanessa. But I refuse to be a part of it anymore.

'I used to think I respected you, Vanessa, and wanted to be like you, but I was wrong. I didn't respect you, I feared you, and there's no way I'd want to be anything like you anymore. You don't care about anyone but yourself. All this is because you selfishly bought a bit of useless land.' I stretch my arms wide. 'But one day your actions will bite you on the arse and you'll find yourself on your own. Is that why you cling onto Tyler? You think he's sleeping around and yet you're still with him, celebrating an anniversary that hasn't even happened yet.'

'You're overstepping the line now, Becky. And you're *this close* to being fired.' Vanessa growls the words as she holds up her finger and thumb to demonstrate my precarious position. But I won't back down this time.

'*My name is Rebecca*. And you can save yourself the bother of firing me, because I quit.'

Chapter 40

The freshly-carved Jack-o'-lanterns look beautiful as they pass, each design unique to its owner, their battery-operated candles glowing and flickering in the evening light. The festival has been a huge success, but I can't quite bask in the glory. Maybe in a few days, once the shock of losing not only my job and future prospects but my best friend in one afternoon has died down. Because Vanessa accepted my resignation without a murmur of protest before she headed off for her romantic getaway. And when I finally managed to get hold of Emma, she confirmed my worst fears. She'd found my file on Vanessa's desk after I'd left for Little Heaton, switched the front cover to display her own name and taken credit for my hard work.

'How could you do that to me?' Even as she was saying the words, I couldn't comprehend the facts. 'We were friends.'

'We *are* friends.' I'd wanted to laugh at the absurdity of Emma's words but I didn't have it in me. 'But I deserved that promotion too. You always go on about how fed up you are being Vanessa's PA, but what about me? I've been stuck on that reception desk for two years. My talents are being wasted just as much as yours are, and it isn't as though you were ever going to do anything with that file. You had it in your hand, for goodness' sake, and you still didn't show it to Vanessa. You didn't make her see that you're creative and talented. You let her walk all over you, and you'll always let people walk all over you.'

But that isn't true, not anymore. Because I finally did stand up to Vanessa; I just wish I hadn't had to sacrifice my job in order to do so.

'This is beautiful.'

I turn to see Stacey standing beside me, looking wistfully out at the sea of lit-up pumpkins. Oliver passed by a moment ago, helping a little boy carry a pumpkin that was bigger than his head.

'You've done an amazing job.'

'Thank you.' I turn away from Stacey and watch the parade. So much has happened over the past few weeks, my stomach is in knots and I don't think I'll be able to untie it again. 'There's been a great turnout. I'm pretty sure we'll have raised enough to cover the extra cost of the land.'

'Really?'

I don't dare look at Stacey – the hope in her voice is hard enough to take. 'But whether or not Vanessa will stick to her side of the deal is another matter.' My eyes are firmly on the pumpkin parade, though I'm no longer taking in the details. 'I quit my job today, so Vanessa isn't my biggest fan.'

'What happened?' I'm expecting Stacey to blow up, but she sounds genuinely concerned and when she touches my arm with her hand, it all becomes too much and the emotions I've been bottling up since the confrontation this afternoon rises to the surface. The frustration and anger, the hurt and betrayal, the grief of letting go of a long-held dream all manifest themselves as a gush of tears. Pulling me aside, Stacey guides me towards a hay bale and pushes down gently on my shoulders until I'm sitting down. I tell her everything that has happened, trying and failing to stop another flood of tears. It's all been for nothing. I've hurt people and let them down, and for what?

'It hasn't been for nothing.' Stacey has been rubbing soothing circles into my back as I recount my afternoon from hell. 'Look at what you've achieved.' She indicates the pumpkin parade, which is about to come to an end and make way for the firework finale. 'Everybody has had such a wonderful time today, and even if Vanessa decides not to sell the land after all, so what? We'll work something out.'

'But I've let you down, again.'

Stacey shakes her head. 'You've done no such thing. You've done everything you possibly could for the sanctuary, and I'm so grateful for that. It's out of our hands now.'

'You don't hate me?'

Stacey nudges me with her elbow. 'Of course I don't hate you, you dork. And there's someone else who doesn't hate you. In fact, I'd say he's pretty smitten with you.' She points out her brother, who's relieving the little boy of the giant pumpkin and giving him a high-five.

'I'm not so sure about that, but it doesn't matter anyway. I'm leaving tomorrow.' My shoulders slump and I'm conscious of a fresh wave of tears building. 'I can't say I'm looking forward to living with my un-housetrained flatmate again.'

'Then don't go.' Stacey shrugs, as though it's a simple answer to my problem.

'I can't stay in Vanessa's guesthouse.' I'm not entirely sure I have the right to stay there tonight, actually, but she didn't demand her keys back and it totally slipped my mind until now.

'Stay with us. It isn't as though you have a job to get back to.' She pulls a face. 'Sorry.'

'Are you serious?' Even as a temporary measure, it would be better than returning to my grotty flat.

'I will expect help with the animals as rent payment.'

'No problem. I've missed those guys.'

'And I should warn you that we've taken in a pig with a flatulence problem ...'

'I've lived with a bloke who chews his own toenails, leaves his dirty underpants on the kitchen counter and wouldn't know one end of a bath from the other. A pig with a flatulence problem would be bliss in comparison.'

'Great.' Stacey throws an arm around me and pulls me in tight. 'Do you want to tell Oliver the good news?' She tries to keep her smirk under control as she nods at her brother, who's making his way over.

'Talking about people being smitten ...' Which has the added bonus of diverting attention away from me. 'Are you ever going to do anything about your massive crush on Dominic? Because I don't think it's completely one-sided.'

'You don't?' The smirk has vanished from Stacey's face. She's looking scarily blanched of colour, even in the dim evening light. I thought she'd be jumping up and down in jubilation, but she looks like she's about to throw up on the grass.

'Who do you think threaded a million fairy lights in the trees?' I point towards the perimeter of the field, which is lit up in multicoloured lights. It looks magical. 'And who do you think set up the generators and supplied the materials for the stage and helped to build it?'

'That doesn't mean he likes me.' Stacey's voice is barely above a whisper, which is unlike my feisty friend. 'He's just a good guy.'

I roll my eyes. 'He did it for you, you dork.' I catch Stacey's eye and we both grin.

'Do you think so?'

'*Yes.*' I sit on my hands so I don't take her by the shoulders and give her a good shake. 'So one of you needs to do something about it.'

Patting me on the knee, Stacey eases herself up off the hay bale. 'I'll think about it.' She holds a hand up in greeting to her brother before she scurries away.

'Was it something I said?' Oliver drops into Stacey's vacated space on the hay bale.

'I think that was her subtle way of giving us a minute so I could tell you I'm staying in Little Heaton for a little while.' I clear my throat and look down at my feet. 'In case you were interested.'

'Obviously I'm interested.' Oliver's fingers brush against mine, but he makes no attempt to take hold of my hand. 'I've really missed you this week.'

'You have?'

I see Oliver nod out of the corner of my eye as I'm too scared to make direct eye contact. 'I've had nobody to whoop at board games.'

I laugh. I can't help it, and it feels good after the day I've had. 'There's a giant Connect Four over by the coconut shy. Fancy your chances?'

'Always.' Oliver gives a one-shouldered shrug. 'But I'd rather kiss you first.'

And he does. Just like that. No drama. No drunken passes. No revelations blowing up in our faces. Just a lovely kiss that's been a long time coming, with a firework scattering pink and green glitter in the sky to mark the occasion.

Epilogue

The butterflies take flight as soon as I step on the train, but the anticipation intensifies as we leave each station along the way behind. It's a familiar journey by now, one I make most weekends and often mid-week, and I could lose myself in a book or tune into the conversations going on around me, but I'm alert, my eyes watching as the towns turn to countryside, buildings making way for fields, people and vehicles for sheep, cows and horses. I've seen this view as winter took over from autumn, turning the golden yellows and rusty reds of the trees to bare branches dusted with snow and frost, watched as commuters added more and more layers, padding out their bodies to protect against the harsh weather. Umbrellas, woolly hats, thick gloves, sturdy boots became the norm, but over the past couple of weeks they've started to slip away. The hats were the first to go, followed by the gloves and the boots. The umbrellas are still shaken on platforms on rainy days, but I don't expect them to disappear completely. Spring may have brought milder weather and blue skies, but this is Britain we're talking about here.

The train pulls into the next station and I'm on autopilot as I start to gather my things; handbag, holdall, satchel containing my work files. I've made this journey countless times. I don't need to know which station we're leaving behind or the next one we'll be approaching in five-and-a-half minutes. It's simply second nature to pack up and make my way to the doors by now.

Oliver's waiting for me at the station, and my step quickens as I catch sight of him, the butterflies in a chaotic flurry as the smile widens on his face. He relieves me of my satchel and holdall before he kisses me, not caring that we're causing a holdup of those eager to get home and kick off their Friday evening routines.

'Sorry.' I pull Oliver out of the way, trying not to clock the glares and tuts as people flow past. You'd think we'd been parted for weeks, months, instead of the two days that have passed since we said goodbye at the station. *Two days.* Is that all it's been? That can't be right.

'I should warn you,' Oliver says as we make a move towards the car park. 'Stacey's in a flap and Mrs McColl is on the warpath.'

'What's happened?'

'The new girl dropped her best crumble dish and cracked it in two yesterday. While the crumble was still in it. Apparently, it went *everywhere*. Mrs McColl has been apoplectic about it ever since.'

'Mrs McColl is usually apoplectic about something or other. I meant what's happened with Stace?'

'Nothing in particular. Unless you count Tammy digging up the broad beans again.' Oliver opens the boot of his car and places my satchel and holdall inside. 'It's just Stace. You know how she gets when we've got an event coming up. She flaps.'

'It's all going to be fine.' I slip into the passenger seat and rub my hands together. It's spring but still quite chilly.

'*I* know that, but you know what she's like.' Oliver starts the engine and cranks up the heating. 'Plus, it's the first event since the development was completed.'

Vanessa did sell the land to Stacey after all, and waived the extra cost in the end. I wasn't sure whether to hug the woman or fall down in shock, but as I haven't actually seen Vanessa since I picked up my bits and pieces from the office shortly after my resignation, I decided to simply celebrate with Stacey and Oliver instead. The outbuildings on the land have been renovated, creating a new café and gift shop, and an education suite which is proving popular with schools and community groups. There's a new allotment, which Mrs McColl has taken charge of and Tammy, the not-so-tiny kitten, has adopted as her playground. When she isn't stalking the chickens around the yard, she likes nothing more than digging up the seedlings for sport.

'She needs to calm down.' I switch on the radio, smiling when I hear the opening to The Lightning Seed's 'Change'. 'That's what I'm here for.'

After quitting my job at Vanessa Whitely Events, I thought my life – and my dreams – were over, but it turns out this was just the beginning. After licking my wounds in Stacey's spare box room for a few days, Mrs McColl gave me a stern talking to (in which she basically told me to stop moping about the place and get a grip), and I started to search for positions in events. This time, I narrowed down my search, honing in on positions that were specific to my knowledge and experience. I wouldn't settle for a job that was vaguely connected to events this time. I had the qualifications and now, thanks to the autumn festival, I had a bit of experience too.

Finding my dream job wasn't easy, and I was lucky that Stacey and Oliver let me stay with them for a couple of rent-free months, but eventually I was offered a position at a small events company based in Warrington. We don't organise the big, flashy events like Vanessa, but I adore my job and the supportive team I work alongside. I now have my own flat a short bus ride from work as it was too much of a commute travelling from Little Heaton every day and back again, but I spend most weekends in the village with Oliver. Lately, there's been talk of Oliver moving into my one-bed flat.

'Is everything good to go?' Oliver pulls out of the station's car park and heads towards Little Heaton. 'No hiccups?'

I shake my head. 'Everything's going smoothly.'

Tomorrow, the animal sanctuary will be hosting its Easter family open day, which I've taken the lead on organising. It's the first time my boss has let me loose on a project, and hopefully, if all goes well, it won't be the last.

*

Mother Nature has looked down kindly on us today, sending a gloriously sunshiny day with a gentle, cooling breeze as we set up for the open day. Tammy is threading her way through my legs as I hide foil-wrapped eggs around the yard, trying her best to upend me. As lovely as the cat is, she can be a little minx and is definitely full of character. While her brothers found new homes once they'd been weaned, Stacey decided to adopt Tammy for herself and she's now become part of the animal sanctuary family. She's even struck up an unlikely friendship with Bianca, the sanctuary's feistiest chicken.

'Balloon modeller's here.' Stacey stumbles across the yard behind a pile of boxes. 'Dianne's taken him across to the café.'

'Is that wise? Isn't Mrs McColl still on the warpath?'

'Hmm, maybe you're right.' Stacey dumps the boxes by one of the trestle tables. They wobble but don't collapse in a heap. 'Let's hope we don't see him running screaming from the building.'

Dodging Tammy, I place an egg on the chicken coop's roof, making sure it won't roll away, while Stacey opens the box on top of the tower.

'Hello?'

The voice is sort of familiar behind me, but it *can't* belong to Vanessa. It's far too meek to belong to my former boss. But when I turn around, there she is, standing rather awkwardly in the doorway of the house.

'I thought I'd pop over and see if there's anything I can do to help?' She steps cautiously into the yard, walking slowly towards Stacey while her eyes flick nervously in my direction. Who is this woman? She looks like Vanessa. She dresses like Vanessa, in designer gear that looks severely out of place in the yard, but her manner isn't akin to the Vanessa I know, nor is her offer to help out.

'That'd be great. Thanks.' Stacey beams at my former boss and indicates the open box beside her. 'Could you put out the craft supplies on these two tables while I go and check in on the café?' Stacey catches my eye, and I know she's going to check in on Mrs McColl and make sure she hasn't made anybody else cry (the poor new girl was sobbing in the loos for over half an hour after Mrs McColl's latest tirade).

'I'll come with you.' I scurry after Stacey, almost tripping over the damn cat. 'What was that about?' I lower my voice as we head towards the new café across the yard.

'What, Vanessa?' Stacey glances behind her and I nudge her with my elbow.

'Of course Vanessa. What's she doing here?'

Stacey frowns at me. 'She's setting out the craft stall.'

I roll my eyes. 'Are you being purposefully dense?'

'Maybe.' Stacey grins at me and threads her arm through mine. 'Seriously though, this isn't the first time she's helped out. She comes over quite often. Whenever she's in the village, really.'

'Since when?'

Stacey shrugs. 'I think it was around Christmas.'

I snort. 'Do you think she was visited by three ghosts and told to mend her ways before it was too late? First she sells you the land for what she paid for it, and now she's volunteering.'

Stacey shrugs. 'Who knows, but I appreciate the help.'

'What exactly does she do here?' I can't imagine Vanessa mucking out the barn, or cleaning up chicken poop.

'She doesn't do anything too messy, obviously. I can't get her out of her designer shoes, for a start.' Stacey pushes open the café door and we listen out for sounds of distress. Luckily, there aren't any and we step inside. 'It's mainly admin stuff, really. She's much better at keeping track of the accounts than I'll ever be.'

'Why am I only hearing about this now?' I place a couple of eggs on the windowsill; I may as well while I'm here. 'And why haven't I seen her here before?'

'Because you're usually loved up with my brother.' Stacey mimes sticking her fingers down her throat. 'Nothing else matters when the two of you are together. It's sickening.'

'Like you're not the same when Dominic's around. You practically get cartoon love-heart eyes whenever he steps into a room. And he's been just as bad since you two *finally* got together.'

'Have you *seen* the man? Can you blame me? He's a god.' Stacey sighs happily before giving her head a shake. 'What were we here for again?'

I shake my own head and make my way to the back of the café, where the balloon modeller is nibbling at one of Mrs McColl's bunny-shaped biscuits.

*

The open day is in full swing, with children dashing across the yard as they search out the little chocolate eggs I've squirrelled away. The animals have been on their best behaviour and haven't, as far as I'm aware, snaffled any of the foil-wrapped treats themselves. Not even Violet, and that pig will eat *anything*.

'Rebecca, over here.' I spot my sister and her husband over by Elsie's tombola, which isn't difficult as she's pretty hard to miss these days. I head over, giving her a quick hug that still feels a bit strange, and not because she's eight months' pregnant and looks as though she's about to pop. Our sisterly relationship is fledgling, but we've both been working at it since I called Kate the day after the autumn festival.

'I guess I just wanted to tell a member of my family who wouldn't respond to the news with indifference or aggravation,' she'd said after telling me about the pregnancy.

'You've told Mum and Dad then?'

Kate had given a humourless laugh. 'Mum quickly moved the conversation on to the cruise she's going on after Christmas – I don't think she even bothered to congratulate me first – and Dad doesn't think it's the right point in my career for me to be having children. He hasn't spoken to me for two weeks and counting.'

Dad still hasn't come round to the fact he's going to be a grandfather in the next few weeks, so it looks as though he's going to push his 'perfect' daughter away too. Still, the news has brought Kate and I together again, and I can't wait to be an aunty.

'This all looks amazing.' Kate looks around the yard as she threads her arm through mine. 'You should be very proud of yourself. I'm proud of you.'

'Really?' I can't help sounding cynical. 'Even though I'm not a doctor?'

'*Because* you're not a doctor.' Kate screws up her nose and leans in close, lowering her voice. 'I never wanted to study medicine, you know, but I wasn't strong like you.'

You could seriously knock me down with one of Bianca's feathers right now. 'What did you want to be?'

Kate's cheeks start to turn pink. 'I quite fancied being an air hostess when I was younger. Can you imagine Dad's face if I'd have told him?'

We share a look, and I can't help giggling at the thought. 'It's not too late, though.'

Kate shrugs. 'Maybe one day, but I think I'm going to concentrate on this one rather than a change of career right now.' She pats her rounded stomach.

'Fair enough.' We're wandering towards the café when I remember I have a gift in my pocket for my sister. 'Here, this is for you. I saw it in the gift shop.' I hand over the cheap ring with a deep blue setting. 'It's a mood ring to replace the one I lost when we were kids.'

'That was you?' Kate laughs as she slides the ring onto her finger. 'Thank you. I'll treasure it.'

'Rebecca?' A hand reaches out and touches my arm. 'Can I have a word?' I start at the sound of the meek version of Vanessa's voice again. She's smiling at me, which is still unsettling after all this time.

'Okay.' I turn to Kate and tell her I'll meet her in the café in a minute or two before following Vanessa to a quieter part of the yard.

'Stacey tells me you organised the open day. You've done a great job.' The smile from my former boss was unsettling enough so her unexpected praise is truly disturbing.

'Thank you, but it wasn't just me. It was a team effort.'

'But you took the lead, yes?' The smile on Vanessa's face droops when I nod. 'I should have seen your potential while you were working for me, and I definitely shouldn't have put my trust in Emma.' *Me either*, I think, but I don't voice it. 'She did steal your ideas, didn't she?'

'She admitted it?'

Vanessa rolls her eyes. 'As if, but it didn't take a genius to work it out. She didn't have an original idea of her own once you left. Putting her on the team was one of the biggest mistakes I've ever made. Trusting a word that came out of her mouth was another. Did you know it was Emma who convinced me it was poor Sonia who was having an affair with Ty behind my back? She kept whispering in my ear until I believed it, stupid cow that I am. It was her the whole time.'

'Emma?' My jaw almost hits the deck. 'And Tyler?'

Vanessa nods and sighs heavily. 'At it for weeks behind my back. No wonder he kept whisking me away for romantic week-ends away and taking me out for expensive dinners. Guilty conscience. And I was daft enough to fall for it.'

'How did you discover the truth?' It's none of my business, obviously, but I'm morbidly curious.

'I found them in a rather compromising position in the haunted house at the Heron Farm Festival.' Vanessa shudders. 'They deserve each other. Not that it lasted – Ty's dating a minor soap star now, according to the gossip mags, so good luck to her. And Emma was working in a call centre for PPI the last I heard.' Vanessa reaches out, and I instinctively flinch, though she simply places a hand on my arm. 'Is there any chance you'd come back?'

'To Vanessa Whitely Events?'

Vanessa nods. 'Not as my PA, obviously. I already have a new one of those, not that she's a patch on you. But no, I have an opening in the team. It's yours if you want it.'

It's all I ever wanted, to be part of Vanessa's creative team. It was The Dream. But dreams change.

'Thanks, but I'm happy where I am.'

Vanessa nods as she removes her hand from my arm. 'Thought as much, but worth a try.' She gives a sad smile as she starts to back away. I could leave it at that. Move on and forget the whole business with Vanessa ever happened. But Vanessa has made a concession today, and I could do the same.

'Thank you, for selling the land to Stacey. And without making a profit.' Stacey's used the extra money we raised at the festival to update the former education suite so she can now house more indoor animals. There are currently five guinea pigs awaiting new homes, as well as a recuperating ferret.

'It's my pleasure.' Vanessa looks around the yard. 'It's down to you and your home truths that did it. I did used to think only of myself, but losing you, poor Sonia – who won an industry award last month, did you hear? – and that pair of vile creatures in a matter of days really highlighted how right you were in everything you said. And I've actually grown quite fond of this place. Did you know I've sponsored Violet?'

My eyebrows shoot up my forehead. 'The pig?' The smelliest animal at the sanctuary by far.

'But I only have to pay towards her upkeep.' Vanessa holds up her manicured hands. 'I absolutely don't have to clean up after her or anything gross like that.'

Part of me wants to laugh, because it's just so typical of Vanessa, but I don't, because she's doing a noble thing. She's choosing to help in a way that's comfortable for her.

'That's great, Vanessa. I guess I'll see you around?'

Vanessa nods, the smile returning as she backs away again. We'll never be the best of friends – probably not friends at all – but we can at least be civil when we inevitably bump into each other in the village.

'There you are!' Oliver wraps his arm around my waist as Vanessa disappears into the crowd. 'Stace and Dominic have challenged us to a paired game of Giant Jenga. You up for it?'

I give a spluttery laugh. 'Are you kidding? Let me have a quick cup of tea with Kate and make sure she's not about to give birth and then we'll kick some ass.'

Oliver kisses me on the cheek before he takes my hand in his to lead me across the yard. 'This is why I love you.' He winks at me. 'Not the only reason, obviously, but a pretty major one.'

We head across to the café, and for once I'm not bothered in the slightest whether we win or lose the game, because I feel like a winner no matter what right now.

Acknowledgements

Firstly, a massive thank you to everyone who helped to name the (numerous) animals in *The Accidental Life Swap*. I thought it'd be fun to ask for help naming them on my Facebook page and I was taken aback by the response! Thanks to everyone who took part (far too many to list!) and the following people who provided the names used in the book: Sharon Smith (Daisy), Gemma Tierney (Chow Mein), Gisele Le Corre (Bianca), Maggie Rollison (Patty), Anne Maria Seymour (Claude), Rae Kenny-Rife (Pumpkin), Jo Jackson (Sophie), Melissa Elizabeth (Tommy, Timmy & Tammy), Stephanie-Jayne Matthews (Rupert), Patricia Scott (Honey) and Maggie Ewing (Violet). When my daughters found out I was asking for help naming animals, they insisted their names were used, so thank you to Rianne and Isobel too!

As I started to plan the book, I put a call out in my newsletter for one of my subscribers to have a character named after them, so a humongous thank you to Stacey Rowe for lending her name.

Thanks also to my family for all the support and cheerleading. Special thanks to my mum, my husband, Chris, and Rianne and Isobel (again), and my writing companion, Luna.

As always, thanks to my editor, Charlotte Mursell, and the HQ Digital team. I really, *really* couldn't do this without you guys.

Finally, the biggest thanks to you, the reader. I hope you enjoy *The Accidental Life Swap* as much as I've enjoyed writing it.

Turn the page for an exclusive extract from
The Single Mums' Picnic Club, another enchanting
read from Jennifer Joyce …

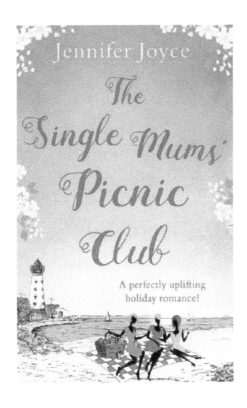

Jennifer Joyce

The
Single Mums'
Picnic
Club

A perfectly uplifting
holiday romance!

Chapter 1

Katie

'What do you mean, you don't like cheese sandwiches?' Katie blinked at her daughter, unable to comprehend the information she had just been given. 'Since when?'

Hadn't Lizzie polished off the double Gloucester with onion and chive from the cheese board just a few days ago? The double Gloucester with onion and chive that Katie had been looking forward to? She'd deliberately left it until last and the deep disappointment at finding the empty wrapper in the fridge was still there, as was the annoyance, bordering on rage, that her children seemed unable to use the flipping kitchen bin to dispose of empty wrappers. The whole kitchen showed their abuse of the family home, from the puddle of milk seeping towards the edge of the countertop to the dirty breakfast dishes dotted around the room; a bowl plonked on top of the microwave, a plate spilling toast crumbs on the table, a butter-sliced knife smearing grease on the floor. Katie despaired, but she was hardly a domesticated goddess herself right now, as evidenced when she gathered up the dirty plates, bowls and cutlery and yanked opened the dishwasher. It was full. And the contents inside were far from clean.

Lizzie dumped the offending clingfilm-wrapped cheese sandwich down on the kitchen counter, missing the milk puddle by mere millimetres. 'Can't I have Nutella instead?'

Ha! If only. Katie had discovered the empty jar in the cupboard during the early hours, when she'd been in dire need of a stress-generated snack, and had almost howled with fury. She suspected her oldest child was the culprit of this particular crime, so she'd enacted her revenge by wolfing down three segments of the boy's squirrelled-away Chocolate Orange. Elliot hadn't clocked the theft yet so, having calmed down since her hunger-induced haze of rage, Katie was hoping to replace the pieces before he did.

'It's cheese or nothing, I'm afraid.' After dumping the dirty dishes in the sink, Katie grabbed the sandwich and dropped it back into Lizzie's open Tupperware box. 'You're lucky we had any bread in for sandwiches at all.'

It was January now – the first day back to school after the festive break – but Katie was still submerged in the fog of Christmas, where routine things like grocery shopping flew out of the window and more relaxed eating habits became the norm; five-a-day now related to different versions of chocolate treats, and grazing replaced structured mealtimes. The bunch of blackened bananas lounging in the fruit bowl hadn't enticed anybody while there was an unhealthy supply of festive indulgences on offer.

'Mu-um!'

Lizzie's protests about the cheese sandwich situation were swallowed by the holler of her fifteen-year-old brother from the top of the stairs. Katie winced. Had he discovered his depleted Chocolate Orange already? She'd planned to dash to the supermarket after her morning's appointment (she desperately needed to stock the kitchen with foodstuff that contained vitamins after two weeks of eating crap anyway) and replace the nabbed segments before Elliot noticed, but it looked like she'd been rumbled. She should have nipped the chocolate-for-breakfast in the bud as soon as Boxing Day was over, but she'd rather enjoyed indulging too, to be honest.

'Where's my tie?'

Katie released a giant sigh of relief. She was still safe.

For now.

'Didn't you put it away safe in your underwear drawer at the end of term? Like I told you to?'

Lizzie sniggered as she clicked the top of her Tupperware lid into place. 'Elliot doesn't even have an underwear drawer anymore, Mum. Most of his clothes are on the floor and any that have made it into drawers are in shoved in at random. When was the last time you saw his room?'

She was in it only a matter of hours ago, actually, creeping around using the torch on her phone to guide her, but she'd been so delirious with hunger, so set on her mission, she hadn't stopped to survey the state of her teenage son's bedroom.

She didn't tell Lizzie this.

Life didn't used to be like this for Katie. She didn't used to sneak around the house, hunting sugar fixes in the dead of night because she was stressed and unable to sleep. She hadn't felt like a harassed madwoman back then, one who always seemed to be on the verge of tears or an empty Nutella jar away from throwing back her head and howling. Eighteen months ago, her life was pretty perfect. She'd enjoyed her job as a bookkeeper at the haulage firm she'd worked at for most of her adult life, she'd had a fantastic husband who was an amazing father to their son and daughter, and they had a gorgeous Georgian property on the seafront of Clifton-on-Sea, a small seaside town in the North West of England. Life was idyllic, with the promenade across the road and the beach beyond, the cliffs just a few minutes' walk away with their stunning views, the harbour with its restaurants and fresh fish and chips at the other end of town. And the house was everything she'd ever dreamed of when she'd imagined starting married life with Rob; large, airy rooms with high ceilings and original fireplaces, a homely kitchen with a sofa at one end and high-gloss cabinets and worktops at the other, and a master bedroom overlooking the sea. Yes, life had turned out perfectly for Katie. Okay, so her boss – who also happened to be her father-in-law – thought it was appropriate to refer to the female members of staff as 'birds', and she'd barely caught sight of Rob since he'd started an introduction to French course at the community centre, but she was happy. She'd thought Rob was happy too, until she learned it wasn't just French he'd been introduced to at the community centre, but the stunning, stretch-mark-free and legs-up-to-here tutor. French, it transpired, really was the language of love, and Katie had been dropped like a hot pomme de terre.

Bastards, the pair of them.

'It isn't there!' Elliot was back at the top of the stairs, yelling down an update on the tie situation.

Katie dropped the milk-soaked kitchen roll into the bin after making sure she'd mopped up every last drop and headed out into the hallway to peer up the stairs. 'It must be in your room somewhere. Have a good look.'

Elliot sighed, long and hard. 'I have looked. It isn't there.'

'It must be. Look again. Properly. But please hurry. We have to leave in …' Katie craned her neck to look at the kitchen clock. With a yelp, she dashed back into the kitchen to rifle through the basket of clean washing that had yet to be sorted into piles, locating a ruffled blouse that she could get away with wearing without having to iron it. Katie – and the kids – had to be out of the house in less than five minutes and she wasn't even dressed yet. Wasn't parenting supposed to get easier once the kids gained a bit of independence? She couldn't remember feeling this frazzled when Elliot and Lizzie were babies, but then she'd had youth on her side back then. And a husband to share the load. Rob and his infidelity were the gift that kept on giving.

'Mu-um!' Elliot was back at the top of the stairs before Katie had even stepped foot out of the kitchen with the blouse in hand. 'It isn't up here.'

'It must be.' Unless Elliot's tie had grown legs and scuttled away (many objects in the May household had a tendency to sprout limbs and hide themselves away, mostly remote controls, the pens Katie kept in her handbag, and every single teaspoon they owned).

'I've looked everywhere. It isn't in my room.'

'Where else would it be?' Katie didn't hang around for an answer. She needed to throw herself into some smart-ish clothes and get the hell out of the house before they were all late. She was in the middle of wrestling on a pair of black trousers (they'd fit before Christmas, she was sure. She really needed to cut out the sweet stuff) when Lizzie poked her head around her bedroom door, dangling a bottle-green tie with the school's crest embroidered on the front between her fingers.

'Where did you find it?' Lizzie and Elliot attended the same school and wore the same uniform, but Katie knew the tie belonged to her son as it was still knotted for ease (or laziness, to be more accurate).

'On top of the fridge.'

Katie opened her mouth to question why Elliot's tie would be on top of the fridge, but it was a useless enquiry. She wasn't sure why half the things happened in this house any more.

'Great. Thanks. Can you give it to Elliot and get your stuff ready? We need to leave. Now.' Katie yanked the trousers over her hips, ignoring the sound of ripping threads, and prayed she'd be able to zip them up.

By some miracle, Katie managed to coax the zip to fasten on her trousers and throw on her blouse while only overrunning by a couple of minutes. Lizzie was already waiting in the car as she ran from the house, yanking a hairbrush through her shoulder-length hair, with Elliot – now wearing his tie and with a slice of toast clamped between his teeth – throwing himself into the front passenger seat as Katie started the engine.

'I'd rather get the train.' Elliot tugged at the triangle of toast and chomped on it as though the bread had offended him somehow.

'You can get the train home later, and I won't be offering chauffer service every day. It's only because I need to go into town anyway.' Katie wound down her window despite the freezing temperature outside. She'd grown up in the small seaside town, but she never took her surroundings for granted, and the smell of the salty air still filled her with joy. She'd fallen in love with the house that would become her family home because of its large kitchen, its en suite master bedroom and the beautiful period fireplace in the living room, but mostly she'd fallen for its seafront location. She would never grow tired of throwing open the curtains in the morning to be greeted by the golden sand and the rippling sea beyond. It was a breathtaking sight, even on a gloomy January morning.

'Why are you going into town so early anyway?' Lizzie asked from the back seat. 'Have you got another interview? Or are you signing on? Are we skint?'

'We're not skint. We're fine.' Coping, at any rate. Rob was still covering his half of the mortgage and providing for his kids (he hadn't abandoned them completely, no matter what Katie thought of him) and they'd had a bit of extra income from their holiday let over the festive period. Katie had stuck it out at her father-in-law's haulage firm for a couple of months after Rob left her, but eventually she'd felt she had no choice but to leave as she felt herself turning into a paranoid wreck. Who'd known about the affair? Her father-in-law, probably, but what about Lesley in payroll? Or Nancy down on reception? She'd handed in her notice, sure she'd be able to find a new job quickly with her qualifications and experience.

She was still job-hunting, more than a year later.

'I have an appointment, that's all.' Katie didn't mention the appointment was with her solicitor as she didn't want Lizzie worrying about divorce proceedings. 'Jack! Hello!' She waved out of the window as her neighbour staggered out of his house with a child pulling on his hand as he tried to manoeuvre a buggy onto the path with the other. An older child was already flinging open the gate, even as his father instructed him not to. Katie flashed him a look of solidarity.

'How's the boiler getting on?' Jack had stooped over to chat through the car's open window, but he straightened almost immediately as his eldest child took the opportunity to bolt. 'Leo! Wait there! Don't go round the corner!' Jack stooped again once his son slowed down. Leo came to a complete standstill to examine what Katie suspected was a splatter of seagull poo on the pavement. 'Sorry. First day back to school chaos.'

Katie grimaced. 'Been there myself. Surprised we made it out of the house at all.' She met Jack's eye and they shared a wry smile. 'Anyway, yes, the boiler is fantastic, thanks to you.'

Katie had been in a bit of a flap when the boiler had decided to take a break from its duties a few days ago, but Jack had stepped in, repairing the aging beast and insisting on only charging for parts (neighbours' rates, apparently).

'You're a life saver.'

Jack laughed and shook his head. 'I don't know about that.'

'We're all very grateful, anyway.' She looked at her kids. They didn't seem particularly grateful; Elliot and Lizzie were fiddling with their phones (nutrition wasn't the only thing that had slipped over the school holidays. The pair had become superglued to their technology since the end of the autumn term), oblivious to the conversation taking part. 'We'd better get going. Don't want to be late and I think Leo's about to ...' Jack turned as Katie's gaze paused down the street, where Leo was crouched, finger poised to prod at the splatter of seagull droppings.

'Leo! No!' Jack, still clinging onto his daughter's hand and the buggy, tore off down the street as Katie pulled away from the kerb. If the traffic was kind this morning, they wouldn't be too late.

The traffic was horrendous, but luckily Katie managed to drop Elliot and Lizzie off at the school gates just as the bell rang to signal the start of the day. She watched as they legged it towards the building before setting off again. With Clifton-on-Sea being a small town, the older kids had to commute to the secondary school in the next town over, where Katie had enlisted the help of a solicitor in the divorce proceedings. There was a solicitors' office in Clifton-on-Sea, but Katie – and Rob – had gone to school with one of the solicitors, and the other one had a sister who cut Katie's hair (when she actually got round to booking an appointment at the hairdressers), meaning the May family's business could end up as prime gossip at Shelby's Hair Design if she'd opted to use them. Instead, Katie had gone for a more neutral solicitor, one who didn't know about the time Katie had been caught smoking behind the gym at school or that her natural hair colour was mousey and starting to turn grey.

'So sorry I'm late.' Katie burst into the reception area of the solicitor's office, panting from the dash over from the car park on the outskirts of town. She swiped the hair that was sticking to her forehead away. 'I'm here to see Helen Robinson. I have an appointment. Katie May?' She posed her name as a question – which felt apt as lately she wasn't quite sure who she was anymore.

'Take a seat, Ms May.' Katie flinched at the use of the term 'Ms', but she plonked herself down on one of the cheery blue tub chairs by the window and picked up one of the magazines stacked on the small, round table in front of her. She used the opportunity to get her breath back, taking in deep breaths fragranced by the vase of creamy roses and lavender freesias sitting on the reception desk. She'd only dashed over from the car park, but she was practically wheezing with the effort. Christmas had really taken its toll on Katie's fitness. Perhaps she should join the gym as part of a belated New Year's resolution? She'd already vowed to get out more and meet new people after being stuck in the house for a year but regaining some sort of fitness would benefit her wellbeing too.

'Helen's ready for you now.' The receptionist was already striding towards one of the doors at the back of the reception area as Katie threw the magazine back onto the pile, and she held it open with a perfectly manicured hand so Katie could pass through to Helen's office. Katie couldn't remember the last time she'd filed her own nails, never mind paid someone to do the job for her.

'It's lovely to see you again, Katie.' The solicitor was smiling as Katie sat down opposite her, but her smile dimmed as she opened the file on the desk in front of her. 'But it isn't good news, I'm afraid.'

Chapter 2

George

George's stomach was in knots as she led her five-year-old son through the school gates. It was too loud, too busy, as children whizzed by and kicked footballs across the vast playground, their voices mingling to form one thunderous hum. Thomas seemed so small – too small – and she clutched onto his gloved hand that bit tighter. It was cold and dreary that morning, still dark despite the morning edging closer to nine o' clock, with a sky full of grey clouds threatening to spill fat, icy raindrops, and it matched George's mood perfectly.

'Are you looking forward to your first day at school?' She kept her voice bright, pushing down her anxiety so she didn't pass it onto her son. She was sure he'd be apprehensive enough without her own emotions bogging him down further. 'You'll get to make lots of new friends, and your teachers are lovely, aren't they?'

They'd had the opportunity to visit the school before Christmas, to see the classroom and meet the teachers, so it wouldn't be quite so unsettling when Thomas started at Southcliff Primary at the beginning of the new term. That was the theory – George wasn't convinced it had panned out in practice. She was a nervous wreck, so she could only imagine how daunted poor Thomas was feeling.

'What are you looking forward to most?' George bent down to hear Thomas's answer over the drone of the playground noise, sure his voice was going to be little more than a whisper, his words strangled by fear and distress at this new, terrifying experience. But Thomas was beaming up at George, a set of tiny, white teeth on display as he threw his free hand high up in the air.

'I want to paint! And play! And look at all the books!' He sucked in a breath as he caught sight of the wooden play equipment in the far corner of the playground. 'Mummy?' Thomas was tugging on her hand and looking up at her with the big brown eyes he'd inherited from her. George was glad he'd mostly taken after her and not the father he didn't even know. 'Can I go and play?' Thomas pointed across the playground, to the small wooden climbing frame surrounded by wood chippings.

'Yes, sweetheart, of course.' George forced her hand to release its grip on his little hand, but she pulled him into a hug before he could leave her, her fingers finding the comfort of his familiar curls. 'But just for a few minutes, okay? You have to line up when the whistle blows, remember?'

Thomas nodded, but he was already tearing off, leaving her standing on her own. She glanced around the playground and suddenly felt ancient. Most of the mums were at least a decade younger than her, some even two. Clad in skinny jeans and spiky-heeled boots, they made George feel old and frumpy in her worn leggings and supermarket-brand canvas pumps. Still, she'd be heading straight off to work once Thomas's class was inside the school, and fancy clothes didn't really suit a cleaning job.

George looked across at the climbing frame as she made her way further into the playground, and her heart melted a little bit when she saw Thomas giggling with one of the other boys. See, he was making friends already. He would be fine.

If only the same could be said of George, who was rooting

around in her handbag for a clean-ish tissue to dab at her eyes. Thomas was taking to school like a duck to water, but his mother was very much in need of a lifejacket to keep her afloat. She wanted nothing more than to scoop up her little boy and scurry to the safety of their home together.

'Everything okay?'

Startled, George almost jabbed herself in the eye with the tissue. She gave a quick dab to mop up the stray tears and presented the owner of the concerned voice with a beaming smile. 'Yes, of course. Everything's fine.' She held up the tissue and rolled her eyes before she dropped it back into her handbag. 'Hay fever's playing up, that's all.'

'Hay fever?' If George had been able to look at the bloke now walking alongside her, she would have seen a slight frown appearing very briefly as he took in the miserable winter morning.

'Yep.' George nodded as she stared down at the concrete floor, watching as her pumps trailed over the painted-on hopscotch grid. 'Winter hay fever. Not all that common, but still as debilitating as its summer cousin.'

She cringed as the words tumbled from her mouth, willing her lips to seal themselves shut.

'Unlucky.'

He was humouring her. Letting her get away with her phony excuse. But at least he wasn't openly mocking her. Not yet, anyway.

'Don't I know you?'

George hoped not. It was one thing making an idiot out of yourself in front of a stranger, but she didn't want to have to relive this experience again.

'No, I don't think so.' She smiled politely at him and slowed her pace, hoping he'd accept her answer and move on. But he slowed his pace too, stooping so he could take a proper look at George as she returned her gaze to the concrete.

'I do know you!' He gave a soft, triumphant laugh. 'It's ... um ...' He screwed up his face as he tried to conjure her name. 'Jill?

No.' He shook his head and tapped his fingers on the handles of the buggy he was pushing. 'Jane? Janine?' He shook his head again and sighed. 'Can you help a guy out here?'

George wasn't sure she should. She wasn't in the habit of giving out her details to random blokes. Or any blokes at all, come to think of it.

'Got it!' He stopped suddenly, his eyes lit up as he pointed at her. 'It's George, right?'

George turned and looked at him properly, taking in his height, his stocky build, his slightly too long brown hair and the beginnings of a beard lightly sprinkled with grey. There was something vaguely familiar about the eyes and the way they sparkled as he smiled down at her.

'Sorry.' He shook his head, the smile dimming. 'You must think I'm some sort of mad stalker.' He held up a hand. 'I'm not, I promise. We – Leo, Ellie and I – used to go to the parent and toddler group at the community centre.' He pointed first to the girl standing beside the buggy and then ahead at his son, who was charging towards a stray football with a roar. 'It was about … three years ago?'

George bobbed her head up and down slowly. She and Thomas had attended the weekly Little Bees and Butterflies group up until a couple of weeks ago.

'It was a fun group, and it certainly helped Leo burn off some energy.' Ahead, Leo drew back his leg before pelting the football into the railings with another roar. 'I wanted to take the little one …' He turned the buggy slightly, where another small girl sat, padded out with a thick coat, woolly hat and matching mittens. 'But I've had to take on as much work as I can lately so I haven't managed to get there.' He pushed the buggy forward and started to stroll towards his son. 'I remember you brought in some cakes one time.' His eyes narrowed. 'Sticky toffee, I think it was.'

George nodded. 'It was Thomas' birthday so I baked some little buns for the group.'

'They were delicious.' He laughed. 'Must have been if I remembered all these years later.'

George felt a warm glow inside despite the chill in the air. She'd always loved to bake, though she rarely had the opportunity to receive feedback from anyone other than Thomas, who was always very enthusiastic about cake, whether it was homemade or shop-bought.

'I haven't seen you at the school before. Has Thomas just transferred?'

The warm glow cooled. Although Thomas was five now and had been eligible to attend school full-time for over a year, she'd kept him at home with her for as long as she possibly could. Thomas was probably going to be her only child, and she wanted to cherish every single moment with him that she could, but she did sometimes worry that she'd made the wrong decision in delaying his formal education. She looked around the playground now, at the small clusters of children, the friendship groups formed back in reception – back in nursery, even – and Thomas was the outsider. Had she been selfish in keeping him to herself for so long?

'No. It's his first day at school.' George raised her chin slightly, ready to do battle about her choices if she had to. 'He's starting in Miss Baxter's class today.'

'Leo's in Miss Baxter's class too.' He pointed across the playground to his son. 'I'll tell him to look out for Thomas, make sure he's settling in.'

The shriek of a whistle pierced the air, ending the conversation before George could thank him, and George leapt into action, tearing across the playground to make sure she squeezed her son tight before he left her for the day.

Where was that tissue?

Thomas was already in the line before she reached him, turning to chat to the boy behind him. He didn't seem to mind the separation, which was a good thing, obviously. Even if it did break George's heart just a little bit more.

'Thomas, sweetie.' She crouched down and pulled her gorgeous boy into her arms, inhaling his smell of shampoo, Paw Patrol bubble bath and fabric softener. 'You be a good boy, okay? And have fun. I'll pick you up later and you can tell me all about your day. We'll have cake, yes? And hot chocolate with marshmallows. We can go to the park. Or the beach hut. Whichever you'd like.'

There was a hand on her shoulder. It was the man with the buggy, whose name she hadn't thought to ask. 'He'll be fine. Honestly.'

She managed a wobbly sort of smile before she crouched again to press a kiss to Thomas' curls, blinking back tears as she stepped away. She waved manically as the class filed inside, stretching up on her tiptoes, watching those familiar curls disappear as her precious boy was swallowed by the school.

'It does get easier, I promise.' Her new companion raised a hand in farewell before he turned the buggy and headed back through the gates. George hung around for a few minutes in case she could snatch one final glimpse of Thomas, but it was no use. With a heavy heart and watery eyes, she shuffled out of the playground and made her way to work.

Chapter 3

Frankie

It still amazed Frankie that her children, who had shared a womb for nine months and were born just eleven minutes apart, could be so different. Finn was currently clinging onto her thigh, tears and snot merging on his top lip as he threw back his head and wailed, mouth surely wider than was physically possible, while his twin sister waltzed into the nursery, clumsy fingers trying their hardest to unzip her winter coat. Her hat and mittens had been discarded on the floor in her eagerness to play with the other children in the toddler room.

'Good morning, Finn!' The early years assistant flashed Frankie a sympathetic smile before she leaned down to pick up Skye's abandoned garments. She secured them onto Skye's labelled hook and turned to Finn with a toothy smile, her held a hand out to the still-wailing little boy. 'Shall we go and play? Poppy's already here. She's been asking about you!'

Frankie expected Finn to unpeel himself and take Keeley's hand. She was his favourite member of staff at the nursery, with Poppy being his play/craft partner of choice, but still Finn clung on, the wail reaching a higher pitch as he squeezed his eyes tight.

It wasn't uncommon for her son to kick up a bit of a fuss when it came to being left at nursery in the mornings, but it wasn't usually this prolonged.

'It'll be the Christmas break. The holidays can sometimes set them back as they get used to being with Mum and Dad all day.' Keeley crouched down to Finn's level and injected more cheer to her ever-bright voice. She didn't spot Frankie's flinch at the 'and Dad' addition. 'Shall we go and do some painting? You can paint Mummy a beautiful picture to take home later!'

Finn wasn't convinced, but Frankie really had to get going. She was already behind on her work schedule due to the nursery closing for Christmas, so she couldn't afford to stand around, no matter how much the guilt jabbed as she peeled Finn's little fingers from her thigh.

'Good boy!' Keeley scooped Finn up before he could grab hold of Frankie again, avoiding his flailing arms as he frantically reached for his mum. 'Give Mummy a big kiss and then we can go and have some fun!'

Keeley was very good at shutting out the screams emitting from the toddler, but the forlorn sound broke Frankie's heart. She wanted nothing more than to succumb to her young son's needs, to take him in her arms and soothe away his tears with cuddles and kisses.

'He'll be absolutely fine in a couple of minutes, I promise.' Keeley was already backing away towards the toddler room, as though sensing Frankie was about to crumble. Finn started to thrash his little legs, but she held on tight. 'He'll be running around with Poppy in no time. Happens all the time.'

Frankie gave a slight nod of her head, but she made no attempt to leave. Every instinct was telling her to grab hold of her son and reassure him. What must be going around his little head? Did he feel abandoned? Rejected? She could take him home. Fit her work around his needs, even though this had been virtually impossible over the Christmas holidays. She'd been so exhausted after running around after two two-year-olds that she hadn't been able to work in the evenings as planned. She'd attempted to, fighting against the urge to flop down on the sofa with the tub of Quality Street and a glass of wine, but her brain was too frazzled to do much more than check her emails. This was the very reason the twins went to nursery in the first place.

'Seriously, Frankie.' Keeley smiled serenely at her, as though she wasn't struggling to keep hold of a very wriggly toddler. 'He'll be fine. You can always give us a ring to check later.'

Frankie nodded again, and this time she took a step back. A teeny step, but a step all the same. She did need to crack on with her work, especially with a deadline looming. She'd phone the nursery when she got home – it was only a ten-minute walk away – and if he was still upset, she'd rush back and collect him.

'Bye, Finn. I'll see you soon.' She pushed a smile onto her face and somehow managed not to break down in tears herself. She craned her neck to catch a glimpse of Skye as Keeley pushed open the door to the toddler room, but her daughter had marched off to play without a backwards glance. From one extreme to the other. 'Love you.' She raised her hand in a quick wave before she turned and hurried away from the nursery and the heartbreaking sounds of her son's sobbing.

Nobody warned you about this bit. They told you all the gory details of labour and birth. The horror stories of night feeds and teething and the terrible twos (doubled, when you had twins). But they didn't prepare you for the gut-wrenching moments when you had to leave them in the care of somebody else. They didn't prime you for the guilt of being anything other than the child's mother.

Finn was perfectly fine when Frankie phoned the nursery six-and-a-half minutes later. She'd run all the way home, taking a short-cut through the park, and hadn't even bothered to ditch her coat before she dialled Parkside Day Nursery, panting and slightly sweating despite the bleak, early January chill.

'Are you sure he's okay?' Frankie had been told that Finn was now happily splatting paint with bestie Poppy, but Frankie couldn't seem to quell the nagging doubt that she was doing Something Wrong, a feeling that had plagued her for the past year. She could never quite shake off the feeling that she was failing her children, that she wasn't good enough despite her best efforts. She'd moved to Clifton-on-Sea for a fresh start, but the feelings of inadequacy had moved with her. Most notably, and the concern Frankie could easily identify, was the worry about her poor babies' lack of a two-parent family. Perhaps this was the reason Finn was so clingy now? Did he feel abandoned? Rejected?

'He is absolutely fine.' Keeley's voice was upbeat, but then it always was so it offered little consolation. The lack of screaming in the background, however, was definitely a comfort. 'He cried for, like, another minute. Two, max. And now he's having a brilliant time with Poppy.'

'Good.' Frankie swallowed the urge to ask if the paint Finn was using was toxic-free and nudged the front door – which she hadn't paused long enough to close – with her foot and unzipped her coat as she moved through to the kitchen. The breakfast dishes were still piled in the sink – another Something Wrong. 'You'll phone me if he needs me, won't you? Because I work from home. I can be there in ten minutes. Less.'

'Of course, but there'll be no need. Finn was just thrown off kilter because of the Christmas break.'

'Yes, I'm sure that's all it is.' Frankie didn't necessarily agree, but she didn't like to come across as a neurotic mum, even if she felt like one a lot of the time. She'd been horrified the first time Skye had marched out of the nursery, her wrist held in the air as she showed off her crafting skills. She'd created a

305

bracelet by threading a mishmash of buttons and large wooden beads onto a length of elasticated cord. Where the nursery saw the opportunity to experiment and unleash the children's creativity while practicing those all-important motor skills, Frankie had spotted a choking hazard the embellishments could have caused.

She'd managed to push down the fear and panic, but it had been there, and continued to present itself on a daily basis.

'I'll see you this afternoon then. About three?' Frankie didn't usually pick the twins up until at least five, but she needed to ease herself back into their routine. And to be honest, three o' clock – almost six hours away – seemed like a stretch.

'We'll see you then. Have a good day!'

Frankie was about to ask after Finn one last time, just to really put her mind at ease, but the phone line was dead. She stared at her phone for a moment, contemplating ringing back – just for a super-quick call – but she came to her senses and shoved the phone into the pocket of her jeans before whipping off her coat and flicking the kettle on. She washed the dishes while she waited for the kettle to boil. There wasn't actually a lot, just a couple of bowls and spoons, two plastic beakers, and a small plate – she really needed to stop beating herself up. She took her cup of tea into the office. Her office was actually a desk and a set of shelves squeezed into an alcove in the corner of the dining room, but it served its purpose and gave Frankie the space she needed to work as a freelance brand designer. Before the twins, she'd worked in a swanky office in the centre of Manchester, but she couldn't face the long hours and the commute once her maternity leave was over, so she'd decided to set up on her own. It had been a risky decision, but one that was paying off, especially since the move away from her home town. She had a healthier balance between her work and home life, and it gave her more of a sense of ease being so close to her children. Of course, on days like these, it took a great effort to switch from mum mode to professional, but she managed to push aside her worries over Finn and concentrate on her latest task of designing a new website for her client. It was almost half past one before she came up for air, her shoulders and lower back aching, cup of tea cold. She winced as she stood, one hand massaging her back while the other reached for the cup. Her work had been largely neglected while the nursery had been closed over Christmas and the New Year, and she'd forgotten quite how stiff her body became as she hunched over her desk. She normally counteracted this with yoga and regular runs along the beach, but she pushed the thought away as she headed across to the kitchen. She'd placed her young children in nursery so she could work, so the thought of wasting that time on such frivolous acts when her son had been so miserable at being left that morning made her stomach knot with guilt.

No. She'd simply have to put up with the discomfort for now. Perhaps she'd do a bit of yoga once the twins were in bed tonight. Or a long, hot bath might do it. She couldn't remember the last time she'd allowed herself anything more than a quick shower; there was always something more important to be getting on with than lazing in the bath.

She flicked the kettle on and poured the forgotten tea down the sink before opening the fridge in search of something to eat for lunch. There wasn't much inside, apart from a few wrapped segments of a Chocolate Orange, the Chomp from Skye's selection box, and half a bag of limp-looking Brussel sprouts. There was butter, but she groaned when she remembered she'd used the last of the bread for her toast that morning. And the cupboards were in a worse state than the fridge. She'd used up everything over the festive period (including a slightly out-of-date tin of Spam) as she couldn't be bothered going to the effort of getting herself and the twins washed, dressed and bundled up in winter coats. They'd spent the past week surviving on non-perishables and she hadn't faced the shops to stock up yet.

'Bugger.' Frankie closed the cupboard and sighed. It looked like she was going to have to venture out after all. And if she was heading out anyway, what was the harm in killing two birds with one stone and going for a little run as well? The fresh air would do her good and help to keep the creative cogs turning.

She raced up the stairs before she could allow the guilt of indulging in a bit of self-care to set in, changing into a pair of leggings, a long-sleeved T-shirt, and the hoodie her brother had bought her for Christmas. After shoving her trainers on her feet and making sure she had her purse, keys and phone (just in case Finn needed her), she was ready to set out. She started off at a gentle pace as she jogged down to the seafront, easing herself back into the exercise after a week or two of excess eating, and she immediately felt her shoulders loosen. It was hard work after holing herself up for the past couple of weeks, and there was a definite danger of rain as the grey clouds darkened, but it was so freeing being out in the open, the sounds of the waves growing closer with each step. She was soon on the promenade, the wind whipping at her hot cheeks, her mouth stretched into a smile despite her exertions. She loved this feeling. She wished she could bottle it up for those times she felt trapped in the house with two mischievous toddlers rampaging around the rooms. Not that she would ever admit this out loud. Motherhood was precious. A gift. She knew she was incredibly lucky to have two happy, healthy children. That she was there to witness them growing up. Not everybody had that luxury.

Oh, but sometimes she missed the old Frankie. The fun Frankie who could drink her brother and his mates under the table at the pub. The Frankie who would meet her friends in town for endless afternoons of coffee, cake and gossip. The Frankie who could go to the toilet without being followed and quizzed about what she was doing. She loved her children so much, but she couldn't help mourning the loss of the woman she was before, if only from the privacy of her own thoughts, and only briefly before she felt like a complete monster.

She picked up her pace, enjoying the scream of pain from her thighs as it overtook all thoughts and emotions. The old Frankie was gone, never to return, and there was no point dwelling on it.

Dear Reader,

Thank you so much for taking the time to read this book – we hope you enjoyed it! If you did, we'd be so appreciative if you left a review.

Here at HQ Digital we are dedicated to publishing fiction that will keep you turning the pages into the early hours. We publish a variety of genres, from heartwarming romance, to thrilling crime and sweeping historical fiction.

To find out more about our books, enter competitions and discover exclusive content, please join our community of readers by following us at:

🖤 @HQDigitalUK

📘 facebook.com/HQDigitalUK

Are you a budding writer? We're also looking for authors to join the HQ Digital family! Please submit your manuscript to:

HQDigital@harpercollins.co.uk.

Hope to hear from you soon!

If you enjoyed *The Accidental Life Swap*, then why not try another delightfully uplifting romance from HQ Digital?

Pig

1. Smokey (Jake Tierney)
2. Miss Cameron (Matthew Tierney)
3. Blossom (Leyanne Bunting)
4. Wilbur (A Michele Mays)
5. Bacon (Trish Hills)
6. Mabel (Trish Hills)
7. Percival (Elspeth Pyper)
8. Marley (Tina Low)
9. Tabatha (Samantha Burden)
10. Rasher (Sarah Rothman)
11. Benedict (Priti Draper)
12. Parker (Rachel Broughton)
13. Trotter (Sue Van Eerden)
14. Violet (Maggie Ewing)
15. Peggy (Birgit Pitson)
16. Pickles (Gloria Mitchell)
17. Hector (Marylyn Hammersley)
18. Charlotte (Karen Clarke)
19. Charlie (Karen Clarke)
20. Apple Sauce (Chris Cahill)
21. Arthur (Mary Anne Lewis)
22. Patrick (Rachel Burton)
23. George & Gemma Tierney (Sharon Smith)
24. Peppa (Gemma Tierney)
25. Vera (Jane Lambert)
26. Boris (Fee Tierney)
27. Fred (Lorna)
28. Prudence (Sue Parsons)
29. Emma, Mickie, Tina, Rob, Mollie, Shaun, Megan, Keiron, Ronnie, Doreen, Sharron, Anne, Albert, June, Rasher, Gammon, Porkie (Michelle)

30. Lillian (Christine Jackson)
31. Florence (Janet Cocker)
32. Freddie (Janet Cocker)
33. Emma (Maggie Philipo Rollinson)
34. Edward (Maggie Philipo Rollinson)
35. Barry (Alison Hamilton)
36. Rosemary (June Cahill)
37. Sparkie (Elizabeth Whatman)
38. Spencer (Wendy Crystal Waring)
39. Pork Chop (Lorna's husband)
40. Horatio (Angela Galvin & Christine Tierney)
41. Bertie (Lisa Robinson)
42. Freda (Liz Mason)
43. Little Legs (Sandra Cahill)
44. Gip (Tracey Wrigley)
45. Stan (Christie Barlow)
46. Matthew (Anita)

Rabbits

Stewie (Jake Tierney)
Roger (Sharon Smith)
Jessica (Sharon Smith)
Pip (Cheryl Williams)
Squeak (Cheryl Williams)
Bramble (Cheryl Williams)
Jelly (Cheryl Williams)
Donnie (Cheryl Williams)
Marie (Cheryl Williams)
Samson (Cheryl Williams)
Delilah (Cheryl Williams)
Paisley (Rae Kenny-Rife)
Juniper (Rae Kenny-Rife)
Jerry (Maria Taylor)

Halliwell (Maria Taylor)
Honey (Patricia Scott)
Amber (Patricia Scott)
Toffee (Patricia Scott)
Fudge (Patricia Scott)
Florence (Clare Turner)
Twitch (June Cahill)
Rocky (Christine Matthews)
Reggie (Christine Matthews)
Snowy, Blackie, Bambi, Bugsy, Rex, Lady Flossie, Sparkle, Twinkle
& Flopsy, Topsy, Tim, Rosie, Jim, Buttons, Paddington, Aunt Sally,
Worzel
Betty (Melissa Elizabeth)
Bertie (Melissa Elizabeth)
Laurel (Nathan Holloway)
Hardy (Nathan Holloway)
Floppy & Hoppy

Big Ears (Sandra Cahill)
Mayhem (Trish Hills)
Magic (Trish Hills)
Bob Tail (Margaret Sherwood)
Bunny Boy (Margaret Sherwood)
Marley (Tina Low & Katy Dawson)
Ginger (Sienne Pilling)
Biscuit (Sienne Pilling)
Cookie (Sienne Pilling)
Cream (Sienne Pilling)
Ralphie (Sienne Pilling)
RiffRaff (Leyanne Bunting)
Flopsy (Sarah Bennet)
Mopsy (Sarah Bennet)
Daisy (Claire Biggs)
Bon Bon (Claire Biggs)

Bunny (Claire Biggs)
Willow (Christine Jackson)
Warwick (Christine Jackson)
Thumper (Sarah Rothman & Gemma Tierney)
Oreo (Gemma Tierney)
Cinnabun (Gemma Tierney)
Rampant (Gemma Tierney)
Velma (Gemma Tierney)
Willma (Gemma Tierney)
Stitch (Gemma Tierney)
Milow (Gemma Tierney)
Fluffy (Gemma Tierney)
Hunny Bunny (Gemma Tierney)
Ann Summers (GT)
Theo (Mandy James)
Leo (Mandy James)
Flip (Hayley Black)
Flop (Hayley Black)
Corinthian (Priti Draper)
Rimini (Priti Draper)
Rosie (Stephanie-Jayne Matthews)
Rupert (Stephanie-Jayne Matthews)
Cupid (Elaine Fitzpatrick)
Valentine (Elaine Fitzpatrick)
Minnie (Kaisha Holloway & June Cahill)
Mickey (Kaisha Holloway)
Mavis (Katy Dawson)
Fluffy Tail (Kirsty Harding)
Twinkle Butt (Kirsty Harding)
Hop (Maxine Phipps)
Scotch (Maxine Phipps)
Winkles (Cheryl Saunders)

Kittens

1. Smudge, Splodge & Sprinkles (Sarah Rothman)
2. Ronnie, Reggie & Rosie (Sharon Smith)
3. Jemima, Jaffa & Bertie (Maxine Phipps)
4. Scampi, Teddy & Bears (Stephanie-Jayne Matthews)
5. [Larry, Curly & Mo] [Bagpuss, Jess & Minky] (Adrian Tierney)
6. Tipsy, Topsy & Tiddles (Mandi Davison)
7. Magic, Logan & Bella (Trish Hills)
8. Mary, Mungo & Midge (JJ Martin)
9. Poppy, Branch & DJ (Rachel Broughton's daughter)
10. Sonny [sonny bum], Flo [imposter cat] & Lola [Lola Bear] (Leyanne Bunting)
11. Tiger, Pudding & Waffle (Hayley Black)
12. Tabatha, Buddy & Harry (Samantha Burden)
13. Charlie, Lexi & Leighton (Charlotte)
14. Simba, Coco, Missy & Oscar (Gemma Tierney)
15. Colin, Freddie & Tessa (Caroline Morris)
16. Beautiful, Benny & Bashful (Gloria Mitchell)
17. Spike, Mixture & Minx (June Cahill)
18. Binji, Ralph & Sassy (Maggie Ewing)
19. Tommy, Timmy & Tammy (Melissa Elizabeth)
20. Bella, Bobby & Brian (Christine Matthews)
21. Smokey, Bad Puss & Sylvester (Matthew Tierney)
22. Pumpkin, Spice & Sugar (Kate Phoenix)
23. Sun, Moon & Stars (Denise Watts)
24. Darcy, Sid & Joannie (Mary Anne Lewis)
25. Jack, Daniel & Coke (Sandra Cahill)
26. Coffee, Toffee & Cream (Sienne Pilling)
27. Bran, Stan & Pickle (Heather Donaldson)

Hedgehogs

1. Hettie (Katy Dawson)
2. Mrs Tiggy Wrinkle (Gemma Tierney & Matthew Young)
3. Mr Pickle Pants (Gemma Tierney)
4. Sonic (Jake Tierney & Matthew Young)
5. Shadow (Jake Tierney)
6. Mr Pickles (Shell Cunliffe)
7. Henrietta/Ettie for short (Caroline Morris & Holly Vockings & Jo Jackson)
8. Spike (Maxine Phipps & Matt Cooper & Angie Saunders & Sarah Rothman & Stephanie-Jayne Matthews)
9. Rodger (Gemma Metcalfe)
10. Marley (Tina Lowe)
11. Hubert & Sylvia (Leyanne Bunting)
12. Pins (Susan Scott-Swift & June Cahill)
13. Needles (Susan Scott-Swift)
14. Ouchy (Matt Cooper)
15. Henry (Holly Vockings & Stephanie-Jayne Matthews)
16. Harry (Holly Vockings & Maggie Philipo Rollison)
17. Charlie (Trish Hills)
18. Winnie (Cheryl Saunders)
19. Elsie (Maggie Philipo Rollison)
20. Sophie (Jo Jackson)
21. George (Jo Jackson)
22. Nina (Susan Cunningham's daughter)
23. Gota (Susan Cunningham's daughter)
24. Sprinkles (Sarah Rothman)
25. Mr & Mrs Flea Bag (Adrian/Michelle)
26. Mr & Mrs Rollie (Adrian/Michelle)
27. Mohawk Mohican (Adrian/Michelle)
28. Forest (Christine Matthews)
29. Pumpkin (Rae Kenny-Rife)
30. Spice (Rae Kenny-Rife)

31. Churchquill & Clemmie (Rae Kenny-Rife)

32. Trubo (Matthew Tierney)

33. Patrick (Matthew Tierney)

34. Button (Mary Ohana)

35. Twinkle (Mary Ohana)

Sheep

1. Hamish (Sharon Smith & Anne Woodthorpe)

2. Judge (Leyanne Bunting)

3. Adrian (Jake Tierney)

4. Florence (JJ Martin)

5. Basil (Jo Jackson)

6. Lambert or Sinead (Gemma Tierney)

7. Sheila (Katy Dawson)

8. Dolly or Shauna or Ernie or Bertie or Hotpot (Adrian Tierney)

9. Larry the lamb (Rachel Kennedy)

10. Cuddly (Gloria Mitchell)

11. Claude (Anne Maria Seymour)

12. Ewenice (Denise Watts)

13. Skittles (Leila Kay)

14. Baaaarbara (Trish Hills & Deryl Williams)

15. Custard (Stephanie-Jayne Matthews)

16. Edgar (Tracey Vage)

17. Gabby (Fiona Squire)

18. Winnie (Cheryl Saunders)

19. Sean the sheep (Sarah Rothman)

20. Leona, Lily, Little Lamb & William (Kim Feasey)

21. Stu (Dianna Jeffrey)

22. Nigel (Matthew Sylvester)

23. Pom Pom (Amanda Collins)

24. Bathsheba (Chris Phillips)

25. Barbarella (Jackie Holt)

26. Gert (Wendy Allen)

27. Beryl (Melissa Elizabeth)
28. Stan (Ginny Parish)
29. Sherlock/Shearlock (Debbie Lund)
30. Pegasus (Susan Cunningham)
31. Ping, Winnie, Rubarb, Addie (June Cahill)
32. Flora (June Cahill & Christine Jackson)
33. Chops (Katie Lonsdale)
34. Winston (Katie Lonsdale & daughter)
35. Dojo (Charlotte)
36. Arthur (Hayley Wild-Rigby)
37. Herbert (Anne Wood)
38. Tabatha (Samantha Burden)
39. Brian or Winnie (Jennifer Whitehouse)
40. Gavin (Andrew Cahill)
41. Woolly (Sue Van Eerden)
42. Tushel (Mary Ohana)
43. Mewriel (Fee Tierney)
44. Minty (Rachel Brain)
45. Boris (Maxine Phipps)
46. Maggie (Joanne Seymour)
47. Rosemary or Juniper or Paisley (Rae Kenny-Rife)
48. Prudence (Jane Lambert)
49. Rodney (Glynis Bell)

Chickens

1. Gemma (Jake Tierney)
2. Petunia (Hannah Benbow)
3. Elsa (Rachel Kennedy)
4. Mathilda/Matilda (Rachel Kennedy & Katy Dawson)
5. Trump (Tracey McCann)
6. Putin (Tracey McCann)
7. Corbyn (Tracey McCann)
8. Tilly (Trish Hills & Joanne Seymour & Gill Forsythe)

9. Cluck Rogers (Matthew Tierney)
10. Hen Solo (Matthew Tierney)
11. Violet (Leyanne Bunting)
12. Joan (Leyanne Bunting)
13. Evelyn (Leyanne Bunting)
14. Henrietta/Henny for short (Shell Cunliffe & Katy Dawson & Rachel Kennedy [Henny Penny])
15. Penelope/Penny for short (Shell Cunliffe)
16. Jennifer/Jenny for short (Shell Cunliffe)
17. Tabatha (Samantha Burden)
18. Olivia (Katy Dawson)
19. Mitzi (Kaisha Holloway)
20. Yolko One/Yokey for short (Sarah Rothman)
21. Tikka (Gemma Metcalfe & Chris Cahill)
22. Hetty (Sue Van Eerden & Maggie Ewing & Lynda Livesay Randall)
23. Betty (Sue Van Eerden & Maggie Ewing & Lynda Livesay Randall)
24. Maud (Sue Van Eerden & Maggie Ewing & Gill Forsythe)
25. Peggy (Sue Van Eerden)
26. Huey, Duey & Lewy (David Cahill)
27. Eliza (Maggie Philipo Rollison)
28. Maggie (Maggie Philipo Rollison)
29. Patty (Maggie Philipo Rollison)
30. Betsy (Fiona Squire)
31. Hilda (Fiona Squire)
32. Dotty (Fiona Squire)
33. Holly (Susan Oddie)
34. Dolly (Susan Oddie)
35. Molly (Susan Oddie)
36. Chow Mein (Gemma Tierney)
37. Mary (Jo Jackson)
38. Mungo (Jo Jackson)
39. Midge (Jo Jackson)

40. Chicken Little (Michelle Tierney)

41. Fluffly (Michelle Tierney)

42. Michelle/Shell for short (Tina Low)

43. Nugget (Karl Bowman)

44. Satay (Karl Bowman)

45. L'orange (Karl Bowman)

46. McQueenie (Caroline Duncan)

47. Bianca (Gisele Le Corre)

48. Bernard (Gisele Le Corre)

49. Chipp (Gisele Le Corre)

50. Teacup (Sharon Speake)

51. Snowcap (Sharon Speake)

52. Martha (Sharon Speake)

53. Mrs Cluckins (Jan Baldwin)

54. Jessica (Liz Raine)

55. Jemima (Liz Raine)

56. Jasmine (Liz Raine)

57. Rosy (Gill Forsythe)

58. Meg-hen (Lynda Livesay Randall)

59. Claude (Lynda Livesay Randall)

60. Rose (Caroline Duncan)

61. Lily (Caroline Duncan)

Donkey 2

Daisy (Sharon Smith)
Alma (Birgit Pearson)
June (Jake Tierney)
Luna (Hannah Benbow)
Sassy (Suzie Jay)
Freda (Lianne Jayne Faulkner)
Beryl (Maxine Phipps)
Cheeky Charlie (Claire Ann Davies)
Rosie (Trish Hills)

Maggie (Helen Rees)
Betsy (Katy Dawson)
Mabel (Shazza Andrews)
Winnie (Cheryl Saunders)
Fred (Frank Baldwin)
Freya (Anna Scally)
Lola (Jayne Moulster)
Dory (Michelle Tierney)
Dottie (Nita Hearn)
Elsie (Anne Wood)
Myrtle (Wendy Fontenoy)
Bianca (Gisele le Corre)
Dinky (Maggie Philip Rollison)
Gerty/Gertrude (Amanda Jane Clarke)
Donna (Caroline Avery)
Lacey Mae (Christine Jackson)
Dollie (Denise Watts)
Wilma (Gemma Macey)
Dottie (Nicky Aldridge)
Charlie Jo (June Cahill)
Lydia (Lynda Livesay Randall)
Assumpta (Rachel Dingwall)
Angelica (Debs Carr)
Gloria (Jenni Bird)
Doreen (Melissa Elizabeth)
Cleopatra (Sharon Cawdron)
Tess/Tessa (Denise Andrews)
Hamish (Jackie & Steve Meredith)
Geraldine (Rosie Alice)
Biscuit/Bikki/Cookie (Sienne Pilling)
Barbara (Jo Kempster)
Ann (Gayle White)
Mischief (Jayne Cook)
Nelly (Emma Kirk)

Cheeky (Holly Vockings)
Treasure (Leyanne Bunting)
Tilly (Jackie Jackson)

Lightning Source UK Ltd.
Milton Keynes UK
UKHW011825191222
414174UK00005B/563